The Trouble with Murder

A Zoe Grey Novel

By Catherine Nelson

For the dreamers.

Hold onto your dreams. Never give them up.

They make you who you are.

Author's Note

The characters, entities, and events in this story are entirely fictitious, or used fictitiously. No character or event is intended to represent any real person or event, past or present.

Acknowledgements

I must first and foremost thank my mother and my brother.

I still remember their reactions the first time I confessed my passion for writing. My mom looked as if a couple things made more sense, and she said, "Oo-oh." My brother looked more than a little impressed, and he said, "So *that's* what you've been doing in there?"

They have embraced writing as a critical part of me with no questions asked. And that confirmed for me I was on the right path. I know the time and attention I give to this craft has frustrated, confounded, and occasionally disappointed them, but they have *never* wavered in their support or encouragement. I am truly blessed and eternally grateful.

I must also thank my grandmother. Her excitement and enthusiasm have touched me more deeply that she'll ever know. I would not be to this point in this journey if it weren't for her. She has supported my dream and encouraged me to pursue it. She'll never know what that means to me. I can't thank her enough.

I must also thank my friends. Mandi was the first person to read anything I'd ever written. Without her encouragement and enthusiasm, it's unlikely anyone else would have ever read anything. Nancy has read most everything I've written, and I have relied on her more significantly than she knows. Sabrina has been a wellspring of encouragement, optimism, and strength. She has held me up and motivated me when I've needed it most. Erin O. has provided endless support. Her excitement has renewed my conviction more than once.

All of these women have given me honest feedback and acted as brainstorming sounding boards when I've gotten stuck or needed inspiration. Their input has been invaluable, and has helped shape the book into what it is today. They cannot know the extent of my gratitude.

Erin S. was practically a stranger when she read this story, and that made everything real somehow. She has since become a friend, and her encouragement has reminded me why I write stories in the first place. That means more than she could ever know. I cannot thank her enough.

Andi also became a friend as a result of this book. I asked her to keep an eye out for typos as she read it. She embraced that request, and it became a passion for this project that has truly touched me. I appreciate that passion more than she knows.

I hope to make them all proud.

The Trouble with Murder

1

I was late. I'd agreed to meet Stacy Karnes at six. It was ten minutes past, and I was another ten away. Traffic was light; maybe I could cut that time in half. I hoped she would still be there when I arrived. Some people wouldn't be.

I hit END as the call dropped to voicemail. I'd already left a message. Stacy wasn't answering her phone.

Stacy had called me that morning and asked to see the apartment. She had pressed me for a same-day appointment. Something in her voice had caused me to agree, even though it required me to work late. Already crammed full, my schedule hadn't afforded me the time I'd needed when a new client had walked into my office that evening. Now I was late.

I turned into the parking lot off Elizabeth Street. The building, a three-story affair built with contemporary lines four years before, had originally been designed for senior living. At the time, it had been called Harriett Valley Estates, named for Harriett Van Patten, a local socialite who was of both the right age and financial status to bankroll such a project. She'd even lived in the building herself until her death a year ago.

But Elizabeth Street, not far from the Colorado State University campus in Fort Collins, Colorado, is hopping with dozens of fast food places, twice as many bars, and a hundred other businesses all drawing great numbers of college-aged customers. And when catering to college students, it isn't profitable to shut your doors at six o'clock. The seniors had found constant disruption and occupancy fell.

After Mrs. Van Patten died, no one fought very hard to hang on to the Estates idea. White Real Estate and Property Management had purchased it, renamed it, and begun leasing it to college students. I became the primary leasing agent and property manager for the location, now called Elizabeth Tower Apartments. With only three stories, it isn't much of a tower, but no one thinks anything of this since it isn't in a valley, either.

The lot was nearly full. I parked in one of the many handicap places White Real Estate had yet to repaint and jumped out. My foot hit the sidewalk as an ear-piercing scream rang out.

I felt my heart leap in my chest then settle into a run, hammering against my sternum. My hair was standing up and an involuntary shiver slithered down my spine. I'd never heard such a scream.

I continued for the door, looking around the lot. I couldn't tell where the scream had come from. I saw no one. But I noticed I was walking faster all the same.

Perhaps it had been a prank. The proximity to campus and so many bars couldn't be ignored, as Harriett Valley Estates property managers had discovered. Drunken college kids were notorious for playing pranks. But I couldn't overlook the uneasy feeling that lingered. And it told me this was something else.

I yanked open the lobby door, built extra wide to accommodate wheelchairs, and strode in. I barely cleared the threshold when I stopped dead. In front of the elevators to my right, a figure dressed in black was kneeling over a young woman sprawled on the floor.

"Uh-oh," I heard myself breathe.

The figure had lifted his or her head at the sound of the door. For one of the longest moments of my life, the figure stared at me, cold, dark eyes burning through the slits of the black ski mask. I stared back. I tried to think, tried to keep breathing. But mostly I just tried not to blink.

Then the moment was broken and time moved again. The figure jumped up, attention fully on me now. Dressed in head-to-toe black, it was difficult to discern any significant details apart from one. The six-inch knife in the figure's right hand, stained with dark red blood, was quite recognizable.

The figure ran toward me and I dropped into a defensive stance, falling back on years of training. The figure closed the distance between us and swung the knife at my chest. I stepped aside, used my left arm in an outward block, and thrust the heel of my right hand forward. Air rushed out of the assailant's lungs in a *whoosh.*

At the same time, an elevator bell dinged and the stairwell door crashed open. The lobby was suddenly full of cheerful, carefree chattering. And people.

The figure struggled to get upright and staggered for the door. Three people stepped off an elevator to my left while two more emerged from the stairwell. The attacker stumbled out the door.

I hurried toward the victim, glancing at my inadvertent rescuers. One of them, a tall blonde I'd signed to a lease two months ago, was holding a cell phone. I pointed to her.

"Call 911."

I dropped to my knees beside the victim and took in the dark red stain spreading across her gray CSU sweatshirt. Several more people arrived in the lobby, many of them gathering around us, staring, talking, pointing.

"Anyone have a towel or anything?" I asked the group at large.

Mostly people just stared back, wide-eyed and confused. A few others shook their heads.

A guy pushed to the front of the crowd as he balled up a shirt. He dropped to his knees opposite me wearing jeans and nothing else.

"Great," I said, reaching for it. I noticed my hands were visibly shaking. "Hold it here and press." I pulled the shirt down to her abdomen and he applied pressure. For all the good it would do. The blood was practically pouring out of her.

"Where's that ambulance?" I demanded, trying to find the blonde woman in the crowd around me.

"It—it's on the way!" someone croaked urgently. A male. I didn't know who or where he was.

I turned back to the girl and placed two fingers against the side of her neck. I felt her pulse beat under my fingertips. It was beating fast. Pumping the blood out of her body that much faster.

She was pretty, dressed in jeans and a sweatshirt, about my age, maybe younger, with shoulder-length blonde hair.

"Anyone know her?" asked the man holding the shirt, looking around.

There were negative murmurs and head-shakes all around.

I thought I knew who she was.

But who would do such a thing to her? And why? Had this been a random attack or was she specifically targeted? I didn't know which would be better—for her or for me.

My brain jumped ahead and I realized once the police and EMS became involved it would be difficult for me to get any information about the girl. Anything I wanted to know, I needed to learn in the next two minutes.

Driven by something I didn't want to name and a need to confirm my suspicion, I looked around for her purse or wallet. There was nothing on the ground near her.

The crowd suddenly split and a kid shot out. He dropped to the floor beside me, his attention on the girl.

"I'm an EMT!" he shouted. "I know CPR!"

The girl didn't need CPR, but I didn't point this out. Instead, I rose and stepped away. I had something else to do.

Squeezing out of the group, I found myself standing in front of the elevators on the west side of the building. This was presumably where the girl had been standing when she'd been attacked. But I saw no purse or wallet unaccounted for on the floor or nearby chairs. Perhaps she hadn't brought one.

What woman doesn't carry a purse? I asked myself as I moved toward the south side of the lobby. Maybe it was in her car. I hadn't brought mine into the building either. Then I spotted it.

A large desk had been constructed in the southwest corner of the lobby. At the time of the seniors, a building employee had been stationed there to assist and direct residents and visitors. TV monitors under the counter had displayed security camera feeds from the dozens of cameras installed around the building. Harriett Van Patten hadn't necessarily minded the noise of the surrounding college students, but she hadn't trusted them, either. She'd insisted on a state-of-the art security system and someone to man it.

Most of the system's functions were no longer utilized and the desk had been unmanned since we'd bought the building. Now it just held pamphlets, brochures, and the occasional coupon. And a bright yellow handbag that seemed to be without an owner.

Skirting the crowd, I reached the counter. Inside the bag I found a wallet. My gut clenched uncomfortably as I read the name: Stacy Karnes. Thinking quickly, I pulled my phone from my pocket and snapped a photo of the ID. A cursory look through the other items in the wallet showed credit cards with the same name, a CSU student ID, and a Social Security Card. I photographed it all.

I returned the wallet and hunted around a bit more, finding little of interest. Conspicuously absent was her cell phone. I'd tried calling her on the drive, but she hadn't answered. Maybe she'd forgotten it at home. But I wanted to confirm, *needed* to confirm. What if she'd had it with her, had answered my call? If she'd known I was running late, would she have waited in her car? Would that have kept her safe from whoever attacked her?

I pushed back through the crowd and squatted beside her. The "EMT" rattled off useless but important-sounding information about her condition. I mostly tuned him out. A quick feel revealed the phone in her back pocket. She'd had it on her the whole time. Why hadn't she answered?

I swiped it and retreated back to the counter. In a true stroke of luck, the phone was unlocked. I heard sirens in the distance and managed a couple photos before I stuffed her phone into her purse and mine into my jacket.

Then the party really got started. Through the lobby doors I saw a fire truck arrive, followed closely by a police car, then an ambulance a minute behind it. Everyone had their lights flashing, which danced over the walls. In two minutes, the number of people in the lobby doubled. Probably every person in the building had gathered to watch the action firsthand. Uniformed personnel occupied the remainder of the space.

Three big, buff men dressed in yellow bunker gear, boots, and navy t-shirts with Poudre Fire Authority logos carried large bags of equipment in from the fire truck and gathered on the floor around Stacy. They were soon joined by a man and a woman from the ambulance. Meanwhile, one of the police officers, who looked like he worked out with the firemen, seemed to be in charge. He issued directions to the others, directions which consisted largely of clearing the lobby, containing the crowd, and separating witness from bystander.

The EMT-kid refused to be cut out of the action as the firefighters settled around Stacy.

"I'm in the EMT class," he said to them. "I'm almost done with my clinicals. I can help."

The firemen shared a glance and fought to conceal smiles. One of them settled an oxygen mask over Stacy's face while another cut open her right sleeve and secured a blood pressure cuff around her arm.

"Is that right?" the third asked as he cut Stacy's sweatshirt in half from hem to collar. Three ugly wounds gaped in her belly, all of which still bled freely. "You wanna help?" he asked as he pressed thick dressings to Stacy's abdomen. "Why don't you hold c-spine?"

"Nothing in the assessment indicates any possible c-spine damage," the kid said, though he jumped up anyway. He repositioned himself and dropped back to the floor, holding Stacy's head between his hands, keeping it in-line and still.

"C-spine damage can occur by the most unexpected injuries," the first fireman said, as if passing on a priceless morsel of information.

The kid bobbed his head up and down eagerly.

I was ushered outside with everyone else. Stacy was loaded onto a gurney and wheeled away. A minute later, the ambulance rolled out of the parking lot. The fire engine left a short time later.

Last to arrive was a van with CRIME SCENE UNIT painted on the side. An attractive but nerdy-looking man got out and carted two huge kits inside, where he then set to work. He took photos and set up numbered, yellow markers.

While the others pushed to the front, trying to see what was going on, I stayed back. I didn't really want to see any more. I'd seen enough—more than enough. And as manager of the building, I figured I'd see plenty more before it was all said and done.

I sat on the curb with my arms around my knees. The crowd ebbed and flowed in front of me. I wanted to leave, but the police weren't letting people go yet. Not to mention I couldn't get my truck around their vehicles clogging up the lot.

My phone chimed softly. I pulled it out and sighed. 7 P.M.: LINCOLN CENTER! DON'T FORGET THE TICKETS!

I'd forgotten to cancel the reminder when I'd given away the tickets. They had been a gift from a client, and I'd planned to spend the evening with Patrick. I quite enjoy a symphony every now and then.

Patrick and I had dated for six months. Last month, he'd gone to Hawaii for a family event. When he got back he'd quit his job, packed his stuff, and told me he was moving. Something to do with the ocean. He was gone a week later.

Probably we broke up, even if he never said as much. This move-to-Hawaii thing seemed pretty permanent.

I sighed again and put the phone back in my pocket. Given my dating history, the Hawaii thing was pretty mild. And I hoped the couple going in our place enjoyed the show. It was supposed to be a good one.

———————————

It didn't take long for the police to determine who had seen anything and who hadn't. There had only been six people in the lobby who saw the masked figure, five of them arriving just as the figure ran out. I was the sixth. At the direction of the officer in charge, the other two officers sent people away when it was established they hadn't seen anything. They were permitted to return to their apartments, guided through the lobby between yellow cones. They were also permitted to leave. They were not permitted to stand around the parking lot within fifty feet of the building. Most people trekked back upstairs.

When the crowd had dispersed and officers stood taking statements from the last two witnesses, the officer in charge, dressed in a navy blue uniform, came over to me. I was struck first by his height: easily six-five. I'm five-eight and I felt tiny standing beside him. He was a few years older than me and exceptionally fit. The bulletproof vest accounted for some of his bulk, but judging by his biceps, it wasn't all vest. His wavy dark hair, cut longer than most cops', was slightly messy, and his face was scruffy. His green eyes had a mesmerizing quality to them. The little brass nameplate on his shirtfront read ELLMANN.

"I'm Detective Ellmann," he said. His voice was deep and sure. He pulled a notebook and pen out of his breast pocket. "I need to ask you some questions."

"Detective? What's with the uniform? Don't detectives wear bad suits?" I looked him over, taking a closer look at his badge. Sure enough, it said DETECTIVE.

"Sometimes detectives wear uniforms." This was clearly a sore subject. "Mind if we get back to the matter at hand?"

"Sure. Is the girl going to be okay?"

"Don't know yet. But her injuries are serious. What's your name?"

"Zoe Grey."

"Do you live in the building?"

"No. I work for the property management company. I was scheduled to show Stacy an apartment."

And I'd been late.

"Do you know Stacy?"

I shook my head. "No. She called my office this morning asking for the appointment. That was the first time I'd talked to her."

"I understand you were the first person in the lobby after the assault. Can you tell me what happened?"

I told him what I'd heard and seen, everything I knew of what happened, which amounted to a whole lot of not much. He dutifully scribbled notes in the small notepad. When I felt the interview was winding down, I asked if I could leave.

He studied me for a beat, and I had the distinct impression he saw the thing I didn't say. I didn't like it. Usually, I'm much better at making sure this can't happen. I attributed this fluke to the fact that I was still slightly stunned and unprepared for police scrutiny.

Nearby, another officer concluded an interview and sent his witness on her way. Spying Ellmann, the officer ambled over. As he did, his eyes flicked my direction and he looked me up and down. I felt a wave of disgust roll through me.

"Ellmann," the officer interrupted. "We've talked to everyone." His nameplate said PRATT.

Pratt was about six feet tall, with dirty blonde hair and brown eyes. He was very slender; even the gun belt and assorted cop paraphernalia were unable to hide how narrow his hips were.

"You the one who saw the whole thing?" Pratt asked me.

I nodded.

Something dark seemed to skitter across his brain and he tried to suppress a smirk.

"Since you touched the body," he said, again looking me up and down, "we should probably take your clothes into evidence. I'll bag them."

Body? Stacy had been alive when she left. Had that changed?

It seemed Pratt volunteered to see me in the buff a little too quickly.

"No," Ellmann snapped before I could respond. "Why don't you take measurements of the parking lot?"

It sounded a lot like the fireman's c-spine direction to me, but I might have misinterpreted. Maybe parking lot measurements would prove useful to the case.

"Stacy's dead?" I asked after Pratt had sauntered away, obviously grumpy. There was fear and sorrow in my voice that surprised even me.

Ellmann looked back to me, his eyes slightly wide. That was the only indication of what he was thinking or feeling; everything else was carefully secured behind his well-practiced cop-face.

"No, she's not dead," he said. His tone was reassuring, certain. "Last I heard from the hospital, she's in surgery. I'm not sure yet what her prognosis is."

I exhaled, unaware I'd been holding my breath.

Oh, thank goodness.

"Are you sure you don't know her?"

I looked up at Ellmann and nodded. "Yeah, I'm sure."

"I have everything I need for now. If there's anything else, I'll be in touch." He reached into his breast pocket and pulled out a card, which he gave to me. "Call if you think of anything, no matter how small. And you'll need to come to the station tomorrow to sign some paperwork."

I tucked the card into my pocket, then picked my way across the parking lot back to my truck. The lot had cleared considerably, though a small group of people was still gathered on the sidewalk just beyond the police boundary, watching. I climbed into the truck, then maneuvered out around the remaining emergency vehicles and drove home.

Home as it stood now wasn't a comforting thought for me, although I planned to remedy this on Saturday, when I moved into my new place. The house I would live in for two more nights was large: five bedrooms, one of which was a separate, private guest suite. There was also a two-bedroom apartment above the garage. Every one of the five bedrooms was currently occupied. So was the apartment.

When I was eighteen, I'd moved to Denver for the man I'd thought I was going to marry, and while the relationship hadn't worked out, the new job had. It was my first taste of property management, and I discovered I had a knack for it. I rose through the ranks quickly and was making an obscene amount of money. Among other things, I began purchasing property.

My mother has never been much of a mother. It wasn't long before she'd needed a place to stay. I wouldn't have thought much of this except at the time my brother, Zach, was still in her charge. So I'd purchased a house here in Fort Collins and moved them in, renting out the apartment and guest suite to help cover the mortgage. I'd debated bringing Zach to live with me, ultimately deciding against it because I didn't want to uproot him from the only life he'd ever known, and the metropolitan part of Denver I was living in then wasn't the type of place where teenagers could ride their bikes in the streets.

But this is why kids shouldn't make decisions like these, because I realized later what Zach had really needed was a mother and a role model, not his friends or afternoon bike rides. His first run-in with the police at age fifteen had gotten my attention. His second a month later got me packing.

Initially, I'd rented a condo. But it became clear that simply being nearer wasn't making an impact. Zach was arrested for the first time for smoking marijuana two weeks after I'd moved back. I really didn't want to live with my mother again; there was a reason I'd moved out when I was seventeen. But I'd proven time and again I'd do anything for my brother, and at that time, the simplest thing was to store my stuff and move into one of the open basement bedrooms.

I'd planned on the arrangement being temporary, just long enough to put Zach back on the right course. But that had proved a more difficult task than my twenty-one-year-old self could have anticipated. Zach barely graduated high school, got arrested a couple more times, did a brief stint in juvenile detention, and had his driver's license revoked. Finally, at twenty, he seemed to have grown up a bit. He'd held a job for eight months without any incident and almost perfect attendance. He'd gotten his driver's license back. And he had enrolled in community college where he was going to class regularly and making a considerable effort to maintain decent grades.

All of this meant I could move out without feeling as if I was abandoning him again. He was even talking about renting a place of his own with a couple of his buddies. So most my stuff was already packed, and Saturday couldn't come soon enough.

I was considering taking a short vacation. Not to go anywhere, but just to have time off work. Life had been exceedingly stressful for me lately. And so very monotonous. Somewhere along the line I'd settled into a routine, and now it consumed my life. I thought a few days off work would be nice. I could relax, settle into my new place, maybe do some fun stuff, something new and different. As the house loomed nearer and nearer, the idea sounded better and better. I made a mental note to speak to my boss about it tomorrow.

As usual, the house was as bright as noon when I returned. Didn't matter that it was nearly midnight. I grabbed my bag and shuffled to the door, doing my best to prepare myself for what I knew was waiting. Mostly I failed miserably.

"Where the hell have you been?" my mother snapped when I came into the kitchen. She was dressed in sweats, a rag in one hand and cleaning products in the other. The kitchen smelled strongly of bleach, with scents of other cleaners choking the air.

"And why are you dressed like that?" Her familiar tone was harsh, unkind, accusing. "What kind of trouble have you been getting into? You're *always* in trouble. Ever since you were a baby. Not like your brother; no child sweeter than that boy. Sometimes I wonder how *you* could be mine."

I looked down at myself as I shuffled to the cupboard. (I didn't want to look, but I couldn't help it.) My black trousers were wrinkled, and I suspected the smudge on my right knee was blood. My blue top was equally rumpled and hanging off my shoulders slightly crooked. It was easy to understand my mother's alarm, given my current state and the vain importance she placed on appearance.

I pulled down a glass and filled it with ice water.

"We'll talk about it later," I said, hardly aware of her tone anymore, but not wholly able to ignore it, either.

"No, we will not! When are you going to grow up? Some of us have *real* jobs and responsibilities. At least your brother is trying to make something of himself. When are you going to do the same? You're *always* in trouble."

Someone had put the record on the player, but it wasn't aligned correctly. The record turned, played the same few lines, then circled back to play them again. Always the same few lines.

"I know," I said, leaving the kitchen. Most of the defeat and sorrow I heard in my voice was the result of what happened to Stacy Karnes. But not all of it. In any case, there was no point engaging her; she couldn't be reasoned with when she was in this state.

The guest suite door opened and Donald poked his head out. He was one of two unrelated people currently living in the house. Not an altogether bad guy, I was fonder of Donald than any of the other renters, past or present. He was five-nine with a slight paunch, in his late fifties, had perfectly trimmed—if outdatedly styled—gray hair and brown eyes that were always seen through thick, dark-framed glasses.

"What's all the racket? I heard yelling." He looked me over through bleary eyes as he adjusted the glasses on his nose. "What happened to you?"

"Work turned into a witness-for-the-police thing when I sort of saw a woman stabbed. How was your day?"

He shrugged and stuffed his hands into the pockets of the red plaid bathrobe neatly tied around him. "Boring."

"Lucky bastard."

2

I rolled out of bed after hitting the snooze button three times. I hadn't slept well. I'd had vivid dreams that were ugly and destructive.

My life got off to a rocky and violent start. From violent, it phased to uncertain, but always it was hard. I've been seeing a therapist regularly to help deal with what that means. Normally, I'm rather well-adjusted, all things considered. I still have patterns of learned behavior I have to work to overcome, but usually I'm successful and can function without major incident in polite society.

But when I experience violence, physical or emotional, whether I'm a participant or an observer, the result is the same. The dreams, sometimes better described as "nightmares," return, and I find I can be irritable, my temper short. From the moment I'd heard the scream last night, I'd known what I was in for. Walking into that lobby, physically confronting the attacker, and seeing Stacy Karnes's body had cracked some of the retaining walls, and my past was seeping back out. I would need to get it under control, and fast.

The coffee pot was empty, as usual. Every morning I was the last to get up, and every morning I found the pot empty. Eternal optimist that I am, I always secretly hoped there would be a cup left, but there never was. Skipping it, I went back downstairs to shower.

I stripped my clothes off and caught a glimpse before I went to the shower. Frowning, I walked back to the mirror. I didn't like what I saw. Perhaps it was merely the result of my uncharitable mood brought on by the lack of sleep and caffeine, but I didn't think so. That wasn't the whole story, in any case.

I'd noticed a slight weight gain after returning home. My family life has always been a huge source of stress for me, and stress seems to negatively affect my metabolism. The weight gain had continued until Barry Paige had been hired, at which point it exploded. See, Paige takes his position as my supervisor more seriously than necessary. In the last eight months, I'd gained thirty pounds. That's more than a woman should gain while pregnant. I'm not pregnant. It was as if the stress I was feeling from every direction had shut off my metabolism, allowing every ounce I ate to slide right down to my butt and stick. My butt and my stomach and my thighs and that place along the back of my arms. Didn't matter that I'd become more conscientious of what I was eating. I'm five-eight most days, five-nine on good days; I don't have a lot of extra height to accommodate or offset the additional weight. And in the last two years, the additional weight totaled forty pounds. All right, forty-seven.

Today it looked more like seventy. This was how I knew I was feeling unfriendly. The stress had brought gray hair, too, though I'm only twenty-five. And my skin had been nearly flawless until recently. Now there are noticeable lines around my eyes and mouth. These irritate me most.

I saw the look in my eye then turned away from the mirror. My eyes fluctuate between deep green and hazel depending mostly on my mood. Just then, they were burning green: a reflection of the strong emotion I was feeling.

I stood under the water for several long minutes, until I was thoroughly soaked, then reached up for my shampoo. I knew the instant I lifted the bottle what I'd find, but (optimist, remember?) I popped the cap and held my hand open, squeezing all the same. Nothing came out but a *swish* of air.

Not to worry. I always keep an extra bottle of everything stashed behind the tampons under the sink. Dripping wet, I got back out and pulled the cupboard doors open, searching for my hidden cache. I couldn't find anything. Confused, I removed everything until I'd reached the back of the cupboard. The only items remaining were deodorant and body wash.

I replaced the items I'd removed and went back to the shower, colorfully cursing Bradley, the college student renting the third bedroom in the basement. He shared a bathroom with Zach and me, one he hardly ever cleaned, and he had a habit of helping himself to whatever he could find. It hadn't been until he'd brought his boyfriend home that I'd understood why he was always using *my* products.

A quick search of the available items in the shower left me with one option. I picked up Zach's shampoo-and-body-wash-in-one and sniffed at the top. It smelled like a man; no way around it. But I had to wash my hair with something. With a sigh, I squirted some out and lathered it through my hair. I needed to have a conversation with Bradley sometime soon. And I was seriously considering raising his rent. Had I been planning to stay past tomorrow, I would evict him instead.

I twisted my long hazelnut-colored hair up and tied it in a knot on top of my head, pinning back my long bangs. (Probably it was good Bradley wasn't home when I got out of the shower.) My hair is a hot mess as often as not. Reminiscent of a 90s-era Julia Roberts; it is thick, wavy, and has a mind of its own. Today, of course, it would have to stay up in order to cut down on the Axe smell. I did the best I could to make it look presentable then left it to air dry. Out of habit, I tucked two extra hairpins into my pocket, just in case I needed reinforcement later.

Early in life, my mother had instilled the importance of such vain undertakings as makeup, hairspray, push-up bras, and control-top pantyhose. While I'd given up most of that as a gesture of rebellion, I still can't bring myself to leave the house without mascara. And for work, I always wear complete makeup. It just doesn't feel right not to. So, I did the makeup thing in a hurry, then pulled together a passable outfit of brown slacks and a green top. I grabbed my bag and hit the door.

My first appointment was at eight. It took some negotiating, but the late walk-in client from the night before had finally agreed to come back first thing this morning. It meant coming in an hour early, but to get him out of my office, I'd agreed.

I checked my mirror and changed lanes, grimacing at the recurring thoughts of the night before. I wanted to blame the walk-in client for making me late to meet Stacy Karnes, but that wasn't fair. Sure, his timing had been unfortunate, but I should have been firmer about cutting the meeting short. I was responsible for keeping my own schedule, and I was responsible for being late.

I couldn't help but think about how different things would have been had I gotten there on time. I'd been a mere moment too late to intervene before Stacy was stabbed. Had I left on time, had the lights and traffic been different, had I arrived a minute earlier, would Stacy be lying in the hospital today? I couldn't help but think not. I realized, had I been any earlier it could just as easily have been me lying in the hospital today. Or the morgue. I also knew I couldn't help the fact Stacy had been in the lobby at that specific time. But she had been there to meet me, and that left me feeling more than a little responsible for what had happened to her. I knew this sense of responsibility and the associated guilt were the heaviest assaults against my retaining walls.

Traffic wasn't cooperating. My goal had been to stop for coffee on the way to the office, but all hope evaporated when I caught the third consecutive red light after leaving my house. If this continued, I'd be late as it was. Being late wasn't something I tolerated well under the best of circumstances. After last night, I didn't think I could tolerate it at all. I pulled my cell phone from the cup holder, wishing it were a perfectly blended, chocolate-flavored coffee instead, and dialed the office. The receptionist answered on the second ring.

"White Real Estate and Property Management. This is Sandra. How may I help you?"

Sandra York was new, having started six months ago. Overall, she did an acceptable job, but she wasn't a natural for the role, and she wasn't highly motivated to compensate for any deficiencies.

"It's Zoe. I need a favor. I have a meeting at eight; I left the info on your desk last night. Can you call the guy and let him know I'll be five minutes late?"

"There's a guy in the lobby. Let me make sure that's not him."

She put me on hold and I listened to elevator music for two minutes. I also managed to catch another red light. She came back on the line just as the light turned green.

"Wasn't him," she said. "I'll call him."

The four cars in front of me began moving. I put my foot to the gas, easing it down while I let my left foot off the clutch. The truck rolled forward, then the engine died. Hoping I'd stalled it, I twisted the key. The engine sputtered but failed to catch.

In my heart, I knew this wasn't something simple. I hit the hazard lights in response to the angry horns sounding behind me then tried the key again. The result was the same.

"Perfect," I sighed, leaning back against the seat. "Sandra, I'm going to need you to reschedule that appointment all together. I'm going to be more than five minutes late."

"Well, how late are you going to be?"

"I hope to make my nine o'clock, but I may need you to reschedule that one, too."

She sighed. "Fine. Let me know." Then she hung up.

I dropped the phone back into the cup holder.

"Yes, I'm fine," I said to the steering wheel. "No, I don't need anything. Thank you. Your concern is touching."

I was northbound on Shields in the far right lane, just south of Drake. About a block ahead there was a turnoff into a parking lot. I stepped out of the truck. A passing motorist belted his horn at me and flipped me the bird. I smiled, blew him a kiss, and waved. Shedding my jacket, I rolled down the window and took my position in the open door.

Despite how heavy a vehicle is, especially an old one like mine, I've never found them difficult to push, especially not my truck. This has been handy considering I've spent a lot of time in the past few months pushing it. I got a few more honks and hand gestures, and a kid hung his head out the window and shouted something dirty as he flew past. No one stopped to help.

Once in the parking lot, the truck picked up momentum. I jumped inside and allowed it to roll as I manhandled the steering wheel, directing it to the far right of the lot, where it rolled to a stop across three spaces. Climbing back out, I walked around and lifted the hood. I stepped onto the bumper and peered over the innards of the truck.

I have very little mechanical prowess but I figured it was merely due diligence to have a look and eliminate all obvious problems. I didn't know the names of any of the parts I was looking at or their functions, but I would have been able to tell if a hose was hanging lose or wires were sticking out somewhere. Of course, I saw none of those things. I also knew the tank had gas.

I'd found the 1978 International Scout II by happenstance. Shortly after moving back to Fort Collins, I'd listed my Mercedes for sale on Craigslist. Wanting to sell the thing quickly, I'd initially listed it low. But I realized soon enough that wasn't drawing the kind of attention I needed—just lots of looky-loos wondering why the pretty, two-year-old Mercedes was so cheap. So I relisted and overpriced it. This cut interested phone calls by more than half, down to a more manageable number and seriously interested parties.

About four people had already looked at the car by the time Stan had called and I'd met him in the Target parking lot. But there was something about Stan that I'd liked. He'd wanted to buy the Mercedes for his wife. Stan had been crazy about his wife, that was obvious to anyone after about five minutes. Her car had recently been totaled and she had been driving his truck, leaving him with his Scout. She'd hated the Scout and refused to drive it.

The Scout had been either carefully restored or impeccably maintained, I'd known from first glance. Talking around an ever-present cigarette between his lips, Stan had told me he had purchased the thing new in '77 and had taken exceptional care of it. A mechanic, he had done all the work himself. His wife may have hated it, but the Scout was a thing of beauty; hunter green with a white removable hardtop and Army-tan interior. And at that time, everything had worked as well as it had the day it rolled off the manufacturing floor.

He'd noticed my interest, and he must have already known he was dying. I had come prepared to deal, and, like I said, there was something I liked about Stan. I'd knocked a big chunk off the price and he'd thrown in the Scout.

For the next year, I took the Scout back to Stan for everything: oil changes, new windshield wipers, tire-pressure checks. He never charged me very much, and I always left the truck with him for the day, let him tool around in it for old time's sake. When he got too sick to work, he gave me the name of a new mechanic: Leonard Krupp. Krupp was old school and could work on a vehicle as old as the Scout.

But the wear and tear must have finally caught up to the thing, because it had been to visit the new mechanic routinely since. I occasionally consider offering to sell it back to Stan's wife, even though she always hated it. Sometimes I dream about driving it over to Krupp's, when it's running, and sending it crashing through the front window of his garage. I've considered pushing it into Horsetooth Reservoir more than once.

When reality finally settled back around me now, I walked back to the cab and retrieved my phone, dialing the number for the towing company from memory.

After arranging for a tow, I called Krupp to tell him the truck was coming back. He didn't answer. I left a message.

Now I needed a ride. I never bother to call my mother. Zach was at work. Friday mornings my best friend, Amy, worked out of town. I knew she'd come get me if I called her, but I reserved calls like that for emergencies only. I tried my friend Sadie, but the call went to voicemail. I didn't leave a message. Then I called Donald. Not only did he answer, but he agreed to come get me.

"Works out perfect," he said. "I was out cruising. I'll be there in ten minutes."

A small groan escaped me before I could bite it down. I knew what "cruising" meant.

———————————

Donald is a lot of things, sentimental being one of them. In addition to his daily driver, he owns a 1979 Lincoln Continental. The car had belonged to his mother before her passing more than a decade ago, but he'd been unable to get rid of the damn thing. Most days it sits at the curb outside the house collecting dust and the occasional parking ticket. Every once in a while, Donald will take it for a little morning spin, cruising up and down College Avenue, just to keep it in running order.

The truck was being loaded for transport when the road boat floated into the lot, Donald at the helm. The thing is nineteen feet long from bumper to bumper and the copper color of a freshly minted penny, with a matching vinyl roof.

The tow truck driver stared openly at the Lincoln for a moment then turned to me. I smiled, waved, and climbed in beside Donald. He sailed the Lincoln home.

"What's wrong with your truck?"

I shrugged. "No idea. It just died."

"Want to borrow the Lincoln?"

Because it was Friday, I'd be lucky if my mechanic got around to looking at my truck today. Realistically, it would probably be Saturday, maybe even Monday. All said and done, it could very well be a week before I could bring it home. Did I want to drive the Lincoln for a week?

"That's generous of you, but I'll be okay. I've got the scooter."

"You sure?"

Donald glanced at me, and I noticed the childlike sparkle in his eyes as he maneuvered the Lincoln.

I couldn't help but chuckle.

"Yes, I'm sure. Thank you. I'll let you know if I change my mind."

Donald tipped his head back slightly and seemed to take in a long breath.

"Say, you wearing Zach's jacket or something?" he asked. "I smell his perfume."

"Yeah, borrowed his jacket." I left it at that.

When we arrived at the house, Donald docked the copper barge at the curb and we disembarked. Donald was, as always, neatly dressed like an accountant. Donald isn't an accountant, but he always looks like one: button-down shirts, sweaters most of the year, khakis, and dark-rimmed glasses.

He cast a fond, loving glance at the Lincoln before disappearing into the house. I went into the garage.

The garage was a three-car tandem design. Two spaces were occupied by my mother's cherry red Saab and Donald's daily driver, a Ford Edge. If it were me, I would have parked the Lincoln in the garage. Monstrosity or not, the thing is a classic, and sitting exposed on the street year after year isn't doing anything good for the value. Although, I have to admit, the paint is as shiny as the day it had been applied.

At present, only the Edge was in residence. Donald works from home three days a week, including Fridays, and my mother was at her office. Despite her condition, she takes her job seriously, which is about the only thing she takes seriously, and she rarely misses work.

The tandem space was used as storage for yard equipment, an extra freezer and refrigerator, miscellaneous items, and a 1963 Cushman Trailster.

The Trailster had belonged to my paternal grandfather. He'd purchased it after developing a fondness for Cushman products during World War II. During the war, Cushmans were airdropped into war zones for use by the soldiers. My grandfather swore a Cushman Airborne saved his life. When he was no longer able to ride the Trailster, he'd passed it to my father. By that time, scooter travel had long been out of vogue. Mostly the scooter had been stored, though occasionally my father had taken the thing out for a ride. A few times, he'd even taken me.

My grandfather had taken exceptional care of the scooter, but my father, who hadn't had a caring bone in his body, had been rough with it. During his tenure, it hadn't been properly stored or maintained. Neither had he been a cautious rider. The Trailster had been wrecked more than once. The way I feel about my father has always prevented me from pouring any kind of love or attention into the scooter. But because it is a classic, and because I have a few fond memories of my grandfather, I can't bring myself to get rid of it, either. So it sits, covered in the corner of the garage.

I removed the dusty cover and stared down at the yellow scooter, scuffed and marred from misuse. A piece of the front fender was missing, the left handle grip was badly cracked, and one mirror was bent. The driver's seat was worn from use, and the material on the passenger seat had a long tear in it. The entire thing was dusty, and there was dirt caked onto the lower parts of the frame. Apparently, it hadn't been washed before it was last stored.

Grabbing the handlebars, I walked the thing out into the sunlight of the driveway. The design of the Trailster is more motorcycle than scooter, with its high handlebars and top-mounted gas tank. And, actually, because of the limited definition of "scooter" by Colorado law, the Trailster is considered a motorcycle.

I twisted the gas cap off and checked the gasoline. By no small miracle, it was still crystal clear and odor free. I went inside and pulled my backpack out of the closet. Then I stuffed my purse into it and slung it on. I got the vintage, open-faced, brown leather helmet my father had always worn out of its storage place and wiped it off, doing the same with the goggles. My father had always wanted a son. He had never forgiven me for being something else, but occasionally he had taught me all the boy things he'd wanted to teach a son. On even rarer occasions, he'd treat me like a daughter and act as if it was okay that I was his. One such occasion included presenting me with a pink, flowered helmet and taking me for a ride on the scooter. The day had ended in blood and tears (both mine), like so many before and after it. I still have the pink helmet, but I don't wear it.

I fit the helmet over my head, fastening the chinstrap. I brought the kickstand up and prepared the kick pedal then gripped the handlebars for balance as I threw my weight down on it. The engine coughed then, with a series of crisp pops, chugged to life. Stowing the pedal, I pulled the goggles down and accelerated out of the driveway, once again on my way to work. I buzzed into the lot and parked at eight fifty-five.

———————————

"Geez, what happened to you?" Sandra asked when I walked in. She had her perfectly-painted lips slightly curled.

Sandra is thirty going on fifteen. She's petite, pretty, unnaturally blonde, and fashion savvy. She likely spent an hour on her hair alone each morning. Ditto for her makeup. In the six months she'd worked here, I hadn't seen her wear the same pair of shoes twice. I confess, I don't even own enough shoes anymore to do that for two weeks. Well, maybe two weeks. But certainly not three. Okay, definitely not a month.

"We can't all look like beauty queens," I said, blowing by her toward my office.

She took an indiscreet whiff as I passed. "Were you with a man?"

I didn't like the level of accusation in her tone. What the hell was wrong with me being with a man, if that's where I had been?

Without responding, I let myself in the door and dropped my stuff on my desk, then raised the blinds and opened the windows. It was May, and our weather was unseasonably warm, the daytime highs reaching into the eighties more often than not. Today would probably be one of those days. But this morning there was a pleasant breeze blowing and the office was stuffy. After settling myself in, I went back to Sandra's desk.

"Were you able to reach my eight o'clock?"

She shook her head. "No. I left a message, but he hasn't called back."

Weird, I thought. *He was so eager last night.*

"Maybe he changed his mind," I said. "Do I have messages?"

Sandra shuffled through the items on her desk and finally located a stack of pink WHILE YOU WERE OUT notes under the current edition of *Cosmo.* She shuffled through them, sorting out mine, then handed them to me. The picture of efficiency.

I glanced at the clock.

"Heard anything from my nine o'clock?" I asked. "He's late."

She shrugged and turned a page in her magazine.

"Nope."

Right.

I walked back to my office. The other offices were occupied, most with doors open and voices drifting out. The office at the end of the hall belonged to Barry Paige. Paige was the director of the Fort Collins division of White Real Estate and Property Management. He'd been doing his job a few months longer than Sandra, but he wasn't any better at his than she was at hers.

Mark White, a real estate tycoon and the owner of White Real Estate, had originally offered me Paige's position. He'd just expanded the company to include Loveland and wanted someone who would help bring growth. I would have done just that, but I'd had to refuse. Under Paige, our division had grown a measly seven percent. I would have more than doubled that number in the same time. As it was, my numbers accounted for four of the seven percent. I'm not sure White has totally forgiven me for turning him down.

When I was eighteen, in my first year of college, working as a CNA in a nursing home in preparation for what I believed would be a long nursing career, a close friend at the time, Brandi, had introduced me to a man named Matt. A few years older than me, Matt had lived in Denver and worked for Colorado Property Management Group as a leasing agent for one of the pricier apartment complexes. Taylor Swift sings a song about being fifteen and believing someone when they say they love you. The same holds true when you're eighteen. He told me he loved me and I believed him. Simple as that.

I'd finished my second semester of school and hadn't enrolled in a third, my nursing career on hold. I'd quit my job, taken a position with the same company, and moved to Denver. I'd been assigned to a different site, one that was less pricey and a good starting place. I was pretty motivated, but it turned out I was pretty good at that sort of work. Maybe it's genetic. My maternal grandfather had been a salesman all his life and could literally sell ice to an Eskimo. My mother also seems to have this gene.

Being closer to Matt, I'd believed our relationship was getting stronger. After six months, he'd begun talking about wanting to marry me. He'd officially proposed after eleven months. Of course, I'd agreed.

I'd thought my life was shaping up to be exactly what I wanted it to be. I was engaged, had begun a career, and the money was pouring in. I was making more than most college graduates. I was doing all the things I wanted: taking vacations, paying off my car, buying nice clothes and jewelry, saving for a wedding. I even bought a house, then a condo, then later a second house. I'd gotten a serious elevation in economic status and was thrilled to explore what that meant.

My success caused me to get noticed by the higher-ups and advance within the company. After working at Colorado Property Management Group less than a year, I'd been appointed to a management position overseeing nine of the properties. The Northern Denver Region, as it's called. I'd been responsible for hiring, firing, the budget, and everything else. Turned out I wasn't half bad as a manager, either, and I'd certainly liked the doubled income. I was able to pay off the condo and one house entirely and make a serious dent in the debt on the other.

Ultimately, I'd been a fool. Matt's interest in me was just a way for him to get closer to Brandi. And despite being my friend, she'd begun a relationship with him behind my back, one that carried on for several months. I'm ashamed to say I didn't catch on until Brandi wound up pregnant. A scheduling slip-up connected the dots for me; Matt was the father.

I'd been heartbroken, but mostly out of spite, I'd kept my job and stayed in Denver. Matt had prided himself on his job and his stats. So I'd thrown myself into work, and quickly climbed the ladder, earning two major promotions and an income twice as big as his.

I'd continued to immerse myself in the lifestyle of wealth and success, but it had lost a lot of appeal after that. Through the tint of heartbreak, all I'd seen were miserable people trying to ease their pain with objects, money, status, and power, myself included. For a moment, I'd almost lost myself in that world.

When I finally broke free, I knew I never wanted to go back. But after bouncing around from one minimum wage job to the next, I'd finally taken a position with a small, local company working for Mark White. I liked this job, and I did good work, but I couldn't let myself get drawn in. Accepting White's promotion would have put me a step closer to a life I didn't want.

Paige's door was closed, but I could tell the windows were open; he was in. Paige rarely made appointments so early. Actually, Paige rarely made appointments. Appointments mean work. White is one of the only people Paige meets with.

As I turned into my office, glancing at the messages, I wondered if White was meeting with Paige now.

I had three messages. Two of them were from residents in Elizabeth Tower. They both expressed concern regarding the safety of the building.

The building had been wired for exceptional security when it had been for senior living; the cameras and other security measures still in place. The only pieces of equipment currently being used were the three-dozen security cameras. The controlled access doors had been disabled, along with the rest. After Stacy was stabbed, it had crossed my mind the people living in the building would be upset. I'd even considered the idea of posting a security guard, if only for temporary measure. I didn't foresee the attacker making a return visit, but there would be no explaining that to hysterical and terrified college kids. Or to their parents.

I returned to my desk and scrolled through my address book until I found the number for a commercial security company we'd used in the past. I called and set an appointment for noon.

I had accepted that my nine o'clock had stood me up when I heard the front door. Just in case it was him after all, I went and poked my head out of my office. A woman in her late twenties trailing two children under five spoke briefly to Sandra then another agent came to greet them, leading them down the hall into an office.

Sandra saw me standing in the doorway.

"She's the first person to come in all morning," she said.

I nodded and turned away, then stopped.

"You said there was a man in the lobby this morning," I said. "When I called."

"Oh, that," she said, waving a hand dismissively. "That was a cop. He doesn't count."

The most frightening part of that statement was that I followed her logic.

"What did the cop want?"

She shrugged. "Asked to see Barry. He was here quite a while."

"Who? Did you get a name?"

"Uh, something with an *E* I think . . . uh . . ."

"Ellmann," I said softly to myself.

She snapped her fingers. "Yep, that's it. Ellmann."

3

After concluding a showing, I grabbed lunch and took it back to the office. My concentration had been divided all morning. I couldn't stop thinking about Ellmann dropping by to see Paige.

Why was Ellmann meeting with Paige? I assumed it had something to do with Stacy's assault. Why wasn't he addressing his needs with me? I was the site manager. It had been me she was meeting. I'd been something of a witness. Paige hadn't been there. What could he know of it? He knows so little of anything at all.

These thoughts continued to pester me as I munched a salad and sipped coffee. Then a face appeared in my open door.

"There's no one at the desk," the man said apologetically.

So typical for Sandra to walk away without telling anyone.

"I'm sorry about that," I said, standing and walking around the desk. "What can I do for you?"

"I'm here to see Zoe Grey."

"That's me."

The man was around thirty, over six feet tall, and obviously fit. He was dressed in well-fitting blue jeans, black boots, and a black polo shirt with a company logo embroidered on it. His brown hair was neatly cut and carefully styled with gel. His blue eyes sparkled with a hint of amusement, as if he knew something the rest of us didn't. He was clean-shaven, and his features indicated his Italian ancestry.

He smiled as he offered me his hand.

"Joe Pezzani. I'm from Wolf Security Concepts."

"Great, thanks for coming. Please, have a seat."

I thought I saw his nose twitch slightly, though he refrained from comment. Maybe I needed to ride around for a while without the helmet, let my hair air out some.

I went back around the desk and set the salad aside. He lowered his long frame into a chair opposite me and smiled again. I picked up a pamphlet on Elizabeth Tower and passed it to him.

"Last night there was an assault in the lobby of that building," I began. "There have been concerns from the residents about their safety. I'd like to post a guard in the building after dark for a few days, maybe a week, to appease them. I don't want them to be afraid in their own homes."

He was listening, nodding, glancing through the information on the pamphlet.

"You sound like you think it's a wasted gesture."

"I don't think it's a waste if it makes them feel safe."

"But you don't think a threat exists."

I leaned back in my chair and re-crossed my legs. "No, I don't. I believe last night's assault was an isolated incident. I'd be very surprised if anything like it ever happened again. But that isn't what's important."

"It's a big building," he said. "Lots of people in and out. What sort of security do you have in place?"

"The building is fully equipped. The only piece we're currently using is the cameras. I don't think it's important to control traffic. I'd just like there to be a presence."

He nodded. "Okay, no problem." He set the pamphlet on the desk and reached for the briefcase he carried, withdrawing a small packet. "It gets dark around eight these days, light around six. Would you like to start with two days? Three? The whole week?"

"Let's do a week, and make it six to six. There's a high level of activity in the evenings, and it would be good for the guard to be noticed."

"Sure." He was filling out the top form quickly, with familiarity.

Through the open doorway, I heard another door open followed by two sets of footsteps: one purposeful, one hurried. Paige's office door. He'd been in another meeting when I'd returned to the office. With two meetings, this was shaping up to be a busy day for him.

"Let me take care of this," Paige pleaded. "It's been a long time coming anyway, and now *this*."

Mark White strode by, Paige on his heels like a yapping lap dog.

Paige shook the paperwork clutched in his hand, but the CEO wasn't looking at him or it.

"I told you," White said with a ring of finality, "I'll handle it. I'll let you know when I've made a decision."

White blew through the front door, slamming it shut behind him, probably before Paige could follow.

Pezzani looked at me, eyebrows raised. "Someone's not happy," he said as he turned back to his writing.

No, I thought, *but Paige doesn't handle it well when he doesn't get his way.*

"All right," Pezzani said, sitting forward. "I'll set this up for three people to do twelve-hour shifts for seven days, starting tonight. One will work three nights; the other two will do two apiece. This will provide them some familiarity with the building and the residents. If you'd like to extend the service, I'll assign the same guys, for that purpose. Sound about right?"

"Sounds gr—"

Paige stomped down the hall and into my office, oblivious to Pezzani. He shook the same documents he'd tried to show White at me then threw them down on my desk. I wasn't having a real great day anyway, but fighting with Paige always makes for a shitty one.

"Oh, come on," I hissed as I pushed away from the desk, paper raining from my lap to the floor.

Where was the professionalism? Professionalism seems to have died out with my mother's generation. Personally, I find this sad, and irritating.

Paige is egotistical and pompous and belligerent on his best days, and in such a hurry to climb the ladder he doesn't care who he steps on. He doesn't care about doing good work or doing the right thing; he cares about how everyone else's work makes him look. Naturally, we'd butted heads from the get-go. On top of it all, Paige is a jerk. But I believe it's possible to be all of that *and* professional.

I looked at Paige. He was practically vibrating he was so excited. That is always bad.

"Know what that is?" he sang, as happy as a kid on Christmas morning.

"Why don't you tell me?"

A disgusting, satisfied smile split Paige's weasel-like face.

Another bad sign.

"I've been waiting for months for some reason, *any* reason, but this is better than anything I could have dreamed." He smiled wider. "You're fired."

Yep, bad.

Probably this was a mess that could be sorted out. But I pretty much thought this would officially flush my day down the crapper. I could always count on Paige for that.

"Excuse me?" I said.

Pezzani slipped the documents he'd been holding into his briefcase and stood. He watched both Paige and me closely. I wondered what he saw.

"You are a constant pain in my ass," Paige said. "You always argue with me and think you know better than me. I know you're after my job."

Pretty much everyone knows better than Paige, five-year-olds included. Case in point, I *don't* want Paige's job.

"The good news is I finally got something on you! Not even White can turn his back on it."

"And that would be?" I asked.

"You falsified documents and stole twenty thousand dollars from this company! I can finally fire you!"

"Wait a minute!" I shot back. Now *I* seemed to forget Pezzani's presence. Leaning over my desk, I pointed an angry index finger directly at Paige's nose. "I don't have any idea what you're talking about. I didn't steal anything. Sure, I hate working for you, but I was perfectly content making you miserable by showing you up. What would I gain by stealing from White? Stealing isn't my speed." Not anymore.

"What about the evidence that says otherwise? You gonna try to tell me it's all a lie?" he demanded, waving an angry hand over the desk, indicating the papers he'd thrown at me.

"Yeah!" I answered. "I haven't stolen so much as a paperclip from this company."

Actually, that isn't true. I've *borrowed* several items from the office, including paperclips, staples, sticky notes, the occasional highlighter, and once or twice I've used company resources to look up background on people I wasn't planning to lease anything to. What I hadn't done, however, was embezzle twenty thousand dollars. I can't even remember what twenty thousand dollars looks like. Had it been me who'd figured out a way to embezzle money, I would never have made it to twenty thousand. I'd have stopped at five, maybe ten. That would have been more money than I'd had in years; it would have bought a lot of shoes. I would have taken it and split. The very fact I kept showing up everyday was evidence I had done nothing of the sort. Idiot.

Paige walked around the desk and, at my height, came practically nose-to-nose with me. His pinched features were distorted with joy, a happy twinkle in his eyes.

"I didn't like you from the beginning," he hissed. His breath was rancid and hot on my cheeks. It was hard to resist the urge to step away from him. "You're nothing but a spoiled brat who throws a temper tantrum every time you don't get your way."

I temporarily lost control of my thoughts, enjoying a moment of blissful insanity. I saw myself slug Paige. I saw his eyes roll back in his head and him drop to the floor like a sack of potatoes, out cold. Through a colossal exertion of will power, however, I managed to keep my hands to myself.

Pezzani easily wedged himself between Paige and me.

"Why don't we take a walk?" he said.

With unexpected speed and agility, he reached under the desk and grabbed my bag, then closed his huge hand around my upper arm. He began steering me around the desk and down the hall. I attempted twice to free myself, my attention still on Paige. Fire burned inside me as the look of satisfaction spread deeper into Paige's face.

"We'll finish this later," I said.

Paige just laughed.

Pezzani had me out of the building and in the parking lot before I even registered a change of scenery.

"Let me go," I snapped, jerking my arm. His grip held firm.

"Not until I'm sure you won't go—" The rest came out in an anguished *whoosh.*

In a move similar to the one I'd used last night with the masked assailant, I applied a small amount of pressure to Pezzani's diaphragm, doubling him over and causing him to immediately release his grip on me. I snatched up my bag and slung it over a shoulder. I was shaking with adrenaline and anger.

Pezzani leaned forward, his hands on his knees, and sucked in air. After a long moment, he forced himself upright, rubbing at his diaphragm. There were tears in his eyes when he looked at me.

"Your thank-yous suck," he said.

"Hilarious. You shouldn't have interfered."

"Oh, yeah, sure. It would have been better to knock the guy out."

"I don't know what you're talking about."

"Please. I saw the way you were looking at him."

When had I become so transparent?

"Still, it was none of your business."

"He would have jumped at the chance to press charges. Ever spent a night in jail?"

Yes. I was not interested in a repeat stay. But that was not the point.

I rolled my eyes and turned away from him. As I did, something caught my attention. Framed in one of the office windows, Sandra York was watching Pezzani and me outside. Our eyes met briefly, and a look very much like a sneer contorted her face. An instant later she turned away, looking pleased with herself.

A thought occurred to me then, but it was so farfetched, so ridiculous, I dismissed it.

"Let's have those forms," I said.

"You just got fired."

"First, Paige doesn't have the authority to fire me. Second, our deal was complete, aside from a signature, before he interrupted. I intend to sort this out, and I don't want to lose a bunch of residents in the meantime."

"You're asking me to lie," he said, digging the documents out of his briefcase and handing them to me.

"Oh, please. Don't be so dramatic. I'm asking you to do the right thing."

I scribbled my name on the forms where indicated then handed them back. "I expect a guard in that building at six P.M. this evening."

"You're bossy for being unemployed."

"You're hysterical," I said, digging the helmet out of my bag. "A word of advice: you shouldn't manhandle people. It can be dangerous." There was no sympathy or remorse in my voice.

"You're upset; I get it," he said lightly, waving a dismissive hand in my direction. "You'll thank me tomorrow."

"Yeah, right."

I sat at a table in the window of Dazbog Coffee on Harmony Road, sipping a frozen mocha. Dazbog is my favorite coffee place, and having been dragged out of my office before I'd finished my first cup, I could justify the indulgence.

I'd calmed down considerably, but I was still plenty pissed. From the coffee shop, I'd called White. He hadn't answered any of his numbers, and I'd left messages at all of them. More than my job status, my concern was White thinking I stole from him. I couldn't imagine White would believe I'd embezzled from him, but I wanted to confirm.

I took a drink then raised the phone. My mechanic should have gotten to the garage and seen my truck by now. But he hadn't called me. I dialed his number and waited. I was irritated when the call dropped to voicemail again. Obviously I didn't quite have my temper under control just yet.

Maybe it would be a good idea for me to burn off some steam. My thoughts returned instantly to the extra weight I'd criticized that morning. Briefly, I scowled at the perfectly blended coffee drink on the table in front of me, involuntarily envisioning it sliding down my throat and right to my backside. It seemed I could benefit from some physical activity in more than one way.

I left the coffee shop and scooted over to 24 Hour Fitness. After the beefcake at the front desk gave me a detailed tour of the facility, I was set up with a woman in her thirties, who I guessed was blessed with natural slimness and was more concerned with her dyed blonde hair, tanned skin, and designer clothes than with exercise. And she'd definitely picked up on the Axe, which I could see didn't help her opinion of me. We didn't talk much while she took my information.

Then I spent thirty terrible minutes sweating and panting on an elliptical machine. When I reached the point of either puking or crying, I hobbled back out to the scooter and decided to head home and finish packing. Tomorrow was moving day, and I still had quite a bit to box up. Sitting astride the Cushman, I used the collar of my new 24 Hour Fitness t-shirt to wipe away the sweat still running down my face and dialed Margaret Fischer, the leasing agent I was working with for my rental.

"It's Zoe Grey," I said when she answered. "I wanted to make sure we're still on for tomorrow."

I heard a couple pages shuffle, then she said, "Oh, yes. I've processed your application, so everything's set as far as that goes. As we discussed, a security deposit of eight hundred dollars and the first and last month's rent is all required up front."

"Or I could just sign over my first-born child," I said.

She didn't reply.

"How's nine o'clock?" I asked.

"Fine," she said, a little coldly. "I'll meet you at the property then."

I didn't have keys yet. Fischer was unwilling to hand over the keys until I handed over a couple thousand dollars. I was unwilling to give her any money until I was sure the agreement would go through. We'd arranged to do the paperwork first and the key/money thing on the day of move-in.

I was stuffing the phone back into my backpack when it rang. I crossed my fingers it wasn't Fischer calling back to announce she would no longer be leasing me the house, that our deal was off. Instead it was Mark White.

"I take it you got my message."

"I did. And I'm glad you called. There are some things I need to speak to you about. Can you come by my office?"

White has a pleasant, smooth voice, which I suspect is part of the reason he does so well in business. Today he sounded drawn. Theft and subsequent legal troubles didn't suit him.

"What time?"

"The sooner, the better."

"I'll be there in ten minutes."

I kicked the Cushman to life and motored out of the parking lot.

Mark White has an office in the Key Bank building on Howes Street downtown. Real estate mogul that he is, he has lots of business ventures. He oversees them all from this central location. I parked on the street, which was relatively empty, and went in. When the elevator let me out on the fifth floor, I made a left and let myself into White Real Estate headquarters.

A smart-looking brunette greeted me then pushed a series of buttons on her keyboard. As usual, Tandy, White's long-time secretary, looked perfectly attired and groomed, as attractive as she was intelligent. I have always liked and respected her. Today, however, I noticed her hair seemed a little flat and her suit slightly wilted. Even she was feeling the stress of the current situation.

A minute later, I heard a door open, and White strode out to meet me. Our greeting was awkward. Then I followed him into his office.

"Can I offer you anything? Coffee? Water?"

He settled behind his desk and smoothed his tie before folding his hands on the blotter. Always as smartly dressed as Tandy, he, too, showed small signs of wear that would have gone unnoticed by anyone who hadn't seen him at his usual best.

"No, thanks."

"Thank you for agreeing to meet me," he said. "I'm sorry I wasn't able to call you back immediately."

White is nearing sixty, but only a handful of people actually know this. He looks forty-five. No doubt his religious workout routine and green goop vegetable shakes play a part in that. Maybe some genetics, too. Tall, trim, athletic, he's barely graying around the temples, and his brown eyes are clear and sharp. He smiles easily, most days, and has a friendly, open face. Behind it is a shrewdly intelligent mind that has taken him far in life.

"I'm sure your life is more complicated since this morning."

He leaned back in his chair. "You have no idea. I can't believe—" He stopped and sat forward again. "Let's start at the beginning. First, I know you didn't take that money."

"Thank you," I said. That was a big relief.

He shook his head. "But I'm afraid it isn't that simple." He took a breath. He seemed uncharacteristically hesitant to tell me what was on his mind. "You should know, after Paige 'fired' you, he took all the 'evidence' to the police." He used air quotes as he spoke, and his face clearly conveyed his annoyance.

"Paige," I said on a sigh. I should have known.

"Berry Paige has officially been suspended. My attorneys tell me I can't fire him. Not at this point, anyway. Either way, he's finished at White Real Estate. But the damage has been done. The case he laid out for the police seems pretty black and white. You are the one and only suspect. And they're moving on it pretty quickly."

"And why wouldn't they, when everything came gift wrapped and tied up with bows?"

"I've been trying to focus on problems I can deal with," White went on. "I have an independent accounting firm reviewing my books. As soon as Paige showed me those documents, that was the first call I made. I want to know where that money came from and where it went. They should have information for me soon.

"Meanwhile, I have a business to run. I can't close the Fort Collins office while this is sorted out, so I need someone to take Paige's position. I'm also opening a Weld County office in Greeley next month. I'm going to need someone to run it."

Translation: I'm offering you either job; take your pick.

"Why don't you have Spinulli take over for Paige?"

Frank Spinulli is Paige's equivalent in the Loveland division of White Real Estate and Property Management. He's better than Paige and might one day be as good as me.

"Eventually I will fold the Loveland and Fort Collins divisions into one," White said. "But that isn't a strategic move right now. Growth from the Fort Collins office has been less than ideal, far less than projected. I need someone who can make up for lost ground and gain more still. You're that someone."

"Is promoting me right now a good idea?" It would be hard to manage the office from jail, which was where the police seemed to want me.

"I think it will be good to see the company is backing you. I told the police more than once today I know you didn't take the money." He gave me an apologetic look. "Unfortunately, it's going to take more than my word to convince them. Plus, I need you. What's it going to take, Zoe? I don't mind telling you I'm in a tight spot here; I'm willing to make a deal."

I'd been considering a vacation anyway. And I don't mind admitting, after the last couple days, some time off held its appeal. I'm normally one to plow ahead, but I decided to take advantage of the opportunity. White was willing to deal; he'd give me what I asked for, even if it wasn't what he wanted.

"I'd like to think about it," I said.

He was nodding as if this was good news.

"Absolutely. Take all the time you need."

"I'd like two weeks off. I've got some things I need to sort out."

He didn't like this request, but he granted it. Apparently "take all the time you need" didn't mean two weeks.

"Fine. I'll have Henry Davis step in for the interim for Paige, then we'll make more permanent arrangements in two weeks."

"Davis is an all right guy," I said reassuringly. "He's learning quickly, and he has some good ideas."

"I know. He's a serious candidate for the Greeley office, assuming I don't get my first choice."

I stood. "Will you let me know what your accountants find?"

White stood with me, then moved around the desk. He pulled a card from his pocket. "Of course. You'll be my first call. I asked my attorneys to represent you, but they tell me it's some kind of conflict of interest in this case. They gave me this guy's name; apparently he's one of the best. Call him. I'll pay for it."

I accepted the card, slipped it into my pocket, and tried for my most positive, confident smile. "Thank you, but I'm sure it isn't necessary. I've done nothing wrong."

"Better not to take any chances."

I left the office and returned to the Cushman. I was stopped by the first light. My head was busy with a hundred thoughts, most of them slanted by my own problems, but in moments of inactivity, some of those thoughts consistently veered to Stacy. As I sat waiting, I wondered how she was doing. Guilt pulled at me. When the light changed, I buzzed down to Mulberry and made a left. The hospital was only a short distance away.

I knew I needed to let the whole thing go. I knew I'd done all I could, given the circumstances, and that I couldn't go back and change anything. But the feelings persisted all the same. The police were looking into her case, and if the way they picked apart the crime scene was anything to go by, they appeared to be taking the attack seriously. There should have been no doubt on my part that they would discover the assailant. But someone needed to answer for what happened to Stacy Karnes. I wanted to make sure that happened.

4

Traffic from the front door of Poudre Valley Hospital is funneled down a long hallway to a desk manned by purple-shirted volunteers during regular business hours. Today was no different; a hunched-back volunteer with blue hair and thick glasses sat there. A sign told me this was the place to ask about patient room numbers.

"Can I help you?" the volunteer asked from her chair, her voice warbling with age.

"I'm looking for patient Stacy Karnes."

"Do you know which floor?"

"No, I'm sorry, I don't." Though I guessed she'd be in ICU. That seemed appropriate given her injuries. I said as much to the volunteer, who had turned her steadied attention toward the computer hulking before her small, fragile frame.

With fingers knotted from arthritis, she tapped out a few keys and clicked at the computer. I felt the Earth move under my feet in the time I stood there waiting.

"All right," she finally announced with such victorious pride I couldn't help but smile. "5608. Fifth floor, Medical. Do you know where that is?"

"Yes," I lied. I thanked her for the information and hurried away from her desk toward the elevators. The line had grown behind me, and I didn't want to spend any more time there.

I crowded into the first available elevator car with a large Hispanic family, a young couple I guessed to be newly dating, and some teenagers. I was pretty sure at least one of the teenage boys was wearing the same scent as me: Axe Phoenix. The couple and I got off on the fifth floor, the last stop. The couple knew where they were going and quietly made their way down a hall to the left. I followed the posted signs until I arrived at the Medical Unit. Then I navigated by room numbers, counting off doors until I arrived at number eight.

I glanced up and down the hall, but there was no one in sight. And I saw no one at the desk. I wanted to ask if Stacy was up for visitors, but I didn't have the patience to wait for any more information.

The door was open an inch or two and I heard voices inside. I knocked and pushed the door open slowly, listening. A sure voice rang out.

"Come in!"

Whoever this woman was, it was clear she was used to being in charge.

Some instinctual part of me was compelled to obey. Another, more familiar, part wanted to rebel. In the end, I pushed the door open.

"Okay," the voice was saying. "This will be Carrie with those pain meds. Last cold wipe here. Good. Now, take a deep breath and try to relax. You'll feel some pressure."

I saw two people dressed in scrubs standing on either side of the bed, which had been elevated to waist-height. I saw bare feet on the end of the bed. Bare, *hairy* feet. And they seemed too big.

The woman on the far side of the bed, a brunette in her forties wearing clear gloves, pulled a beige-colored, flexible tube out of a white plastic container positioned on the bed between the feet. She glanced up at me briefly as she gripped the tube. I noticed there was something clear and jelly-like dripping from the end.

"Oh," she said, having realized I was not the person she was expecting. "Can I help you?"

After a couple steps, I saw enough to put it together.

With her other hand, she was holding a penis. Bringing her hands together, she put the end of the tube into the end of the penis and shoved. My mouth dropped open as the patient shot up off the bed.

"Aaaahhhh!"

The sound had come from both of us. Him in a scream, me in a panic.

The patient (obviously a male) with pain etched into every part of his face, struggled against the second scrub-clad figure who tried to push him back down on the bed. He caught sight of me, question in his eyes. But I was already moving backward.

I banged into the door, which had drifted shut. Crying out again, I spun around and practically flung myself through the doorway. I jerked the door closed behind me then stood leaning against the wall, my hands over my eyes. I knew the image was permanently burned into my brain.

"Can I help you?"

The frosty tone cut into my thoughts, drawing me back to the present.

I peeked through my hands and spied a woman an inch taller and several pounds lighter than me who screamed "high-maintenance." Everything from her hair and makeup to her skin and nails to her clothes and shoes cried time, money, and deliberateness. I instantly disliked her. And I had the depressed feeling she would give me further reason for this opinion by the time our exchange was through.

"I was just leaving," I said, attempting neutrality. I pushed myself from the wall and sucked in a deep breath as I started walking.

"Who the hell are you?" she snapped. Then I saw her flinch slightly, her nose working. She'd picked up on the shampoo. "What were you doing in my husband's room?"

What were the chances the man in the room I'd been mistakenly sent to also wore Axe Phoenix?

A long, painful howl rolled out of room eight. Both of us looked at the door. I took a subconscious step backward.

"Baby!" she cried under her breath. Then she turned back to me, fire in her ugly brown eyes. "What did you do to him?"

Standing up a little straighter, pushing my shoulders back a bit further, I stared at her head-on and gave a little smirk. "He has enough company at the moment, and he's more than entertained. Guess he wasn't expecting you back so soon." I infused this with enough suggestion to cause her blood to boil. It would be temporary, but I was satisfied.

She wanted to have a few more words with me, but her jealousy and hatred consumed her. Spinning on her expensive heel, she marched her (slightly dimpled) bottom, stuffed into pants just a bit too small, through the door into the room.

I couldn't help but laugh softly to myself as I turned to continue on my own way. I was greeted by a young blonde girl smiling at me.

"I see you've survived your run-in with the Wicked Witch of Medical."

"Aw, and I hoped it was just something *I* brought out of her."

The girl laughed and shook her head. "Not even close. I've never seen her that mad before, though; you really got under her skin."

I've heard this before.

"You must not be a friend of the family."

I shook my head. "No. The volunteer sent me to the wrong room."

And I'd suffered permanent damage. Maybe it all worked out for the better that I'd never finished college and become a nurse. Had I, it would have been *me* doing the penis-and-tube thing. I shuddered involuntarily.

The blonde nodded knowingly, as if this sort of thing had happened before. She indicated I should follow her as she walked to a nearby computer.

"Which patient are you looking for?"

"Stacy Karnes."

"Karnes with a *K*?"

"Yes."

"That's the problem. The volunteer heard Barnes with a *B*. She sent you to Stacey Barnes. Was it Millie? Sometimes she forgets her hearing aids."

I confessed I didn't know the name of the blue-haired volunteer. The blonde looked up the correct room number and sent me with directions. I thanked her and beat a hasty retreat. Suddenly I was ready to run out of the hospital and never return. But I hadn't done what I'd come to do yet. So instead of *1*, I hit *4* when I got back on the elevator.

Stacy was, in fact, in ICU. Now that I was on the right unit, I counted off room numbers until I found Stacy's. This time I peered inside cautiously before going in; lesson learned. Inside I saw a middle-aged man and woman sitting together beside Stacy's bed, their hands grasping hers. I guessed these were her parents. The woman in particular bore a striking resemblance.

Taking a deep breath, I knocked softly on the open door and stepped inside. They both turned to look at me, and I saw their eyes were wet and bloodshot. I couldn't imagine what they were going through.

"Can we help you?" the man asked.

"I'm sorry to intrude, but I was there when . . . it happened. I've been worried about her. How is she doing?"

They rose and walked toward me. He grabbed my hand and shook it, squeezing it tightly. She wrapped me in a tight hug. They were both crying again.

"We can't thank you enough," he sobbed. "Who knows what would have happened if you hadn't been there."

Who knows what would have happened had I been there on time.

The woman was crying now, too. They clutched one another's hands. This wasn't what I'd envisioned. And I was uncomfortable.

"I'm sorry I wasn't there sooner. How is she?"

"The doctors say it could be much worse," the man began, turning to look at Stacy. "She was in surgery for six hours, but they say they got everything cleaned out and closed up. They had to remove a small portion of her intestine, and her liver was bleeding pretty badly, but nothing truly vital was damaged. So, we just have to wait."

"Is she going to be okay?"

"You bet," he said firmly. The woman was bobbing her head in affirmation. "Our Stacy, she's strong. She's a fighter."

"I'm glad to hear that." I was truly relieved. And now it was time to go. "I don't want to take too much of your time. I better go."

The woman sniffed and wiped at her nose with a tissue.

"You're welcome anytime. If there is anything, anything at all, that you ever need, don't hesitate to ask."

The man nodded vigorously in agreement.

After another long minute of thank-yous and hugs, I finally pulled myself away from the parents and headed for the door.

I retreated to the elevators. My mind was a whirlwind of thought. I wondered where the police were in their investigation and if any progress had been made. I wondered who their suspects were, and what they were doing to follow up. Not for the first time, I wondered why Stacy had been in that lobby to begin with. Why had she wanted to see the apartment? Why did she want to move? I remembered her voice on the phone. "Panic" was too strong a word, but she was stressed. She wouldn't take no for an answer; she'd been determined to submit her application and see the apartment that day.

What was bothering her? Why was she in such a rush? Was she running? Did that have something to do with her attack? Was her attacker someone she knew? I tended to think so, but that was mostly because I couldn't fathom a masked attacker randomly stopping by the lobby of Elizabeth Tower to stab someone. Who did she know that could do something like that?

What am I doing? I asked myself. *Am I trying to figure out who assaulted Stacy Karnes?*

If I was doing this, *why* was I doing it? Did I think finding the person responsible would make me feel better, would absolve me of some degree of guilt? I couldn't deny somehow *that* math added up in my head. But I had other things to figure out, things in my own life, like my job. My musings were interrupted when I saw Detective Ellmann turn the corner and walk toward me.

He was dressed in jeans and a t-shirt, his gun and badge casually clipped to his belt. And he was hot. I had no other choice than to admit it to myself. I was also very much aware of the fact that I was dressed in my sweaty gym clothes and still smelled like a man.

"What are you doing here?" he asked.

"I didn't know you also policed the hospital and its visitors."

He stopped in front of me and planted his hands on his hips. He wasn't amused. And I saw him discreetly sniffing at the air. Undoubtedly, he'd also detected the Axe. Despite the fact my hair was still wrapped tightly on my head, it was pretty powerful.

"Tell me you're not here seeing Stacy Karnes."

"Nope. Stacey *Barnes*. The volunteer sent me to the wrong room."

He sighed and rubbed a hand over his eyes. "You can't be here; you can't visit the victim of the crime you're involved with. It looks bad and complicates things."

"Involved? Whoa. You can't seriously think *I* hurt her, . . . can you?"

"It doesn't matter what I think. We're investigating an assault, maybe an attempted homicide; we have to rule everyone out. That includes you."

I sighed and did a mental head slap as a couple pieces fell in place.

"That's why you were at the office this morning, talking to Paige," I said. "You can't talk to me because you think I had something to do with it."

"I need to rule you out," he repeated. "And you still need to come to the police station and sign paperwork."

"The sooner you 'rule me out,' the sooner you get back on track."

"Right. When were you planning to come to the station?"

"Isn't it sort of a twenty-four-hour place? I have stuff I need to do, so I can come by later tonight."

He reached into his pocket and withdrew another card, which he passed to me. "I wouldn't want you to inconvenience yourself or anything," he said, stepping around me. "Call me when you're planning to come in and I'll meet you there."

"It's on my list," I shot back. "I'm going to get my hair and nails done now, then I have a massage and shopping to do, but maybe sometime after that, you know, unless something else comes up."

He lifted a hand and waved it without slowing or turning around.

I was almost overwhelmed by the urge to give him a hand sign of my own but managed to resist, taking the elevator and exiting the hospital without any gestures.

———————————

It was a relief to discover the house empty when I got home. I had no idea where anyone was, and I didn't care. It was two o'clock in the afternoon, and, with any luck, they'd all stay gone for another couple hours.

I went to the garage and pulled cardboard boxes from behind a large stack of plastic storage bins. I'd saved them from my last move, knowing I'd need them again. I carried an armful back inside to the basement and taped them together.

The bookshelves had already been cleared and the knickknacks wrapped up. I took a box to the desk and arranged things inside, filing away loose papers in the drawers. It was mostly mindless work, and I felt my thoughts drifting. I knew their direction, and I didn't want to go there. I put my iPod on its base and called up my favorite playlist then cranked the volume.

I took two more boxes and went to the closet. I tried singing along while I stuffed sheets and other linens into them. Inevitably, my mind wandered.

What I knew about Stacy Karnes was minimal. She was currently renting a house near campus and was interested in moving. On the phone, I'd asked her if her lease was up, and she said she'd found someone to sublet. Elizabeth Tower wasn't too far from campus, but it wasn't as near as her current place. And while the apartments were competitively priced, she would end up paying almost three hundred dollars more.

Back at my office, I'd started a file on her. After speaking with her, it was clear she was sold; looking at the place was merely a formality. I'd run a background and credit check on her. The results were in her file. From what I recalled, her criminal history was nonexistent, and her credit was in good standing, even if her score was on the low side. That isn't uncommon for people her age.

It was May. May was a very busy month for move-outs and new leases because of school, but still it seemed strange for Stacy to be moving. Typically kids move the last week of May, not the first.

I realized this was more a gut feeling than a position based on facts. But her lease wasn't up, she hadn't gotten a new job, she wasn't moving in with a boy- or girlfriend. Why did she suddenly want to move?

I was moving because I had ugly thoughts about the people I lived with more often than I felt was healthy. "Stressful" didn't begin to cover what it was like living with my mother. Bradley and the others didn't help anything, either. Was it possible Stacy was moving to get away from her roommates? Given the amount of rent she was currently paying, she had to be one of at least three—more likely four—people living in the same place.

I left the boxes and walked away from the closet, pulling out my laptop. I sat at the empty desk and brought up the *Fort Collins Coloradoan* website. Stacy's attack didn't make the front page of the newspaper, but I did find a little blurb about it. It was minimal, lacking insightful or significant details, and reported the police were withholding the name of the victim. This told me nothing new, so I opened dexknows.com. I didn't have access to all the same search systems from home as I did from the office, but I could still dig up some basic information.

I searched the last name *Karnes* and the first initial *S* and got a few hits. After reviewing the photos I'd taken, I saw one of the results matched the address on her license. Next, I did a reverse search of the address and wrote down the names that came up. I also did a reverse search on all of the phone numbers in her call history, only a couple of which back to landlines, for which I also wrote down names. I searched county property records and discovered the house Stacy rented was owned by William Rivas. He might be worth talking to; he could know why Stacy Karnes was suddenly so interested in moving.

Next, I Googled Stacy's name. One of the top hits was for Facebook. I opened a new window and brought up facebook.com, signing in as my friend Jill. I don't have a Facebook page, and Jill always uses her dog's name as her password. People should never use the names of family members or pets as passwords; they are too easily discovered by people with more malicious intentions than me. I used the "search for more friends" function to bring up Stacy Karnes's page. I couldn't believe how much information was accessible via Facebook; I scribbled several pages of notes.

Her boyfriend was Tyler Jay. When I typed him into Dex, I got nothing back. I couldn't find a Facebook page for him, either. I typed his name into Google and hit pay dirt.

One of the top results was a link to the Larimer County Sheriff's Office website. It took me to the county's most wanted list. Tyler Jakowski, a.k.a. Tyler Jay, was at the top. I had to consciously snap my mouth closed as I read the page. Jakowski was wanted on suspicion of murder, six counts of felony assault, two counts of rape, and a slew of other things. His physical description was listed and his mug shot provided. At the very bottom of the page it said, "$15,000 reward for information leading to the apprehension of Tyler Jakowski."

Fifteen thousand dollars? Interesting. More interesting was the question of his possible involvement in the attack on Stacy Karnes. According to the information I'd just read about Jakowski, he certainly had it in him to stab a woman. Karnes's Facebook page reported no troubles in their relationship, but perhaps she hadn't updated it yet. Or maybe her recent feelings were on Twitter, which I wasn't interested in checking. Or maybe Stacy didn't put her every emotional whim online. Maybe he was mad at her for dumping him. Or maybe she had an as-yet unrecorded criminal history to match his and their latest scheme had caused some sort of disagreement between the two of them that turned physical.

If I were wanted for murder, among other things, where would I go? If I had the means, I'd get the hell out of Dodge. But what if I had a significant other? Would that be reason enough for me to stay? If it were, where would I go? Where did most boys go when they got into trouble? If the boys I knew were any way to judge, the answer was home to Mama.

I spent ten more minutes digging into Tyler Jakowski and filled several more pages of notes. I was fairly confident I had some decent places to start looking.

Looking for what? I asked myself, getting up from the computer. *Why would I go looking for Tyler Jay, a dangerous criminal?*

He might have something to say about what happened to Stacy, I answered as I threw some more linen into a box. He was capable of stabbing a woman. Actually, he was capable of more—much more, according to his wanted poster. And what if he was responsible? Did I want to be that close to him?

The rational side of my brain kicked in with a reasoned argument. Tyler's wanted poster listed him as five-ten. It had been difficult to discern last night because the figure was completely obscured by black clothing and everything happened so quickly, but, standing barefooted, I am five-eight. When I'd come face-to-face with the dark-clad figure in the lobby, I'd been wearing heels that added two inches to my height. The attacker had been shorter than me; of that, I was certain. Still, it wouldn't hurt if I saw Tyler Jay myself.

This argument persisted as I filled the last of the boxes I had stashed. When they were full, I dragged out plastic storage bins and began filling them. I had a stack of pants in my arms when I heard the doorbell. I deposited the stack into a bin and stood as the bell ring for a second time. I was halfway up the stairs when the visitor began pounding on the door.

"Yeah, yeah, yeah," I muttered under my breath as I walked. "If I didn't know better, I'd think my house was on fire."

"Police!" a gruff voice barked. "Open up!"

Just what my day needs, I thought. *More police.*

I threw the lock and yanked the door open. I stared out at the man on the porch, making no effort to conceal my irritation.

"What's the emergency?" I snapped.

He held open the jacket of the inexpensive, tan-colored suit he wore, showing me the badge clipped to his belt. I glimpsed a holstered gun to go with it. Now *this* guy looked like a detective.

"Detective Hensley," he snapped back. "Fort Collins Police Department. I need to speak with Mrs. Grey. That you?"

"Why all the racket?" I pressed. "What if no one was home?"

"The garage door is standing wide open." This was all he said, as if it was explanation enough. "Are you Mrs. Grey?"

He was relatively lean for a cop, though his gut seemed to be slowly getting away from him. He was in his forties, not quite six feet tall, and had dark hair that was starting to gray. He seemed as annoyed as I was, and I wondered if he'd arrived that way or if I'd brought it out of him. On the one hand, it seemed fitting; he'd brought it out of me. On the other, it didn't seem prudent to annoy detectives who came beating down your door.

He lifted his eyebrow expectantly and waited.

"Mrs. Grey is my mother, and she's not home at the moment. I'm Zoe Grey." This wasn't the first time my mother had run up against the law. At least he wasn't here for me. "What did she do now?"

"You're the one I need. Please open the door. I have some questions to ask you."

Bummer.

It wasn't the first time I'd heard a cop say those words, either, and unfortunately I didn't think it would be the last. Talking to cops who think I've done something wrong is one of my least favorite things to do. This is followed closely by talking to cops who know I've done something wrong. These encounters weren't any more pleasant when I knew I'd done nothing wrong. Cops aren't great conversationalists.

"Did Ellmann send you?" I sighed and moved away from the doorjamb, leaving the door open. "I mean, it's just paperwork."

"No. What paperwork?"

Behind me, I heard Hensley step inside and close the door.

"Never mind."

I went to the kitchen and pulled a glass from the cupboard. Hensley came in behind me, no doubt taking in the house around him with the keen eye of a detective.

"Are you here alone?" he asked casually. "Or do you have company?"

It was the Axe; I was positive.

"Just me," I said, mentally moving "shampoo" to the top of my shopping list.

I wasn't sure what state the house was in, but I knew my reaction to having him inside would tip him off whether he saw anything or not. My mother, while in her manic states, kept everything cleaned to a blinding polish. But she didn't have the best judgment and often brought home things she shouldn't have, things of the chemical variety. I crossed my fingers nothing had been left in plain view and went to the water dispenser in the fridge.

"Water?" I asked.

"No, thanks."

I carried the glass to the breakfast bar and climbed onto a stool. I indicated the others, and Hensley took a seat. He reached into his jacket and withdrew a small notepad similar to Ellmann's. Did they issue those with badges? He flipped back several pages.

"Twenty thousand dollars of White Real Estate and Property Management's money is unaccounted for," he said casually. Any annoyance he'd felt earlier was either gone or strategically hidden beneath his well-practiced neutral cop-face. "Know anything about that?"

I took a sip of water and shook my head. "No, I don't. It was just brought to my attention this morning."

"I have documents on my desk that indicate otherwise."

"Someone went to a lot of trouble to cover their tracks, then. I don't steal." Not anymore, anyway.

"Don't you?" the cop asked. He flipped another page then stopped. "You have a history of theft."

He was bluffing, and doing a damn fine job of it; I was a little bit impressed. My last arrest had been at the age of eighteen and wasn't for theft. Everything before that was sealed in my juvenile record. It was possible for the police to petition a judge to unseal those records, but there would have to be a very compelling reason to do so. I doubted my implication in the embezzlement was sufficient. Still, had I not known this, I would have believed he knew more than he did. I made a mental note to watch what I said.

"You're a terrific liar," I said, smiling conspiratorially.

"It isn't a lie."

"As far as you're concerned, I've been arrested one time, and that was for assault, not theft."

"A judge has unsealed your record." A wild stab in the dark, and while I knew it was precisely aimed, he did not.

Hensley was a good interrogator. He had no doubt wrapped up more than a few cases by just talking with people, causing them to incriminate themselves. I would have believed him had I not known better. *That* was a little intimidating.

I shook my head. "My lawyer would have been notified as a matter of procedure. He would have then called me. Since I haven't heard from him, I know no such thing has happened."

"You seem quite familiar with the law, Ms. Grey. Have you had legal training, or is it all from experience?"

"I pay attention."

He waited a beat, but I said nothing more. He flipped to a different page in the notebook and tried another track.

"I looked at your financials," he said. "You're making ends meet now, but times are a little lean for you, comparatively. You were once making more than a hundred thousand dollars a year. Did you get tired of this low-rent way of life? Twenty grand would go a long way in putting you back into your former lifestyle."

"Twenty thousand? Are you kidding? Let me hit the highlights for you. The last year I was in Denver, I made a hundred and fifty thousand dollars, which you already know. Twenty grand is a drop in the bucket when you're pulling down almost eight times that. So, if my end goal were to go back to that lifestyle, and I chose theft as my means of doing so, twenty grand wouldn't make a dent. More importantly, I have absolutely no interest in going back to that lifestyle. Mark White begged me to take Barry Paige's job. The salary he offered me would have been a hell of a lot more than twenty grand, but I turned him down." I reached for my glass. "Have any more theories?"

"From what I hear, you don't think much of Mr. Paige. Maybe stealing the money was your way of flipping him the bird. Or maybe you have some kind of problem with Mr. White."

"It's no secret I think Paige is a waste of space and a tool to boot. But this money was stolen from White Real Estate, not Paige, and I have no problems with Mark White or the company. Furthermore, embezzling from White Real Estate would have played right into Paige's hands because he's been looking for a reason to fire me since we met. I wouldn't make it so easy for him. And, if I were truly guilty, I never would have left my fingerprints, so to speak, all over everything. Whoever is responsible drew big, red arrows pointing right to me. Why would I do that to myself? Why would I not even *try* to cover my tracks?"

"Embezzling money can be tricky. Or maybe you never believed you'd be discovered and didn't bother to be sneaky."

I snorted. "That's the mark of a novice. Anyone with a criminal history is thinking one thing when they break the law: don't get caught. The only way I would have stolen that money would have been if I was positive it wouldn't lead back to me."

"But you didn't steal it?"

"No. I've learned a few things so far in life. One of them is you have to earn your way. Stealing is not earning."

It was a hard-learned lesson, but it'd finally sunk in.

Hensley was scribbling notes, and I thought I could almost see the wheels turning. With anyone else that would be a relief, but with cops it always gives me a sense of unease. Their minds are trained to pick apart everything, turn everything around, suspect everyone. I don't like when I'm the suspect.

"So you have a moral problem with stealing?"

"All I'm saying is I have principles." I sighed. "You said you looked at my financials. Did you find twenty thousand dollars?"

Of course not.

"Yes," Hensley said.

I felt the bottom fall out of my world. The blood drained from my face, and I gripped the counter as a wave of dizziness washed over me. I prayed I'd misheard.

"Excuse me?"

"I did check your bank accounts. There are deposits totaling twenty thousand dollars from Wednesday and Thursday. Fifteen thousand was transferred out to accounts we've traced back to the Cayman Islands. The other five is still in your account."

My brain scrambled to keep up.

"No, that can't be right," I said.

"Did you make the deposits into the wrong account? Like you said, you would have intended them never to be discovered."

"No, I didn't make any deposits. Oh, shit," I said as realization struck. "You seriously think I did this."

"Yes, I do. So far, everything I dig up points straight to you."

I suddenly felt sick.

"But what about the books?" I asked, grasping at straws now. "Won't you go over the accounting records? There is no way twenty thousand dollars was stolen from the company in two days. That's too obvious. More likely, it was siphoned off in small amounts over a period of time. If the records show that to be true, can't you trace where that money went, find who really stole it?"

"We're looking at the books now. Is that what you did: siphoned the money off slowly, in small amounts?"

"What? No. The books will show you, I didn't steal any money."

"If there are any inconsistencies, we'll find them. But I have a feeling we're going to find the money leads back to you, one way or the other."

If I was seriously being considered a suspect, that changed everything. For one, I needed to stop talking. If Hensley wanted to ask more questions, he was going to need a warrant to hand to my lawyer.

"I've said all I'm going to," I said. "Please leave."

"Formal charges of fraud and embezzlement will be filed against you. The paperwork the company has proving your guilt is pretty thorough and convincing."

I reached into my pocket and withdrew the card White had given me a few hours before. I slid it across the bar to Hensley. "Contact my lawyer if you have more questions."

I carried my glass into the kitchen and stood staring at Hensley across the counter, my arms over my chest and a dark look on my face. In no rush to comply, he stared back at me for a beat or two, then slowly closed his notepad and returned it to his pocket. He picked up the card, studied it carefully, and slipped it into his pocket with the notebook. Then he eased himself off the stool and strolled to the front door.

When he was gone, I threw the deadbolt and spun on my heel for the stairs.

5

A smarter person might have been scared of being convicted of a felony and sentenced to prison. Maybe I'm not that smart. Mostly I was pissed. But prison was the furthest thing from my mind. I wanted to know who had really stolen that money. Then I wanted to have a talk with them about pointing the finger at me. I didn't appreciate the finger-pointing.

When I hit the front door, I saw some thunderclouds had rolled in and it was beginning to drizzle. I grabbed a jacket and the Cushman then buzzed away from the house.

As I rode, I reflected on my day. It hadn't started well and had only gotten worse. I called Amy to commiserate because this always makes me feel better. I used a hands-free earbud and hoped she could hear me over the wind and the engine.

Amy Wells and I grew up together. We'd known each other since before either of us could walk, and at that age it doesn't take much to form a friendship. But whatever bond existed between us, it had sufficiently held us together for the last twenty-four years. Her life had been just as hard in its own way. This hardship was one of our binding threads. Amy is the only person who knows my life story, knows everything about me, my every sin, and loves me anyway.

The line rang then dropped to voicemail. I hung up without leaving a message. It was Friday night, and chances were good she had plans with her fiancé, Brandon. Overall, I think Brandon's an all right guy, and he's probably perfect for Amy, so it doesn't bother me too much that she spends so much time with him.

Wal-Mart isn't my favorite place to shop, but I needed a couple things, and I didn't want to go to more than one store. That is one thing Wal-Mart has going for it: one-stop shopping. I took Lemay Avenue north past Mulberry and pulled into the parking lot, which is huge and poorly designed. I buzzed the Cushman into a motorcycle spot, killed the engine, and pushed down the kickstand. A thin man with leathery, weathered skin, frizzy, gray hair tied in a long ponytail, and full riding leathers eyed the Trailster as he strolled over to his Harley.

"Great bike," he said. Prepared for sarcasm, I glanced up only to find sincere reverence in his eyes. Perhaps he also had a history with Cushman scooters.

"Thanks."

We nodded to one another, then I hurried into the store. A particularly rough gust of wind whipped around me as I hit the sidewalk and ducked inside.

The enormous warehouse-like building that is Wal-Mart is a fluorescent nightmare with a horrible soundtrack. There are directional signs hanging everywhere, but none of them actually point to anything. It's hard not to feel like a rat in a maze in this store.

My first stop was the shampoo aisle. Then I went looking for electronics. Finally I spotted the TVs mounted on the exterior wall; I never did see a sign.

After a trek through the department, I saw thousands of electrical devices and components, even answering machines. Who uses answering machines anymore? But I didn't find what I was looking for. I didn't find any employees, either.

In the neighboring shoe department, I finally spotted one: a woman who looked busy. Watching as I walked over, I realized she merely *looked* busy, a skill she had no doubt honed to shiny perfection her entire working life. She was actually accomplishing very little.

"Excuse me," I said, attempting to be polite (benefit of the doubt and all that). "I have a question."

She cocked a hip to the side as she turned to face me, planting one fist on said (ample) hip, and stared at me. The name badge pinned to her shirt at her right (also ample) breast read WANDA.

"Yeah? How can I help you?" Her tone left no room for doubt about her interest in helping me.

I bit back my kneejerk response. And despite my best effort, the words "game on" flashed on and off in my mind. "I need help in electronics. Is there someone available?"

"His name's Cody," she said, turning away from me again.

I took a breath. "Cody doesn't seem to be around. Would you be able to call him for me?" I eyed the small walky-talky clipped on her belt.

"Well, *I* don't know where he is."

I was quickly losing my patience. Patience isn't my strong suit, anyway. Between the hospital ordeal and Hensley, I was just about taxed.

"Does Cody wear one of those little radios?"

"Yeah," she said, shrugging but not turning back to me. "We all got one."

I waited a beat, long enough to be sure she had no intention of helping me, then stepped forward and yanked the radio off her belt.

"What the hell, lady?" she demanded, spinning around to face me once more. She tried to swipe the radio out of my hand. "Give that back."

Our exchange had drawn the attention of nearby customers. Most pretended to be shopping while really watching us. And it was too late to turn back now; at this point, I felt I was committed.

I stepped back and looked at the radio. It wasn't even on. I switched it on and hoped it was on the right channel, since it was unlikely Wanda would give me any information.

"Yo, Cody," I called into the radio. "It's Wanda in shoes."

A few seconds later the radio crackled and a voice came over the line.

"Go for Cody."

I wasn't sure if this was expected radio-speak or if he was just being funny.

"Customer in electronics needs assistance. You got that?"

"On it. Cody out."

I was pretty sure now Cody was just being funny, and I have to admit, if I had to use radios all day long, I would resort to the same tactics.

I winked at Wanda then left, still holding the radio. The walk (or hike, depending) back to electronics was quiet and I encountered no one. I looked around for some sign of Cody when I arrived in electronics but found none, so I went to the register counter in the middle to wait. Several other customers had gathered, milling around like lost sheep, waiting to check out or ask questions. Why do people shop here?

After a minute ticked into two, I lifted myself up to sit on the counter and wondered if I'd been stood up. Why was *I* shopping here? Just as I wondered if RadioShack was still open, a young man, not yet twenty, tall and lanky with pimples on his face, wandered over. He openly looked me up and down. Then he tipped his head at me.

"You the one who needed some help?" His voice was a bit nasally, and he probably got mixed up with his sister on the phone, if he had a sister.

"I'm looking for a digital audio recorder. I can't seem to find one. Do you have any?"

"A what?" the kid asked.

I sighed. "You know, like a tape recorder, for taking notes and stuff."

"Like messages?" he asked. "Well, we call those *answering machines*, and they don't use tapes anymore."

I took a breath and tried again, exercising exceptional restraint, I thought. (Patience: not my virtue.) "If I wanted to record my professor's lecture, what would I use?"

"You're in college?" the kid asked, again looking me over. "Shouldn't you be done with school by now?"

What the hell is wrong with kids these days?

"What about my question?" I asked.

"Well," the kid said, shrugging and turning away as he spoke. "We got these things over here, but I'm not sure it's what you're looking for."

I hopped off the counter and followed Cody. He stopped and pointed to several items laid out on the shelves in front of us. I squatted down for a closer look. The first box I saw read in bold letters DIGITAL AUDIO RECORDER. Imagine that.

I confirmed I'd found what I needed, and Cody took his leave, carrying Wanda's radio with him. I quickly compared the items and chose one, mostly based on price. The stupid little thing was pricey. I managed to purchase it without encountering any more major hang-ups then sat in the parking lot inserting batteries and trying it out. Convinced it was in working order, I stuffed everything into my backpack and buzzed out of the lot.

———————————

It was too early to continue with my get-out-of-jail plan. Instead I cruised over to Stacy's place.

There were several lamps on throughout the house. The windows and doors were open to let in the cool evening air. The wind had persisted throughout the afternoon and now the air was muggy. I parked across the street a couple houses down and sat, waiting, watching. There was a lot of activity in the neighborhood, but no one seemed to pay me much mind, although the scooter drew a few looks.

After a few minutes, I saw a girl in cotton shorts and a hooded sweatshirt, her dark blonde hair piled messily on top of her head, rise and walk across the front room of the house. I could see the blue lights of a TV flashing on the walls. When she returned, she was sipping something from a glass. She crossed the room and dropped out of sight again. So far, she was the only one I'd seen, though Stacy shared the house with three other girls. I decided to give it a shot.

I crossed the street and knocked on the screen door. A moment later the girl I'd seen appeared before me. She was five-six and had pretty brown eyes, except I saw something dark flash in them; it looked a lot like fear. More noticeable was her surprise. This was followed closely by confusion.

She was obviously wondering who I was and what I wanted, so I attributed her guarded manner to her suspicion, but that didn't feel quite right.

"Can I help you with something?"

"Is Stacy home?" I asked.

Something in the girl's presentation changed, then she seemed to work herself up, as if she would burst into tears. After a moment of thought, she pushed the screen door open and waved me in, returning to the other side of the room. She sat down on a brown leather sofa, which I suspected was the real deal given the faint leather scent in the air. She drew her knees up to her chest and wrapped her arms around them as I sat in a nearby chair, also leather, also real. And very comfortable.

"I'm sorry to tell you," she said softly. "But Stacy was attacked. She's in the hospital."

I feigned surprise, widening my eyes. "No!"

Reading people and lying are two skills I'd honed to perfection early on in life. Then, they had been survival tools. Later, I'd used my power for evil. Now, I try to use my powers only for good. I thought this qualified.

"Yes!"

"I can't believe it! What happened? Is she okay?"

I took in the room as well as the girl. The spaces I could see from where I sat were well furnished, and everything seemed rather expensive. Certainly, these weren't the furnishings of a typical college crash pad. One or more of the people living here had money. It was possible someone's parents were funding their college experience; I'd seen that more than once as a leasing agent. But I suspected that wasn't the case for Stacy.

The girl shook her head. "No one really seems to know yet. The police are looking into it but don't have much. She was stabbed last night. She's in critical condition."

"I can't believe it," I said again. "I just saw her in class, you know? How unreal."

Something else flashed in her eyes, but it was gone almost before I registered it.

"Tell me about it. I've been freaking out since I heard."

"Why? Are you afraid something might happen to you?"

She shrugged and glanced at the dark windows, all of which were open. "Maybe. You know, the cops don't know what happened. Maybe it wasn't random."

Her tone made it clear she had a theory she wanted to share. It didn't take much prompting for her to do so. But it didn't feel like a girl confiding a private speculation, which furthered my suspicion.

"If it wasn't random, then what? I mean, Stacy seems like such a nice person."

"Oh, she is, you know, it's just that . . ." The girl shrugged again, searching for the right words. "She maybe got mixed up with a bad guy." She sighed. "Stacy would deny it to the end, but her boyfriend isn't a great guy, you know? I just, uh, I just wondered when I heard, that's all."

"Had they been fighting or something?" I asked, continuing my performance. "Is he dangerous?"

"I don't know. I just know a couple days ago he was in a big hurry to get out of town. He wanted her to come with, but she didn't want to just pack up and leave. She's a pretty good student and actually likes school. From what I could tell, he wasn't planning a vacation, you know?"

No, he was planning to skip town, trying to stay one step ahead of the cops looking for him.

"Geez! What's this guy's name? Does he go to school here? Would I know him?"

She shook her head. "No, he's not a student. His name is Tyler Jay. He's got lots of tattoos, most pretty cheap-looking, and a nasty scar above his left eye. He gives me the creeps, always has. I always worried he was going to hurt her."

"And now you think he might hurt you?"

She shivered, but it didn't feel quite genuine. "I don't know, I really don't. I hope not. He has no reason to."

I wasn't the only expert liar in the room. I couldn't help wondering what, exactly, she was lying about, and why.

"And you think he may have hurt Stacy because she wouldn't go with him?"

"It's only one theory. You know, the cops aren't sure it was random."

"What makes them think it was targeted?"

She shrugged. "I don't know. She was in an apartment building on Elizabeth when it happened. She still had her purse."

"Was she visiting someone? Maybe they saw something."

Another flash of something, there and gone before I could really identify it. But her eyes darkened a couple shades.

"I don't know what she was doing there. We don't know anyone in that building."

Didn't the roommate know Stacy was moving out?

I shrugged. "Maybe she was looking at an apartment or something."

"Why would she look at an apartment?"

Her tone and the cold look in her eyes caused another red flag—or five— to fly up in my mind.

"I don't know, but if she didn't know anyone in the building, why else would she go there?"

She reached out and grabbed hold of that thought easily. "That could be, I guess. She didn't mention it to me. She could have been there to visit someone she worked with. Maybe someone from the restaurant lives there."

"She told me which restaurant she works at but I forgot."

"The Olive Garden."

I snapped my fingers as if I suddenly remembered. "That's right. Geez, I just can't believe this. Do you know which room she's in? I think I should go visit."

"She's not awake yet, but they say she can hear us talking to her." She gave me the room number I already had.

I departed a few minutes later, returning to the Cushman. The roommate, Tina Shuemaker, hadn't given me much information on the boyfriend, Tyler Jay. Despite casting suspicion on him, she wouldn't say anything else about him, like where he lived, worked, or hung out. I wondered if she truly didn't know. But her credibility had been damaged early on in our conversation, so I had my doubts. All she'd said was Tyler drove a black Cadillac Escalade.

Not having snooped quite enough for one night, I motored over to a different neighborhood and found one of the addresses I'd come up with for Tyler Jay. It wasn't the most upstanding part of town, but it was mostly respectable all the same. I saw no sign of any unruly, tattooed characters or Escalades around or near the place. Next, I drove past the house I felt sure belonged to Tyler's mother. It was in a slightly classier neighborhood, but I saw nothing helpful or suspicious on my cruise past. A light was on in the rear corner of the house, in what I imagined was a bedroom. There were no Escalades on the street or in the driveway. I decided it would be worth it to make the trip in the daylight so I could ring the doorbell and speak to the occupant.

What will you do if Tyler answers the door? I asked myself.

I still hadn't come up with a satisfactory answer by the time I arrived at my next destination.

6

I buzzed over to my favorite Mexican food place near the mall in the center of town. It wouldn't hurt to kill another hour, and I was hungry. Ellmann wanted me to sign paperwork, but after our meeting at the hospital, I wanted to put him off. It was paperwork. It would still be there tomorrow.

The hostess and I greeted one another by name and chatted as she picked up a menu, probably out of habit, and led me through the restaurant to a two-person booth in the bar. I sat facing the entrance and watched as people came and went in the hall beyond. The bar was full, nearly every stool and table occupied. A soccer game played on every TV screen. There were regular cheers and jeers from groups around the room.

Gabriella was my waitress, and after a moment spent catching up, she took the menu I hadn't looked at.

"The usual today?" she asked. "Or something different?"

"The usual."

She smiled and nodded. "Oh, hey, why do you smell like a man? Is there something you're not telling me?" She bobbed her eyebrows suggestively, hope evident in her heavily-painted brown eyes.

"No. Ran out of shampoo and had to borrow my brother's."

"That is so boring it has to be true. Who would lie about something like that?"

She left to get my drink, and I pulled the pile of notes I'd made out of my pocket, spreading them over the table before me. I munched on chips and salsa while I reviewed them, trying to sort things out in my head. My attention focused on Stacy Karnes and Tyler Jakowski, and I made a new note here and there as I worked through the information. I had just about decided what I would do next when I glanced up.

I'd been keeping a pretty close eye on the traffic in the hallway, more out of habit and curiosity than anything else, but I was stunned to see a familiar man walk in and speak to the hostess. My eyes rolled involuntarily, and I dropped the chip I'd picked up back in the basket.

Joe Pezzani spotted me over the hostess's shoulder and a stupid grin spread over his face. I couldn't help the sigh that escaped me. A minute later, he was carrying his to-go bag in my direction. The hostess watched him then saw me. She did a palms-up gesture and shrugged her shoulders: an apology and a what-do-you-want-me-to-do message all in one. An instant later, Pezzani was sliding in the booth opposite me.

"Fancy meeting you here," he said, setting his carry-out bag on the table.

"Yeah." My tone was flat. I leaned back in the booth and crossed my arms over my chest. "Fancy."

"You're not here with someone, are you?" he asked.

I was saved from answering the question again when Gabriella returned carrying my dinner. I set the notes aside, and she put the plate down. She smiled at the newcomer.

"Will you be staying?" she asked.

We answered at the same time. I said no and he said yes. Gabriella, obviously confused, looked between us then settled on me.

"He's cute," she said. "What's the harm?"

She turned and left.

He smiled like a thief.

I rolled my eyes.

I didn't know anything about this guy. And what he knew about me wasn't necessarily flattering.

I leaned forward slightly and lowered my voice. "Are you stalking me?"

He smiled and laughed. "You think quite a bit of yourself, don't you?"

I shrugged. "Maybe I just don't think much of you."

He laughed, his blue eyes sparkling.

Gabriella returned with a fresh basket of chips. She batted her eyelashes at me with a barely perceptible incline of her head toward Pezzani before she left. I did another eye-roll.

"It's kind of a mess over at White Real Estate today," he said. "That guy Davis, he doesn't seem to have a grip on things yet."

"It's his first day and the circumstances are bad. Give him a minute to adjust."

He shrugged. "Just what I saw."

"Why are you here?" I asked.

"For dinner, obviously. I love their chili rellenos. On my honor, I'm not stalking you. It's coincidence."

"No such thing."

He was looking at me, his blue eyes searching my face carefully. "I stopped in to grab dinner."

He seemed to be telling the truth. But I truly don't believe in coincidence. Yet, in this situation, what other explanation could there be?

Pezzani stood and picked up his carry-out.

"Enjoy your dinner," he said. "Maybe I'll see ya around sometime."

I was still wondering what he meant when I left the restaurant myself. As I climbed onto the scooter and buzzed out of the lot, my eyes inadvertently flitted to the mirrors, watching for signs of being followed. I saw nothing that appeared suspicious, but it was dark, and I'm anything but an expert. Plus, I wasn't exactly inconspicuous on the scooter; I could easily be followed from a distance.

My phone rang. It was Amy. I fit the earbud into my ear and answered.

"Saw you called," she said. "What's up?"

I shrugged. "I'm kinda having a shitty day." I hit the highlights, catching her up on the latest news.

"What's this Joe look like?"

"Amy, come on. A girl could die."

She sighed. "I realize that, but I can't do anything to change that. So come on, is he cute?"

We chatted for a while, then she had to go. Brandon was waiting on her. His family was in town, and they had plans with them all weekend: dinner tonight and a big family gathering tomorrow. Amy didn't really know his family very well, and she was worried about making a good impression.

It was just as well. I didn't want to talk about Pezzani anymore, and she didn't want to talk about Stacy anymore. Plus, I'd arrived at my next destination.

———————

The look on Sandra York's face when I'd seen her watching me from the office earlier had continued to flash in my mind. Her self-satisfied sneer brought with it several speculations I'd initially dismissed because they were so ridiculous. Now that prison was a real possibility, I was highly motivated to find the real thief. This led me to follow those early speculations through to the end. There were some holes, but I thought I'd found enough pieces to see a picture.

All I had was a working theory, though, so I needed to have a conversation with Sandra. I wasn't going to prison. I sure as hell wasn't going to prison for something I didn't do.

I found the house with no trouble then parked at the curb. Sandra had thrown a party once and invited everyone from the office. I'd made a brief appearance, which I'd regretted. Now I was pretty sure she was going to regret having given me her address.

The house was completely dark; no one was home. I pulled the recorder from my backpack and tucked it into my back pocket then made myself comfortable in the porch swing. Inhaling deeply, I eased back into the swing and rocked gently, sure my wait would only be a few minutes.

Two hours later I was still waiting. And I really had to pee. Bad. I was contemplating peeing behind the neighbor's large front-yard bush. Then the wind picked up. When the rain started, I'd had enough.

I hustled to the curb and fetched the Cushman, steering it up the driveway then manhandling it up onto the porch.

I decided to use Sandra's bathroom and continue waiting for her inside. I intended to have a conversation with her even if I had to wait all night. But if I was forced to wait that long, I might as well be comfortable.

Getting into the house wouldn't be a problem. I hadn't used those talents in a while, but would be like riding a bike. Of course, everything would be easier if I could just find a key.

The absence of light helped conceal my movements and offset the chance of a neighbor noticing me and misunderstanding my intention. I confirmed the door was in fact locked then had a look around. But I found no spare key hidden underneath any of the flowerpots, rocks, or the doormat.

I ran through the rain around to the backdoor. It too was locked, but there were just as many potential hiding places for a key on the patio. Under the second flowerpot I picked up, I found what I was looking for. Smiling, I snatched the key, noticing the mark it had left on the cement. I let myself in then replaced the key and the pot.

I stopped in the first bathroom I came to, drying myself on a borrowed towel and pinning back my wet bangs with a hairpin from my pocket. Then I looked around the house.

I'd been struck last time I was here by how expensive Sandra's furnishings were. Far too expensive for what I know her income to be. This confirmed I'd at least come to the right place; Sandra knew more than she was telling. The chances were good some of what she knew pertained to the missing money.

In the master bedroom, I found a king-size four-poster bed covered in silk sheets and down comforters. Everything was tidy and neat; even the bed was made. I guessed Sandra had a housekeeper who made regular appearances.

Since I had to wait, the bed was as good a place as any to do it. Forgetting about my wet clothes, I climbed onto it and sighed as I gently sank back into the mattress and closed my eyes. In that moment I thought Sandra was the biggest witch I'd ever met, and I no longer felt bad for never liking her. Nice people don't have beds like hers.

Almost an hour later, I heard the garage door. I lay still, listening. The kitchen door opened and closed, then sharp heels clicked against the floor. A light went on and then off again after a few minutes. Then I heard footsteps on the stairs. I sat up.

Sandra came into her bedroom and flipped on the light, now carrying her shoes in her hand. She took several steps before she finally saw me. She gave a start, and a mean look colored her face.

"What the hell are *you* doing here?" she demanded.

"I know, I know, you thought you'd finally gotten rid of me." My tone was sympathetic, as if I understood her plight perfectly. "This bed is *so* comfortable. Wow!"

"I'm calling the police."

"I wish you would. It will save me the time."

"You were going to call the police because you broke into my house?" she asked, moving into the doorway of the closet where she dropped her shoes.

Her hair was a tangled mess, her makeup smeared, and her clothes wrinkled. The late return home and the state of her appearance left me with one conclusion.

"How's Barry?" I asked casually. "I hope I didn't scare him."

She scoffed and shrugged indifferently. But not soon enough. "How should I know?"

"Because you were still at work with him after I left. Or were you with him after hours tonight? Putting in a little overtime, there, Sandra?"

I could see I'd struck the nail on the head.

"You don't know what you're talking about. I'm calling the police."

"What's stopping you? I just wanted to give you a chance to explain your side of the story before I called them myself."

She took a step toward me. "What story?"

"The story of how White Real Estate came to be missing twenty thousand dollars."

Her eyes widened slightly and she gaped at me. "You don't actually think *I* stole that money, do you?" Then the corners of her mouth tipped up in a smile. "Everyone knows *you* did it."

I smiled and winked. "You and me, we know the truth, don't we? You've got some pricey stuff in here. Especially these linens," I said, rubbing a hand over the soft down comforter beside me. "These are *great*, by the way."

"I like nice things, so that proves I stole the money?"

I shrugged. "If you say so. Like I said, I only wanted to give you a chance to explain."

"You won't really call the cops," she challenged.

I laughed. "Of course I will. I've got nothing to lose now. You saw to that."

"Oh, please! You were so miserable in that job; everyone could see it. I did you a favor. You should be grateful."

"I don't hate the job," I countered. "I hate Paige." And the memories the job regularly brought up. "Sending me to prison isn't a favor. Besides, this wasn't about me. You needed a fall guy for your crime. Someone must have started to get suspicious, and I was perfect. Like you said, it was no secret how much I disliked Paige. Everyone would believe an embezzlement story; it's the ultimate revenge. You falsified documents, forged signatures, successfully pointed the finger at me. But it won't work."

A horrible smile spread over her face. "Oh yes it will. Checked your bank account lately? The cops will, if they haven't already. They'll find the couple thousand you held on to after transferring the balance to an offshore account they'll never be able to look at."

I smiled back at her, just as wickedly. "This isn't your first time, is it? A look at companies you've worked for in the past will likely turn up other embezzlement cases. Once the police establish a pattern and trace that deposit into my account back to your computer at work, or maybe Barry's, it won't take much more for them to figure out what really happened."

"Don't you ever give up?" she snapped. "It's over! Everything is airtight. Everything points to you. The cops won't look past all the nice, neat little pieces."

"Maybe not. But I will. And they'll pay attention when I put together just as many nice, neat little pieces pointing back to you."

"From your prison cell? I doubt it. I'll be set up in a new place, a new company, living off the money you stole, while you make license plates or whatever prisoners do."

"You'll have to be more careful next time. You stole twenty thousand dollars, but you'll probably only take away ten, maybe twelve, after all the cleanup is said and done. Framing me is costing you."

"Tell me about it. But believe me, I won't make the same mistakes next time. Barry was a stupid choice, for one. Everything is much easier if the fucking CFO is transferring the money out for you." She gave me a patronizing smile. "But that's nothing you need to worry your pretty little head about. You need to worry about how you'll look in orange and how you'll make new friends and live in tight spaces."

I got up and started for the door. Then I turned back.

"Out of curiosity, was I convenient, or did you pick me deliberately?"

She smirked. "Barry had you picked out from the beginning." Then she leaned forward and whispered. "He doesn't like you."

I smirked back. "I know. Give him a message for me, will you?"

"What message?"

"Tell him I said, 'checkmate.'"

Outside, I pulled the recorder from my back pocket and turned it off.

7

The next day, or rather later that same day, just after seven in the morning, my doorbell rang. Given that I'd spent most of the night waiting for the thieving witch Sandra to return home, I hadn't been in bed very long. And what time I had spent there had been fitful, my sleep plagued with more disturbing dreams of memories past.

I smashed a pillow down on my head and rolled over. I noted distantly that my shirt was damp; I'd been sweating. My alarm was set for ten. It was Saturday; I thought sleeping until ten was reasonable. Especially since this was the first day of my vacation.

The doorbell persisted, however, followed by angry banging on the front door. It reminded me vaguely of the way Hensley had attacked the door the day before. But two visits from the same cop in eighteen hours was unlikely, right?

I threw myself out of bed and stumbled to the door with my eyes still half shut. I knew without consulting a mirror I looked . . . bad. Mornings aren't really my thing. Let this be a lesson to whomever it was pounding on my door.

I heard a sharp voice in between rounds of banging.

"Ms. Grey! You need to open the door."

"Is the house on fire?" I called back, my tongue still thick with sleep.

"No. Open the door."

"Is someone bleeding to death?"

"No. If you don't— "

"If there's no emergency, come back in three hours."

"Ms. Grey, it's Detective Hensley. Open the door or I will."

Uh-oh.

I fumbled with the locks then yanked the door open and winced at the bright sunlight.

"Do you know what time it is?" I demanded.

Hensley chose to take my remark as a sincere inquiry and not the sarcastic gibe it was. He looked at his watch.

"Seven twelve."

"Oh, you've got to be kidding me!" I groaned, sagging against the doorjamb.

Hensley had another officer with him: a young, uniformed man I didn't recognize. They both looked serious, as if they meant business. The sleep was clearing from my brain quickly now, and I pretty much figured their visit wasn't good.

"I need you to come with me to the station," Hensley said. "I need to ask you some questions."

I was wearing sweats and a t-shirt, and I looked no better than I had the first time Hensley had seen me. The officer seemed to be considering whether or not I was crazy. At the moment, I wasn't sure, either.

I spun around and headed for the stairs. I heard both men hurry into the house then thunder down the stairs behind me.

"Where are you going?" Hensley asked sharply.

"Can I get my keys and some shoes before you drag me off to jail?"

I went into my room and grabbed my bag and tennis shoes from the floor.

"I'm not taking you to jail."

"You mean that's not our first stop," I corrected.

I shut my bedroom door then went into the bathroom down the hall.

"What are you doing?" Hensley asked.

"Relax, Detective," I said, walking in and setting my stuff on the counter. "You'll give yourself a stroke."

I caught sight of myself in the mirror and cringed. Bad was an understatement.

I grabbed a band from the drawer and tied my hair up. Pieces stuck out all over, but it was fine for an early morning interrogation and jail. I fished out a pin from the drawer and pinned my bangs out of my face, both cops looking on carefully, as if waiting for me to pull out a weapon I kept stored there.

A minute later we were piled in two cars, the officer in a marked Crown Vic, and Hensley and me in an unmarked Crown Vic. I sat in the back while Hensley drove. We were separated by a metal grate. The backseat smelled like urine and vomit, and there was a suspicious-looking stain on the floor behind the passenger seat. The only highlight was Hensley had refrained from using handcuffs. Technically, I wasn't under arrest. But I had no doubt that was his intent after a bit of questioning.

The officer went his own way while Hensley drove me to the police station located on Timberline Road, just north of Drake. The building was new and characteristically modern, with lots of pointy angles, metal, and glass. I think the tax dollars could have been put to better use, but I'm not in charge of making those decisions.

Hensley parked in the back and led me in through a rear door. We rode the elevator to the second floor then made our way down a long hallway. We arrived at a door marked CRIMES AGAINST PROPERTY and went in, coming to a small lobby of sorts. The desk in front of the door was empty, the secretary having gone home for the day, or the weekend, and only a few of the desks and offices in the space beyond were busy with activity. Offices and conference rooms lined the perimeter of the space. Black letters painted on the glass doors identified each one. In the middle, a dozen mismatched desks were crammed together, with narrow walkways snaking between them. Hensley led me to the far wall and into a room marked INTERROGATION.

These rooms are intentionally cold and intimidating, and this one was no different. There was a single metal table bolted to the floor with a large steel ring welded to the middle of it, used for securing handcuffs. There were two plain metal chairs on either side of the table, and Hensley deposited me in one of them. He called to someone nearby and told him to watch the door then stepped away. The guard, a plainclothes man in his forties, remained outside and paid me little attention, instead continuing to read through the thick file he held.

Hensley returned a few minutes later with a stack of files in his hands, which he arranged over the opposite side of the table. Then he sat and pulled his notepad from his pocket, flipping to the page he wanted. A business card fell out and he held it up.

"Want to call your lawyer?"

The card I'd given him yesterday.

"No. Not yet." No sense racking up a huge legal bill if I could clear things up myself.

"You have the right to legal counsel."

"I can invoke at any time."

He set the card aside and consulted this notepad.

"Do you know why you're here?"

"Do I get three guesses?"

"You're in enough trouble as it is. You might want to cooperate, make things a little easier for yourself."

"I'm not going to make it any easier for you to put me in prison," I said seriously.

"One step at a time."

"Don't you want to arrest me?" I asked. Then it hit me. "Sandra called you."

"Yes," he said. "She's filing charges against you for breaking and entering. She says you broke into her house last night. Do you know anything about that?"

I had to admit, I liked her style. Always on the offense.

"Breaking and entering?" I smiled. "We work together. She told me about the key she keeps under a pot. I went by to see her last night, but she wasn't home. I wanted to wait for her, but it started raining. I used the key to let myself in."

"She claims she doesn't leave keys lying around, and that she wouldn't have told you about them if she did."

"I'm not surprised. I went to ask her about the twenty thousand dollars missing from White Real Estate."

"Why ask her about the money?"

"Because I didn't steal it. I thought she might know something."

"Did she?"

I reached into my bag and withdrew the recorder. I set it on the table between us and pressed PLAY. We listened as the conversation replayed. Nothing in his expression changed, but he began shifting in his seat when Sandra finally confessed. I hit the STOP button and looked at him.

"See, she's using her little report to keep you guys busy, focused on me."

He sighed and set the notepad aside. "Did you put the key back?"

"Yep. Wasn't there, huh?"

"She's saying it never was."

"See the concrete?" I asked, remembering the mark the key had left.

He didn't answer, but he didn't need to.

"Okay, so what now?" I asked. "Can I go?"

The detective reached forward and picked up the recorder. "I'm sure this will help clear up a few things," he said, slipping it into his jacket pocket.

"I made a copy of that," I said, pointing to his jacket. "In case it 'disappears' or anything."

He shot me a dark look.

I wasn't long on trust for Hensley. If left up to him, I would have been arrested and charged with a felony. That didn't give me a whole lot of faith in the system.

"I'm just saying," I said, raising my hands. "I told you I didn't know anything about the missing money, but you didn't believe me."

"*Everyone* who sits on that side of the table says that," he shot back.

"But you didn't even bother to look past the nice, neat package Paige handed you. A little extra effort seems worth it for that one person who is *actually* telling the truth."

"I'll have someone give you a ride home," he said, gathering his things.

"What about that breaking and entering bit?"

He stood. "Filing a false police report is a crime. It's something I will take up with Ms. York when next I see her."

I couldn't help but smile.

———————————

Hensley called an officer to drive me home, but no one could pick me up for fifteen or twenty minutes. I agreed to meet the officer in the lobby then decided to look up Ellmann. I still needed to sign paperwork, and since I was already there, I couldn't find any good reason to put it off. Even though I did look for one.

Ellmann had instructed me to call him when I arrived, but so far I hadn't done anything else he'd told me to do, so I didn't see any reason to start now. I wandered out of Hensley's division then stopped a middle-aged guy dressed in jeans and polo shirt in the hallway. He gave me directions, his quintessential mustache dancing as he spoke.

I thanked him then moved away, finding the door marked CRIMES AGAINST PERSONS. It stood open, so I walked in. As I passed another empty receptionist's desk and entered another bullpen, I experienced déjà vu. This space was a mirror image of the one Hensley worked in. The differences were the number of desks and the level of activity. While property crimes had simply been occupied, this division was *busy*. More than twice as many people were at work in here, and there were possibly twice as many desks. The arrangement of working spaces crowded together seemed to defy the physical laws of science; so many desks could not possibly fit into the allotted space.

The directions I'd been given turned my attention to the far corner. There, with his back to me, I spied the figure of the detective I sought, his size making him hard to miss. He was sitting at his desk, a smaller man in a suit standing beside him, both of them intently watching the computer screen. I slipped quietly through the maze of desks and stopped behind them, watching over Ellmann's shoulder. The computer screen was split in half, the scene playing out from opposite angles.

I knew what this video was. This was the security camera footage from Elizabeth Tower.

Stacy Karnes stood at the counter browsing through a brochure she'd found there, her purse sitting where I'd later found it. The time readout on the screen said 1813. After reaching the back of the brochure, she put it down and looked around. She pulled her phone from her back pocket and glanced at it, possibly checking the time since she wasn't wearing a watch.

Why hadn't she answered the phone? I thought, my guilt weighing heavily on me.

Stacy tucked the phone back into her pocket then picked up another pamphlet. Behind her, the lobby door opened and the masked assailant walked in.

The person in the mask seemed to speak to Stacy. Stacy put the pamphlet down and turned around. I was no expert, but she didn't seem overly concerned until she laid eyes on the figure, and then I could only guess it was the ski mask that upset her. Did that mean she knew the person? Had she recognized the person's voice? I didn't know yet, but I was more determined than ever to find out.

After turning around and seeing the mask, Stacy lifted her free hand and clamped it over her mouth, taking a step backward. The figure withdrew a gloved right hand from the front pocket of the hooded sweatshirt, holding a knife. The knife I'd seen covered in blood. The assailant stepped forward, pursuing Stacy. Unexpectedly, Stacy raised her right foot and thrust it forward, connecting with the assailant's belly. It wasn't a move born of skill or practice, but of an instinct to survive. The figure doubled over and stumbled back momentarily. Stacy sprinted for the door. The assailant recovered quickly, however, and grabbed the hood of Stacy's sweatshirt, pulling her backward.

Stacy spun around to face the attacker, attempted to fight the attacker off, but the attacker sunk the knife into her belly once, then twice. I saw her mouth open and knew she was screaming. It was the scream I'd heard in the parking lot, the scream that reverberated in my dreams, and the scream echoing inside my head now. The assailant stabbed her a third time and she collapsed. When she was down, the assailant squatted, raising the knife above Stacy's chest. Then suddenly the assailant stopped and spun around toward the door. I knew the assailant was seeing me.

On-screen, I walked into the lobby and stopped. For a beat, my eyes were locked with the assailant's. Then the assailant jumped up and ran toward me. I watched as I dropped back into a defensive stance and brought my arms up. My physical encounter with the figure was brief. I blocked the blow, landed one of my own, then the stairwell and elevator doors burst open. The attacker stumbled for the door then out into the night.

I watched myself issue the order for the blonde to dial 911 and cross the lobby to Stacy. I knelt beside her then reach out to check for a pulse. The newcomers on scene fell in around us and pretty much blocked Stacy from view. A moment later a guy peeled off his shirt then pushed through the crowd, dropping out of sight. I knew he was pressing his shirt against Stacy's abdomen at my direction. After another minute, the EMT-kid shot out of the stairwell and barreled through the crowd, dropping out of sight as he knelt beside Stacy. I remembered well what he was doing.

Then the crowd shuffled, and I emerged near the elevators. I seemed to be looking for something, thinking. I moved around toward the counter, having spied Stacy's purse. There, I proceeded to rummage through it, pulling items out of her wallet and snapping photos. After a brief search, in which I clearly looked for something I didn't find, I pushed my way back into the crowd and return a minute later with Stacy's phone. My every movement was in plain sight of the camera. There was very little question about what I had been doing.

I wondered if this was the first time the police were watching the footage. I guessed it was. If Ellmann had seen any of this before, he would have been down my throat demanding to know why I'd been snapping photos of a dying girl's ID. I could pretty much guarantee that was about to happen now. Although, Ellmann hadn't spotted me yet; there was still time to turn around and leave, delay the interrogation by another few hours. Then a man in jeans and a shoulder holster stepped up next to me, and I knew any chance of escape had just been squashed.

"Hey, Ellmann, looks like you've got a visitor," Shoulder Holster said, obviously amused.

Ellmann and the man in the suit spun around, instantly assessing the situation. It was about that long before I saw the anger and annoyance fill Ellmann's eyes. For whatever reason, I didn't find him as difficult to read as Hensley, though they both did the neutral cop-mask thing well.

Instinctively, I took a small step back. I felt my leg bump against something hard, solid, and knew it was another desk; they were crammed in here like freaking sardines. Quick escapes were severely hindered by this poor arrangement.

"This looks like a bad time," I said lightly. "You seem busy. I'll come back later."

"You were supposed to call me," he said, standing.

I shrugged. "I was right around the corner, literally. I thought I'd drop by, see if you were in."

I took a step to the left, the way I'd come, squeezing past Shoulder Holster, who was laughing out loud now.

"I'll come back when you're not so busy," I said again, taking a couple more steps. "I can see you're busy."

Without taking a step, Ellmann reached out a long arm and closed his enormous hand around my entire upper arm. His grip wasn't tight, but I could feel the strength in it. It'd be a chore to get free unless he released me.

"You're here now," he said. "I'd hate for you to have come down here for nothing."

"I assure you the trip wasn't wasted. I had other business to take care of."

"We'll talk now."

He began steering me back out of the maze and then to the right, instead of the left and toward the door. In the far corner, I saw two rooms with INTERROGATION stenciled on the glass and felt myself break out in a light sweat at the thought this was where I was being dragged now. One interrogation room per day was my limit. I let out the breath I'd been unknowingly holding when we sailed past those rooms and through a door marked BREAK ROOM.

It was essentially a kitchen. Counters and cupboards lined two walls and there were a dozen small round tables spread throughout the rest of the space, each with two or three chairs. I could see standard kitchen appliances, making the kitchen fully operational. There were three coffee pots on one end of the counter, all three of which had dark brown liquid in them, and at least one was on; the smell of burnt coffee filled the room. Two tables were currently occupied.

"I need the room," Ellmann said.

Without a word of question or protest, the others cleared their tables and left. Ellmann released me then went to the door and threw the bolt, locking us in, or everyone else out—I wasn't sure which. And I didn't know which I preferred. He turned back to me and stood with his hands on his hips. I crossed my arms over my chest defiantly.

"What the hell were you doing?"

I'd done a lot of things for which he was likely to demand an explanation and didn't know to which he was referring now. And, while I'm no expert in surviving police interrogation, I have a handle on the basics. I never offer more information than asked for, lest I give away information previously unknown.

"You'll have to be more specific."

"Sadly, it's true; you've done so *many* things." He took a breath. "I don't know how long you were standing behind me, but you know I saw the footage; I saw what happened in that lobby. Can you please explain to me what you were doing in her purse and with her phone? At first glance, it appears you're rifling through a dying girl's belongings, searching for something worth pocketing."

"Maybe you should have taken my clothes that night, then. I took nothing from her."

Except a bit of information.

"You don't strike me as the aimless type, so I don't think you weren't snooping without reason. You were looking for something. What?"

I shrugged. "Emergency contacts. You know, I thought maybe I could find the numbers so EMS could just pass them along to the ER staff."

This was the first answer that popped into my head. I ran with it.

"And then you took pictures? Why? If you found the numbers, ER staff would have found them, too."

"I noticed the battery light flashing. I only took pictures so the information would be accessible after her phone died. I was only trying to help. There was so much excitement, and everything happened so fast after the ambulance got there, I just forgot about the photos."

I've become a good liar. Better than good, actually. Sometimes I scare myself.

What surprised me, though, was that I almost felt bad lying to Ellmann. I was actually starting to like the guy.

He walked forward toward the nearest table, shaking his head the way a person might do after explaining something simple to someone else who just didn't get it. It wasn't the first time I'd had that effect on someone. Usually I see that expression on my boss or supervisor's face.

"You know you smell like a man?" He lowered himself onto a chair and looked up at me.

I nodded. "Axe shampoo," I said. "Phoenix, specifically."

He just looked at me.

"My gay roommate used all my shampoo. I didn't figure this out until I was already soaking wet, so I had to use *something*. My brother uses this stuff."

He nodded, then his thoughts moved on to something else. Likely back to the topic we'd been discussing a moment before. Suddenly he seemed tired compared to the last time I'd seen him. And his dark hair was sticking up in tufts around his head from where he'd dragged his hands through it. I wondered if he'd slept since Stacy had been attacked. I realized I was asking the question before I could stop myself.

"Have you slept? You don't look so good."

He looked at me. "Thanks. Your compliments make me feel all warm and fuzzy inside."

"Right," I said, taking the chair across from him. "That's obviously some sort of boundary you don't want to cross. I get it. Sorry."

He sighed and leaned his elbows on the table, running his hands over his face and back through his hair, leaving a fresh chunk standing on end. "I'm crossing all sorts of boundaries. For instance, I should be having this conversation in an interrogation room, on tape and on record, after I've read you your rights."

"I appreciate you not doing that, by the way."

"Actually, it was selfish. I thought if I stood any chance at all of getting a straight answer out of you, it would be in an informal conversation, which, incidentally, requires far less paperwork. I get the impression you'd be a pain in the ass if we went the other way."

"I can't imagine why you'd think that," I said. He had no idea how right he was. Or maybe he'd spoken to Hensley.

"Look, I need you to consent to a search of your home and vehicle. Actually, *you* need that. And since you saw the security footage, we need to do it now. Even a first-year law student could argue the problems with letting you go home now and doing a search later."

"You want to search my house?"

"That won't be a problem, will it?"

I sighed and slumped into a chair. "This sucks."

"Detective Hensley came to see me. Seems like you've gotten yourself into quite a bit of trouble in the last twenty-four hours."

"An arguable point." I shrugged. "I'd been thinking recently my life had become monotonous, boring."

"How do you feel about it now?"

"Way less boring," I confirmed.

8

The station lobby was a zoo. A baby was crying, three children were running around screaming, a man was yelling, a woman was complaining. I stood beside Ellmann watching Troy, the nerdy-looking guy I'd seen at Elizabeth Tower, motor the Crime Scene van out of the parking lot and head north on Timberline. I'd given him a spare key and directions to the mechanic's shop.

Ellmann was dressed in a similar uniform to the one he'd worn the day before: jeans and a t-shirt. I thought detectives were supposed to get around in cheap suits and bad ties, like Hensley, but I had yet to see Ellmann dressed that way. Of course, I'd only known the man two days; it was possible this judgment was premature.

"This take long?" I asked over a hysterical shriek. I was still staring at the place where the van had disappeared from view.

He nodded toward the door then held it open for me and followed me out. From the sidewalk, the chaos of the lobby was muffled.

"Not too long, usually."

"Don't you need to be there?"

He shook his head. "Troy doesn't do his best work when we stand over him. It's faster if we give him his space. What's wrong with your truck?"

"No idea. Trouble is, my mechanic can't seem to figure it out, either. He spends more time with the damn thing than I do these days."

"You need a new mechanic. Mine's pretty good, if you want the number."

"I'll keep it in mind."

"You eat breakfast yet?" he asked.

I hooked a thumb over my shoulder toward the lobby. "Yeah, I hit the Continental Breakfast buffet before I checked out."

He chuckled. "Right. I know this great place . . ."

He turned and began walking down the sidewalk toward Timberline. I fell in behind him because I had nothing better to do. And however long "not too long, usually" turned out to be, it would go by much more quickly over breakfast with Ellmann than standing alone on the sidewalk in front of the police station. Plus, I was hungry. More than that, I needed a cup of coffee.

We walked north along Timberline to Burger King a block over.

Inside, we found only a few other breakfast-goers, all of them obviously cops. Ellmann ordered some supersized egg-bagel combo thing with extra everything and a bucket of coffee. He'd obviously eaten here before.

"And for you, ma'am?" the teenager behind the counter asked, looking at me.

I really hate being called "ma'am." It makes me feel old. Of course, to a seventeen-year-old girl, *everyone* over the age of eighteen *is* old. So, maybe all was right with the world.

"That sounds good," I said, stepping up to the counter. "I'll have the same."

Her finger stopped over the touch screen of the register, and she looked up at me. I noticed Ellmann was looking at me, too. I glanced from one to the other then shrugged.

"What?"

This wasn't typical of the way I ate, however, most everyone would assume it was, given the extra forty-seven pounds I couldn't hide underneath baggy t-shirts and sweats. Either way, it sure wouldn't help me with the forty-seven-pound problem.

The girl did some order-entering while Ellmann and I did some arguing. He handed his card to the girl to pay for the whole thing, and I wanted to pay for my part. I dug some cash out of the bottom of my bag, but he wouldn't accept any of it.

The girl returned carrying two trays piled high with cholesterol, calories, and certain death. Ellmann turned away from me and reached for one of them. I quickly stuffed the cash into his back pocket and reached for the other. He immediately gave me a small head shake, but seemed resigned to his defeat.

We carried our trays to a corner table where we both moved for the same seat—the seat that would afford a view of the entire restaurant and both doors. I thought we'd have to throw down until Ellmann suggested the next table over. There we both sat in the booth against the wall, side by side, each with a clear view of the place.

"Do you always argue about everything with everyone?" he asked after swallowing a bite.

I sipped at the coffee. Thank goodness it had been the least expensive item, because it tasted like recycled motor oil that would double as gasoline in a pinch.

"You bring it out of me."

"I'm not sure if I believe that or not."

I was halfway through my bagel thing when the door opened and two more cops walked in. They were dressed in suits, by far the most expensive suits I'd seen so far. One was charcoal gray and the other a dark pinstripe. They spotted Ellmann, took me in for a moment, then started toward us. I felt Ellmann tense beside me, but nothing about his outward presentation changed. Had I not been sitting next him, I would have had no idea anything was off.

The men were in their late twenties or early thirties. The guy in the charcoal suit had light brown hair; the other blonde. And they wore enough cologne to choke a horse.

"Look at this," the brunette said to his companion. "Do you believe it? Our very own Ellmann, out on a date." He turned to his friend. "They grow up so quickly."

The blonde snickered. "A *breakfast* date," he clarified, bobbing his eyebrows suggestively.

"Don't you clowns have anything better to do?" Ellmann asked. "Maybe some police work or something?"

"Oh, that's right," the brunette said. "I forgot dating is a sensitive issue with you."

I cut in before Ellmann could respond. "Speaking of dating, how long have you two been together?"

Both men puffed up considerably at my suggestion.

"I'd guess a few years," I went on. "You know, you're starting to look alike. That happens. My grandparents, for example, looked so similar people thought they were siblings. And I'm ninety percent sure they *weren't* siblings, but who can know for sure? It was a different time."

The blonde flushed, either from embarrassment or anger—my bet was embarrassment. The other's eyes had turned cold and dark. Malevolent.

"We are not a couple," the brunette hissed.

"Hey," I said, raising my hands in front of me. "I'm not judging. Look at the Romans, for instance. They were a mighty people, and fond of same-sex sexual relationships. Actually, they were fond of sex, period, but still. And they weren't the only culture. Who's to say where we'd stand on issues like that today if it weren't for the Catholic Church? I guess it's fair to say we'd see a lot of things differently if it weren't for the Catholic Church. Like birth control. Anyway, the point is, to each his own. All that really matters is that you're happy. Are you happy?"

"No," the blonde spat. "We're not happy." The statement had been intended to defend their sexual orientation and the boundaries of their relationship, but it didn't come across that way, and he knew it the instant it was out of his mouth. It only flustered him more.

Ellmann was grinning from ear to ear beside me.

"I'm sorry to hear that," I said. "My advice? Get counseling. Those marriage counselors really know what they're doing. You obviously love each other, so you're bound to work it out. Don't give u—"

"Shut up!" the brunette snapped, the features of his face pinched and red.

"Uh-oh," I said. "Was it something I said?"

There was a brief moment of confused and angry mutterings before the pair finally spun around and all but ran out of the restaurant. The brunette gave one last look in through the window. I smiled and waved, giving him a big thumbs-up. A few seconds later, there was the screech of tires as their car peeled out of the lot (and away from me).

I sighed with satisfaction then reached for my bagel.

Ellmann was smiling.

"That was great." He took a bite.

"I only feel a little bit bad."

"Why feel bad at all?"

"Because they actually *are* sleeping together. Who are we to judge?"

He froze. "What do you mean they're sleeping together?" he finally asked.

"The blonde one had the distinct look of a kid caught with his hand in the cookie jar when I first mentioned they were a couple. There were signs of embarrassment from both of them, lots of anger, but under all of it, fear. Fear of being discovered." I shrugged. "I hope they actually are happy together."

Ellmann didn't say another word to me until we were at my house with Troy and the crime scene team.

———————————

My primary objective today was to get moved. If I hadn't needed a new place to live before, I definitely would after the police search. I had called Margaret Fischer during breakfast and rescheduled our meeting. I didn't want the search to jeopardize our deal. Then I called my brother.

I couldn't use my truck, and it would take way too many gas-guzzling carloads to haul everything over in the Lincoln, despite the impressive cargo space (the trunk could comfortably accommodate eight suitcases or six dead bodies). I needed a truck. After breakfast, I somehow managed to talk Ellmann into dropping me off at Home Depot on Harmony. I gave him my house keys and promised to be right behind him.

I found Zach, dressed in his bright orange apron, helping a stooped old man in the electrical department. He gave me his keys, and I bought two more rolls of packing tape. I made it three steps out the door when I heard a voice behind me.

"Look who it is."

I looked back and saw Joe Pezzani. He was dressed similarly today as he had been when I'd seen him in my office, and he looked just as good. He settled his sunglasses in place as he walked out into the sunlight.

"Wanna give me that line about not stalking me again?"

He stopped beside me.

"It's possible *you're* stalking *me*," he said. "I'm working."

He did have his security company uniform on, so maybe this was another coincidence. But how many times could I *coincidentally* run into the same guy?

"How did it go for the guard last night?"

The wind shifted, and I caught a whiff of something wonderful-smelling. I was pretty sure it was him. I was just as sure I didn't smell very good under the still-fragrant Axe. I hoped the wind didn't shift again until I was long gone.

"All reports were negative: nothing out of place, nothing unusual, nothing suspicious."

"Good. Hopefully that will help calm everyone's nerves a little bit."

"This isn't really any of your business anymore, though, is it? I mean, that Davis guy is handling everything, or trying to."

"I was serious; Paige can't fire me. I'm still employed. Therefore, it's still my problem."

I didn't see the need to mention my vacation. Probably that would just confuse the situation for him.

He chuckled softly. I turned and continued toward the parking lot.

"I need to be going," I said. I had a date with a cop and a crime scene investigator.

Pezzani fell in step beside me.

"Listen, I was thinking we should stop meeting like this."

"Yeah?" I said without slowing. "Well, that's easy. Next time you think of following me, don't. Just stay home."

"Despite myself, and you, I find you interesting. I was thinking next time we could meet on purpose."

I chuckled. "What, like a date?"

"Yeah. What do you think?"

I glanced up at him. He was being sincere. Who the hell was this guy?

"You're serious."

He pulled his phone from his pocket. "Yes. What's your number?"

After a brief, internal debate, I acquiesced. I reasoned that I had given Pezzani, possible stalker, my phone number because it was the fastest way out of the conversation and the parking lot. Ellmann was likely already at my house, and I could only hope my mother wasn't home. I didn't want to entertain any other possible explanations for having given Pezzani my number.

"Where's your truck?" he asked as I climbed into my brother's Dodge Cummins.

"The shop."

"What's wrong with it?"

Why did everyone ask that question? I didn't know what was wrong with it; that's why it was in the shop.

"No idea."

We said our goodbyes and I roared out of the lot.

When I got home, the crime scene van and Ellmann's navy blue Charger were parked at the curb. I saw no sign of my mother. So far so good.

While Troy and his two helpers methodically searched the place from floor to ceiling, wall to wall, starting in my bedroom, I tried to stay out of the way. I made coffee and passed it around. For a while I stood with Ellmann in the kitchen, both of us drinking our coffee silently. When nothing of interest was found in either my bedroom or the bathroom, I went downstairs to take a shower (and wash my hair).

When I emerged again, I heard yelling upstairs. My heart instantly beat faster, and I experienced the usual fight-or-flight response these types of situations regularly bring out in me. Swearing under my breath, I hustled upstairs and into the kitchen, where my mother had Ellmann and Troy cornered. Troy's helpers were standing nearby, staring conspicuously at the spectacle before them. She was hurling questions at them so quickly they couldn't respond.

"Mom, what are you doing home?"

Bridget Grey is tall, like everyone else in the family. (I had gotten shorted on that gene, literally, standing at least three inches shorter than all my relatives, past or present. But I look a lot like both of my parents, so that eliminates the UPS man.) At five-eleven barefoot, she was easily more than six feet tall in the heels she wore today. Her hair, kept perfectly blonde by the slew of chemicals she treated it with every few weeks, had been shoulder length and attractively layered until a couple weeks before. This had been the beginning of her unmedicated upswing into mania. She'd gone to an expensive salon on a whim and instructed the girl to chop it off. Now it's chin length, shorter in the back and slightly longer in the front, and styled dramatically.

She has blue eyes, and her choice of makeup during these states is to wear night-out makeup during the day and even racier styles at night. Her side of the family is all rail-thin and not particularly strong, in any sense of the word; they traded capability for appearance, something I'd noticed none of them really minded. No exception, my mother had worn a size three before having children and now wears a four.

Today she was dressed in an expensive black pencil skirt split up the back to mid-thigh. She wore a pushup bra, a red scoop-neck blouse with strategically placed ruffles calling attention to her cleavage, and a tailored black jacket that cut her narrow figure and accentuated all of her best features. No one can say the woman is anything but gorgeous.

She wheeled around and marched forward, her attention wholly focused on me now, much to the relief of Ellmann and Troy. Ellmann was still on alert, however, and watchful.

"How dare you question me! It's my house! I'll come and go as I please! The better question, young lady, is what the hell is going on here? Why are these men here tearing my house apart? Who gave them permission to do that?"

I was familiar with this routine. She could fire off questions so quickly she seemed to have no need for breath. But I could assert myself enough to interrupt. Whether there was wisdom in that or not.

"I gave them permission."

"How dare you!" She spun back around and pointed an angry finger at Ellmann, who had trailed her across the kitchen. "This is *my* house! How can *she* give permission? It has to be *me*. And, I don't give permission. Get out!"

Ellmann was catching on.

"If we leave now," he said quickly, "we'll come back with a court order, and you won't be able to keep us out. That looks much worse."

She swung back around to me.

"What are they looking for?" she snapped. "What have you gotten mixed up in now? You know, you're such a troublemaker. The police are always looking at you for something. When are you going to straighten out your life? Your brother, now *he's* making something of himself."

The same record, spinning 'round and 'round. Always the same few lines.

"They don't actually think I did anything wrong." And this whole little act of hers wasn't entirely about me.

"This is my house!" she said again. "Get out! All of you, get out! Including you, you little brat." She stomped over to me and slapped me, her open palm smacking hard and sharp against my cheek. The stinging sensation lingered.

Before I could respond, Ellmann clicked handcuffs on her wrists, against her wild and ugly protests. She flung and jerked and kicked, but Ellmann easily guided her to the door and out of the house. I could still hear her screaming after the front door closed behind them. She was screaming about calling her lawyer. I really hoped she didn't do that. She had reason to worry about the police searching the house, though. Who knew what they would find in her room?

I looked at Troy, who still stood against the kitchen counter wide-eyed and open-mouthed.

"Are you almost finished?"

Maybe I should have been more worried about her, about what she kept in the house, about what kind of trouble I might get into for it, but I found I was beyond all that.

"We, uh, we still need to finish most of this level, and the garage. But . . . with the lady of the house revoking consent, we won't be able to move forward until we have a court order. Despite how sure Ellmann made getting one sound, it's highly unlikely we will, given the circumstances."

The front door opened and closed.

"Go ahead and finish. I gave consent, and I haven't changed my mind."

"But it isn't legal if the house doesn't belong to you," Ellmann said from behind me.

"Then it's legal," I said. "I own the house."

I left the kitchen and returned to the basement to resumed packing. The clock had started ticking, and it was counting down fast. And I still had quite a bit of work to do.

"So, you own the house, huh?"

I looked up and saw Ellmann leaning against the doorjamb of my bedroom, his hair brushing the top.

"Yes."

I was standing in front of the closet, stacking more clothing into a plastic bin.

"If you own the house," he tried again softly, "why are you the one moving out?"

"It's complicated. Let's just say it's easier."

Once the bin was full, I crammed the lid on and lifted it. Ellmann came over and took it from me, carrying it out of the room and setting it near the door. He used tape to reinforce the lid.

"Thanks," I said, pulling the next bin over and reaching into the closet again.

"What did she mean when she said you're a troublemaker? That the police are always looking into you?"

He took up his place in the doorway again.

"She resents me almost as much as I resent her. She hasn't been able to see things fairly where I'm concerned for the past thirteen years. Maybe longer."

I hauled hanging items out of the closet by the armful, dropping them unceremoniously into the bin.

"Is that when she started comparing you to your brother?"

"No, she's been doing that since the day he was born. The resentment started when I was twelve."

"What happened?" he asked.

I stuffed one more armload into the bin, squashed the lid on, and held it closed while Ellmann taped it. I let him carry it out and set it on top of the other. Then I retrieved another bin and resumed my task.

"I know if I don't tell you, you'll just look it up, but that's fine with me. It's not something I talk about."

"All right, change of subject. Why are you in such a rush to pack?"

"Because anything I want to keep I need to have out of here by the time she gets back. She doesn't respond well to being slighted, especially in her current condition, and especially by me. She'll retaliate. Maybe she'll have a big bonfire in the backyard, maybe she'll drench everything in gasoline or bleach." I shrugged. "Hard to say. She's done that and a lot more."

"No pressure, then, right?"

"You don't have to help me. I've gotten pretty good at packing over the years."

He shrugged. "I'm here, and I've got nothing better to do."

"By the way, what did you do with my mother?"

"Put her in the car. But don't worry," he said. "I cracked the window."

9

"This is a great place. How'd you find it?"

Joe Pezzani and I stood in the kitchen of my new place off Drake, east of College, sipping bottled waters, the only edible thing in the house.

I had nearly finished packing everything when Ellmann had called to say my mother had just spoken to her attorney. Knowing her release was imminent, I'd asked Pezzani for help with the move. There had been more to do than I could do alone, and I'd wanted to avoid another run-in.

Amy would have come to help me had I asked, but I knew this thing with Brandon's family was pretty important. My friend Mercedes Salois is a nurse and works nights at the hospital. She'd worked the night before and was sleeping. I couldn't call my brother, whose truck I was already borrowing. And Donald isn't big on physical labor. So, to both his surprise and mine, I'd called Pezzani.

"I went to another management company in town and asked what they had available. Finding this place was just luck."

"Didn't want to take something your company manages?"

I shrugged. "It was an option. But sometimes that's complicated. This way is usually simpler."

Working with Margaret Fischer was certainly simple. She was predictably by-the-book. But it wasn't pleasant. For either of us. I wasn't fond of her and, sadly, I didn't think she liked me.

That morning, after the search team had left, I'd had to call Fischer because I was running late for our rescheduled appointment. I'd thought she would be in good shape if that was the worst thing that happened to her today. Still, she'd done a lot of glaring and sighing until I'd given her a check and she'd given me the keys.

"And you like simplicity?"

"Generally speaking, yes."

We made dinner plans for the following evening, my treat as a thank-you for the moving help, then Pezzani left. I grabbed a fast shower, threw on jeans and a top, and hit the road. The one thing I hadn't been able to spend a lot of time packing was food, and that was something I was going to need. I began compiling a grocery list in my head, the total adding up quickly by my mental math. I wasn't getting paid for my vacation. For the next two weeks, I would be living off my savings. Not the most ideal situation considering I'd just taken on the expense of an additional household. Maybe I needed to go back to work and accept White's promotion.

No, I thought. *What I need is money.*

Immediately, my thoughts drifted to Tyler Jay and the fifteen-thousand-dollar reward. I would soon be burning through my savings; another fifteen large would go a long way in reducing my stress level until I got things figured out. Grocery store forgotten, I pulled the pages of notes out of my bag, glancing over them as I drove. I had a few possibilities, but the best bet seemed like his mom's house. If Tyler Jay was still in town, I thought the chances were good his mother would know where he was. It seemed pretty likely she would know where he was even if he wasn't in town. What I didn't know was if she would tell me.

I knew nothing about Tyler Jakowski, aside from the fact that he was dating Stacy Karnes and was Larimer County's Number One Most Wanted Fugitive for a whole slew of violent crimes. Tina Shuemaker had said he had a scar and a lot of cheap-looking tattoos. I wondered now if he'd gotten any of those in prison. At a stoplight, I quickly went over the information I'd pulled off the Internet about the names Tyler Jakowski and Tyler Jay. There wasn't much aside from a few newspaper articles, primarily from the *Fort Collins Coloradoan*, regarding Tyler Jakowski and his suspected involvement in various crimes. I hadn't made note of any reported gang affiliation, but I suddenly wondered if that was because I'd overlooked it or simply hadn't dug deep enough.

I found the house I believed belonged to Tyler's mother and parked a couple doors down. I sat for a moment taking in the neighborhood. Located in the center of town, just off Prospect, this subdivision is middle-class. The driveways have minivans and SUVs parked in them, and the yards are full of bikes and toys.

The lots in this neighborhood are slightly larger, the houses having been built in the '70s, before cookie-cutter designs. The house was a tri-level, painted a cheery yellow that had faded over the years. The windows and gutters appeared clean, and the yard was maintained. There was a late-'90s Honda Civic CRX parked in the driveway with aftermarket exhaust, rims, and spoiler, the windows tinted beyond legal limits, and twin white racing stripes splitting the shiny black paint from bumper to bumper. I didn't think

Tyler's mom, whatever kind of woman she was, would drive a souped-up Honda with such horribly atrocious rims. At least, I *hoped* she wouldn't.

Taking a deep breath, I exited the truck, walked up to the front door, knocked, and waited.

I saw movement behind the curtains in the windows on all three levels of the house. It confirmed I was on the right track. A woman a few years older than my mother, dressed in worn and comfy-looking jeans, opened the door and stared through the screen at me, taking in even the most minute details. Her entire demeanor was guarded, cautious.

This was definitely the right place.

"Can I help you?"

"I really hope so. I'm a friend of Stacy's, and I'm trying to find Tyler. Is he home?"

I watched her face closely, seeing her eyes flick involuntarily to the left, at something inside the house.

"Tyler who?" she asked. Mom wasn't a very good liar.

"Tyler Jay. Stacy told me to find Tyler if anything ever happened to her." I was pulling this out of my ear on the fly, hoping anything I learned would be more than I'd had before, even if I didn't hit pay-dirt straight away. "She's in the hospital. It's serious."

Something in her shifted, softened. I wondered if she'd met Stacy. Either way, she seemed saddened by thoughts of Stacy's injuries.

"I'm sorry to hear that, but I don't know any Tyler."

Her eyes flicked to the side again, and this time they lingered for a second or two. Then I heard movement. A large man came into view, blocking the woman from sight. He pushed the screen door open and stepped out onto the small porch, forcing me back down the steps and onto the sidewalk.

He was about my age, well over six feet tall, built like a refrigerator, and dressed in baggy, black shorts and a black tank top. His chest, arms, and neck were tattooed with symbols and designs largely meaningless to me, though I got a distinctly "gang" vibe from them. He was of Hispanic descent, though not wholly. His skin was more tanned than brown, his hair and eyes brown but not dark. His hair was short and slicked back from his forehead. It looked like he was trying and failing to grow a moustache. I stared up at him, struggling to keep all signs of intimidation hidden, wondering who he was and what he planned to do to me, because he wasn't Tyler Jay, and I suspected he knew where Tyler was.

"Who are you?" he asked. His voice was surprisingly soprano for his size.

"My name is Jennifer. I go to school with Stacy. Are you Tyler?"

My go-to fake name is Jennifer. It had been ever since I'd started sneaking into clubs during my unruly teenage years. In my high school class, practically one out of every three girls was named Jennifer, half of them brunette.

"Derrick," he answered. "You go to CSU? Aren't you a little old to be in college?"

Old? Old?!

I'd been getting this old bit a lot recently. Starting immediately, I'd need to be more aggressive about getting my stress level under control. Because obviously it was the stress that had aged me.

"I got a late start," I said lightly, shrugging. "Took some time off after high school. Do you know where Tyler is?"

"Look, little girl, you better run along, now."

"I'm sorry to bother you; I'm just trying to help out a friend. She's not doing well. The doctors don't know if she'll make it. I really need to find Tyler. Can you help me?"

I'm not sure why asking, "Can you help me?" tends to soften people, but it does. It doesn't always mean they'll do what you want, but it almost always means they'll feel so bad about *not* doing what you want that they try to make up for it by doing something else. Whatever the reason for the response, I take advantage of this phenomenon regularly. Even now I saw this big man's face relax and his eyes soften. His stance was less confrontational, and he was obviously trying to decide how to respond.

"Look, girl, Tyler knows about Stacy already, okay? You can't tell him anything he don't already know. So, don't worry about it no more. That's the best thing for you. Just walk away."

"He already got the message?" I asked, hopeful. "Maybe she asked more than one person to give it to him. She said it was important, I think about money, but I'm not really sure. I'm just glad he knows. I know it was important, and I'd feel really bad if I didn't do this for her, especially if she dies. Gosh," I said suddenly, as if realizing this was a possibility for the first time. "I really hope she doesn't die."

I shifted my weight between feet, sniffed, and quickly blinked my eyes a few times. I wanted to give the impression that I was emotionally distraught at the thought of Stacy Karnes passing away. I might have just looked like a girl too old to be in college who had to pee and was fighting an attack of allergies.

The man sighed and stepped off the porch to stand in front of me, lessening the difference in our heights almost imperceptibly. He was suddenly very uncomfortable, no doubt worried I would burst into tears. He obviously wanted to avoid that outcome.

"Hey, it's too soon to know anything for sure," he said. "Stacy's strong; she could pull through."

I nodded and sniffed again.

"Now, since it was so important to her, why don't you tell me the message, and I'll get it to Tyler?"

I shook my head. "I'm sorry, but she was very clear: speak to Tyler directly. She said there would be others who would want the information. She said to ask for him here because his mom would always know where to find him."

It was a huge gamble. Everything could blow up in my face if the woman who lived in this house was not actually Tyler's mother. All I really had to bolster my guess was the fact that Tyler was about my age and the woman who had answered the door was about my mother's age. It was thin, so very thin. I held my breath while the man took in my words.

Through the open screen door, I saw another man step into view. He glanced at me then took in the street with the eye of an experienced fugitive. This man, tall and lanky, with cheap-looking tattoos and a scar over his eye, was the same man from the photo on the wanted poster. This was Tyler Jay.

"I'm Tyler," he said in a deep voice, husky from cigarettes. "What's the message?"

"If you're really Tyler," I said, "tell me what Stacy's tattoo looks like."

"She doesn't have any tattoos."

From the way he said it, I was fairly sure he was telling the truth. Of course, I was all too aware this was also a gamble, since I didn't actually know the answer.

"All right, then," I said, satisfied. "She said if anything ever happened to her, I was supposed to find you. She wanted me to tell you she tucked something away for safekeeping in your spot. That's it, nothing else. I sorta guessed it was money, since I know she works so much, but she never did say."

Something I'd said hit home with him; I could tell by the small change in his eyes. Wasn't *that* a stroke of luck.

"How do I know this is a real message?" he asked. I resisted the urge to panic. "Why would you deliver a message for her anyway? She never mentioned you, so I doubt you two are very close."

I cleared my throat and shuffled my feet nervously. "Uh, well, she sort of walked in on me with a certain professor once. We were . . . well, you know. Anyway, she said she would spread it all over campus if I didn't do her a favor. Hey, look, if that sort of thing got around, I'd be kicked out! The professor would be fired, and she'd probably never find another job. I figured doing this one little favor was a small price to pay."

I have no idea where I come up with this stuff.

"Wait," Derrick said. "*She*? The professor was a woman?"

I looked at him innocently. "Yeah. Why?"

A stupid grin spread over his face and he shook his head. "No reason."

I turned back to Tyler, who was also grinning slightly. Boys are so dumb. "So, listen, I'm sorry to come over like this, but I just wanted to deliver on my end of the bargain. I'm really sorry about Stacy. I actually like her. You know, she's okay when she's not blackmailing you."

Tyler chuckled softly. "She must have picked up a few things after all, little Miss Goody Two-Shoes. Thanks for the message. I'll make sure she knows you came through if she . . ."

He couldn't bring himself to say what I struggled to think about myself, and I didn't even know the girl. Tyler might have been a bad and dangerous guy, accused of all sorts of horrible crimes, but he was just a man underneath all that, and he seemed to really love Stacy. I kind of felt bad for him; it hurts to lose someone you love, or to worry about losing them.

I just nodded. "Thanks."

I turned and walked back to the truck, got in, and drove away as fast as I could without appearing to be running for my life.

———————————

I drove to King Soopers on College and sat in the truck while I dialed the phone number that had been listed at the bottom of the wanted poster. I had been expecting to speak to a real person, given the fact that Jakowski was such a wanted man, but instead I reached a recording and was instructed, in detail, about what to leave in my message. I recited all the requested information and hung up. I wondered how long it would take for the reward money to be paid. I also wondered why the police and sheriff's office had been unable to find Tyler. After a few minutes on the computer, I'd had a few doorbells to ring. Tyler had answered the first one.

I'm not a huge fan of law enforcement anyway, my past being what it is, but I do have a certain respect for the people who do it. That had taken a serious hit in the last couple days. Hensley would have railroaded me because it was the simplest thing to do. No one could find Tyler, yet I'd done it without even really trying. What were Stacy's chances of finding justice? Was Ellmann really trying to track down her assailant? Or would he simply continue to focus on me because that was simpler? I had been in the lobby, and Stacy had been there to meet me, but that was the extent of my involvement. The security footage clearly showed I was not the one to attack Stacy. And while there had been some unusual activity in my bank account recently, a quick check would prove I'd not paid anyone to do it, either.

If left in the hands of the police, would Stacy's attacker be found and punished? I couldn't deny I had my doubts. This left me examining my options.

King Soopers was crowded with the after-work rush, but I managed to survive without any hand gestures or colorful language. I piled the hundred dollars worth of groceries into the truck and went home. Then, in an effort to get the most of my new gym membership and take the forty-seven-pound problem seriously, I threw on sweats and paid a visit to the elliptical. I spent thirty sweaty minutes considering whether or not there was anything I hated more than the elliptical. Just about the time I decided there wasn't, and that I was going to ralph, the timer ticked off the last minute, and I shuffled back out to the truck. I returned home, set the coffee pot timer for nine, showered, and hit the hay.

I knew I hadn't been asleep very long when my phone awoke me. My whopping headache told me so. I also didn't need to look at the time to know it was late. Late-night phone calls are almost always bad news.

"Yeah?" I answered without opening my eyes.

"Zoe, I need help."

It was my brother.

I pushed the covers back and sat up.

"What's wrong?"

"Can you pick me up?"

"Where are you?" I asked as I got up. I switched on the lamp sitting on the floor beside the bed and winced at the light.

"College and Mulberry."

"I'll call you when I get there."

"You won't miss us."

That sounded ominous.

I wish this was the first time I'd ever gotten a late-night call about my brother. But it wasn't even close. And while I always hope it will be the last, I have no illusions.

I could see the blue and red strobe lights from half a mile away. Northbound traffic on College was unaffected, while southbound traffic was down to two lanes and eastbound traffic on Mulberry down to one. A team of uniformed officers was directing traffic.

Donald's Lincoln was nosed up against the southbound traffic light, blocking traffic in the same direction. The light was leaning at a forty-five degree angle, the lights hanging crookedly and flashing signals at eastbound traffic. Two ambulances and a fire truck completed the party, emergency response personnel everywhere.

A tall officer I recognized from the Elizabeth Tower incident waved me through the intersection. I complied then hung a right into the Safeway parking lot, squeezing through a large group of gathered rubberneckers, staring and pointing, some snapping photos and taking videos with their phones. I snagged the first parking space I found (handicapped) and hopped out.

Dodging a string of oncoming traffic, I cut across and hustled up to the officer.

"What are you doing?" he asked over a chorus of horns. "You're going to get hurt."

"My brother," I said, trying to keep the worry out of my voice. I pointed at the Lincoln. "That's his car." For all intents and purposes, anyway. Zach had borrowed it from Donald because I was currently borrowing his truck. "Is he okay?"

The officer, whose nameplate read FRYE, kept one eye on traffic, continuing to move vehicles through while he spoke to me.

"Don't worry," he said seriously. "They're all fine. EMS has them in the ambulances. As far as I understand, none of them need medical care."

"None of them? How many were there?"

"Eight, I think. All in various states of inebriation."

"Drunk? And driving?" My worry was quickly giving way to anger.

"If it makes you feel any better, they only killed the light pole; they didn't hit anyone else, and no one was hurt."

"It doesn't."

I spun on my heel and marched toward the first ambulance, parked on College, south of the intersection. I cut through traffic as two other officers yelled at me about being in the street. Ignoring them, I stormed the ambulance. I saw five young faces, most of which were familiar to me. None of them belonged to my brother.

"I'll be with you in a minute," I said, pointing my finger at each of them.

The second ambulance was parked on Mulberry, just west of College, in an eastbound lane. There was a uniformed man standing in the open back door talking to someone sitting on the bumper. When I got closer, I could see two others sitting inside with a female attending to them. My brother was sitting on the gurney. He spotted me the instant I rounded the door.

"Wait, okay?" he said, spreading his hands and getting up before I could do more than take a breath. "Before you freak out, let me explain."

"You better think long and hard about every single word that comes out of your mouth right now," I said.

He jumped down and stood in front of me. He's a head taller than me and lean, like our mother, with light brown hair and blue eyes, that were currently bloodshot. He'd been experimenting lately with a goatee I didn't like. He wore jeans and a t-shirt, and I could smell the alcohol on him.

He sighed and took a breath.

"It's not as bad as you think."

"I think you were driving drunk and hit a light pole, which could have just as easily been a car full of children."

"No one got hurt. See, we went out," he said, waving a hand at the first ambulance. "It's Hayley's birthday; we were celebrating. At first it was just five of us. I was the only one with a car we could all fit into, so I ended up driving. Then we ran into a few more people. And after we hit a few more places, I knew I shouldn't be driving. So I gave the keys to Devin. He had the least to drink of all of us."

I turned and looked at the Lincoln French kissing the light pole then looked back at Zach.

"How dare you, Zach. That isn't your car. How could you be so disrespectful?"

He scoffed and shot a look at the Lincoln. "That thing's made of steel, Zoe. Not even a bulldozer could dent it."

I took another look and privately agreed the Lincoln appeared unscathed. And, actually, the damage to the light pole seemed worse than expected. But that was not the point, and I wasn't willing to let it go.

"If there is any damage to that car, you're paying for the repairs. You're also going to tell Donald what you've done."

"Fine. Donald'll understand. Second, don't lecture me, Zoe. I don't need it."

"The hell you don't. Anybody who runs around doing stupid shit like this needs a hell of a lot more than a lecture. What the hell were you thinking, letting a drunk person drive? Getting in the car while a drunk person was driving? People could have been hurt, or worse. *You* could have been hurt."

"I told you, Devin wasn't drunk."

I pointed at the light pole. "Try selling me that line one more time."

"He just lost control of the car, that's all. It's a mammoth car; he wasn't expecting it."

"You mean his reflexes were dulled by alcohol. That means he's drunk. You know better than this."

"Whatever," he snapped. "I knew you'd freak out."

"That's my job. I'm supposed to freak out. Now, hand it over." I held out my hand.

He looked at it and tried for a blank expression, but I saw guilt flash in his eyes. "What? What are you talking about?"

"Whatever ID you used to get into the bars tonight."

"No idea what you're talking about."

"You're twenty years old, Zach. Give it to me."

He stood, staring at me with a cold look, his chin tipped up defiantly. I held my ground, giving him an equally cold look. Finally, with childish indignation, he reached into his pocket and pulled out a card. Slapping it into my palm, he turned and stomped back to the ambulance, climbing up beside his buddies to commiserate.

I tucked the fake ID into the pocket of my jeans and went back to the other ambulance. Devin was sitting on the bumper beside Hayley. The two had been an item briefly, but the fact that Hayley actually liked my brother had ultimately come between them. Devin was basically a good kid and had been basically a good friend to Zach since they'd met in middle school. Hayley, however, was bad news, and she had a way of dragging everyone down around her. For a time, one of those people had been Zach. I thought he'd finally broken away from her. I was genuinely surprised to learn they'd been out together tonight.

Devin spotted me and immediately looked down at his feet, his shoulders slumping a little. At least he had the good sense to be ashamed of what he'd done. Hayley, on the other hand, sat up a little straighter and stared at me head-on.

"I'm really sorry, Zoe," Devin said. "I shouldn't have been driving; I know that. But that car, I mean, it's so damn long, and it doesn't steer . . ." He rubbed a hand over his face then pushed it back through his hair. His eyes were moist as he looked at me pleadingly. "I'll help pay for the damages."

"You're damn right you will. Do you realize you could have killed someone? Could have killed yourself or anyone else in the car? Did you think of that?"

He shook his head as he dropped his gaze again. "I'm sorry."

"Hey," Hayley snapped. "Back off. You're not his mother."

I turned on her. "I'm sure you remember I take issue when Zach is put in danger."

She scoffed and rolled her eyes. "How can I forget? You're fucking crazy, bitch."

"Right now, my crazy isn't focused on you. Would you like that to change?"

Her mouth snapped shut, and the wheels of her alcohol-polluted mind began turning. She sat back, surrendering.

I turned back to Devin, holding out my hand.

"Let's have it."

Unlike Zach, he made no attempt to deny or protest. He reached into his shirt pocket, pulled out the ID, and handed it over.

"Where'd you guys get these?" I asked, tucking it away with the other.

"Bought 'em from a guy downtown. Hundred bucks apiece."

"You're going to tell your parents about this," I said. "All of it."

Devin groaned and bent forward, his head in his hands. "I'd rather go to jail."

"Don't worry," I said. "I'm pretty sure you're going to jail, too."

Frye walked up to me, a tow truck driver on his heels. I recognized the tow truck driver; he'd towed my truck more than once, including yesterday morning. Zach saw the group gathering and joined us.

"I thought that thing belonged to you," the driver said, hooking a thumb over his shoulder toward the Lincoln. "I mean, how many of those things can there be?"

"Will it fit on your truck?" I asked.

"Ah, it doesn't need to be *towed*," Zach said. "Look at it. It's fine."

"Actually, the kid's probably right," the driver said to me.

"But we need to move it," Frye said. "It's blocking traffic."

No kidding.

"The keys in it?" I asked.

The driver nodded. "Yeah. I'll hook it up if you can't drive it."

"Do me a favor," I said to Frye as I walked away. "Keep an eye on him."

Frye looked at Zach then nodded to me. Zach rolled his eyes and crossed his arms.

The driver climbed into his truck, parked behind the Lincoln, and backed up, giving me some room. I boarded the road-boat and turned the key. The gas-guzzling engine that topped out at a hundred and fifty-nine horsepower roared to life. I levered the transmission into reverse and gave it some gas, angling the wheel as I backed away from the pole.

I felt it the instant the bumper separated from the pole. Then I heard a deep, agonizing moan over the rumble of the engine. Looking at the pole, it seemed to almost shutter. Then, as if in slow motion, it began to move. It fell, crash-landing in the middle of the intersection, barely missing a small VW Beetle and instead smashing into a parked police car, snapping the light bar and caving in the roof. The blue and red lights winked out as the traffic light flashed to green.

I saw Zach's mouth fall open as he stared at the pole and police car. And I was pretty sure Devin burst into tears. The tow truck driver appeared beside the open driver's side window.

"Didn't see that coming," he said, staring at the pole. "Did you?"

If Devin hadn't been destined for jail before the destruction of the police car, he certainly was after. And it turned out the tow truck driver hadn't made the trip for nothing. Frye issued tickets for drinking to all the kids who were underage, then let them go home with sober rides, mostly parents. And I was pretty sure he confiscated a few more fake IDs. Devin was arrested and taken to jail for his parents to bail out. I parked the Dodge legally then climbed aboard the Lincoln with Zach and drove him home.

Zach didn't speak to me the entire trip. Once home, he marched off to his room and shut the door without so much as a backward glance. It was three o'clock in the morning, but my mother wasn't home. It was entirely possible she wouldn't come home tonight. Glad she wasn't there to yell at me and too exhausted to drive anywhere else, I crashed on the basement sofa and fell asleep almost instantly.

10

It was Sunday. At seven o'clock, there was the sound of sharp heels clicking against the tile and someone hitting my feet. I shot up and peered through one blurry, barely-open eye at my mother standing at the end of the sofa with her hands on her hips.

"What's wrong?" I mumbled.

"Aren't you going to church?" she asked. "After what you did last night, you need to go to church."

I groaned and fell back against the pillow.

"You're going to hell." She said this with the authority you'd expect from the gatekeeper herself. "You're a troublemaker. You need to go to church."

The same record, the same lines.

I rolled over and smashed a pillow down on top of my head. I knew I fell back to sleep, because I awoke sometime later to a sharp pounding on the front door. Vacations are supposed to be about sleeping in and relaxing, being lazy. So far mine sucked.

There was another round of pounding, and I adjusted the pillow, pressing it against my head.

What does Hensley want now? I wondered, until the sleep cleared enough for me to realize Hensley shouldn't want anything now that his case was closed.

Upstairs, I heard the front door open and Donald speak to the visitor. The visitor's voice was muffled, and I couldn't make out the reply. A moment later, the door closed and there were footsteps on the stairs. I rolled over in time to see Ellmann cross to my former bedroom and peek inside, finding it empty. Maybe they taught cops how to knock on doors at police school.

I threw the blanket back and swung my legs over the side of the sofa.

"I don't live here anymore," I said, my voice hoarse from sleep.

He came to stand at the end of the sofa, the same place my mother had stood earlier. He was dressed in jeans, t-shirt, and a ball cap.

"I need to talk to you."

"You look pissed."

"I just came from the hospital. Stacy Karnes woke up briefly but then went into cardiac arrest. She's back in critical condition, and it doesn't look good."

I looked at him, confused, rubbing sleep out of one eye. "I'm sorry to hear it," I said. I felt genuine sadness for Stacy and her family. "But what does that have to do with me?"

"While I was there, I ran into Stacy's roommate, a girl named Tina Shuemaker. She told me all about some girl who came by her house asking all sorts of questions about Stacy and her boyfriend. She described the girl pretty well. You wouldn't happen to know anything about *that*, would you?"

"And if I did?"

He sighed and grabbed the cap off his head, running a hand back through his hair. "So that's what you were really doing when you ransacked her purse. You were looking for her address. Why would you do that?"

"Hey, hey, hey," I said. "I didn't *ransack* her purse."

"Is that the only part you heard me say?"

"Okay, look. I might have wondered what her name was, so it's possible I looked for her driver's license. I might have found it and happened to noticed her address. I might have wanted to express my condolences to her family, so it's possible I went to that address. Her roommate might have been home."

"Hypothetically?"

"Exactly! *Hypothetically*. And, in that hypothetical scenario, I didn't do anything wrong."

"Why the interest in her boyfriend?"

"Hypothetically, I might have wanted to offer condolences to him, as well."

"Is it also possible you wanted to have a face-to-face with him so you could determine if he was the one who attacked Stacy?"

Among other things.

"Do you think he's the one who attacked Stacy?" I asked.

I didn't. Tyler Jay was way too tall and too slim. And he didn't seem to recognize me. Surely the person who came after me that night would recognize me if I walked up to his or her door.

"It's one theory we're running down," he said. "Tell me, did you offer Tyler Jay your condolences?"

I sighed. I think I had known, even if only in the very back of my mind, Ellmann would learn about my phone call to the tip line.

"*Hypothetically,* maybe."

"*Maybe* you can explain about the message you left on the tip line regarding the whereabouts of Tyler Jay, who happens to be a very wanted man in this county."

"It's possible I might have run into a guy named Tyler Jay. It's also possible I thought you guys would want to know where he was."

Ellmann bit back his response then sucked in a deep breath. After a long pause, he slowly exhaled.

"Zoe, Tyler Jay is a very dangerous man. He kills people. A growing number of people think he *enjoys* killing people. You can't be 'running into' guys like him."

"Well, what does it matter now? You guys arrested him, right? He'll be in prison for a very long time."

Ellmann shifted, and I saw it in his eyes before he could wipe it away.

"Are you kidding me?" I asked, shooting up off the sofa.

"We went to the address you gave, but by the time we got there, he was gone. His mother won't say a word. He's in the wind, probably long gone by now."

I threw my arms up. "Unbelievable. What use is that stupid tip line then?"

"Tyler Jay will turn up eventually. We're looking for him harder now because of his possible involvement in this case; we'll find him. In the meantime, I have to offer you a friendly piece of advice: stay out of this case. Next time, it won't be friendly. Do I make myself clear?"

"Crystal."

"Between you and me," he added, his voice a bit softer, "the boyfriend isn't a nice guy. I don't want anything to happen to you."

"Why? Would you feel responsible?"

"Yes, I would."

"Sort of like I feel now, about Stacy being attacked. I was late for our meeting. I should have been there sooner."

I dropped back down to the sofa.

Ellmann sat down beside me, placing the hat on his knee. He spoke softly.

"If you'd been there any sooner, chances are good you would have wound up in a hospital bed right beside her. Maybe worse. What good would that have done?"

I couldn't keep the tears out of my eyes. I looked up at him, searching his eyes and face.

"I still feel responsible. I see her in my dreams."

"Don't get hung up on that. It'll only drag you down."

He was right. But it wasn't that easy.

We sat quietly on the sofa for several minutes before my guilt subsided enough that my surroundings came back to me.

"Shit," I said, hopping up.

"What's the matter?"

"Uh, we need to go." I looked at my watch as I grabbed my bag. My mother could come home at any time, and I didn't want to be there when she did.

"Worried about your mother?"

"Aren't you?"

He shrugged as he stood and returned the hat to his head, as if he'd had more dangerous run-ins. "She's actually the reason I needed to talk to you."

"Yeah? What about her?"

"I need to know if you're interested in filing charges against her for the incident in the kitchen yesterday."

"Charges? Is there some reason I should?"

He looked down at his shoes, searching for the right words.

"You have to stand up for yourself," he said. "You can't let people hurt you anymore."

He'd looked into me after our chat yesterday. Found out what I didn't want to tell him myself. That being true, I was rather surprised to see him again so soon. What he now knew about me was, to say the least, a turn off. More often, people found it scary. Some irrationally believed I'd do the same to them. For a cop investigating a crime to which I was distantly connected, no doubt it cast me into further suspicion.

"Believe me, people don't hurt me anymore. She's the single exception."

"I know what happened thirteen years ago, and I know you had several charges filed against you for assault and battery when you were in your late teens."

"Those files are sealed," I said, thinking back to the conversation I'd had with Hensley not so long ago. "How do you know what's in them? Or are you guessing?"

"Relax." He held a hand out in front of him, palm toward me. "I had a friend take a little peek, just to see what the charges were. Nothing was opened; I don't know any details."

I wondered if Hensley had the same friend.

"Well, there you go; I don't let people hurt me anymore. Of course, I'll admit it's harder with my mother. You can't hit your mother."

He shrugged in such a way that implied he knew mothers beyond that rule and was trying to decide if mine was one of them.

"You could file charges," he said. "And, if you wanted, I could help you get the house back. I mean, it doesn't seem right that you own two houses in the area and still have to rent a place."

Ah. I was beginning to understand a little better now.

"I was being honest yesterday; it's simpler if I move. Let her stay here."

I walked around him. He turned. "If it's leverage you need, I have some. After our search yesterday."

I stopped.

When Hensley had dropped by unannounced, I'd been concerned about what he might spot lying around. But by the time Ellmann, Troy, and Troy's helpers had shown up to actually search the place, my mother's habits had been the least of my concerns. No doubt they had uncovered a whole host of illegal substances in her room, perhaps elsewhere in the house. For the first time, I was truly fearful of what the cops had found in this house. In the end, it was *my* house. I'd just barely scraped out of trouble with Hensley, but Ellmann's case was still far from closed. And if I was held responsible for whatever had been found, I might not be so lucky a second time.

Slowly, I turned back to face Ellmann. I was practically sweating with the exertion it took to keep my face neutral. Or maybe the sweating was from fear.

"What did you find?" My mouth was dry, and I couldn't hide that, no matter how hard I tried.

"Everything I found was in her room and bathroom," he said, his hands up. I knew he was trying to reassure me, but it wasn't working, not by a long shot. "After I detained your mother, I ran her name, saw her priors. Suspicious of what could be found, I searched her room myself. Troy and the others have no idea what I found, and it's won't show up in any report. I could use it to have a conversation with her, however. Help her understand the wisdom in finding her own place."

"No." I said it too quickly and too sharply. I took a breath and tried again. "Look, I appreciate what you're doing, but please, let it go. You don't know her lawyer; the man's a snake. Whatever you try to do here while operating in the gray, he'll turn back on you. Nothing will change with her, and you'll be out of a job. Or writing parking tickets downtown—whatever happens to cops whose careers have been ruined. Please, let it go."

He stared at me for a beat. He wanted to press it, but he resisted. Finally, he nodded.

"Let me know if you change your mind in the future."

I didn't think him hanging onto whatever drugs he'd found in my mother's bedroom was wise, for the reasons I'd just mentioned. It wouldn't have surprised me if she tattled to her attorney, who would then pull Troy's report and find no such substances included in it. His twisted and malicious mind would immediately know the drugs didn't just disappear. He could easily make a fuss, discover them in Ellmann's possession. And whatever Ellmann had found would not be minimal. Anyone caught with that amount of product would be in seriously hot water, especially a cop, who could then be accused of stealing from a crime scene.

But Ellmann seemed to trust me to a degree, so I could do nothing but return the favor. He was an adult, had been a cop for a while, and seemed to know what he was doing. I had to trust that he did.

I crossed to Zach's door and knocked. There was no sound from inside, and no one answered. I opened the door and saw the bed was empty; Zach was gone. I had a sinking feeling I knew what that meant.

"Son of a bitch," I muttered under my breath as I closed the door and turned back to Ellmann. "Look, I really appreciate the thought and concern, but I don't need anyone to rescue me. Think you're the only one with leverage?" I kept my voice soft, gentle, considerate of the fact that he was reaching out to me and I was batting his hand away, even if part of that response was out of concern for him. "You know, I've never had help, never had a rescuer, so I wouldn't know what to do with one now. Anyway, given the kind of trouble my mother can get into, it's probably easier keeping her here. Besides, despite it all, I would feel bad if I kicked her out. She'd have nowhere to go."

"She's an adult. She can buy or rent a place like everyone else. She can afford it."

"So I'm not the only one you looked into. It's like I told you yesterday, it's complicated. I don't think I'm going to press charges."

I went to the stairs. Ellmann was behind me. He nodded his head as if I'd given him the answer he'd expected, even if he was disappointed.

"She didn't think so, either. But she *is* going to file a complaint with my superiors regarding my 'unnecessarily cruel treatment' of her yesterday, so I'm looking forward to that."

I led the way to the front door.

"I'm sorry. I thought it was great, but I guess everything comes with a price." I looked up at him. "Remember what I said about her attorney."

He shrugged. "Remember the night we met? You said something about a detective wearing a uniform. I was working off a reprimand from a particularly scathing complaint. So, your mother's isn't the first, and it won't be the last. Occasionally they're even true. Between you and me, it was worth it. You know . . . your hair looks nice down. You should wear it that way more often."

I was surprised by the compliment. It took me a full minute to recover. "Thanks," I said as I opened the front door and stepped outside. I saw the curb where I'd docked the Lincoln a few hours before was now occupied by Ellmann's Charger. "That little shit."

"Problem?"

"How do you feel about giving me a ride?" I asked. "And can we stop for coffee? I'll buy you a cup."

———————————

Ellmann pulled into the Safeway parking lot, and my heart sank as I saw the shiny copper of the Lincoln glinting in the morning sun like a beacon for distant and weary travelers. There was no sign of Zach's truck. Cussing a blue streak under my breath, I thanked Ellmann for the ride, grabbed my coffee, and got out. I stood for a moment, staring at the wonderment of automotive engineering, before I realized Ellmann hadn't moved.

"You don't have to wait," I said, turning back to him.

He was leaning against the open driver's side window. "It seems like the right thing to do," he said with a shrug. "And I can't help it; I worry about you."

I don't think of myself as being so pitiful. And I didn't really like that Ellmann did.

I walked to the passenger side of the Lincoln and dropped to a knee beside the rear wheel. I'd already checked my bag; the Lincoln keys were gone. Zach had taken them from me, not gotten an extra pair from Donald. And Donald had been gone by the time Ellmann and I had left the house. I reached up under the skirt and dragged my fingertips along the wheel well.

Donald had once talked about how forgetful his mother had become in her old age. She was always losing her keys and locking herself out. He was concerned about his own memory, feeling it, too, was beginning to slip, and he had asked me about hiding a house key somewhere on the porch. He'd already hidden a key to his car in one of the wheel wells. He'd told me these were the same things he'd done for his mother when she began locking herself out.

Finding nothing, I stood and went to the front wheel. I could only hope the hidden key was still on the car. It seemed like a long shot, given that the car had been parked at Donald's curb for quite some time, but it was the best I had going for me.

"Wanna call a locksmith?"

I looked up at Ellmann as I stood. I could get the door open; that wasn't the problem. I could even hotwire the car, but that wasn't a good long-term solution, and I didn't think Donald would be too understanding. In any case, I didn't want to explain how I could do either of those things, to Donald or to Ellmann.

"If I can't find a key," I said, moving to the last wheel, "I'll need to call a cab."

"Good thing I waited, then," he said. "And lucky for you I've got a stack of paperwork on my desk I'm avoiding."

I'd just about given up hope when my arm brushed against something sharp. I reached for it with my hand. There, toward the front, was a small rectangular box that didn't belong. Gripping it, I gave it a tug. It budged slightly but held strong. Shifting my weight, I grabbed the thing and pulled for all I was worth. Finally the damn thing broke free.

My hand was filthy. The small box was unrecognizable under years of dirt and road grime. Still kneeling, I knocked the box against the asphalt, breaking loose some of the caked-on dirt. When I could see enough of the box, I worked to pry the pieces apart. After some sweating and a lot of swearing, I got the lid back far enough to get the key out. I held it up to Ellmann.

"Victory."

"Congratulations. It was close there for a second."

I stood and dusted off the knees of my jeans. "I always win."

"I'm sensing that. Stay out of trouble."

He pulled his head and arm inside then buzzed the window up as he drove out of the lot.

I walked to the door, hoping the key in my hand was in fact a car key and not the old woman's house key. With my fingers crossed, I slid it in the lock. A breath seeped out of me when it turned and I saw the lock pop up through the glass.

That afternoon, I pulled out my laptop. I'd been thinking about White's offer since I'd left his office. It was a good one, but the bottom line was, I'd been doing property management for a long time now. I'd gotten into it as a means to an end, and I'd stayed in it out of spite. It was a constant reminder of my foolishness and subsequent heartache. White was probably never going to stop pushing to promote me. I was probably never going to want a promotion.

I thought the best plan for my two-week vacation would be to line up alternative employment. I really hated to leave White and White Real Estate, but I thought it might be best for him, all things considered, and I knew it was probably best for me. It was also nice to know I had a good job waiting for me if I couldn't put anything together in time.

I spent some time updating and polishing my resume then went onto the King Soopers website and completed an application for a management position. While shopping last night, I'd learned the company was hiring. King Soopers wouldn't be my dream job, but it was a place to start. For good measure, I hit a couple other websites and submitted a handful of other applications.

I had a couple hours to kill before dinner with Pezzani, so I climbed aboard the Lincoln and floated over to Tyler's mom's house. Ellmann was probably right; Tyler was probably long gone. That would be the smartest move. But I got the distinct impression Tyler was hanging around for some reason. Maybe that reason had something to do with Stacy Karnes. Whatever else Tyler was or had done, his feelings for Stacy were genuine. I had seen real pain in him when I'd spoken to him the day before.

As I sat and stared at the house, my mind wandered. I thought back to the day before and my meeting with Tyler. He and his crew had been keeping a pretty close eye on the street, it seemed. They were being extra cautious. So why had Tyler come out and spoken to me? Had he sensed I wasn't a threat? For all he knew, I could have been a cop.

But if I'd been able to get to him, how had the cops missed him? Had something about our conversation tipped Tyler off that his location had been compromised? Or had he decided to move on simply as a precaution, because he *had* exposed himself when he'd spoken to me? I couldn't decide which scenario I thought most likely, and my brain continued to turn the problem over.

I was almost positive Tyler's mom would prove the best way to track Tyler down a second time. However, the lead seemed like a dead end today. Maybe because it was too soon. Maybe because it was Sunday. I didn't know. I decided to bag it for the time being. On my way home, I sailed past the other addresses I had linked to Tyler Jay, just in case he happened to be sitting on the front porch or an Escalade was parked in the driveway. Of course, neither of these was the case.

As I drove, my mind drifted back to Stacy. Ellmann had said she'd gone into cardiac arrest this morning and was back in critical condition. I was pretty certain that meant something bad. I was scared it meant she would die.

This train of thought naturally led me back to the lobby of Elizabeth Tower and the night she was stabbed. I wondered again what would have happened had I been on time. And I wondered why Stacy had been there at all. Why was she looking for a new place to live? Why did she want to break her lease and move?

On impulse, I hit the blinker and hung a left, heading back to Stacy's house. I'd already spoken to Tina Shuemaker, but Stacy lived with two other girls. I could only hope one of them might have some insight into Stacy's life.

Today the house was shut up and the curtains drawn. There were two cars in the driveway and several more parked at the curb, so I suspected someone was home. I had no way of knowing if any of the vehicles belonged to Tina, but I crossed my fingers she wasn't there. I'd hate for her to report me to Ellmann a second time.

I docked the Lincoln and went to Stacy's door. Two minutes later, a tall, athletic brunette opened it and peered out. She smiled as she pushed the screen door open.

"Hi," she said.

I smiled and handed her a card I pulled from my pocket. "Hi. My name is Zoe Grey. I'm a leasing agent for White Real Estate and Property Management. Stacy Karnes applied for a lease a couple days ago, and I'm just doing a bit of background. Are you her roommate?"

The girl stepped back and waved me in. "Come in. Yeah, I'm Kelsey. I've lived with Stacy since freshman year. I didn't know she'd found a place." The girl studied the card for a beat. I hoped she wouldn't ask why I was working on a Sunday. Or dropping by in person. That would be awkward.

Kelsey shut the door behind me, and I could feel the difference in temperature; the house was pleasantly cool. I followed her into the same living room and took up the same chair as my last visit. She settled in the same place Tina had. She set the card on the table then smiled at me.

"So, how can I help?"

"As part of the application process, I just need to ask a few questions of Stacy's roommates. You've known Stacy quite a while. Did you know she was planning to move?"

Kelsey seemed guarded, as if she was taking extra time to choose her words. She involuntarily shot a look through the open doorway that led to the rest of the house. I wondered again who else was home.

"I knew she was thinking about it. But I thought she might wait until the lease was up."

"Do you know why she wants to move? She didn't indicate she'd gotten a new job or anything on her application."

"No, it's nothing like that." Another quick glance at the doorway. "It's for personal reasons."

"I understand there are four of you here. Are any of Stacy's other roommates here? I'd love to speak with them as well."

"Uh, sure. Well, I mean, Tina's not here, but Ashley is. I can go get her."

"That'd be so helpful. Thank you. I can try to talk to Tina some other time."

Inwardly smiling at my good fortune, I waited while Kelsey went to fetch the third roommate. There was a brief silence followed by the sound of voices and associated footsteps growing closer until Kelsey reappeared in the living room with a short, blonde girl beside her. This new girl, Ashley, was blessed with blue bedroom eyes and pouty lips, all natural along with her blonde hair. She also had curves in all the right places. It was obviously she'd learned long ago how to exploit all her assets. Trailing her were three puppy-eyed, college-aged boys, and it was pretty clear what was on their minds.

"I'm Ashley," she said, following Kelsey to the sofa.

"Nice to meet you," I said. I introduced myself again then gave her the same bullshit line I'd given Kelsey about completing Stacy's application. "We were just talking about why Stacy's looking for a new place. Is she having any problems? We like to know about these kinds of things before we sign anyone to a new lease, you understand."

Ashley shrugged. "Tina's a bitch."

Whatever Kelsey had been tiptoeing around was obviously of no concern to Ashley.

"Tina's that way to all of us, but she is worse to Stacy. Been that way for a while now."

The trio of boys bobbed their heads up and down in confirmation. Even Kelsey was in agreement, though not quite so openly. It seemed possible she feared Tina, feared even the idea of this conversation getting back to Tina. Did one girl truly make their lives so miserable?

"Honestly, we've all looked at moving out at one time or another," Ashley went on. "I guess Stacy can afford it now. I know I can't."

"Stacy hadn't told any of you she'd found a place?" I asked.

There were headshakes all around and a couple murmured nos.

"Who might have known? Who would she have told?"

I didn't think her attack had been random, but I couldn't explain why I felt that way. I guess I didn't like the idea of violence happening anywhere for no reason. But that was only part of it.

Ashley shrugged and looked to Kelsey, whose face was slightly blank. I wondered if the girl was good at whatever sport she played, because she seemed a little timid in the real world. But who could tell; maybe she was the best soccer or volleyball player in recent history.

"Stacy has a lot of friends," Ashley said. "And she's close to her family. But I think if anyone knew, it was her boyfriend, Tyler. She told him everything."

"That's true," one of the boys piped up. "They're really tight."

Great. The trail led me right back to bad-guy Tyler Jay. How convenient. The only problem was the more I thought about it, the more I doubted Tyler Jay had anything to do with Stacy's attack. In fact, it seemed more likely he didn't know anything about it. I got the feeling if he had, he'd have added another body to his resume, and Stacy would be sitting here in her living room right now.

"Would she have told anyone else? One of her friends maybe?"

"I would just be guessing," Ashley said. "I only ever see Stacy when we're both here, and she hasn't been spending a lot of time here lately."

She looked at Kelsey. Kelsey shrugged.

"That's pretty much true for me, too," she said. "I mean, we'd meet for coffee or lunch or something and talk, but I think she was, you know, kind of afraid, or maybe worried, about stuff she said getting back to Tina. Not that I would tell Tina anything, but still, I think she's been keeping a lot to herself."

"Who are her closest friends?" I asked.

"What does it matter?" Ashley asked. "I mean, who cares if she told someone she was looking at places to live?"

Ashley wasn't just a pretty face. Best not to push too hard.

Changing tracks, I said, "I'll speak to the landlord about her payment history and that sort of thing, but is there anything else I should know about Stacy as a renter? Any other problems or things that might come up?"

"Look, Stacy is a freakishly good person," Ashley said. "She doesn't have any bad habits, she doesn't ever do anything wrong, she doesn't even swear. She's a straight-A student, a perfect employee, and the best roommate. Sometimes I wonder if she's actually human. If you don't rent her a place, you're a moron."

Their goddess had spoken. All three boys bobbed their heads again. Kelsey didn't seem quite as sure this time.

"Is Stacy's boyfriend moving in with her?" she asked.

"No. Why do you ask?"

A brief flash of guilt. "No reason. I just know he's had some trouble, you know, with the police, in the past."

Ashley rolled her eyes. "So what? He didn't do most the shit they think he did, and even if he did, he's crazy about Stacy. He would never, ever do anything to hurt her. And he would do anything she asked him to. He knows how lucky he is to have her." She looked me square in the eye. "If he did move in with her, he wouldn't give you or anyone else any trouble."

I couldn't help myself. I was beginning to really like Ashley.

"I'll keep that in mind," I said as I stood. "Thank you so much for the information. I still need to speak to the landlord, but at this point I don't see any reason why Stacy's application won't be approved."

Ashley stood and all three boys stood with her.

"Yeah," she said. "Let's just hope she lives long enough to enjoy it."

11

I'd lost track of time at Stacy's house. Jumping into the Lincoln, I gunned it for home. Of course, the Lincoln accelerates from zero to sixty at a whopping fourteen seconds, so I didn't exactly make record time. Pezzani was at the curb when I floated into the driveway.

I offered him a sail around town in the Lincoln, but he confessed he suffers from seasickness. Instead, we went in his red Ford Mustang. Not a fan of Mustangs myself, I couldn't deny this car seemed to fit Pezzani somehow.

"Where would you like to eat?" he asked as he reached the stop sign at the end of my street.

He was dressed in jeans and a green shirt. He was either freshly showered or he kept a bottle of something really delicious-smelling stashed in the glove box.

"How about the Olive Garden?"

Ten minutes later we put our name in for a table. When we were seated, our waitress appeared almost immediately. She was short, five-three maybe, with short blonde hair secured in two pigtails, one below each ear. Her blue eyes were painted, and she wore dangly silver earrings. Her nametag read MEGAN.

"What can I get you to drink?" she asked after introducing herself and finishing a brief speech about specials.

She smiled a blindingly white smile and nodded as we gave our order. "Take your time with the menu. I'll be back with those drinks."

We ordered after our drinks arrived, and the girl hustled off again. The restaurant was busy, full of the sounds of conversation and laughter, the clinking of silverware and dishes. Delicious food smells were everywhere and I realized, as my stomach growled, I hadn't eaten all day.

Pezzani and I chatted, and I noticed it was easier, more relaxed, than it had been. I was still guarded, cautious, distant, but I wasn't defensive. Surprisingly, I thought I could actually like him.

Our dinner arrived and we dug in. Everything was delicious. When we were about halfway through, Megan came around to check in and refill our water glasses.

"Hey, I was going to ask you," I began. "Do you know Stacy? I think she works here."

Megan nodded, sadness in her eyes. "Yes. Do you?"

"I just heard what happened to her," I said solemnly. "It's horrible."

"I know!" she gasped. "Stuff like that just doesn't happen here, or at least it isn't supposed to. My parents *freaked*. They wanted to fly out and pack up my stuff the next day."

Pezzani was patiently watching the exchange, amused.

"I know," I said. "I'm totally terrified to go out alone after dark. They still haven't caught who did it."

"Do they even know who did it? Last I heard they didn't know whether it was random or not."

"No, I know. But it has to be random, right? I mean, who would do something like that to Stacy?"

I saw it in her eyes before she could completely play it off.

"I have no idea," she lied. "Stacy is a really great person."

"Oh, my gosh!" I said, then leaned forward and lowered my voice. "You know something! You know who did it! You *have* to tell the police. She could *die*."

"Shh!" she hissed, stepping forward and leaning toward me. "I don't know who did it, I *don't*. I just know she had this fight with another girl, Tina, who works here, okay? They were in the kitchen, and it almost came to blows. The manager almost fired both of them."

Pezzani shifted in his seat.

"Tina, Stacy's roommate?" I asked. "She works here?"

"Yeah. Didn't you know?"

No, I didn't know.

Shit.

It wouldn't be good if Tina knew I was here. It would probably be worse if she knew I was asking about Stacy again. Who knew what kind of trouble she'd start if she saw me a second time.

"Do you know what were they fighting about?" Pezzani asked, taking a sudden interest in our conversation.

Megan shrugged. "I'm not really sure; I only saw the very end. Stacy was really upset, that's all I know. I got the feeling Tina had done something, or maybe said something, but I missed most of it. The manager was pretty clear we weren't to gossip about it, either. If anyone does know, no one is saying."

"But you think Tina had something to do with what happened to Stacy?" he asked.

She shrugged again and stood up, uncomfortable. "I really don't know. I mean, I hope not. Who wants to say they know a person who could do something like that? It's sick."

She was right; it was sick.

And she would be wise to wonder what would happen to her if she went around accusing Tina and it turned out Tina *was* capable of such a thing.

The rest of our dinner was rather uneventful. In the car, Pezzani finally asked me about my interrogation. I explained about Stacy, but I omitted most of the details about my interest in who assaulted her and my genius plan to turn her boyfriend in for an easy fifteen grand.

"So, what's your interest?" he asked. "Are you trying to figure out who stabbed her?"

"What? No." Yes.

"Right."

He parked at the curb outside the house.

"Do you want to hang out for a while? The place is sort of a mess, and I don't have any furniture to speak of, but I could plug in the DVD player or the stereo."

He laughed. "Who could turn down an offer like that?"

We went to the porch and I opened the door. As soon as I stepped inside, I knew something was wrong. A metallic scent I immediately recognized hung on the air, and the little hairs on the back of my neck stood up. I couldn't tell if Pezzani had sensed anything amiss as he followed me in. I reached for the light switch beside the door and flipped it on, bathing the living room in bright overhead lighting.

There, face down on the hardwood floor, was Derrick, the giant man I'd spoken to at Tyler's mother's house. His arms and legs were spread slightly to the sides, and a large dark-red pool of blood had spread around his torso. There were three bullet holes in his back.

I froze. Pezzani stared over my shoulder.

"You know him?" he asked casually.

"Sort of."

"He's dead."

———————————

Pezzani started to call 911, but I stopped him and called Ellmann instead. Ellmann wasn't exactly excited to hear from me. At least, not for the reason I was calling.

"Is this some kind of joke?"

I sighed. "Even I have standards; what kind of joke would that be? I'm serious. There is a dead man in my living room."

"I'm five minutes away. Don't touch anything. In fact, wait outside."

The line went dead in my ear before I could reply, probably so I couldn't argue. I put the phone back in my pocket.

"We're supposed to wait outside."

Pezzani shuffled out, me behind him. We sat on the porch step, waiting. Neither of us said much. Nothing like a dead body to change the course of an evening.

I saw blue and red lights bouncing off the houses around us before Ellmann's navy blue Charger pulled to a stop at the curb. He switched the lights off then climbed out of the car. I noticed he was surprised to see I wasn't alone but worked to hide it, and he hid it well. Pezzani and I stood and moved off the porch as Ellmann approached.

"How was dinner?" Ellmann asked, spying our leftovers.

"Great, until now," Pezzani answered innocently, unaware of the edge in Ellmann's voice. "I have to admit, this is the first time anything like this has ever happened to me."

He offered his hand to Ellmann, introducing himself.

"Detective Alex Ellmann. Pleasure." His tone was slightly flat.

"Alex, glad you could come. Zoe thought you were the man to call."

"It's Detective Ellmann," he said as he passed both of us and went into the house.

He used a latex glove he'd pulled from his pocket to open the door. I caught the door behind him and held it with my elbow, peeking into the house. He stepped inside, glancing from the body to the parts of the house he could see from the doorway.

"Heard anything since you got here?" he asked, reaching for the gun in the holster on his hip.

"No," I told him. "Why?"

"Go back outside and wait there."

He drew the gun and moved slowly into the house. After a few steps he stopped.

"I didn't hear the door close."

"All right, all right," I muttered, backing out of the doorway and letting the screen door bang shut.

Surprisingly frustrated at being excluded from the potentially dangerous search of the house for a murderer, I plopped back down on the step to wait. I heard a couple doors close and the occasional footstep, but I didn't hear any yelling or screaming or gunfire. Seemed safe to say the house was empty. Aside from one large dead man who didn't belong, that was.

Ellmann emerged from the house, his phone pressed to his ear, and squeezed past me off the porch, walking back to his car. He disappeared from sight for a moment as he leaned into the trunk. When he reappeared again, he was no longer on the phone. He walked back to us carrying a clipboard and wearing a grim look.

"Party's about to start," he said. "First of them will be here in a couple minutes." He pulled a stack of forms from the clipboard and handed them to us. "Need you to fill these out. They're witness statements." He looked to me. "Unfortunately, we're going to be here a while, and I'm not sure how long they will hold your house as a crime scene. Is there somewhere else you can stay?"

I sighed.

I'd just moved out of the only place I had to go. I'd been in my new place for a total of two days. I'd just bought a kitchen-full of groceries.

"I'm not staying anywhere else," I said defiantly. "This is my house."

"The dead body is in the middle of it, Zoe," Ellmann said. "You won't be able to get past the crime scene to the rest of the house. You can't stay here."

"I'll sleep in the kitchen and use the backdoor."

Ellmann sighed and pushed his hand through his hair.

"Don't put it past her," Pezzani said.

"I don't," Ellmann said. "That's what scares me."

The first of what would turn out to be a dozen responders pulled to a stop at the curb beside Ellmann's vehicle and hurried up the driveway. Ellmann directed him to begin canvassing the neighborhood. There were no blinds on the windows, and a large caliber gun had been used; someone should have seen or heard something.

"Let's start with you," Ellmann said to Pezzani. "I need to ask you a bunch of questions, but I'm guessing you don't know much, so we'll be able to get you on your way pretty quickly."

I thought this was a poke at Pezzani's intelligence, not a comment regarding his usefulness as a witness, but Pezzani didn't seem to take it that way. Maybe I was reading too far into it.

As I watched them walk away, I found it interesting to see them side-by-side. I didn't know either particularly well, but they seemed pretty different, and yet strikingly similar in many ways. It was also interesting to see Ellmann's reaction to Pezzani and finding us together after a dinner date. I supposed it had something to do with the hero/rescue thing he'd been trying earlier, but it seemed more like caveman-possessive stuff. Where was it coming from?

I sat on the porch writing out an objective report of the facts in relation to discovering a dead man on my floor. As people continued to arrive, Ellmann continued issuing orders, setting people to work on specific tasks. The crime scene people—two men I'd never seen before—were the last to arrive. Troy can't work all the time, I guess. After ten minutes of questioning, Ellmann let Pezzani go. I spoke to him briefly in the front yard before convincing him to go home. He offered me a place to stay twice before he left, and both times I assured him I'd be fine.

"Now it's your turn," Ellmann said, flipping to a blank page in his notebook.

I lifted myself up onto the hood of the Charger, my heels on the tire. He gave me an annoyed look but chose not to say anything.

"Who is he?" he asked.

"'He' who?"

"The dead guy."

"No idea."

He dropped his arms and looked at me. "Zoe, there is a dead man in the living room of the house you moved into *yesterday*, shot and killed by a .45 revolver. Believe me, this is *not* the time to play games."

"I didn't shoot him."

"I don't think you did, but that doesn't change the fact that this could be very bad for you. Tell me straight what's going on."

"Because you can help me?"

He looked at me for a long moment. Probably trying to decide if I'd done something horrible that would be difficult or dangerous to cover up or explain. Finally, he nodded.

"Yes, I can help you. But only if I know exactly what's going on. You're already mixed up in some other very bad business. If you get into too much trouble, there won't be anything I can do."

"Other business?"

"Stacy Karnes, Tina Shuemaker, and Tyler Jay."

I groaned. "You know, I just want to say, for the record, it was horribly inconsiderate for whoever attacked Stacy to do so while she was in the lobby of my building waiting to meet me, okay? It's been nothing but trouble for me."

"Is that because it aggravated some insatiable need you have to stick your nose into everything, regardless of societal norms, political correctness, and the interest of your safety?"

"Now, is that really necessary?"

"Am I wrong?"

"It just sounds *awful* when you put it like that."

"Even so, maybe you can explain what's going on."

I sighed. As I thought about things now, it didn't seem as if I had a lot of choices.

"The man in the living room is Derrick; all I got was a first name. He was with Tyler at Tyler's mom's house when I stopped by. I talked to—"

"Wait, you *talked* to these guys?"

I wasn't sure why I was in trouble. He already knew I went to the house. Why couldn't I talk to them? "Maybe."

"Zoe, driving by his house is one thing, but you can't go knocking on the door of a man like that."

"Did you think I'd spotted Tyler Jay sitting on the front porch sipping iced tea?"

"You could have been hurt."

"I'm fine."

He swung an arm in the direction of the house. "What if those bullets had been meant for you? What if they came here tonight looking to kill you?"

I shivered at the thought then quickly pushed it aside. "That makes no sense," I objected. It was a baseless objection, and we both knew it. "Anyway," I said, "that Derrick guy seemed to be running interference for Tyler, like a bodyguard or something. You know those bad guys; they all have entourages. All I know about him is that he has no taste in fashion, poor choice in deodorant, thinks I'm too old to be in college, and gets extremely uncomfortable if a woman starts crying."

"Funny," he said humorlessly, not looking up from his notes. "Tina described you the same way."

"What way?"

I thought I knew.

"Too old to be in college."

And, I'd been right.

I shook my head. "You know, these kids today, I'm telling you. What's the world coming to . . ."

"It's maybe just a little bit harder for you to lie, I guess."

"It was a rhetorical question," I snapped. "And I'm a damn good liar."

His eyes flicked up at me.

"I mean—"

"Don't," he cautioned softly with a shake of his head.

I didn't.

My friend Mercedes, who goes by Sadie, is one of the most social people on the planet. There is always a party or celebration or get-together for her to go to. When there isn't, she throws one herself. Partying includes drinking, and Sadie is very careful about drinking and driving. She always makes arrangements for transportation home or to stay the night at someone else's place. Tonight when I called her about crashing on her sofa, she told me she was sleeping at a friend's house; she didn't need to tell me she'd been drinking. She went on to say she would be at her friend's house for the next two days, because her apartment building was being fumigated and several large-scale repairs and renovations were taking place. I wasn't totally heartbroken when I found out I couldn't stay there. The one-bedroom apartment is tiny.

I knew Amy was out of town for a short getaway with Brandon after a weekend of fiancé-family stuff. But I didn't think she'd mind if I crashed on her sofa. When I called her, I obviously woke her up. I briefly explained why I was in need of a place to crash and asked if it was okay to use my key.

"Oh, Zoe," she began, "of all the nights to find a dead body in your house. Brandon's parents are staying at the house for a few days while we're gone. They won't mind if you stay there, but I think they'd drive you crazy. How desperate are you?"

"Not that desperate."

I'd met her fiancé's parents once, and I knew they would drive me crazy. They are two of the strangest people I've ever spent time with. I often wonder how Brandon had turned out so sweet and normal-like. The best I can figure is that he's direct evidence miracles *do* happen. Either that or he belongs to the milkman.

The police activity around and inside the house was finally winding down. It had been hours since I'd returned home and found the body. The neighbors had all been woken up and asked probing questions about suspicious activity or persons. Notes had been taken, witness statements filled out, official reports started and some finished. The crime scene guys had made a hundred trips to and from the van, carrying things in and out, documenting every possible detail, collecting every micro-scrap of potential evidence.

The last patrolman, Pratt, who had also been at the scene of Stacy Karnes's attack, emerged from the house after speaking with Ellmann. He nodded to me then climbed into his patrol car and motored away. Of course, not before taking another head-to-toe look. Shortly afterward, the forensic guys started carrying things out to the van. I got the distinct impression the party would be over soon and I'd be officially homeless.

There was no way I was going back to my mother's house, if only because I didn't want to listen to her go on and on about what a troublemaker I was. That, and her manic activities would make any decent sleep difficult. I wasn't sleeping well these days anyway. I was still considering Amy's offer to bunk with the future in-laws, but decided to try one last play. I dialed the phone and waited.

Three rings, four rings, five . . . . Prepared to hang up, the ringing suddenly stopped. The voice on the other end was groggy. Joe Pezzani had been asleep.

"Sorry to wake you up."

"No, actually, I can't believe I fell asleep. I was going to call you . . . geez, hours ago, and see how it was going. How is it going?"

I shrugged. "It's going. Actually, I think it's about over. The coroner took the body a few hours ago, most the cops are gone, and the crime scene guys are packing it in. I think most the neighbors have moved away from their front windows at this point, too."

"Did anyone see anything? Is there anything new yet?"

"No. Or if there is, Ellmann isn't saying."

"Where are you? Are you still at the house?"

"Yes. Actually, that's why I'm calling. I wanted to talk about your offer of a place to stay."

I could tell he was grinning. "I thought you had that covered."

"Yeah, well, turns out this is a really bad time for people to get murdered in my living room. So how about it? Can I sleep on your sofa?"

"Sure. Or you can sleep in the guest bedroom. Your choice."

He gave me directions and we hung up.

Ellmann followed the last three men out of the house. He flipped off the light, locked and pulled the front door closed, then carefully applied a warning sticker to the door and doorframe, intended to prevent entry into the house—or to alert officials that entry had been made. Everyone else piled into their vehicles and drove away as Ellmann walked down the driveway toward me.

"Did you make arrangements?" he asked.

I nodded. I thought maybe it was better not to elaborate. "I did. I'm all set."

"All right. Well, I'm tired; I'm going to get some sleep. Please don't call me with any other emergencies for at least twelve hours. The truth is, you're wearing me out."

"Wearing you out? I called you once."

"You're connected to the messiest, most complicated case I've had in a long time, and it just keeps getting better." He tipped his head at the dark house. "So, like I said, no emergencies or problems of any kind for twelve hours. Can you manage to keep out of trouble for twelve hours?"

"Doesn't sound that hard."

12

Pezzani lived in a condo off Elizabeth and Overland Trail. The front door opened to a three-by-three foyer and a staircase. I followed him up the stairs and to the left, into the open living room and kitchen area. A small hallway on the right led to a loft and several open doors. The rooms beyond—probably bedrooms and bathrooms—were dark. The furniture was distinctly masculine and modern, with lots of black colors, linear designs, and cold metal and glass. A black leather sofa was arranged opposite a large glass entertainment center, which held a big screen plasma TV. The TV was on, the sound muted, and only one lamp was turned on. Despite the cold and dark materials, the place had a rather homey feel to it.

"Feel free to make yourself at home," Pezzani was saying. He walked over to the coffee table, picked up the remote, and switched off the TV. "This is the couch." He waved at the sofa. "Or the guestroom is over here."

I followed him down the hall to the first door on the left. He went in, switching on the light as he passed. In the far corner, he poked his head through another doorway and turned on a second light.

"There is a Jack and Jill bathroom between these two rooms," he explained, "but I use the other room for a home gym and storage, so it's all yours. Clean towels in the closet there."

I walked over and peeked in at the biggest bathroom I'd ever seen. The bedroom was just as huge. The vaulted ceilings and huge windows, even covered by dark drapes, all contributed to the spaciousness of the place. There was a queen-sized bed with a bulky, black bed frame and black linen, a stark contrast to the white walls and floors. A black dresser, bedside table, and armchair with ottoman completed the décor.

"This is a nice place," I said.

"I think I'm finally getting settled in."

"Did you just move in?"

"No, I've been here a couple years."

I chuckled.

He started for the door. "Like I said, make yourself at home. Help yourself to whatever you can find. I haven't been grocery shopping this week, so it might take some scrounging."

"No worries, I'll be fine. I appreciate it."

"I have to work at nine tomorrow, but I should be back around noon. I'll leave a key on the counter. You're welcome to stay as long as you like."

"I should be able to figure something out. The police shouldn't have my house for too long."

"Still, the offer is there."

I thanked him again and we said our goodnights. I dropped my bag to the floor and kicked off my shoes, then climbed onto the bed, fully dressed.

_____

The masked figure was back. It was dark. I was in a house I hadn't seen in years. The figure was coming toward me, slowly, one stalking step after another. The shiny silver blade of the long, ugly knife gleamed in the figure's right hand. The dark eyes visible through the black slits twinkled with joy and excitement. Terror gripped me. I couldn't move. My feet rooted to the floor, I stood helpless, watching, as the figure loomed closer and closer. The knife seemed to get longer with each step.

I could tell the figure was smirking, enjoying the pursuit. Fear, icy and sharp, vibrated through me in waves as the figure reached up and pulled off the mask. My father laughed maniacally as he threw the mask aside and lunged forward, thrusting the knife toward my abdomen.

Shuddering, I shot up in bed, gasping as I threw myself backward in an effort to escape the attacker who no longer existed. I winced as my skull knocked against the heavy headboard, and I desperately tried to stave off panic as I worked to recall where I was. After a beat, it all came back to me.

Still shaken, I reached out and flipped on the bedside light, quickly taking in the room, confirming I was indeed alone. I felt my phone vibrate in the pocket of my jeans and too easily recalled the feeling of fear vibrating through me in my dream. Funny how the mind works.

Fully awake now, I realized I was still dressed, still on top of the covers. I'd intended to just close my eyes for a minute, but I'd obviously passed out. I shot a glance at the clock on the table. 6:02.

"This vacation sucks."

I'd been woken up in the middle of the night for the third consecutive day of it. Not that I was sleeping well.

I worked the phone out of my pocket.

"Yeah?"

"Are you all right?" The voice was familiar. And there was no mistaking the worry in it.

I moved to the edge of the bed, letting my feet dangle, and tried to shake the lingering effects of the nightmare.

"Just tired of being woken up," I said, trying for indignation. "Is this an emergency? If it isn't, call back in a double-digit hour."

"It's Ellmann. This issue might not wait until ten o'clock."

I sighed. "Shit. This better not count against my twelve hours; I didn't call you."

"This isn't about you or me. It's about your mother."

The worry had mostly gone, but now I noticed there was a grim tone to his voice.

"She's not dead, is she?"

"No. Why would you ask that?"

"That's the phone call I always expect when it comes to her."

He was silent for a beat. "I'm sorry to hear that." And he was sincere. "No, she's not dead. She was arrested. She's being arraigned this morning."

I pulled at my shirt. It was soaked through with sweat and sticking to my skin. "Did you arrest her?"

"No."

"Then, so what? It isn't the first time; it won't be the last. Why call me?"

I could almost see him shrug on the other end of the line. "She asked us to call your brother. Somehow I thought it was better to call you."

"Please don't call him," I said, sliding off the side of the bed. "I'll come get her."

"Arraignment's at eight. Need directions?"

"No." Unfortunately, I did not.

"Didn't think so."

"Where's her car?"

"Impound."

"Fantastic."

I hustled into the bathroom, grabbing the duffle bag on the way. Last night, Ellmann had permitted me back into the house once more after the body had been rolled away by the coroner. He'd stood watch while I packed a few days' worth of clothes and needed toiletries, then he'd escorted me back outside.

I hurried through a quick shower then threw on jeans and a short-sleeved top. I skipped all makeup aside from several swipes of mascara (which I just can't bring myself to skip, ever), and left my hair down to dry, stuffing a hair tie and a couple pins into my pocket for later, when it started driving me crazy.

Best I could figure, I'd slept a couple hours, which was basically a nap. I wanted to crawl back in bed, put off my problems for a while, and sleep until mid-afternoon, but, as tempting as that was, I knew it wouldn't solve anything. Not to mention, I doubted I'd get much sleep given the slant of my dreams these days. And I had no doubt that if I didn't go fetch my mother, someone *would* call my brother. I try really hard to keep him away from all this.

I set the duffle bag on the floor at the top of the stairs and went to the desk in the loft. It was neat, with not much lying on it. The laptop was closed. The landline phone was quiet. The lamp and the printer turned off. Only a couple loose pieces of paper and a small stack of unopened mail cluttered it. The office space also held two large black bookcases, which featured an impressively diverse collection of books: everything from contemporary fiction to classics to biographies. A small loveseat was pressed against the wall opposite the desk, a book and a blanket left on one side.

I took a piece of paper from the printer and scribbled a note for Pezzani, walking it into the kitchen and leaving it by the coffee pot, which was still half-full from the day before. I left the house key where it was, grabbed my bag, and locked the door behind me. I boarded the Lincoln and sailed for the north end of town.

The impound lot was my first stop. I walked to the small office and spoke with the attendant. It would cost $79.48 to get the car out. I reasoned it was worth the cost. I paid the fee then accepted the keys. I parked the Lincoln two blocks down, then walked back and found my mother's cherry-red Saab 93.

It didn't take as long at the impound lot as it had in the past, so I stopped for coffee. I drove to Dazbog on Cherry, ordered a Brain Damage because it was shaping up to be that kind of day, then spoke briefly with one of the owners while I waited. Coffee in hand, I returned to the Saab and drove a few blocks south to the courthouse on Laporte.

I wasn't the only one here for arraignment. Apparently it had been a busy weekend. The parking lot was full. I had to park on the street a block away.

I found an unoccupied six inches of bench space outside the courtroom and squeezed in, sipping my coffee. There were benches lining the hallway in both directions and all were full. Additional people stood or sat on the floor. It reminded me a lot of the airport: a bunch of people with other things to do standing around waiting for an unpleasant experience.

The courtroom doors were pushed open by a bailiff in a tan uniform, and we all filed in. I found a seat near the back and settled in for the long haul. The lucky ones would be seen in the first few minutes. The unlucky ones would be seen after lunch. I had no way of knowing which my mother would be.

My mother, in all fairness, had also been subjected to a rough and traumatic upbringing. I'm sure this accounts for her current condition, though there are different schools of thought on that subject. Her father had been abusive to her, which seemed to explain why she ultimately ended up marrying my father, the most abusive man I've ever even heard about. I think the reason I don't have the same condition is because I internalize far less than she does. I'm sort of the angry-out-loud type, and that just isn't her style. More the suffer-in-silence kind, she'd been diagnosed with Bipolar I Disorder in her late teens.

When she takes her medications as prescribed and visits her psychiatrist as scheduled, she does fairly well, with only minimal evidence of her condition noticeable. The problem with Bipolar people is the same as with schizophrenics, I'm told; when they feel good, they stop taking their meds like they should and slip right back into the throes of their diseases. For my mother, this means she alternates every few months between the highs and the lows.

When she's in a high, or manic, state, she sleeps only a few hours every few days, cleans everything excessively, spends money exorbitantly, has sex unreservedly (with anyone who's offering—man or woman), talks too loud, and drives too fast. When she's manic, she's the ultimate partier and all the rage among a certain group of friends, most of them half her age. When she's low, or depressed, she sleeps an average of twenty hours a day and foregoes typical activities of daily living, like showering, brushing her teeth, and dressing in clean clothes. The chores around the house go undone unless I do them.

When she's off her meds, it's almost always a couple weeks into her first true depressive state that she starts taking them correctly again. She enjoys the ups, but not the downs. She just doesn't seem to understand she can't have one without the other, and she never gives up trying.

Because my mother was currently off her meds and as manic as I'd ever seen her, I hadn't been surprised to get Ellmann's call. I didn't have all the details yet, but I'd been telling Ellmann the truth: this wasn't her first arrest, and it wouldn't be her last. Her arrests were almost always drug- or alcohol-related. My mother was a regular in the bars in Old Town, at college parties, and at raves. All of those things have high potential for drawing police attention.

The door behind the bench opened, and an older woman in a black robe climbed up and sat herself in front of the court. We were all instructed to rise while she did this, then permitted to sit when she was settled. At her nod, the bailiff went and opened a door on the left. A group of five men shuffled in. They were all wearing street clothes and handcuffs. They all appeared to have had a rough night. One by one, each case was called. The representative from the district attorney's office stood and addressed the judge, making requests that largely had to do with bail. Those who had defense attorneys stood with them behind the opposite table. Each party made their requests, the judge made a ruling, and the next case was called.

I'm the oldest, five years older than my brother, who was actually an accident. I think it's for this reason my mother feels about him the way she does. He's her miracle, the baby that shouldn't have been. My father had wanted a boy and had been more than a little pissed off when I'd turned out to be something else, something he'd punished me for regularly. He had made it clear to my mother they would continue trying until he got the little boy he wanted and deserved. Even in my mother's broken mind, she'd known having more children with that man would be a mistake. So, in an uncharacteristic moment of clear and selfless thought, she had the delivery doctor tie her tubes, unbeknownst to her husband. Knowing this had happened, it made the existence of my brother just that much more precious.

The reason my father had wanted a baby boy was because domestic violence (perhaps the worst on record, according to local police), hadn't been his only bag. He'd had another dirty little secret: unspeakable acts against little boys.

Now, when I was nine, ten, eleven, I couldn't even pretend to be worldly or wise, but I had recognized the way my father had began to look at my brother was wrong; it had scared me. I hadn't understood at the time what depraved thoughts had been running through his sick head, but I'd known they were bad. After the baby had been born, I'd made a point of standing between him and my father, the way my mother wouldn't, the way she hadn't ever stood between my father and me. There had been very few occasions when the man had laid an angry, hurtful hand on Zach.

Every time I'm called to pick my mother up from jail, the police station, or court, I'm reminded of a night thirteen years ago. I'd gone to pick my brother up from his afterschool class and learned my mother had collected him an hour earlier. By this time, I'd made it a point never to leave Zach unattended with my father. He couldn't even look at Zach without frightening me anymore. I'd bummed a ride home and found the house dark, my mother gone. I'd known something was wrong.

After running through the house, I saw a bar of light under my brother's closed bedroom door. It had been the only light on in the house. Never before or since have I experienced panic like I'd felt at that moment. Without much clear thought, I'd barreled through the door. My fear had been confirmed.

My father had been sitting beside my brother on the bed, dressed in only his underwear. Zach's shirt was gone. Operating on instinct fueled by pure terror, I'd grabbed up a wooden baseball bat lying on the floor and charged my father swinging. He'd raised his arms to defend himself, but the bat glanced off his head. The blow had knocked him back and momentarily stunned him.

Horrified at what I'd done, I'd dropped the bat. I'd grabbed Zach and dragged him out of the room. We'd sprinted down the hall to the office where the crawl space was. For years, the crawl space had been Zach's safe place, the place I'd sent him to keep him out of reach of my father, to make sure he never had to witness what my father was capable of. Zach had been hysterical, confused, and beyond scared. He'd been feeling everything I had felt. I'd wanted to stop and cry, too. But neither of us could have afforded that.

While Zach had locked himself in the crawl space, I'd run to the desk and groped around for the phone in the dark. I'd been able to hear my father shouting from beyond the office door. He'd been increasingly irritated with me by this time because I'd refused to leave Zach alone with him. He hadn't liked me much anyway, but this had just made it worse. Hitting him had been the final straw. He'd sworn to kill me. I can still remember what it felt like to hear him scream those words and have absolutely no doubt in my young mind he truly meant them.

When he'd started breaking through the office door with the bat, I'd forgotten about the phone and run to the gun cabinet. Even though I wasn't a boy, like he'd wanted, when he was in one of his good moods, he had taken me to do boy things. He'd thought guns were a boy thing. From an early age, I'd learned to handle, shoot, and care for them.

My hands had been trembling so badly I'd been unable to get the tiny key in the lock on the cabinet. I'd grabbed the paperweight from the corner of the desk and chucked it at the door. The glass had shattered. He had nearly made it through the office door by the time I put my hands on a gun. His intentions had been clear, and I had understood perfectly that it was either going to be me or him. The thought of leaving him alone with my brother forever made me decide it had to be me.

I'd just reached into the drawer where the magazines and ammunition were kept when the last of the office door had splintered away. He'd run in and taken a swing at me. I'd dropped to the floor as I forced my shaking hands to put the loaded mag in the gun. He'd swung again when I fired the first shot. It had struck him center mass but hadn't stopped him. Anger and hatred had seemed to drive him forward. I'd rolled out of the path of the bat and fired three more shots, my small forearms burning from the exertion of hefting the gun, pulling the trigger, and fighting the recoil. Four black dots had spotted his chest, and blood poured out of them. For a moment he'd stood completely still, frozen. Then he'd collapsed to the floor.

The police had arrived then; a neighbor had called 911 to report the racket. I collected my brother and got him out of the house. The police had taken us to the hospital for evaluation, followed by the police station for questioning. It had taken the police nearly six hours to locate my mother and another three for her to show up. When she had arrived, she'd stormed into the room where I'd been sitting with the detective.

"How could you, you little brat?" she'd shouted. "How could you do this? He was my husband! He was your father! You brat!"

She'd been shrieking, her voice shrill and abrasive. I hadn't responded. I'd been numb then, from what I'd just experienced. But I was also long accustomed to tuning out her ranting, as even then it was nothing new. The detective had gotten up to intervene, but she'd ducked around him, racing up to me and slapping me. After the detective had thrown her out, she'd collected my brother and left. Just like she'd left me at school on a regular basis, she'd left me at the police station on the worst day of my life.

Inevitably, my mind flashes back to that night when I'm called to pick her up. I always want to leave her, the way she'd left me. It's always a struggle not to. Leaving her wouldn't accomplish anything. My mother doesn't learn that way. And I don't think it would make me feel any better, either. Still, it was this that filled my head while I waited for her case to be called. By the time I heard her name, I'd pretty much put it all behind me again, where it would wait to be dragged out again next time.

The case was heard quickly; my mother's lawyer was present.

13

Bridget Grey was dressed in a black miniskirt that barely covered her derriere and a black halter-top covered in rhinestones and sequins. I easily imagined how the top would have glinted and sparkled under the lights of whatever club she'd been in last night. In the sunlight, I noticed her skin had been brushed with glitter, which drew attention to her perfect shoulders and ample breasts. Her heavy makeup was smeared, and it thickly ringed her bloodshot eyes. Her normally prefect blonde hair was matted and gross, sticking up in various places. She only had one shoe, carried in her purse, which she'd managed to hang on to somehow.

Even in her post-party state, she still easily drew the attention of almost every male within her immediate vicinity. And they weren't seeing a woman too old to be dressed as she was, or a woman who had partied too hard. I couldn't help but roll my eyes as the idiots practically drooled over her.

While her lawyer walked her out, the pair discussing something or other, I hiked back to the Saab. When I pulled up in front of the courthouse, my mother and Kenneth Weitz, her very expensive attorney, were standing in the morning sun, waiting. I switched on the flashers and barely had time to get out of the car before my mother slid in behind the wheel.

"What took you so long?" she snapped before slamming the door.

The flashers winked off, the engine roared, and the tires spun, leaving twin streaks of black rubber on the asphalt. An angry horn bleated as my mother jerked the Saab into traffic, cutting off another car.

"You're welcome!" I called to her bumper.

I returned to the sidewalk, where I now spotted Ellmann. As he walked casually over to me, I wondered how long he'd been there. What was he doing at the courthouse at all?

"At least you brought her car this time," the lawyer said.

"Next time, I'll tell the cop who calls me to pick her up to go fly a kite, and then you can bring her home, Ken. How's that sound?"

Weitz smiled a sick, lawyery smile, and I felt my gut roll.

"All I have to do is threaten to call your precious baby brother, and you'll come running, Zoe darling. Who are we kidding?"

Turning on an expensive, no-doubt handmade leather shoe, the attorney waltzed away, probably planning what to buy with the haul he'd just taken for defending my mother in court this morning. Really, the two of them were perfect for one another. Both sleazy, selfish people who lived almost entirely in worlds of their own making.

Ellmann stopped beside me, his hands in his pockets. He was staring at the little lawyer strutting away. I could see something a bit stronger than dislike on his face.

"Bridget was in quite a hurry to get out of here," he said. "The excitement of freedom, or embarrassment?"

I scoffed. "Neither. She wants to get to work. Despite everything, she takes her work pretty seriously, and she's actually good at it."

"At the accounting firm."

"BGW and Associates. She's the *G*. Because of her condition, they didn't want to put her name on the building. At first they would only agree to her as a silent partner. But she negotiated the *G*. It also helps that she's better at their jobs than they are; they need her. Which is why they put up with all her shit. Now, nice to see you, but I need to go."

I turned and started walking. Ellmann fell in stride beside me.

"What do they do at BGW and Associates? Do you know?"

"You looked them up. I'm sure you saw the 'Accounting and Investment Services' part after their name."

"Yeah. But I hoped you knew more."

"Sorry. You know as much as I do. What are you doing here, anyway? Did you come here to interrogate me?" It sounded a bit harsher than I'd intended. Ellmann wasn't the enemy. Actually, from everything I'd gathered so far, he seemed like a pretty decent guy. And I was starting to like him.

"A couple last-minute things to file," he said. "Spotted your mom in the hallway with her snake-oil salesman. You were right about her attorney. Weitz isn't a very nice guy."

"No shit." I hiked my bag up on my shoulder. "Listen, I don't mean to be rude, but don't you have work to do? Like maybe finding whoever put Stacy in the hospital? Or finding Tyler Jay?"

I reached the corner and hit the button for the crosswalk. Ellmann easily kept pace, his legs several inches longer than mine.

"I get it," he said. "You're having a shitty day. I won't take any of this personally. In fact, let me give you a ride."

"What makes you think I need a ride?"

It irritated me that Ellmann always seemed to know what I wasn't saying. Normally, I'm not this easy for people to figure out. Actually, I'm *never* this easy for people to figure out. Amy's pretty good at it, but she's been doing it her whole life. After five years of friendship, Sadie'd told me she felt like she still didn't know me. So what was the deal with Ellmann? I didn't know. And maybe I didn't want to know.

"You obviously drove your mom's car here, which was at the impound lot. So, where else would your car be? Come on, the lot's like four or five miles from here; let me give you a ride. I'm over here." He pointed and rounded the corner, walking toward the other side of the courthouse.

The light changed and the crosswalk signal winked on. Glancing at the light, I sighed and fell in behind Ellmann. The truth was, I was exhausted. I just didn't want to walk that far.

Ellmann had snagged a primo place, one reserved for those who bleed blue. We climbed in, then he cruised away from the courthouse and over to the impound lot. He was about to ask me where I'd parked, until the sun gleamed off the unmistakable copper paint of the enormous barge.

"Never mind," he said, making a left and stopping behind the Lincoln. "When do you get your truck back?"

I shrugged. I had no idea. The mechanic was on my list of people to call today. But who knew; it might be a week.

Suddenly an image of the truck flashed into my mind. It was stalled on the railroad tracks, a steam engine barreling toward it. I could hear the ear-piercing shriek of the train's horn. Then the train smashed into the truck, shattering it to a million tiny pieces that exploded and rained down like confetti at a party.

"Hey, Earth to Zoe."

Ellmann's voice penetrated the thought, and I shook my head. I had no idea how long he'd been talking to me.

"Sorry," I said. "I'm just a little tired."

"That little grin you had there," he said. "You looked like a kid at Disney Land. What were you thinking about?"

"Nothing." I grabbed my bag and opened the door. "Thanks for the ride," I said as I got out. "Again."

"Stay out of trouble, huh? The twelve-hour rule is still in effect."

I shrugged. "No problem."

I got into the Lincoln and my phone rang. Ellmann made a U-turn and disappeared around the corner as I answered it.

"Zoe Grey? My name is Karen Lerman. I'm calling from King Soopers about the application you submitted. I'd like you to come in for an interview."

Excellent. My second such call today. A woman from Hobby Lobby had also called me that morning, while I'd been waiting for my mother at the courthouse. We'd scheduled an interview for tomorrow. Maybe all this meant my day was looking up.

"I have quite a bit of flexibility in my schedule this week," I said. "What day works best?"

"Actually, I was hoping you had time today. Maybe this morning? How's eleven?"

Incidentally, eleven worked for me. I had a pretty open schedule.

I agreed to the time and we disconnected.

I noticed a text from Pezzani. He'd obviously gotten my note.

"Hope the family is okay. Anything I can do? I'm off at eleven today. Wanna have lunch?"

I sent him a quick reply accepting his lunch offer. Then I dialed my mechanic. I knew the shop was open, but no one answered the phone. I left a terse message then started the Lincoln and coasted home. I got to the first stoplight before I realized I didn't have a home to go to.

I called Donald. I knew he didn't mind that I was driving the Lincoln, but I did. It was past time to return it. But I fully realized the dangers of going to my mother's house right now. She's never in a great mood, as far as I'm concerned. Just getting out of jail was likely to put her in a very bad mood. By a stroke of luck, Donald reported she was not at the house, and she had not been home. I started that way, giving him clear instructions to call me immediately if she turned up.

By the time I arrived at the house, I'd received no such call. Donald met me on the porch. I tossed him the keys as I hustled into the garage, slinging the duffle bag across my chest then pushing the Cushman out into the driveway. I called my thanks to Donald, jumped onto the Cushman, and buzzed away.

I had some time to kill before my interview, so I decided to hit the gym. I put in another painful half hour on the elliptical and immediately felt a terrible burning sensation in almost every part of my lower body. I was holding back tears when the counter finally hit thirty minutes. I winced with every step to the locker room then stood in the shower for a long time.

Dressed in my interview best, clothes that had suffered slightly from being hastily packed into the duffle bag, I buzzed over to King Soopers. I wasn't too worried about the fact that I'd pinned my hair up wet, or that my clothes weren't crisply ironed. I understand the principle of always putting the best foot forward, but this was King Soopers, not the Capital Building, or even a bank. I felt sure a few small wrinkles would be overlooked, if they were noticed at all. I followed the instructions Karen had given me. I arrived early, but she seemed in a hurry to interview me anyway.

She led me up the stairs at the back of the building. The second floor was old and undecorated. There was a large open area filled with two tables, a microwave, fridge, and coffee pot that served as the break room. There was also a bathroom and a wall of small lockers. The rest of the space was given over to offices. Some of the offices were labeled with names on the doors while others weren't. The office Karen led me into was labeled BOB DURRAN.

The interview was relatively short. She asked a series of questions, and I answered them to the best of my ability. Then I asked a few of my own. I learned management in this particular store was undergoing reorganization. There had been terminations, layoffs, promotions, demotions, and a host of other changes. Bob Durran no longer worked for King Soopers. Karen usually worked out of an office in Denver but had come up to help get things back on track. This, at least, explained the hurry to get through interviews.

Interview concluded, I carried the duffle bag back out of the store and climbed onto the Cushman. It was too early to meet Pezzani, so I decided to drop in on Stacy again. She was occupying a decent portion of my thoughts, anyway, so I thought it was reasonable to visit.

I bypassed the line waiting for the volunteer—today a man with bottle cap glasses—and got on the elevator. I reached for the button marked *4* and noticed all the buttons were lit. I looked at the only other people on the elevator: a woman and her young son. The kid grinned at me.

Before the elevator delivered me to the fourth floor, it had stopped at three, returned to one, gone to the basement, and stopped again at one. I shot a dark look at the young boy as his mother finally led him out of the elevator. I was pretty certain I could have gotten there faster if I'd taken the stairs. Which also would have been better for me. Go figure.

As I rounded the corner onto ICU, I nearly ran into Tina Shuemaker. She was dressed in jeans, heeled boots, and a ruffled top. Her hair was down—a layered, deliberate mess—hanging past her shoulders. Her makeup was flawless and her jewelry trendy. She carried a large designer bag on her shoulder.

"Oh, hello," I said, stepping out of the way just before we collided.

She looked up, but it took a moment for her to place my face. When she did, her smile was cold and didn't reach her eyes.

"What are *you* doing here?" She made it sound more like an accusation than a question.

"Visiting Stacy, of course. And yourself?"

"The same. What else would I be doing?"

I didn't know. "Is she doing any better?"

Tina shrugged and tried for a sad look, but like the smile, it seemed insincere. "The doctors aren't hopeful. I have to get to class; I'm late."

Then she was gone.

As I made my way down the hall, a series of alarms sounded somewhere. An instant later, people dressed in scrubs and white jackets were jumping up and hurrying out of the nurses' station and down the hall. Vicki Karnes, Stacy's mother, shot out of Stacy's room, panic-stricken. She was forced backward as the wave of people flowed past her.

"Help!" she cried desperately. "Please, help her!"

By the time I made it to the room, all sorts of equipment and people had been convened around the bed. The alarms were still sounding, and the staff was talking over them, calling out information and orders. Thomas stood huddled with his wife in the back of the room, just inside the door. Both of them were crying as they watched, and waited.

Stunned and horrified by the implication of the sounds and hurried activity, I was unable to move, unable to look away. The same way a person is compelled to watch a train wreck. I chalked it up to human nature.

The horrible feeling in my chest and the hot tears burning silently down my cheeks were something else.

_____

East Moon Asian Bistro and Hibachi is one of the new restaurants on Harmony Road just west of the newly constructed Front Range Village. The main entrance is on the west end and opens onto a wide sidewalk leading to the patio and a large fire pit, which was currently unlit.

Inside, Pezzani was waiting on a bench. A smiling blonde girl manned the hostess station. To the right, the restaurant is arranged in typical fashion with booths and tables, many of which were occupied with the lunch crowd. To the left, the restaurant is sectioned off with floor-to-ceiling sheets of glass. On the other side of the glass are large Hibachi tables designed to seat eight diners. Two of them were occupied with large groups, Asian men dressed in black uniforms and red chef hats stood behind each. The occasional burst of flame and skillful tossing of utensils completed the show.

A large bar separates the two sections of the restaurant. The left side of the counter is high, with barstools pushed up to it. The right is much lower, with chairs and fancy plates at each seat. Another Asian man in a black uniform and red hat was behind the counter preparing food. This was the Sushi bar.

Pezzani stood when he saw me, taking me in. He was dressed in what I'd come to recognize as his work attire: black polo with company logo, perfectly fitted blue jeans, and black boots.

"You look nice," he said. But I thought there was a hint of amusement in his voice. I didn't know what to make of that.

I'd stopped crying halfway to the restaurant, but I imagined my eyes were still red. He didn't seem to notice. For which I was grateful. I didn't want to talk about it. I couldn't help but think Ellmann would have noticed, though.

"This is my interview costume," I said, hoping to end the discussion.

We followed the hostess to a booth along the back wall, declining an offer to sit at the bar and passing on the Hibachi experience of it all. Our waitress appeared, introducing herself and reciting the specials. We ordered drinks and she left to get them. We consulted the piece of paper on the end of the table, discussing Sushi.

Before I heard it, I felt it. The atmosphere in the restaurant changed. An instant before, it had been filled with typical dining sounds: the low murmur of conversation and the clinking of silverware on plates. The soft overhead music had created a soothing ambiance. But, as if a switched had been flipped, the entire room fell silent. The only sound remaining was the music, which, in that brief moment, was deafening.

The silence lasted for a millisecond, just long enough to grab my attention. As I looked up, I realized it had been the calm before the storm. There were several gasps accompanied by a chorus of screams. As quickly as the last, another switch was flipped. Suddenly, it was pandemonium. People screamed and clamored, dishes broke, chairs scraped the floor and fell over. At the same time, I saw a familiar figure step around the end of the bar into the dining room.

A figure dressed head-to-toe in black, wearing a ski mask. And the figure had a new accessory: a big, shiny gun.

The figure spotted me and began firing. Self-preservation kicked in, as automatic to me as breathing. Before the first bullet left the gun, I was out of the booth and scurrying across the floor toward the bar. I wanted to put something very large between the shooter and myself.

The shooter charged through the restaurant. Bullets peppered the walls. The report from the gun battered my unprotected eardrums almost palpably. One, two, three . . . . The wall art burst and crashed to the wooden floor.

Pezzani was right behind me. We hit the deck and across the floor for a moment. Then we scrambled, desperate for my shoes to gain purchase on the polished hardwood floor. The shots continued, trailing our forward movement. Eight, nine, ten . . .

In dogged pursuit, the shooter swung the gun after us. Bullets sailed over our heads. They struck the glass panels. The glass shattered and rained to the floor.

Behind the bar, I shot to my feet and sprinted forward, keeping my head down. Pezzani was on my heels. We were between the bar and the glass. The panels shattered in sync with the report of the gun. Each one exploded as we passed. The glass flew everywhere, spraying over my right side.

Thirteen, fourteen, fifteen. Finally, the gunshots stopped. I heard the harmless *click, click, click* of the trigger pulling on an empty gun.

I looked behind me to see if the figure was reloading. Still clutching the gun in his or her right hand, the figure sprinted forward but made no effort to reload. I stopped, turning to face the figure. I could see nothing in the gloved hands apart from the empty gun. However, I kept my eyes peeled for a knife.

The black-clad figure charged forward, black eyes burning into me. I dropped into a familiar defensive stance. Suddenly, the figure's eyes cut to my left, toward the door. Without slowing, the figure tore by, barreling through the exit. I hurried after him or her. I hit the sidewalk in time to see the figure jump into the passenger side of a small, white compact car. The car tore out of the lot with a screech of the tires.

My chest heaved and my already taxed muscles burned. I bent forward and put my hands on my knees, sucking in air. Yesterday, when I'd returned to the house and found the dead guy, I hadn't really considered that I'd been the target. I couldn't say for sure the attack in the restaurant had been directed at me, either, but it seemed plausible. At least, I was now willing to consider it. What I didn't know was why someone was trying to kill me. Neither did I know who that someone might be.

Standing upright, I went back inside. Pezzani was at the hostess station talking on the phone, the hostess hysterical beside him. I noticed he had red gashes on his arm and face from the glass. Looking at my arm for the first time, I saw I was in the same condition. Some of the wounds were rather deep. Pezzani hung up then noticed me.

"Police are on the way."

Fifteen minutes later, I was sitting on the bumper of the ambulance beside Pezzani, an EMT tending to the worst of my lacerations. The parking lot was crammed full of emergency response vehicles and rubberneckers. The police were speaking to witnesses, taking statements, and writing reports. Those few who had needed medical care were being tended to in the parking lot, no one requiring serious attention or transport to the ER.

The EMT secured a bandage around my upper arm as a navy blue Charger stopped at the curb behind two patrol cars.

I wasn't surprised to see it here. But I was a bit surprised by the mix of emotions I felt as a result.

Ellmann had on aviator-style sunglasses and a pissed-off look. He crossed the sidewalk to the nearest uniformed officer and spoke to him briefly. The officer used his hands to point in several directions as he responded. In following the officer's finger, Ellmann had looked toward the parking lot and spotted me sitting on the ambulance. He concluded the conversation and started over. He stopped in front of me and planted both hands on his hips. Even through the shades, I could see the unfriendly look in his eyes.

"Oh, Alex," Pezzani said, standing and offering his hand. "Or, Detective Ellmann, I should say. Good to see you again."

Ellmann shook the other man's hand unenthusiastically, so busy glaring at me he barely glanced at Pezzani.

"What happened?" he asked.

Pezzani launched into an account of the event, though I was pretty sure Ellmann had been asking me. I was content to merely listen, letting Pezzani explain while the EMT continued to bandage my wounds. After reaching the end, Pezzani sighed and shrugged.

"That's when the police showed up," he finished.

Ellmann was nodding his head, listening and absorbing the details, never looking away from me. He wasn't taking notes as he typically did, though. I wondered if that meant this wouldn't be his case. I thought it should be, since it seemed connected to the others, but what did I know?

The EMT taped the last dressing and stood. "Several of those need sutures. We can take you to the ER, or you can go on your own."

"I'll go on my own," I said. "I probably shouldn't leave just now anyway." Even if I wanted to avoid the conversation I knew was coming.

"Sounds good." He reached for a clipboard and made several checkmark. Then he held it and the pen out to me. "Just sign this."

I signed the document, relieving the ambulance service of any guilt and legal responsibility regarding my injuries, and handed it back. The EMT signed as a witness then tore off a carbon copy and handed it to me. He shook my hand and wished me well, then turned his attention to other things. Pezzani and I stood, both bandaged on our right sides, and moved away from the ambulance.

"Have you given your statements?" Ellmann asked.

"No, not yet," Pezzani said. "We were sent to the EMTs first."

Ellmann turned and looked around. He waved to an officer concluding an interview, calling him over. The man ambled toward us carrying a clipboard.

"This man needs to make a statement," Ellmann said, pointing to Pezzani. "He's finished with the medics. Will you take him and get him started?"

"No problem. If you'll just come with me, sir."

Pezzani moved off after the officer.

Ellmann reached out and wrapped his hand around my uninjured left arm, guiding me toward the far side of the parking lot, where a six-foot privacy fence had been erected between the shopping center and the trailer park. Only when we reached the curb did he release me.

"What happened?" he asked again, pulling off his sunglasses. He studied the cuts on my face and seemed particularly upset by the laceration on my cheekbone.

I shrugged. "Joe gave a pretty good account."

He just stared at me.

"What?" I asked.

He sighed and tugged a hand back through his hair. "I asked for twelve hours," he said. "*Twelve hours*. How hard could that be? Do you know how long it's been? Nine."

"Hey, you said not to call you for twelve hours. Once again, I didn't call you."

"I said no emergencies or problems. This is both."

"Well, don't be mad at me. I didn't call you. And I didn't ask that gunman to come shoot the place up."

"You're like a walking magnet for trouble. It follows you wherever you go. With you, it's one disaster after another. What will be next? We've already got assault, murder, and now a gunman in a restaurant. I hate to think about what will happen next. I mean, you've got to be running out of lives by now."

My gut lurched, and I winced. Tears sprang instantly to my eyes. Hadn't the hospital called him?

"Actually, it's two murders."

"What?" He hadn't missed my reaction, and now he realized it had nothing to do with his lecture. "What do you mean?"

"I just came from the hospital. Stacy . . . didn't make it." My voice was tight, and with the last few words, my restraint was zapped. I began to sob, tears streaking down my cheeks again.

"I thought you'd been crying," he sighed. "I'm sorry."

Ellmann took a step forward then stopped himself. Instead, he reached a hand out and put it on my shoulder. It was strong, warm, and comforting. I appreciated his small gesture.

He stood for several minutes, waiting patiently while I worked to get myself under control. Then he asked a couple questions. I filled him in on the details I had, few as they were. He was genuinely upset to hear the news. I also suspected a small part of that had to do with the fact that I was upset.

"I asked you specifically not to get into any trouble, and you went to the hospital?" he asked, resuming the lecture. "How does that make sense to you?"

"I'm fine, by the way," I said, cutting off his tirade. I just didn't have it in me to listen to any more lecturing. My tolerance for it is low on my best day. And I was not having the best day.

My words seemed to sober him. He stopped and sighed again, eyeing the bandages then looking down at his boots. When he spoke next, his voice was much softer.

"Are you really okay? Is this the worst of it?" He pointed to my arm.

I nodded as I looked at my arm. I saw now it was shaking. In fact, my whole body ached, my muscles tight and trembling. It was the lingering effect of the adrenaline. And maybe some fear.

"Yes. I'm fine. A few stitches and I'll be good as new."

"I got called because the reports started coming in about a shooter dressed in black with a ski mask, just like my other case, and maybe they're connected. I just knew you were here. And no one could tell me if anyone was hurt. I . . . I was scared."

I was quiet for a beat.

"I'm sorry," I said sincerely. "I didn't ask you to worry about me."

Also, I didn't know how I felt about it.

"Not that it would change anything."

"No," I said. "Trouble magnetism is like a disease with no cure."

Since lunch out had been a disaster, Pezzani and I went back to his house and ordered in. I noticed Pezzani had paused before opening the door, looking out to make sure the sandwich guy wasn't wearing a ski mask and holding a gun. Turned out he was unarmed.

The shooting incident had been unsettling, to say the least. I didn't know whom the figure had been shooting at, though I had my suspicions. I didn't know why the figure was shooting. I didn't know who had done the shooting. I didn't know what, if anything, the shooting had to do with Stacy Karnes. I didn't know if Tyler Jay was connected. If he was, I didn't know how.

All of this bothered me. I've never liked questions with no answers. Actually, most of the trouble I've found myself in throughout my life could very well be blamed on this very phenomenon. And I don't like when people start catching on to the fact that I really have no idea what I'm doing, what I'm talking about, or what's going on.

After lunch, I called my mechanic again. This time he answered. But there had been no progress. I had, naively, expected different news.

I was lying on the living room floor with my legs on the sofa. My arms were flung out to each side, and I had my eyes closed. I was concentrating on breathing slowly and evenly, while trying to organize and focus my thoughts.

My phone, lying somewhere on the floor near my head, started ringing. By the third ring, I was still debating whether or not I would answer. Finally, I picked it up and pressed it to my ear, not opening my eyes.

"Zoe Grey?"

"Yes."

"This is Karen Lerman calling from King Soopers. How are you?"

The woman I'd interviewed with that morning. "I'm well, thanks," I lied. "Yourself?"

"Just fine, thank you for asking. I was calling you back about the job. It didn't take us as long as we anticipated to make a decision. I'd like to offer you the position."

We hashed out a few details, and I ultimately agreed. I'd make decent—if not excellent—money, work thirty-two hours a week, including every other weekend, and be located at the Taft and Elizabeth store. I agreed to start tomorrow.

I'd barely put the phone down when it rang again. I thought it was Karen calling back about something she'd forgotten. I answered without looking at the display.

"Someone was murdered on the property?" a shrill voice demanded. Not Karen Lerman.

I pinched my eyebrows together. "Who is this?

"Margaret Fischer from Fort Collins Property Management. I've been getting phone calls all morning from other renters on that block. They've been telling me all about the police activity and the coroner van and the cops asking them what they knew about the guy who was murdered inside the house I just rented to you. I just got off the phone with the police. They say the house is an active crime scene."

She stopped and waited expectantly, as if I was supposed to say something.

I didn't know what.

"Okay. And?"

"And?" she spat back. "*And* I'd like to know what the hell is going on. Is there a dead person in the living room of the property?"

"No. The dead guy is in the morgue."

She sighed as if she already knew that.

I wondered, then, why she'd asked.

"Who is he? Is he someone you know? Did you kill him? The police won't tell me anything except the place is a crime scene. I have to tell you, there are some serious breaches in contract here."

"Excuse me?" I said, cracking an eye for the first time. "Did you really just ask me if I killed him? What kind of question is that?"

"A valid and relevant one," she quipped. "Criminal activity of any kind is expressly prohibited in the rental agreement you signed. That being the case, I find you to be in violation of the contract, which makes it null and void. You'll have to vacate the premises immediately."

I shot up and scurried away from the sofa.

"*What*? You're accusing me of murder and subsequently evicting me? You have got to be kidding."

My tone had caused Pezzani to wander over from where he'd been working at his desk. He stood looking at me curiously, wondering what had caused my outburst.

"I am very serious. We here at Fort Collins Property Management take murder and all other crimes very seriously. We will not tolerate any crime on our properties. When can you be out? We'll have to have the place cleaned, which, of course, will come out of your deposit."

"That is absolutely unacceptable. I will not be charged for cleaning up after a murder I had nothing to do with."

"We are within the rights granted to us by the contracts and agreements you signed, and we will enforce them fully."

I drilled my finger into the END button.

I mumbled something to Pezzani, told him I'd call him later, then grabbed my bag and left. I whipped the Cushman out of the lot and into traffic, heading to the office of Fort Collins Property Management, and the desk of Margaret Fischer.

With more angry movements, I found Ellmann's number and dialed it. The line rang five times and I wondered if he was intentionally avoiding my call, fearing another emergency or problem, either of which, at this time, would have been well within the twelve-hour window I'd been given. Finally, the call was answered.

"I need the name of that mechanic," I said, skipping everything else, like identifying myself.

"Hello to you, too," he said lightly. He recited the number. "You sound pissed. Your mechanic try to jip you again?"

"No. Well, yes, probably. Whatever. The truck still isn't ready, he hasn't even looked at it, and I need it back yesterday. I'm going to have to move again."

"What? Why?"

I explained.

There was a long silence. "You're joking."

"Again, not something I'd joke about."

I disconnected and dialed the number he gave me. A nice-sounding man answered, and I asked for Manny.

"I'm Manny. What can I do for you?"

"My name is Zoe Grey. I got your number from Detective Ellmann. I'm having a problem with my truck."

"What's the problem?"

I sighed and managed not to roll my eyes. If I knew what was wrong with the damn thing, I wouldn't be calling him.

"It's not running. Currently it's at my mechanic's shop, but it's been there a lot recently, so I'm looking for a new mechanic."

"I'm your guy. Alex is good people; he's done right by me and a couple friends. So, any friend of his is a friend of mine. Can you get it to my place?"

"Yes."

"If you bring it by today, I'll take a look at it. Most problems are simple. My guess, you have a simple problem. Problem is, simple doesn't always mean cheap. Simple just means I can find it faster."

He gave me an address and his cell phone number, and we disconnected. I'd arrived in the parking lot outside the property management office and was sitting on the scooter. I made one more call. My brother didn't answer, so I left a semi-urgent message and tucked the phone into my pocket.

Half an hour later, I stormed out of the office, beat-red and so angry I could have breathed fire if I'd tried. When I'd arrived, Margaret was in her office with the door closed. The teeny-bopper receptionist, who didn't look old enough to drive, had informed me Margaret couldn't be disturbed, and if I wanted to see her, I'd need to make an appointment. In a moment of temporary insanity, I'd stomped around her desk and flung Margaret's door open. She'd been sitting behind her desk, her stocking feet propped up on it and crossed at the ankles, talking on the phone. At the sight of me, she'd quickly ended the phone call and informed me my behavior was beyond unacceptable. I leveled the same accusation at her. We argued for the better part of thirty minutes.

"You signed a contract," Margaret had said.

"Which you deemed null and void."

"Yes, because of the crime."

"The same contract which allows you to keep my deposit."

"Yes."

"The contract that is now null and void."

This was the basis of my argument. She'd fumbled and stuttered and grasped at straws. Then she'd resorted to finger-pointing, and later name-calling. She'd held her ground, though, refusing to give up at all costs.

I finally had to leave. My learned behaviors are violent, all of them. Well, almost all. Just then, the anger and frustration raged inside me, and I knew I was on the edge. The scales were precariously balanced, and a feather on either side would tip them. It would have been all too easy for me to crawl over Margaret's desk and strangle her.

———————————

I drove to my house, or my former house, also known as the crime scene. I parked and went to the side of the house, where I scrambled over the four-foot chain-link fence, snagging my already ruined suit pants.

Ellmann had not put any stickers on the sliding glass door or the garage door. I used my key to let myself in through the garage. Inside, the place smelled like gunpowder, blood, and something I would have labeled "death."

I hurried through the living room, skirting around the huge dark stain in the middle of the floor, and into the bedroom. I found the box I was looking for in the corner under two others. I ripped it open and dug inside, pulling out the medium-sized lockbox. I unlocked it and lifted the lid.

Inside lay three handguns. I wasn't entirely convinced the shooter in the restaurant had been gunning for me. But no one had been killed. That seemed like the intent, so it was reasonable to conclude whoever it was would try again. On the off chance I was the target, I wanted to even the playing field.

I chose the Glock .45 and a full magazine, sliding it into the gun with the heel of my hand. I chambered a round and made sure the safety was on. I also collected two additional magazines and a box of .45 rounds. I dropped everything into my bag and left the way I'd come.

It's illegal to carry a concealed handgun, like I was doing. I had never applied for a permit because I'd never had any need or desire to tote a gun around with me. Until now.

My next stop was the shooting range. I was no stranger to guns, but it had been several months since I'd shot any, so I thought a brush-up session would do me good. After the shooting range and an entire box of .45 rounds, I was feeling a lot more in control of my life and the situation, whatever situation that was.

And after towing my truck to the new mechanic's shop, I was also feeling a lot more optimistic about the future. I couldn't really put my finger on it, but I felt like Manny would actually fix the truck and not try to con me. I wondered if that had something to do with Ellmann, and that Manny would ultimately have to answer to the detective if he cheated me. I wish I could say it was me that had put the fear in him, but I was obviously no threat. Just ask my last mechanic.

Amy was out of town, her future in-laws crashing at her house for the rest of the week, and Sadie's apartment wouldn't be ready for human habitation for another forty-eight hours. With my notes and the newspaper spread out before me, I made several more phone calls regarding my housing problem. I called the leasing agents I'd contacted previously and discovered I had only one hang-up. I didn't know how long my current place would be a crime scene. Until it was released, I couldn't move. So, I ended up back at Pezzani's for a second night.

We watched *X-Files* reruns for a while, munching on popcorn. Pezzani stole a kiss, which was slow at first, more exploratory, then not so slow and hungry at the end. It had been a good kiss. Still, I went to the guestroom alone.

Tired, but too restless to sleep, I sat leaning against the headboard, a piece of paper on my knee. I did math for a while, figuring out how much money I might get back from Fort Collins Property Management, how much money I still had in my bank account, how much money a new move-in would cost, how much money my new job at King Soopers would net me, and how long I could conceivably make it until I no longer had a penny to my name. With these depressing figures on my mind, I hauled out the newspaper and began reading through the help-wanted ads.

I still had the Hobby Lobby interview lined up. Of course, even though the position was in management, it was Hobby Lobby; I didn't exactly see big dollar signs. Realistically, it might not amount to even a minimalistic existence. It might make a good second job, if I could work out the details. That being the case, I'd keep the interview, but also keep my eyes open.

I went to the bathroom and took in the state of my face. I had gone to the ER for the recommended sutures. Twelve in all. I washed all of the open wounds with soap and water then smeared Neosporin over them, bandaging the larger ones. Finished, I returned to bed and picked up my book. Two hours later, I was closing in on the last page and was as wide-awake as ever.

Beyond the bedroom door, I heard a faint scuffle followed by a long creak. The sound itself wasn't cause for alarm, yet all the hairs on my body stood on end. Initially, I assumed Pezzani had wandered out to the kitchen for a midnight snack. But in the time I'd spent here, I'd never heard anything creak like that. It sounded like a person opening a door and trying to be sneaky about it. It also sounded farther away than Pezzani's door on the main level of the house. It sounded like the front door.

Dropping the book on the bed, I rolled to the floor, switching off the lamp as I went. I scurried over to my bag and reached in for the gun, finding it easily. Holding it in my hand, I felt a small measure of the control I'd experienced that afternoon return to me. I was still apprehensive, but the fear was tempered now.

I strained my ears to pick up any other out-of-place sounds while I dug around in the bag for a flashlight. I closed my hand around it and heard what was surely a foot on the staircase. I'd noticed one near the middle sagged every time I'd stepped on it, giving a soft moan. I heard it now. Pezzani had few reasons to leave in the middle of the night. I was sure now someone else was here. I hoped it was a family member or ex-girlfriend or best friend with a key. I feared it was a figure in black wearing a ski mask.

Hearing the step, I went to the door. I had a split-second to make a decision. Option one: wait where I was until the door opened and a gunman appeared. The problem with that was Pezzani. If they went to his room first, they would probably kill him. I really didn't want his death on my conscience, no matter if I was dead or alive.

Option two: post myself in the office and pick off the intruders one by one over the wall of the stairway. This had the tactical advantage. The problem was the level of exposure. I would be a sitting duck, trapped with no escape. If I failed to hit them, they would easily be able to kill me. The fear was tempered, but it wasn't wholly overshadowed.

What's the worst that could happen? I asked myself.

Well, I could get shot. If I got shot, it would be painful. And I could die. Or, I could get shot and just die, in which case it wouldn't be painful. Of course, in either of those scenarios, I'd be dead. I didn't really want that. I was too young to die.

Worst vacation ever, I thought.

After an evaluation of pros and cons, I decided option two was preferable to option one, despite its risks. I might get shot, which would hurt like a bitch, and I might die, the only bright side of that being I wouldn't feel any pain. But my chances of *not* getting shot were better if I took an offensive approach.

Only a millisecond had passed since I'd heard the footstep on the stair. I made a conscious effort to control my breathing, keep it calm and even. Then I reached up and twisted the doorknob.

I pulled the door open silently, listened, and then stood. The gun was raised in front of me, gripped with both hands. I trained it on the stairs and crept silently out of the room. Just as I knelt down in front of the desk, I heard another footstep. It was hard to determine if there was more than one intruder.

A head bobbed up on the other side of the low wall, the ski mask instantly identifiable. My heart skipped a beat. Then it hammered against my ribs. All I could hear was my own heartbeat.

I took a breath to calm myself. Then I heard the step creak a second time. I resisted the urge to pull the trigger, waiting.

Figure One reached the landing and briefly glanced in both directions. Then he or she moved left into the living room. I could see the gun in the figure's right hand. It was the same one from the restaurant.

A moment later, a second head popped up in the stairwell. This one also wore a ski mask. I hadn't heard a third moan from the saggy step.

"You guys here to see me?"

My words were like a starting gun at the races. Suddenly everything happened all at once. Figure Two, still on the stairs, swung around toward me, gun following. At the sight of my gun, Figure Two dropped back down out of sight. Figure One, in the living room, wheeled around. Catching sight of me, Figure One aimed. I switched on the light and hit him or her square in the face. Figure One groaned, eyes squeezing shut reflexively in the mask. But gun up, he or she fired anyway, blindly.

I fell back behind the desk. Bullets whizzed overhead, landing in the wall and bookshelves behind me. I heard movement and knew Figure One was headed my way. I scampered forward on my belly, toward the hallway. By the direction and angle of the bullets, I knew Figure One was close.

We made it to the hallway at the same time. Figure One wasn't expecting me to be at his or her feet, and this was my only advantage. I rolled onto one side, the gun raised in front of me, and fired. Three quick shots. They struck the figure directly in the chest. The gun fell from the gloved hand and hit the floor. An instant later, the darkly clad body followed.

The gunshots had drawn Pezzani; I heard his bedroom door open. Back on my feet, gun in front of me, I hurried backward.

"What the hell—"

I plowed into Pezzani then shoved him back toward his open door.

Figure Two leaned around the stairs and fired off several shots. I fired back, and the figure quickly retreated behind the wall. But I heard a gasp. I'd hit him. Or her.

We reached Pezzani's room, and I dropped to one knee in the doorway. Keeping most of my body inside the room, I maintained my aim on the stairs around the doorjamb. I told Pezzani to call 911. Figure Two leaned around the corner once more. I was ready.

I fired several shots quickly. Figure Two had no time to squeeze the trigger. He or she immediately withdrew behind the wall. Then I heard footsteps. An instant later, the door banged open.

The second shooter was gone.

I jumped up and hurried forward, one eye on the stairs and the other on Figure One in the hallway. When I reached the downed shooter, I squatted and picked up the gun, holding it in my left hand by the muzzle. I stepped over Figure One and crossed to the top of the stairs. They were empty, and the door was standing wide open. I hustled down and peeked out into the darkness, glancing around the parking lot. I got there just in time to see a pair of taillights pull around the corner and out of sight behind another building.

I went back inside and flipped on the lights. I set the confiscated gun on the desk and went to the figure. Squatting, I pressed two fingers to the throat. No pulse. Relaxing slightly, I reached for the mask.

Pezzani stepped out of his room and stood staring, somewhat dumbstruck, at the scene before him. I yanked the mask off and stared down at a face I didn't recognize. The man was young, around my age, with short brown hair and good skin, of obvious Hispanic descent. His face was clean-shaven with only a day's growth on his chin and cheeks. I wasn't sure who I'd been hoping for, but I was disappointed to find this guy. I stood.

"Did you call the police?"

In answer, I heard the faint wail of a siren.

"You should go down and open the door," I said.

I picked up the dead man's gun and moved away from the body. Pezzani hesitated for a moment then moved toward the stairs, stepping around the dead man. He went to the door and pulled it open as the sirens stopped. The blue and red strobes were flashing through the windows, dancing on the walls in a way that was becoming more familiar by the day. I heard Pezzani talking and someone else responding.

I ejected the magazine and emptied the chamber of my gun, then laid both at my feet. I stepped away from them, my hands visible in front of me. There was the voice of a second officer followed by footsteps and the jingling of equipment as somebody climbed the stairs. Officer Frye looked from the body in the hallway to me and then the guns at my feet in one quick glance.

"Okay," he said, nodding. "You step to the right and I'll do the same."

Slowly, as if moving together in some kind of dance, I took one slow step after another. Frye matched my pace. Keeping his eyes on me, he picked up both weapons by the muzzles.

"This one yours?" he asked, holding up the empty one.

I nodded. "I didn't want to touch the other one too much. It belonged to him. Or, at least, he brought it." I inclined my head toward the dead guy.

"Okay. You and I need to go outside now."

"Sure."

I preceded him out of the house, stepping around the body and descending the stairs. When we reached the front door, the EMTs were pulling bags of equipment out of the rig. I followed Frye's directions and walked to the police car parked in front of the condo. The EMTs hurried inside. They were only inside for a couple minutes.

Frye secured both weapons and began giving instructions to everyone else while I waited. I went to the front of the car and sat on the hood. Pezzani stood with another officer a couple cars away. As the conversation progressed, Pezzani began looking over the officer's shoulder at me, his looks varying but equally dark. I was experiencing déjà vu. I'd been here before. I knew what happened next.

The conversation concluded and Pezzani marched over. He was dressed in cotton pajama pants and nothing else, his chest and feet bare aside from the white bandages on his right side. His hair was mussed from sleep, and he was past a simple five o'clock shadow.

"What the hell were you doing with a gun?" he demanded. His voice was intended to be a whisper but was far from it. The anger was obvious.

"Protection," I said. "Thank God I had it. There were two of them. We would have been sitting ducks."

"We?" he said, stabbing his chest with an index finger. "*We*? No, I don't think so. *You.*"

"Actually, it's hard to know. The two times someone has tried to kill me recently, I've been with you. They could just as easily have been aiming for you."

"Recently? Is this a habit of yours?"

"No. It's been a long time."

"How could you shoot that guy?"

"Well, he was shooting at me, so it was just a reflex really."

"He's dead! You killed somebody. How can you do that? Doesn't it bother you?"

"It was actually easier this time. So, that's sort of upsetting."

"This time? How many other times were there? How many people have you killed? What kind of person are you?"

Then it was there, on his face. Disgust and horror. The same expression I see on everyone's face when they find out what I'd done. I was probably just tired, but seeing it on Pezzani's face now, the revulsion and fear and judgment, something in me snapped, and I was beyond pissed. I flew off the hood of the car, planting myself in front of Pezzani, pointing an angry index finger at him.

"Don't judge me! Don't you *dare* judge me. What if I hadn't had the gun? Did *that* ever cross your mind? What if we'd both been asleep and unarmed when they got here? We'd *both* be dead. Did it occur to you that I saved your life?"

I saw a navy blue Charger pull up behind the ambulance.

"This isn't about me!" he shot back. "This is about *you*."

"It was self-defense! What was I supposed to do? Sit quietly and let the bastard kill me?"

Ellmann wound his way through the emergency response vehicles, his eyes on Pezzani and me as our argument continued to escalate. We had also drawn the attention of several others nearby. I saw Frye and another uniformed officer hurrying toward us.

"The cop said you've done this before," Pezzani continued. "How many times? How many other people have you killed?"

The cops reached us a few paces before Ellmann.

"Hey, that's enough," Frye started.

"How many times?" Pezzani demanded. "How many people have you killed?"

"I had no choice," I said. "And you're welcome."

The second cop reached for me. "Come on, that's enough."

I jerked my arm out of his grasp. "Leave me alone."

The cop reached for me again, but Ellmann stepped between us.

"It's all right, Parker. I'll take it from here."

The officers nodded to Ellmann then shuffled back to their interviews.

My eyes were still locked on Pezzani, daring him to ask me again how many people I'd killed, daring him again to accuse me of making the wrong choice.

His disgust was battling his fear. Ultimately fear won.

I felt a piece of my heart break, as it did every time.

"All right, Joe," Ellmann said gently but firmly as he clapped a hand on the other man's shoulder. "Let's take a walk."

Under Ellmann's grip, Pezzani had no choice but to go where directed. Ellmann steered him to a police cruiser parked on the other side of the lot. After securing a babysitter, he returned to me. His face was hard and expressionless, typical for a cop, but his voice was soft.

"Are you okay?"

I was a breath away from tears. I knew if I opened my mouth I'd burst out crying. Instead, I simply nodded and leaned back against the car, crossing my arms over my chest.

Ellmann stood with his hands in his pockets, studying me.

"I'm going to go talk to the first on scene. I'll be back in a few minutes."

Again I nodded, and he was gone.

I lifted myself back up onto the car and sniffed, wiping at my eyes. This was getting ridiculous. I thought about the money I still had in the bank and wondered if it wouldn't be better spent on a trip to Brazil.

15

I stayed until an officer had taken my statement, asked me a thousand questions, and had me walk him through the chain of events three times. Then I repeated everything with Ellmann, who'd taken me inside for a real-life, hands-on version. I'd been fingerprinted and photographed and tested for gunpowder residue. Finally, I was permitted to pack my things and leave. Pezzani was long gone, and I overheard someone say he was staying with a friend. I had no idea where I was going to stay.

Packed onto the scooter, I made my first destination my house, the crime scene. I hopped the fence and let myself in the same way I had that afternoon. I debated taking the whole lockbox but decided this was as good a place as any to keep the extra stuff, given my current degree of mobility. I took the Sig Saur 9mm and all the trimmings. It didn't have the same brute-force stopping power as the .45, but I'd gotten a look at the dead man's chest. If I could shoot that accurately next time, I wouldn't need the brute force.

Feeling slightly more secure, I climbed back onto the scooter and buzzed over to Best Western University Inn on College across from CSU campus. I managed to check in and find my room without incident. I used a fake name and paid cash. The clerk, a college-aged kid with his eye on the small TV under the counter the whole time, didn't ask any questions. After I offloaded all essential items, I pushed the scooter into the room, parking it against the wall between the TV and the door. The scooter was too attention-grabbing and memorable to be parked in the lot all night long.

The room was small but sufficient. There was a single queen-sized bed, a table with two chairs, and an impressively large bathroom with bathtub. I flipped on the TV and dialed up CMT and VH1, flipping back and forth at commercials, singing along with the songs I knew. I wanted the noise and the company.

I sat at the table and cleaned the gun, then reloaded it. It had been even longer since I'd shot that particular gun, but the weight of it in my hand was familiar. I would make a trip to the shooting range tomorrow, but I felt confident in my ability to use it should the need arise between now and then.

I cleaned up then thought about sleep. My ears were still ringing from the second round of gunfire, and I saw the whole thing replay every time I closed my eyes. When I had them open, all I could think about was the argument with Pezzani. I heard the accusations repeat in my mind and saw the disgust and judgment in his eyes. And the fear. I wasn't sure which was worse, but the disgust hurt the most. It hurt even more than the rejection.

TV long forgotten, I was well into wallowing in my troubles. I was feeling sorry for myself and almost completely hopeless. On top of that, I was confused. I really didn't know who those shooters had been after either time. It could just as easily have been Pezzani. Even if I didn't really believe that, it was a valid possibility.

Now on my way to full-blown depression, I thought about a drink. I'm not a big drinker, but I thought a shot or two would help me feel differently about the current state of my life. The only thing causing me to hesitate was the fact that it wouldn't help my thinking. If I'd been followed to the motel, or if anything else happened, I wouldn't be operating at full capacity. That scared me.

Miranda Lambert was singing about being the fastest girl in town when there was a knock at the door. When my heart kicked back into gear, my brain followed. I picked up the gun off the bedside table and crept to the door. It took a whole minute to work up the courage to stick my eye to the peephole. I was so relieved to see Ellmann, I could have fainted.

I unlocked the door and held it open, the gun out of sight behind my back.

"What are you doing here?" I asked.

He was dressed in the same jeans and button-down shirt, but his hair was standing up in tufts around his head from where he'd dragged his hands through it, and he was holding a bottle of Jack Daniels and a case of Bud Light. I looked past him and spotted the Charger parked near the office.

He held up the alcohol. "I need a drink after the past couple days, and I've just been showing up afterwards. I figured you could probably use one, too."

"How'd you find me? I didn't tell you where I was going." In fact, I'd specifically taken precautions so I *couldn't* be found.

"I'm a detective," he said. "It's my job to find people."

I just stared at him.

"I had a friend run a trace on your cell phone. I called the front desk and asked the night clerk about a yellow scooter.

He remembered the 'old motorcycle.' When I got here, I showed him my badge, and I may or may not have threatened him a little. He gave me your room number."

I stepped back, allowing him to pass. I didn't think Ellmann presented a threat, and I very much doubted anyone who did had followed him. Ellmann seemed like he was a good cop, good enough to pick up on something like that. Plus, I thought a shot of that Jack would taste pretty good.

He walked to the table and set everything down.

"Smells like gun oil in here," he said. "Don't suppose that's a gun behind your back."

"And if it is?"

"I would suggest you keep one handy."

I dropped the gun to my side. "Seems like I need them."

He nodded. "It does."

I retrieved the glasses off the bathroom sink and carried them to the table, where I sat with my feet tucked up under me and the gun in front of me. Ellmann twisted the cap off the bottle and poured a generous amount into both glasses, then sat opposite me. We each picked up a glass, raised it toward the other, and drank. The amber liquid burned on the way down, and my eyes watered.

Ellmann held the bottle to me again, but I shook my head. One was more than plenty. I was still scared I'd need to defend my life before sunrise. He set the bottle aside and pulled out a beer. I passed on that, too, so he cracked one open for himself and took a long pull.

"You don't just need a gun to defend yourself, though, do you?"

I set my glass on the table. "It helps when the other person is shooting at you."

"I saw the security footage from the apartment building and the restaurant. You were prepared to physically confront the attackers both times. In the restaurant, it was deliberate; you stopped running, turned to face the gunman."

"He was out of bullets."

"It wasn't just the adrenaline, was it? You've had training."

"Some."

"What kind of training have you had?"

It seemed Ellmann wasn't going to let the issue drop. And, really, I couldn't see the harm in telling him. It was nothing illicit or scandalous, and he already knew more about me than most people. The time to keep information from Ellmann had been before he'd learned of the fatal self-defense part of my past.

"My best friend Amy and I grew up together. The incident with my father, him . . . trying to kill me . . . well, it scared me. Terrified me, actually. Like with everything else, I turned to Amy.

"She'd been studying martial arts for a long time. She'd always begged me to go with her, but I'd always had my hands full at home; keeping an eye on my brother was a full time job. Martial arts had given her a sense of control, a feeling of security. And after the thing with my father, I needed that. So she began teaching me, after school, on recess, on weekends. It helped. I started to feel less afraid all the time, less worried, more confident.

"I began to drift away, devote less time to learning from her. When I was fourteen, there was . . . an incident. With a boy, someone I thought I could trust. I tried to defend myself using what I'd been taught, but it wasn't enough. I'd been ashamed and angry. And the fear came back. So I went back to Amy. The lessons resumed. And after that, my commitment never wavered.

"Amy has two black belts and will test for a third in a couple months. She's won several championships. Obviously, she's still involved in the art, still studies, and does a lot of teaching. Since I've only studied with her, I've never tested for a belt, but Amy assures me I could earn one if I ever want to."

Ellmann took a long pull on his beer then set it on the table. "The good news is, maybe I don't have to worry about you quite as much as I thought."

"What's the bad news?"

He looked at me for a beat.

"One day, in the near future, I want you to tell me a happy story about yourself and your past. Something good that happened to you."

His voice was almost sad. I searched his face, which was not hidden behind a cop mask just then. I was looking for signs of pity but didn't find any. Mostly I saw kindness and caring. Who was this guy?

"I have stories like that," I said.

I realized I was trying to reassure him. Not everything in my past is horrible, even if that was all he'd heard. More surprising was the realization that I wanted to tell him those stories. And I wanted to hear his. I wondered how long he'd be around, what would happen next, what we would do once this case was over. I didn't know much about Ellmann, but I liked him. I wanted us to get to know each other. Given my history with people in general, and with men in particular, that was an entirely foreign attitude for me.

What was happening to me? Maybe it was the alcohol. I pushed my empty glass farther away. I noticed my hand was shaking. But *that* had only to do with what had happened at Pezzani's.

Ellmann noticed the shaking, too.

"Are you really okay?" he asked.

"No," I said quietly. "I'm not."

He sighed. "I'm really sorry about what Pezzani said. He had no right."

I shrugged. "He's entitled to his opinion. What hurt the most—" I choked back a sob and took a breath. "It was the look. The same one everyone has when they find out. It's like they see me as a monster."

"You're not a monster." He leaned forward, his elbows in his knees. "You've been through stuff most people could never imagine, and you've survived. Most people couldn't deal with what you've had to. They see a person they know they could never be. And they make themselves feel better by labeling you a monster."

Tears ran down my cheeks silently. I really wanted his words to be true. But something inside me refused to believe it.

"I'm sorry," I said, getting up as I wiped at my eyes. "Your day's been stressful enough. Hell, your whole week."

"Don't worry about that." He was suddenly behind me, his big hands on my shoulders.

"Why are they trying to kill me? Who are they? What did I do to them?"

"I don't know." He rubbed my arms gently, mindful of the bandages. "But I'm going to find out. And I'm going to stop them."

"I don't need a rescuer."

"I know. Maybe I'm rescuing them."

I chuckled softly.

His touch was warm, comforting. I wanted to melt into him, let him be a source of solace, but I feared I knew what was coming: the same reaction I got from everyone who knew—my mother, ex-boyfriends, past friends, Pezzani. I knew it would break my heart if I let him get close now and he left later. Better he leave now. So I pushed him.

"I killed someone tonight," I said, turning to face him. "I chose my life over his."

He looked at me, his eyes studying mine. I wasn't exactly sure what I saw in his. This wasn't his cop face, but he was guarded. I worried I knew why.

"And I don't feel bad about it," I said softly, tears running down my cheeks. His hands reached for my shoulders again. "I've done it before, and I'd do it again. *That's* the kind of person I am."

Something in his eyes changed, but there was no disgust, no fear, no judgment. Only pain. He was hurting for me, because of what I was going through, what had happened to me.

"You're the kind of person who did the only thing she could do," he said, his voice even and sure. "The kind of person who knows she didn't do anything wrong."

Despite my tough talk, the tears flowed freely, and I sobbed softly.

He pulled me into his chest, wrapping his long arms around me. I felt his strength, his security. I wanted to linger in it, allow him to hold me up, if only for a moment. Still, I hesitated.

I could feel that whiskey beginning to swirl around in my brain now. It had only been one drink, but it never takes much, and the alcohol played on my thoughts all the same.

I pulled away and wiped snot and tears from my face. Ellmann brushed back a strand of hair, his hand lingering on my face.

"Why don't you look at me the same way they do?" I whispered.

"What way?"

"Like I'm a monster."

It obviously hurt him that anyone saw me that way. Why? Had he killed someone? Did he know what it was like for people to look at him that way? Is this why he seemed to see me differently?

"I don't see a monster," he whispered. "That's not why you scare me."

"Why not?"

"Because I've seen the real you. I've caught glimpses of that girl every now and then, when you weren't looking. She could never be a monster."

His eyes darkened slightly, and then I knew why he was so guarded. It was personal. He wasn't guarding Ellmann the cop; he was guarding Ellmann the man.

He wanted to kiss me, but he hesitated. Without thinking, I stepped closer and stood on my tiptoes, giving him permission. And he lowered his mouth to mine.

Suddenly my body was warm in places I'd forgotten about (places Pezzani's kiss hadn't awakened). I wrapped my arms around his neck, and he pulled me closer. When our kisses grew hungrier, he picked me up and laid me on the bed. (If he noticed the extra forty-seven pounds, he didn't let on.) He pulled the gun off his belt and set it on the bedside table, then he paused.

"What about Pezzani?" he asked.

"What about him?"

"What about you and him?"

"No such thing. Never was. Never will be."

He looked relieved. "I thought you were together."

"No." If I was honest, it had been Ellmann from the beginning. I waved a hand between us. "He didn't make me feel like this."

Ellmann just smiled and kissed me again.

Something on the periphery of my consciousness wasn't right. It mingled with the horror playing out in my subconscious. Sweating, panting, trembling, I sat up and scrambled backward. In my dream, my father, whose face I'd been able to see clearly through the black ski mask, had held a gun this time. Instead of chasing me, he brought the gun up and aimed, controlling his breathing, choosing his shot. He'd always been a frighteningly good shot.

With bleary eyes, I quickly took in the room, which I hadn't yet placed. Then I heard the voices on the other side of the door—the reason I'd woken up. The fear was immediate and nearly complete, eclipsing all other judgment and dictating all behavior.

I looked around the room, searching for anything I could use to defend myself or for a place to hide. Outside, there was some shuffling, some more talking, whispers now, then movement against the door. There was some rattling and banging followed by the unmistakable sound of the keycard sliding into the door. Panic seeped in around me like black oil, blotting out all sensory information and stalling my thinking. My heart hammered against my chest.

The lock beeped and retracted, then the handle turned and the door opened. Finally, my attention skimmed over the Sig Sauer on the bedside table. Blindly, I clamored for it, grabbing it up. Holding it in both hands, I swung it toward the door as someone stepped into the room. My index finger began squeezing the trigger.

"Whoa," the person said. "Easy."

His voice was calm and steady, and it penetrated my panic-stalled brain.

Ellmann stood in the open doorway, his cell phone pinched between his ear and shoulder, both hands full: one with a brown bag and the other a drink carrier. He was wearing the same clothes, though the shirt now hung unbuttoned over the t-shirt, and his aviator sunglasses.

Suddenly the pressure from the fear and panic was gone, though I still felt both quite potently. I lowered the weapon quickly and dropped it onto the bed at my feet. My stomach roll with nausea as I realized how close I'd come to pulling the trigger.

With shaking arms, I pushed myself back against the headboard and pulled the sheet over me. Ellmann shut the door and walked to the small table.

"No, not you," he was saying. "Listen, I heard you. I'll do what I can. I need to go."

He deposited what looked like breakfast on the table then put the phone in his pocket.

It was daylight, sun streaming in around the heavy drapes over the windows. I finally remembered where I was and why. I also remembered what I'd done the night before, both at Pezzani's as well as with Ellmann in this very room. Nausea rolled through me again.

Ellmann came over and picked up the gun, returning it to the bedside table. I heard something else heavy drop beside it: his gun. He sat on the edge of the bed and wrapped me in his arms. He kissed my forehead.

"I'm sorry I scared you," he said. I could feel his heart beating just a little too fast. "I didn't even think about it when I opened the door."

He'd thought about the possibility of someone else coming through the door, though. My gun had been on the table when I'd gone to bed. He'd moved it closer.

"It wasn't just you." My mouth was dry, my voice hoarse. "I was having a nightmare."

"Must have been some nightmare. I've never seen anyone look so terrified." His voice was a tight whisper.

Yeah, so terrified I'd almost shot him. I shuddered. And swallowed down the bile that rose in the back of my throat.

"It's over now," I said. I didn't want to think about it anymore. Fear and panic weren't going to get me anywhere, and I had things to do. As I thought about the fact that I was homeless, carless, and in job-limbo, I felt depression calling to me again. Add to that list being marked for death and mixed up in a major crime, and my thoughts went immediately to the Jack Daniels still sitting on the table.

"Did you bring coffee?"

Ellmann didn't push me. Allowing me to change the subject, he kissed my forehead again and got up.

"I walked to Einstein's for bagels and coffee. I don't know what you like, so take your pick."

I smiled. "Sounds perfect. You know, I'm beginning to suspect you're a pretty sweet guy."

He shrugged and grinned. "Don't tell anyone, okay? It'll ruin my reputation."

I got up and dressed, my thoughts inevitably drifting to my reason for being naked in the first place. I'm not the type to fall into bed with someone I know so little about. The night before was very much out of character for me. Maybe it was the trauma of having just used deadly force to defend a second attempt on my life. Maybe it was the hurt of the rejection from Pezzani. Maybe it was the shot of whiskey. Maybe it was the way Ellmann made me feel. I didn't know. More likely, it was all of these things working together. And because I had no experience with this, I didn't know what to do next.

I joined him at the table, discovering the fortunate news that he and I have similar tastes in coffee and bagels. I took my choice of coffee, and Ellmann had his choice of bagel. We were both quiet for a while as we ate and sipped.

"What's the deal with Tyler Jay?" I asked.

He looked up. "We chased down the leads you gave us, but he was long gone by the time we got there. We've got an APB out on the Honda you described, but we're not hopeful. It came back registered to Derrick Bilek, the dead guy in your living room."

"Little car for such a big guy. Are you sure?"

He nodded. "That's what the DMV has on file."

"What about hospitals? I know I hit that second shooter last night. There were a couple drops of blood on the stairs that could not have come from anyone else."

Again he was nodding. "We know. Initial forensics says there were two different blood types. It's way too soon for DNA, so that won't help us right now. No one showed up to the ER at PVH or MCR with a gunshot wound or any other injury that could possibly be a gunshot wound. I've got a guy making the calls to other hospitals like Greeley, Loveland, Cheyenne, Denver, but I'm not sure we'll find anything. He might not be able to go to a hospital."

"Because I killed him, or because he's Tyler Jay?"

"Either. Although, I'd be surprised if he turned up dead. There wasn't enough blood for a serious injury."

"He split the second I hit him. It's possible he wasn't in the house long enough to bleed."

"Anything is possible."

"Aside from Tyler Jay, how does Derrick Bilek tie to Stacy Karnes?"

He was about to take a bite but stopped and looked up at me. Slowly, he set the bagel down. "No."

"No, what?"

"The answer is no."

"What's the question?" I knew the question.

"Whatever you have in mind about Tyler Jay or any of the rest of this mess, the answer is a big no."

"I don't even know what that means," I said. I knew exactly what it meant.

But who was I to let a little thing like Detective Ellmann stop me?

After breakfast, Ellmann left to go to work, and I showered and dressed. I went to the office and arranged for another night. I was climbing onto the scooter as my phone rang.

"It's Manny. Are you able to stop by?"

"When?"

"What are you doing now?"

"What's wrong?" All my little antennas were standing up at attention.

"You need to see this."

"Now's good. I'll be right there."

It was a ten-minute drive from the Inn to the garage. I parked outside the small, dingy office and bypassed the door, seeing no one inside. Both garage bay doors were open, and four men were working inside. Two were working on a Lexus SUV on the lift, while the other two had their heads under the hood of my truck still sitting on the ground.

"Manny?" I called to the group at large.

Both men looked up from my truck. The smaller of the two wiped his hands on a rag as he walked toward me. When his skin was as clean as it would get without the aid of soap, water, and professional-grade degreaser, he extended it to me.

"I'm Manny."

"I'm Zoe."

He was five-six with shoes on, his black hair long and hanging on either side of his eyes. He had brown skin and tattoos covering both arms, visible around the greasy t-shirt he wore. He had hazelnut brown eyes and a goatee. His jeans sagged slightly on his hips and were as dirty as his shirt.

"Let me show you," he said, tipping his head over his shoulder toward the truck.

We walked over and stood in front of it. The other man, who resembled Manny, was still standing beside the truck. We all looked on, and for a moment we were like mourners at a funeral.

"What am I looking at?" I asked.

"We figured out what the problem was," Manny began. "It was the fuel pump. That's simple enough to fix. When we went looking, though, we found a bunch of interesting stuff."

"Like what?"

"Parts that don't go on a Scout. Whoever's been working on this truck changed parts out of the electrical, fuel, cooling, and exhaust systems."

"That son of a bitch," I breathed. "That *son* of a *bitch*!"

"All of that contributed to the problems you were having. How much did the guy charge you?"

"More than four thousand over the last year."

Manny was nodding his head. "Yeah, some of those parts have been in there for a while. Who's this mechanic?"

"Leonard Krupp. Know him?"

Manny looked pained. "You could say that. Listen, this isn't the first time good ol' Lenny's done something like this."

"Lenny was friends with the guy who owned this thing before me," I said. "Stan vouched for him. How could he do this to his friend's car? This Scout is a classic."

"Sometimes money is more important than friendship," Manny said philosophically. "You should ask Ellmann to go visit him with you and get your money back."

"Ellmann? Why would I bring him?"

"The power of the law. Sometimes people respond to that sort of force."

"I'll be more effective without him."

"Really?"

"Yeah, Ellmann has to stick to the law and keep things legal. I'm not really limited that way."

Manny and the second guy both smiled.

"Can you put all these parts in a bag or something?" I asked.

"When are you planning to visit Lenny?" Manny asked.

"As soon as you get the parts out of the truck."

"Give us fifteen minutes. And I want to go with you."

"Usually I'm a solo act, but I'll make an exception on one condition."

"What's that?"

"Whatever happens at Lenny's stays at Lenny's."

He grinned wider. "Deal."

True to his word, the parts were all in a plastic grocery sack Manny had lying around the shop fifteen minutes later. We climbed onto the scooter and motored over to Krupp's garage while Manny's friend started putting the truck back together. I was horrified by the number of parts in the bag: the thing was so full the handles wouldn't meet. I could only imagine the price tag on this garage visit, and I saw the balance of my checking account drop dramatically.

I parked outside Krupp's office and went inside. While there was activity in the open garage, Krupp was visible behind the desk, talking on the phone. An elderly woman sat in a chair, waiting. I walked in as if I owned the place and dumped the parts onto the counter. They bounced and clattered to the floor. Krupp stopped speaking mid-sentence and stared at me open-mouthed. I couldn't be sure of the expression on his face, but my bet was anxiety. The old woman looked scared.

Krupp mumbled something about calling back later and hung up. As he did, his demeanor shifted, and he slid a defensive mask onto to his face. When he looked back at me, he was aiming for indifference—falling short, but aiming all the same.

"What's all this?" he demanded, waving his hands over the parts.

"Your lies."

"Excuse me?"

"You heard me. Evidence of your con. These are all the parts you swapped out of my truck and charged me for." I turned to the old woman. "He's not working on *your* car, is he?"

"Well, uh, actually, yes."

"My advice? Take it to someone else. I recommend this guy." I pointed to Manny.

"How dare you march in here and accuse me like this!" Krupp cried.

Manny walked over to the woman and extended his hand. She placed hers in his, and he gently helped her up, then guided her to the door. He was talking softly to her.

"We have a problem here," I said to Krupp. "You charged me more than four thousand dollars over the last year, and you've been swapping out parts the whole time."

"You can't prove where these parts came from," he said as Manny returned to stand beside me. "You can't prove I put them there. You probably put them there yourself."

"I keep very detailed records, and since Stan died, you have been working on my truck exclusively. That doesn't look so good. You know, Stan's probably rolling over in his grave right about now, you bastard. He trusted you."

Krupp had the decency to look ashamed, if only briefly. His eyes darted to the floor, and he shuffled from foot to foot.

"I would never—"

I cut him off, because we both knew he would, and he had. "The good news is, we can make this whole little problem go away right now."

He looked up again, studying me skeptically. "Oh, yeah? How's that?"

"I'll need my four thousand dollars back. Plus another thousand for my hassle."

"*What*? Are you crazy? There's no way in hell I'm giving you five thousand dollars!"

"That's fine," I said. "I was recently fired, and now I'm on vacation, so I have a lot of time on my hands. I think I'll put my energy into you. I'll start compiling a list of your customers. Then I'll talk to each of them and have Manny here look at their cars. I bet he finds something similar in those cars. Then we'll get a lawyer. The public loves a good tort case like that. THIEVING MECHANIC CAUGHT SWINDLING CUSTOMERS. That will be the headline. How much do you think that will cost? You won't work as a mechanic another day. You'll have to close. Still, that probably won't cover the debt. You'll probably lose your house, too. And your car, your retirement, any stocks or savings—all of it."

Anger seized him then, and he reached under the counter. When he came back up, he was holding a gun and staring down the barrel of the 9mm in my hand. He looked up from the gun and into my face.

"Why don't you pass me that gun?" I asked.

It took a full minute of private deliberation before he finally made a decision. He slowly handed the gun to me, and I took it. He looked defeated.

"Are you going to shoot me?" he asked.

"Don't think I haven't considered it."

He was watching me, trying to gage my intent.

He sighed. "All right." He looked at the gun. "All right, I said. I'll write you a check."

"I don't take checks."

He looked at me.

"Wouldn't you just cancel it by the time I got to the bank?"

He conceded. "Fair enough. I'll get cash."

"Let's take your car. I'll drive."

The trip to the bank and back took less than an hour. Manny and I dropped Krupp back at his garage looking pissed and defeated. I had five thousand dollars burning a hole in my bag, and I was sure I'd be leaving most of it with Manny.

We returned to his garage to find the Scout sitting out front, back in one piece and sparkly clean. In the office, Manny printed the invoice, and we went over it item by item. It ran the length of five pages and took half an hour. We got to the bottom of the page, and I saw the price.

"That can't be right," I said.

He pinched his eyebrows together and pulled the invoice to him, studying the number. "It's right," he said, turning it back toward me.

Five hundred and thirty-nine dollars.

"You replaced close to fifty parts."

He nodded. "Yeah, I know. It took a couple hours, too. But, that's all on there."

I pulled the stack of cash out of my bag and counted off a thousand dollars, putting in on the counter. "Even *that* is less than fair."

He handed three hundreds back to me. "Take these back and you've got a deal."

"I'll take one back."

"Take two."

"Fine."

When things were squared away, Manny and his helpers heaved the Cushman into the back of the truck. I strapped it down then climbed behind the wheel. I waved to Manny and the others then drove away. Suddenly, things seemed a bit better than they had that morning. My truck was fixed, I was four thousand dollars richer, and I had a new gun.

16

Dressed in the requisite outfit of business casual, I reported for my first day of work at King Soopers, donning the black vest Karen had provided. After visiting Krupp, I'd managed to make my interview at Hobby Lobby. The manager, Helen Auwaerter, was paged then emerged a minute later to lead me to her office.

"Oh, my, dear," she'd said when she saw me. "What happened to your face?"

My face was the only part of me I couldn't cover up. I'd worn a long-sleeved shirt, which caused me to sweat like a pig, but I couldn't do anything about my face. I had put a Band-Aid on the largest laceration, covering the sutures, but there were dozens of smaller ones.

"I was beside a pane of glass when it shattered." No need to explain why it shattered.

The interview was over in fifteen minutes, and I wasn't really sure what had happened. I'd presented a copy of my resume and expected questions about my work ethic and experience. Instead, the questions had been strictly about my personality. If I was an animal, which animal would I be? If I had a dream about having a baby, what would that mean to me? If I could change one thing in the world, what would it be?

How did any of this relate to my ability to wear the blue vest and supervise those who punched numbers into the cash register? I had no idea how, or even *if*, the woman had been able to determine my qualification to do said task by the said idiotic questions. She promised to make her decision by the end of the week and let me know either way, but I wasn't holding my breath. I could only hope the King Soopers thing panned out. Because so far, this job-hunting crap wasn't working out too well.

Karen introduced me to a man named Tony, who was to teach me my new job. Tony wasn't quite six feet tall, wasn't quite of average size, had dark hair that was prematurely thinning, and wore glasses. Based on these factors, as well as the limp handshake he'd given me, I assessed him to have a very sensitive ego. As the shift progressed, it became apparent I was correct. I hoped I wouldn't be working with Tony very often (or ever again), because tiptoeing around and trying to filter everything that came out of my mouth was exhausting. Not to mention, I'm not very good at either to begin with.

My official title was "Customer Service Manager," but that, I soon learned, was just a fancy way of saying "babysitter and referee." A great deal of my shift was spent shadowing employees in various other positions around the store. I also learned being hired to a managerial position from outside the company didn't earn me any favor with anyone, certainly not with anyone who had applied for the same position and lost out. I spent three hours at the customer service counter with a woman named Yolanda who had been passed over twice for the job I'd just accepted. "Awkward" didn't begin to cover it. Actually, "hostile" was probably more fitting.

After lunch, I was partnered with a kid named Landon whose job was bagging groceries and helping people out to their cars. Landon lectured me extensively on proper bagging protocols then stood over me with hawk-like focus as I attempted to put into practice what I'd been taught. He was quick to jump on me when I made mistakes. I could have fainted with relief when he went to a neighboring register temporarily without a bagger.

Taking my first deep breath in hours, I addressed the next customer in line.

"Paper or plastic?" I asked the man. He was dressed in an ill-fitting suit and gold jewelry and was talking on the phone.

"Plastic," he snapped.

I made quick work of the items collecting at the end of the conveyer belt, arranging them in sacks of like items to a particular weight designation, as per training protocol. I was actually quite impressed with my handiwork as I loaded the plastic sacks into the cart. It seemed I worked exceptionally well when out from under the eye of critical teenage scrutiny.

"$98.76," the checker said. Zander wasn't much older than Landon, but he was more laid back, with long brown hair that fell forward over his eyes. He was quick to make jokes and smiled easily. He was also pretty good at his job.

The man ended the phone call and handed Zander his credit card.

I put the last of the items into sacks. The man glanced over at me.

"I said paper," he snapped.

"I'm sorry?" I said. "I asked and you said plastic."

"No, I didn't," he said, raising his voice and stepping toward me. "My wife's on some tree-hugging kick and only wants paper; it's recyclable, or some such crap. I said paper."

I looked at Zander and he shrugged.

King Soopers has a very strict the-customer-is-always-right policy. I looked at the cart full of groceries neatly arranged in plastic sacks and sighed.

The yelling had drawn Landon back. He apologized to the belligerent man while giving me a see-what-happens-when-I-leave-you-alone look. I thought he was sending the wrong message, and I made a mental note to discuss it with him later. It's one thing for the customer to always be right, and another thing entirely to throw a coworker, new, incompetent, or otherwise, under the bus.

We transferred the items from the plastic sacks to the paper ones, Landon assisting and once again supervising. He didn't once mention how well organized the plastic bags had been.

While we re-bagged all the groceries, the woman behind the man made clear her impatience at being made to wait.

The last bag was finally packed, and as I settled it in among the others, I asked, "Would you like help out?"

I'd hardly gotten the words out of my mouth or let go of the bag when the man suddenly jerked the cart forward and spoke over me.

"No," he spat. "You've *helped* enough already."

He almost ran over an old lady leaving another register in his haste.

"Have a great evening!" I called in as cheery a voice as I could muster, waving at him as he stomped away.

Zander had already begun ringing up the items of the next order, and they were collecting at the end of the belt. Landon separated them as I looked to the impatient woman.

"Paper or plastic, ma'am?" Landon asked before I had a chance.

"Plastic." Her tone was cold and superior, as if she was disgusted to have to interact with lesser beings like us.

"Plastic?" I repeated. "You want plastic?"

"Isn't that what I said?"

I shrugged as I began filling the first bag. "It's what the last guy said, too. I just wanted to be sure."

This scored me a reproachful look from the vigilant Landon.

By this time, I was counting down the minutes until I was able to leave. When I had thirty-eight minutes on the clock, I heard an announcement overhead.

"Wet cleanup, aisle fifteen. Wet cleanup, aisle fifteen."

Aisle fifteen is the soda aisle, and there are, by far, more wet cleanups in that part of the store than all the others combined. I knew this after just seven and a half hours of employment. I'd also quickly learned soda is a pain in the ass to clean up. By the time the cleanup call went out, a dozen carts had been wheeled through it, and twice as many people had tracked through it, so the whole damn aisle had to be mopped. Still, I had my finger crossed.

"I'll go," I volunteered. "Landon's got this covered anyway."

Tony turned and looked down at me from the small podium on which he stood, raised between the center registers to afford managers a view of the entire front end. He considered something privately for a moment then grunted in assent.

"Fine," he said. "Hurry up."

I wheeled the mop and bucket over to ground zero and counted this cleanup as my fourth wet cleanup in the same aisle today. The horrifying part was that I hadn't been the only one doing cleanups today.

I dragged the cleanup out as long as possible, trying in vain to run down the clock. When I could stall no longer, I put the mop away and returned to the front end, bagging groceries under the impossible criticism of an eighteen-year-old kid with horrible acne until it was finally time for me to go home. I clocked out, grabbed my bag, and used every last ounce of self-control I possessed not to run out of the store.

––––––––––––––––––

Ellmann had said the police followed up on my tip about Tyler Jay and turned up zilch. This was disappointing, and I couldn't help but wonder how long my information, my perfectly good information, had sat in some voicemail box somewhere in digital outer space waiting to be listened to. Considering how "wanted" Tyler Jay was, he didn't seem like a real priority.

I cruised back over to Tyler Jay's mother's neighborhood. I'd been right the first time about the house belonging to her, and about Tyler being there. I had a feeling he hadn't gone far. He seemed like a mama's boy, and whatever this said about Tyler Jay and his emotional health, it was lucky for me. I was willing to bet if Tyler wasn't at Mom's house, she knew where he was. I harbored no illusions about her telling me, but I thought she might give it away all the same. I just wondered how long it would take.

I drove past the house once and had a good look around. The Honda was no longer in the driveway, and the place looked shut up. I turned the corner then parked so I could see the front of the house from a distance. I slid over to the passenger seat and pulled a book out of my bag. I hoped if anyone noticed me, they would assume I was waiting for someone who'd run inside for something forgotten.

It occurred to me sitting outside the house of Tyler Jay's mother was stupid because there was a chance it was Tyler Jay who was trying to kill me. It also occurred to me a certain power would return to me if the hunted became the hunter. I didn't really like being hunted, and I especially didn't like feeling powerless. Hunting seemed scary, too, but a different sort of scary, a sort that seemed more manageable.

Just after six, a Cadillac came down the street. Mom's garage door raised and the Cadillac slipped inside. I made a note of the license plate. The door lowered and everything was still again. The tinted windows on the newer model luxury car had prevented me from identifying the driver. I watched the house and waited. Most the shades were drawn, but an upstairs window on the side of the house was open. I saw a woman appear and pull them closed. It was the same woman I'd seen the last time I'd visited.

Around eight o'clock, I was tired, thirsty, and had to pee so badly I was seriously considering using the empty coffee cup in the cup holder. I'd nearly finished my book and wondered what I was waiting for. There was no guarantee the woman would do anything but make dinner, watch TV, and go to bed. But I wasn't willing to throw in the towel just yet. Mostly because I wanted to prove I was right. Right about what, exactly, and to whom I had to prove it, was still in question.

I practiced some deep breathing to keep my mind off my bladder and finished the book. The sun had set, and I'd required a flashlight to read. My thighs ached from holding it for so long, and my legs were bouncing. I decided to call it quits. At least for thirty minutes. I'd hit the restroom, get something to drink, maybe hit the restroom again, then come back and settle in for a few more hours.

I reached for the key and turned the engine over as Mom's garage door rattled up. It was up in time for me to see her getting into the car with a large paper carry-out bag, and I couldn't help but wonder if maybe I knew what was in it. I had suspected Mom wouldn't *tell* me where Tyler was, but thought she might end up *showing* me. My heart beat a little faster with excitement, and against my will, my brain quickly added fifteen thousand dollars to my bank balance.

I kept my lights off until the Cadillac was to the end of the block, then I started to follow. I'm no expert in the art of tailing. Turned out, Mom wasn't an expert in *spotting* a tail. So we made a good pair.

We drove north. When she hit College, she continued north through Old Town, and I began to experience doubt. It was possible this wouldn't be a short trip. Maybe Tyler wasn't staying in town. Maybe she wasn't going to see him at all. Maybe my bladder was on the verge of rupture for no good reason.

She cruised past Willox and made a right at America's Best Inn, driving to the back of the lot and parking. America's Best

Inn had been El Palomino Motel until a few months ago. The Palomino had been the sort of place that rented rooms by the hour and did a lot of cash business. It had been run down and as infested with crime as it had been with bugs. America's Best had given the place a facelift.

I pulled in and parked in the first slot I found that afforded me some view of the opposite end of the place. I turned in my seat and watched as Mom got out of the car, carrying the large paper bag with her. She climbed the external stairs to the second floor then walked to the third door. She knocked, there was a slight movement in the curtains, then the door opened. She disappeared inside, and Tyler Jay stuck his head out, making sure the coast was clear.

Ha!

Thank you, Mom.

I immediately drove through the parking lot to the gas station next door, where I raced to the restroom. The door to the women's room was locked, so I tried the men's. Unlocked. I hustled inside. When I emerged, a thirty-something man was waiting. He gave me a look.

"Emergency," I said as I passed.

He looked at the door, no doubt worried about what he might find inside.

I left and went back to the motel parking lot. The Cadillac was still there—one of only a half dozen other vehicles. The new ownership had renovated the place, but they hadn't yet reinvented it as a safe or welcoming place to stay. I wasn't sure they'd ever succeed, given the reputation it had and the part of town it was in. I made notes about the makes, models, and license plate numbers of all the cars and left. As I drove, I called the tip line.

————————————

My plan had been to return to my motel room. My day had started unnecessarily early, and it was now nearing midnight. But I knew I wasn't going to have any luck trying to sleep. My last dream and the experience of nearly shooting Ellmann that morning were still too fresh. So, I hit the gym.

Besides the guy at the front desk, who was watching videos on his iPhone, I was the only one there. I eyed the elliptical but decided I was too tired for that. And anyway, my lower half was still sore from my last visit. So I hit the weights instead. To say I had no idea what I was doing was an understatement. But I followed the charts and tried to work both my upper and lower body, front and back muscle groups. After about forty-five minutes, the fatigued, sore feeling was equally distributed throughout my body, so I called it a night.

I went back to my motel room and made another phone call, this time to order pizza. I showered while I waited for the delivery guy, then I ate while watching reruns of *House*. I deliberately chose to ignore how the pizza might negatively affect any progress I'd made at the gym.

House was in the middle of an argument with a new board member when there was a knock at my door. I snatched up the gun and crossed slowly to the door. I braved a peek through the peephole and saw Ellmann standing outside.

Who else could it be? He was the only one who knew where I was. At least I hoped that was true.

I opened the door and looked out at him. He was standing with his hands on his hips looking as pissed as I'd ever seen him. Again, not saying much since I'd only known him a week.

"Tell me you didn't," he said, his voice tight.

"Okay, I didn't."

He sighed and dragged a hand back through his hair. "But you did, didn't you?"

"It would help if I knew what we were talking about; I could participate more in this conversation."

"A buddy of mine called and said there was another message about Tyler Jay's whereabouts. He said the same girl left both messages. That would be you. But you probably didn't just happen to walk past him while shopping at the mall."

"Well, how likely is that? First, I don't spend my free time shopping, mostly because I can't afford it anymore. And second, if I did, I wouldn't go to the mall. Not *our* mall, anyway. It's pretty sorry these days."

"Whatever," he said. "The point is, you went looking for him. I told you he's a bad guy. It's possible he's connected to Stacy Karnes's murder and the two attempts on your life. But you went after him anyway. What were you thinking?"

My temper started to flare.

"I was thinking I was more than a little pissed the police didn't catch him the first time I found him, especially since it could be him that's trying to kill me. I knew exactly how to find him and had the time to do it. Did you guys catch him?"

He shifted on his feet and his expression changed. No. The answer was a big, fat no.

"We sent guys to the motel, but the room was empty when we got there. The manager let us in, and the room had obviously been lived in, but he was gone."

"Are you kidding me?"

I turned away from the door, leaving it open, my leg brushing past the Cushman parked in its spot beside the door. I went to the bedside table to put the gun down. Frustration was boiling up in me, and I thought it best not to be armed.

Ellmann followed me in and closed the door.

"How hard is it to catch this guy?" I asked, venting now. "Why is it you guys can't even *find* him? It's not that hard. I've done it twice. He's supposedly wanted, but no one's really putting any effort into catching him. Obviously calling the tip line is a huge waste of time because no one listens to it. You know, there really should be a *live* person answering those calls. That way someone can send people out right away, you know, *before* the bad guy gets away. Again."

Ellmann sank down into a chair at the table and listened to my tirade. He snatched a piece of pizza, eating it while bobbing his head at appropriate times.

"I understand you're upset," he began.

"Oh, don't use that psychobabble cop-talk stuff on me," I snapped. "This is ridiculous. Tyler Jay is the most wanted man in Larimer County. I've reported his location twice, and he's still wandering around free as a bird. Free to do as he pleases, which might very well include killing me. Why isn't anyone taking this seriously? What's it going to take?"

He'd finished off his piece of pizza.

"I would tell you not to go after Tyler again," he began, "but it'd be like telling a bear not to shit in the woods: pointless. So, instead I'm going to advise you to be careful. Even if Tyler Jay isn't the one shooting at you, he's very dangerous. He's killed a lot of people, most of them just for fun."

I scoffed and threw my arms up. "What the hell good would it do? It would be a waste of everyone's time. If I find him again, I'll have to catch him myself."

At that statement, real fear flashed in his eyes.

"Call me."

"What?"

"*If* you find him again, call me. You know that'll be faster than leaving a message."

The last little bit of fight rushed out of me, and I dropped into the chair across from Ellmann. When he reached into the pizza box for a second piece, I snatched another for myself. We sat in silence eating our pizza with *House* playing in the background.

"How long are you going to stay here?"

I shrugged. "How long is my house going to be a crime scene?"

"We'll probably release it at the end of the week."

"Great, I'll be able to get my stuff. I know the management company is anxious to get the place cleaned up and another renter in."

"I'm going to tell the boys not to bother with cleanup. Let them take care of it. Seems fair after kicking you out."

"I'll just end up paying for it. She's going to take the cleanup costs out of my deposit. I probably won't get back half of what I put down."

The look at that news was anger.

Ellmann's hard to read because he's been a cop so long. He's had a lot of practice hiding his real thoughts and feelings. But I was beginning to understand that Ellmann's a passionate person and feels things in extremes. So, if he let his guard down, even for few seconds, it wasn't hard to see the emotions burning in him. And he seemed to let his guard down a lot around me.

"You didn't tell me that part," he said. The cop-face was back in place.

I shrugged and took another bite. What difference would it have made? I was still out a lot of money, whether he knew about it or not.

"Did you explain things to the lady?"

I nodded. "The discussion turned into an argument, which deteriorated into a fight. She called me some names, and then I left. I was thinking I might take another crack at her. I had pretty good luck with my former mechanic this morning."

He looked at me.

"What happened with the mechanic?"

"I explained the situation to him, and he kindly refunded all of my money." And then some.

"Just like that?" He didn't believe me for a second. I liked that as much as I hated it.

"Pretty much. After he understood the facts, he was quite reasonable."

"And I suppose you've sworn Manny to secrecy."

"You wouldn't check up on me, would you?"

"In a heartbeat."

"Fine. Go ahead and try. Manny knows what happened to Krupp. He should be able to imagine what will happen to him if he spills."

Ellmann looked worried. "Is this Krupp guy . . . still alive?"

"Oh, please. Of course he is. He's just a little unhappier, a few thousand dollars poorer, and in need of a new gun, that's all. Oh, plus Manny poached one of his customers. Anyway, I don't kill more than one person per day. I have my limits."

"Tomorrow will be a new day. I'd hate for the real estate lady to get killed."

"Tomorrow *is* a new day. But killing people isn't all it's cracked up to be, and it doesn't really solve your problems." I sighed. "Let's not be so cavalier about killing, please. I don't feel good about what I've done."

I dropped the uneaten portion of my pizza slice onto the lid of the box, my appetite gone.

Ellmann winced slightly then leaned forward, taking my hand in his.

"I know," he said softly. "I'm sorry. I wasn't thinking."

I gave a small nod, and he squeezed my hand. Then he leaned back in his chair.

"When are you going to talk to her?" he asked, resuming our conversation.

"Probably in the morning." I looked up. I could see the wheels turning. Uh-oh. "Why?"

He shrugged then reached for my unfinished slice. "No reason."

Right.

He raised his eyebrows in silent question, indicating the pizza. I nodded. He took a bite.

"Please stay out of it," I said. "I can take care of this myself."

He chewed thoughtfully for a moment and looked at me. "What if I give you twenty-four hours?"

"And after that?"

"Then it will be my turn to have a talk with the lady. What she's doing is wrong, and that's sort of my job."

"She's a problem for a lawyer and a judge, not a cop."

"Twenty-four hours. Take it or leave it."

17

For the first time in days, I slept soundly without interruption. And it had been two days since anyone tried to shoot me. I was feeling pretty good. Maybe things were looking up.

Ellmann was asleep beside me, his breathing slow and regular. I rolled onto my side and watched him. He lay on his back, his head to one side, his feet hanging off the end of the bed. His hair was messy and his face scruffy. His bare chest rose and fell with each breath.

I leaned forward and kissed his shoulder. Then I kissed his collarbone. I pushed myself up and kissed his neck. I could feel his breathing change as he started to wake up. I straddled him and kissed his cheek and his chin. He began to stir. He rolled his head toward me, and his mouth found mine. Then he was fully awake. As the kiss deepened, the rest of him began to wake up.

More than an hour later, we were still in bed, tangled together, hot and sweaty, blissfully unaware of the rest of the world. Ellmann's phone rang on the table beside his gun and badge. He didn't seem to hear it. Or, if he did, he had no intention of answering it. A while later we lay together, catching our breath. I had a pleasant, almost numb, sensation throughout my body, and I felt lighter than air.

Ellmann picked up the phone and lay back in bed while he listened to the messages. It sounded like several. I'd only heard the phone ring once, but maybe it had been ringing all morning. I didn't know, and I didn't care. He hung up.

"I have to go."

"Sounds like somebody needs you pretty bad."

"Four messages. Did you hear the phone ring?"

"Just once."

"Me too."

"I can be pretty distracting."

"You have no idea."

Twenty minutes later, he was showered, dressed, and out the door, a slice of cold pizza in his hand.

I showered, standing under the water for a good long time, enjoying the feeling I was experiencing. As I dressed, I decided it was more a *humming* feeling than a numb feeling. Either way, I thought it was great.

After grabbing breakfast, I stopped at the shooting range. I'd gone the day before and run through a whole box of ammo, but this was a poor time for slacking off. As if my life depended on it, I purchased another box and shot every last bullet with focus and concentration, because when it came right down to it, my life *would* depend on it.

Then I headed to Fort Collins Property Management. I felt optimistic about talking to Margaret Fischer. My phone rang as I stopped for a light.

"What's the real estate lady's name?" Ellmann asked.

"You said you'd give me twenty-four hours."

"That was the plan."

"Was? What's wrong?"

"The name, Zoe?"

I answered.

He disconnected.

The questions started forming in my mind as I drove to Fischer's office. I wasn't sure what was wrong, but I guessed it wasn't good. I also suspected it had something to do with those phone calls he'd been getting all morning. I parked and went inside.

The receptionist looked the same as she had the last time I saw her. She barely glanced up at me from her computer screen when I walked up to her desk.

"Can I help you?"

"You know . . . Jasmine," I said, reading her nametag. "Your attitude, and Margaret's . . ."

Suddenly, just like in a cartoon, a light bulb went off inside my head. An idea occurred to me for the first time. I couldn't help smiling at my epiphany.

Fort Collins Property Management is a small division of a large company I know well. Several years before, I'd made them a great deal of money.

I couldn't believe I hadn't made the connection before. I still had friends at Colorado Property Management Group; if Fischer couldn't be reasoned with, I'd call in a favor from one of those highly placed friends and have them help me sort this mess out.

"Is there something I can help you with, or not?" she said sharply, enunciating each word carefully.

"I came to see Margaret. Is she in?"

Even before I'd finished asking the question, I started around the desk toward Fischer's office door. Jasmine hurried along behind me, going on about how I have no right to just barge in, and how she was going to call the police, and harassment wouldn't be tolerated, blah, blah, blah. I pushed the door open. The office was dark and empty. No Margaret Fischer anywhere, and no sign she had been in the office today at all.

I backed out and turned on Jasmine.

"Where is she?"

Blah, blah, harassment, blah, blah, blah, police, blah, blah . . .

"Jasmine!" I snapped, getting her attention. "Where is she? Is she coming in today?"

"I don't know!" she finally spat. "She didn't come in this morning, and we haven't heard from her. I can't reach her. It isn't like her."

"Let her know I need to speak to her when she does get in."

I walked through the front door and out to the sidewalk as Ellmann exited his Charger. He didn't necessarily look surprised to see me, but he didn't look happy about it, either. Considering the morning I'd given him, I figured this was about work. What would it have said if it was about me personally?

"What are you doing here?" I asked, walking down the sidewalk toward him.

He was hurrying up to me. He closed his hand around my arm and steered me forward, toward my truck. I'd been headed that way anyway. I didn't understand why I was being escorted.

"What's going on?"

"You need to leave. Right now."

"I'm not going any—"

"Zoe, I need you to trust me," he said urgently, cutting me off as he pulled open the truck door. "I know you don't do that well, but I'm begging you. Please, trust me. Get in the truck and drive away right now."

He shot a look up and down the street, anxiety rolling off him freely.

A sick and twisted part of me wanted nothing more than to stay, just to irk him, to show him I wasn't going to be ordered around. The smarter (more functional) part of me simply nodded and climbed behind the wheel. I was turning the corner when I saw a patrol car pull up and park beside the Charger. I had no idea what was going on, but I didn't doubt Ellmann had just saved me a lot of hassle. And I would never admit it out loud, especially not to him, but I was glad I had done as he'd told me.

Whenever I'm glad to have followed someone else's orders, it only ever means I am in big, big trouble.

Ellmann said the police had gone to America's Best Inn and found Tyler Jay's room empty. I cruised north through town to have a look for myself. I thought it was a long shot, but I needed a place to start, and that seemed as good a place as any. I also wanted to keep my thoughts away from what had happened at Fischer's office and why Ellmann had sent me away.

I turned into the parking lot and drove around once. As I did, I consulted the notes I'd taken the day before about the cars I'd seen in the parking lot. There were a couple more now, which I added to the list—for what purpose, I didn't know—and several were missing. I circled the ones that were no longer in the lot and put squares around the ones that were. I drove over to the gas station and parked.

I spotted a homeless-looking man standing at one end of the building, two large bags at his feet. I approached him, and he eyed me warily. Probably people didn't just walk up to this man.

I reached into my bag and withdrew two fifty-dollar bills.

"Would you be interested in making a hundred bucks?"

More skeptical studying. "What's the job?"

"Walk over to the Palom—I mean, the Inn, and knock on door 217."

"That's it?" He was beyond skeptical.

"That's it. I need to see who opens the door, without them seeing me."

"You a cop or something?"

"No, nothing like that. My ex stole a bunch of stuff from me when he took off last week. I've heard he's still in town, but if he catches wind I'm looking for him, he'll split."

"He must have made off with something pretty important."

"My great-grandmother's antique furniture and artwork, the bastard. More than the monetary value, it has priceless sentimental value."

The man nodded and looked at one of the bags on the ground. "What an asshole. If he's there, you want me to tune him up for you?"

Tune him up? The guy who maybe enjoys killing people? Not a good idea.

"No. If he's in there, I'll hit him right where it hurts."

There was a single nod. "I'll do it." He held his hand out.

I passed him a single bill. "Half now, half when it's done."

"Deal. Can I lock these bags in your truck?"

The lock on the tailgate of the Scout is busted. It broke the day I took Stan for one last ride in the truck. He'd been at death's door, too sick to work for nearly a month. His dying wish had been to drive the Scout once more. He'd had to settle for the passenger seat. I'd always thought the lock had basically fallen off out of sadness. The Scout seemed to love Stan as much as Stan loved it. Foolish, yes, but turns out I'm more sentimental than I let on.

I'd never gotten the lock fixed. Mostly because my half-assed attempts to find an original lock had turned up zilch, and Stan would never have approved of anything else. That, and it seemed unnecessary.

But I didn't mention this to the homeless man. After the bags were secured in the back of the Scout, we split up. He walked to the Inn, and I made my way on foot north along the highway. I strolled past the Inn and watched out of the corner of my eye as my hired helper walked through the lot, scanning doors for room numbers. I stopped behind the six-foot privacy fence separating the Inn's parking lot from the one next door. I hoped it would appear I was waiting for something, like the bus maybe, rather than obviously snooping.

I peered through the old, weathered slats and saw the man climb the stairs and walk to the same door Tyler's mom had, number 217. He knocked and waited. Nothing happened. He knocked again, harder, then tried to peek in through the window, past the curtain. A moment later, he was descending the stairs, and I was hustling back around the fence. I hurried to the office.

"Hi. Can I help you?" The desk clerk was eighteen, maybe, with a pimply face and a math book spread out on the desk in front of him. He pushed his glasses back onto his nose with an index finger and smiled, showing me a mouthful of braces. Zits, glasses, and braces: the trifecta of adolescent hell. Poor kid.

"Yes, I'd like to check in."

"Okay," he said, moving to the computer. "We can take care of that."

"Last time I was here, I stayed in 217. Is it available?"

"Um . . . let me see." There was some typing and some mouse-clicking. "Yes. It is."

"Great. I left my wallet in the car. I'll just go grab it."

The kid eyed the bag on my shoulder. "Okay. I'll be here."

I left with no intention of returning.

———————————

I swung by my house the crime scene and found it actually *was* a crime scene. Which confirmed my problem was much bigger than I had originally anticipated.

It was déjà vu. There were patrol cars, a coroner's van, and a crime scene van. A dozen people were standing around on the driveway, sidewalks, and front yard, talking and pointing. I could see the front door was open, and there were more people moving around inside. I didn't see Ellmann's car.

It was obviously a bad time to drop by. The books I'd been after could wait. So I dropped by Tyler Jay's mom's house instead. Twice in a row I had struck pay dirt there, and I figured the odds were pretty good a third time would pay out. It was just a matter of time.

With nothing to distract me, my mind wandered. I only made it about ten minutes. My mind ran rampant between ideas and questions, most of them on subjects I wanted to stay away from. Finally, I dug a piece of paper out of my bag and scrounged up a pen.

I feared Margaret Fischer was dead. The activity at the house made me think another body had been discovered there. There was a reasonable connection between Fischer and the house. It didn't seem totally far-fetched to think it was *her* that had been found dead.

I thought the better question was, why? Of course, I still wasn't clear on why the last guy had been killed there. But the list of reasons for Fischer to visit the house was pretty short. Perhaps she'd wanted to have a quick look around to help her calculate what she would charge me for cleanup. So, then, who killed her? She wasn't a threat. Or was she? If she was a threat, what had made her so? Did she know something? Did she see something? If it was the same people who killed the first guy, what were they doing back at the house?

I jotted down notes: questions, thoughts, random ideas. I then circled some and drew lines between them, illustrating a connection. There weren't enough clear connections to satisfy any of the questions I had. I worked at this a while longer, then my phone chimed. Time to go to work.

The lot was full when I arrived. I snagged an open spot near the front (against policy), grabbed my vest, and went inside. My heart sank when I spied Tony perched at the podium.

The day proved to be a repeat of the one before. I spent the first part with Tony. Then I was sent to the customer service desk. Finally, I was paired once again with Landon. Walking into King Soopers was starting to feel like my own nightmarish version of *Groundhog Day*.

Under Landon's ever-critical eye, I managed to bag an old woman's groceries without inciting comments or complaints from either her or Landon. It was the first such occurrence that day. After I placed the last bag in the cart and my offer to help the lady out was refused, a page went out for the dreaded wet cleanup in aisle fifteen. Something in the way the person said the word "cleanup" caused a foreboding feeling to bubble up in my gut. I also knew before looking up Tony was going to charge me with the task.

"You, Zoe! Can you get that cleanup?"

Tony was standing at the edge of the podium, looking at me expectantly. A king overseeing his minions. I really didn't like being a minion. But the cleanup offered a reprieve from both him and Nazi Landon.

"Yep! I'm on it!"

I collected the mop and bucket, as well as several other items, and trudged to the end of the store. I could hear evidence of the mess from two aisles away; shoes were sticking to the floor with each step. I turned down the aisle and saw a six-pack of Dr. Pepper sitting in the middle of the floor. As I drew closer, I could see each of the six cans had blown open upon impact, the carbonated contents exploding everywhere. A foamy mist had settled over the tile in a six-foot radius and was dripping from the items on the shelves. I pulled out four wet-floor signs and blocked access to the affected area, much to the aggravation and annoyance of several shoppers.

As I worked on the mess, I thought back to days past. It was always in the middle of a particularly hard or stressful day, while engaged in some monotonous or disgusting task, that I remembered what my life had been like only a few years before. I couldn't help but compare it to my current life: the job, the salary, the status. It was too easy to long for days past, and I had to deliberately remember the reasons my life was different now, force myself to recall that I didn't want it to be like it had been, not really.

"Excuse me."

I had a spray bottle in one hand and a wad of paper towels in the other, wiping off the two-liter bottles of soda covered in Dr. Pepper. I paused and turned to see a short, overweight man dressed in loafers, with no socks, staring at me from behind the barrier I'd erected.

"Can I hand you something?" I asked helpfully, moving toward him, mindful of my step on the slippery floor.

"You can let me pass."

His attitude and tone of voice triggered me immediately, and it was a conscious effort of will for me to maintain my courteous and helpful demeanor.

"I'm sorry, sir," I began. "I'm in the process of cleaning the floor, and it wouldn't be safe. I'd be more than happy to get something for you. And I'm sorry for the inconvenience."

"Who are you to dictate orders to me?" he demanded.

I scrambled to replay the conversation. I felt he had taken a distinct turn somewhere and left me behind.

"I will not take orders from someone like you," he spat, lifting his chin several inches and literally looking down his nose at me. Quite a feat, since I was taller. "If I want to pass, I'll pass."

He threw aside the barrier, causing it to clatter to the floor, and before I could stop him, he was charging forward with his cart. The cart's wheels rolled into the solution I'd sprayed on the floor and began to slide. His loafer came down in the solution next and continued moving forward, after he'd already lifted the other foot off the ground. For one horrifying moment, the man was suspended in some ice-skating trick gone wrong, sliding forward on one foot, the other hanging in the air behind him. He clung to the cart for dear life, hoping to steady himself, but under his weight, the cart began to veer.

Soon his foot was quickly sliding out from under him. In direct relation, his butt began to sink toward the floor, pulling the rest of him down. He was also leaning to the right, pulling on the cart. The end of it swung wildly to the left, toward the shelf. Then he hit the ground, landing with a *thud*, his body bouncing and jiggling. A woman at the end of the aisle screamed.

The cart slammed into the shelf, but he refused to release it. It struck the stacked six-packs of aluminum cans and dragged them from their perches. Before I could blink, a slew of them were free from the shelf, falling toward the floor. They struck and burst open, one right after another—a series of tight little *pops* followed by the sound of pressurized spray. Soda erupted from dozens of busted cans, drenching the man, the immediate area, and me.

The screaming and explosions had drawn the attention of everyone on that half of the store. Wide eyes and gaping mouths and pointing fingers were everywhere. I used a wet sleeve to wipe at my face and succeeded only in smearing the soda over my skin. The man on the ground was cussing, going on about something. Tony, the only other manager on duty, pushed through the crowd and stood at the still-intact barrier, staring at the scene before him. The man managed to get to his hands and knees, slipping and sliding, struggling to get to his feet. He fell twice, landing hard on his knee. Finally, he righted himself and clung to the cart for support, though that hadn't worked out so well last time.

"Are you all right?" I asked. I tried to infuse as much concern into my voice as possible, though my true feeling was the man had gotten exactly what he'd deserved (and then some), a rare joy in life, I've found.

"You did this on purpose!" the man accused in a shrill voice.

"Excuse me?"

"You heard me! You coaxed me in here knowing full well I'd slip and fall."

"Actually, I specifically warned you against it and told you it would be dangerous. You didn't listen."

The man reeled back from my words, indignant. He looked around, searching for someone in the crowd to back him, give power to his claim. His sights settled on Tony, and his face lit up.

"You," he said. "You work here. I want to talk to her boss. She intentionally saw to it that I fell in here."

"I'm very sorry, sir," Tony began, reaching for the man and helping him to the safety of the other side of the barrier. He was making all the appropriate noises to appease the man. "Clean this up!" he hissed over his shoulder at me.

Placing a guiding hand under the man's elbow, he led the man down the aisle and out of sight.

I couldn't resist the urge to roll my eyes before grabbing the mop.

Twenty minutes later, all evidence of the Disaster of Aisle Fifteen (as I'd come to think of it) had been eradicated, aside from what I wore. My clothes were still wet, and my skin and hair were sticky. I'd cleaned up as much as possible in the bathroom before returning to the front end, but it had been mostly useless. When I got back up front, Tony was at the podium, and the man was nowhere to be seen. Actually, the entire front end was relatively deserted. This isn't a busy shopping time; Tony had already informed me of this when he'd explained, then re-explained, staffing.

I checked my watch and found there was less than an hour left in my shift.

"Hey, Tony, what do you say I cut out early tonight?" I plucked at my wet clothes. "Let me go home and get cleaned up."

"Oh, you're going home all right," he said, leaning over the podium and looking down at me. "Clock out and don't come back. You're fired."

I was sure I'd misheard him.

"I'm sorry, what?"

"You're fired," he said slowly, enunciating every syllable.

That's what I thought he'd said.

I wasn't sure he had the authority to fire me, given we held the same position.

"Why?"

"Customer service is our number one priority here, and the customer is always right. We take it very seriously if our employees are rude or hurtful to customers. It just isn't tolerated."

I was reeling.

"You believe that pompous jerk?" I demanded. "You actually believe I would have simply stood by and let him get hurt without trying to prevent it?"

"That's what he said. If the customer is always right, I have to go with his version of the event."

Obviously, I wasn't thinking clearly.

I jerked my vest off and chucked it at him. It was still soaking wet with soda. It landed against his face and chest with a satisfying *smack*, leaving a wet mark on his shirt.

"Unbelievable. You could have told me *before* I cleaned up the mess, you asshole."

I cut between the podium and a closed register, heading for the door.

"You can pick up your paycheck next Monday!"

I managed to walk out without flipping him the bird.

18

By the time I got back to my motel room, I was still pissed. I'd already left Karen Lerman a message about whether I really had lost my job. More importantly, I needed to decide if I even wanted it. Pretty much everything about it sucked.

I showered, washing my hair twice, then threw on some clothes and hit the door. Angry as I was, I had other things to do. Finding Tyler Jay and figuring out if he was the one trying to kill me were at the top of the list. I climbed into the truck and drove to Mom's house. The house looked exactly like it had when I'd left earlier. I wondered if Mom was home.

I tried to read a book I'd purchased on my fifteen-minute break, but I couldn't get into it. My mind refused to focus, instead drifting to all the same thoughts that had plagued it earlier. I pulled the stack of notes I'd compiled from my bag. I read them, then reread them. I made some new notes, drew a few more lines, wrote a few more questions. This was the problem; the list of questions was growing, and I still had no answers.

Frustration boiled inside me, causing me to think about doing foolish things, like knocking on Mom's door again, and this time asking her directly where Tyler was. The idea of facing Tyler Jay again wasn't scary. I knew it should be, given everything Ellmann had said, but I just didn't feel it. I involuntarily imagined Tyler wearing a ski mask. This was more intimidating, but I still wasn't afraid of him. Then my thoughts drifted automatically to the three incidents in which I'd faced someone in a ski mask. I didn't know who that person was, but I felt the beginnings of fear blossom inside me.

I reached into my bag and found the Sig. Pulling it out, I checked the magazine and the chamber. Then I held the gun for a moment before finally tucking it away. Having it made me feel safer, more in control.

As I put the gun away, my phone rang. I knew before I picked it up who was calling.

"I feel like I should start by saying I didn't do it."

"I already know that," Ellmann said. He sounded stressed.

"Oh, good."

"I thought you'd be working."

"I got off early."

"Where are you? I need to talk to you."

I looked up at Mom's house. "I can meet you somewhere."

I could hear him roll his eyes over the phone. To his credit, he didn't sigh. "Have you seen him yet?"

"If I knew what that meant, I would say no."

"Right. Meet me at CooperSmith's."

"That's pretty public. That a good idea for me?"

"Right now, yes."

We disconnected, and I looked at my watch. It was just after seven. I figured chances were slim Tyler Jay and his entourage would come back to Mom's house after ditching the motel last night. How had they managed to disappear a second time before the cops arrived? I quickly added this to my growing list of questions.

It had also been later when Mom had gone to visit Tyler at the motel; probably she'd keep to a similar schedule if she made another visit. Still, Murphy's Law said Tyler Jay and his pals would drive up in the missing Honda or Escalade the instant I left.

The parking situation downtown is pretty much a mess. If you're lucky, you can snag a parking place on the same block as your destination. More often, though, you have to park blocks away. I bypassed College altogether, figuring it would be a waste of time. Instead, I went straight to Remington and found a place just south of Mountain. I parked, grabbed my bag, and hiked across Mountain into the Square. CooperSmith's is on the southwest corner, and it looked packed. Actually, the entire Square looked packed.

Ellmann wasn't lingering outside, so I pushed my way inside and spotted him sitting at the bar.

"I put our name in for a table," he said when he saw me. He looked at his watch. "Should only be a couple more minutes."

All the other stools at the bar were occupied, so I stood beside him. He'd offered me his seat, but I'd declined. I had a night of surveillance planned; I thought it would do me some good to stand while I was able. A moment later, he reached down and took my hand in his. He lifted it to his mouth, kissed it, then squeezed it.

Oh, good, I thought. *At least I know this isn't personal.*

When Ellmann's name was called, we followed the hostess through the crowded dining room to a table for two in the back. We placed our order and waited until the waitress had departed before speaking. Ellmann leaned across the table.

"I don't suppose you saw Margaret Fischer this morning," he said.

"I don't suppose she's the dead body you found in my house this morning," I said.

Surprise blinked briefly in his eyes before he could hide it. "Why am I surprised?" he asked, shaking his head as he dragged a hand back through his hair. "I shouldn't be. It's impossible to keep information from you. It's like the universe aligns itself exactly so you can learn what you shouldn't know. It's like you have some kind of gift, or maybe just incredible luck."

"It's a gift and a curse."

"Not the best time for jokes," he said. "You're in serious trouble."

"That sounds about right," I sighed. "I didn't have anything to do with anything, but why would that matter?"

"Fischer's secretary said she had planned to stop by your house on her way home yesterday. She wanted to have a look around so she would know what needed to be done when the crime scene was released."

"She go in the house?"

"Yes, we found her in the living room, not far from the existing bloodstain. The sticker on the front door had been cut. We don't know if Fischer cut it or if she found it cut when she got there."

"If she found it open, she could have walked in on someone doing something they didn't want anyone to see. Maybe that's why she was killed."

"It's a theory I'm working. Personally, I think it fits better than most the others. But I've learned murder is never as simple as we'd like it to be and never as complicated as it seems to be."

The waitress arrived and delivered our food. Again we waited for her to leave before resuming the conversation.

"When was she killed?"

"Last night sometime. Coroner is saying between six and eight."

I sighed. "Great."

"What?"

"My alibi is me doing something I shouldn't have been doing, alone."

"What were you doing?"

"I was sitting outside Tyler Jay's Mom's house. It was around eight o'clock when she drove over to the Palomino."

"America's Best Inn."

"Whatever. I must have called the tip hotline around eight-thirty."

"Eight forty-three. I checked."

"Still, not very solid. I suppose I'm in the suspect pool."

"You *are* the suspect pool."

My turn to be surprised. "Come again?"

"The gun used to kill Fischer was a 9mm we found beside her body. It's registered to you."

———————————

Dinner didn't get much better. I also thought my budding relationship with Ellmann was about to change. I was wanted for questioning in the murders of both Margaret Fischer and Derrick Bilek, even though I had an airtight alibi for Bilek's murder. It seemed like a no-brainer bad career move for a cop to be hanging out with a murder suspect. I had to admit, that made me sad. I really liked Ellmann.

After dinner, I returned to Tyler's mom's house. It had long since gotten dark, but I didn't pull out a flashlight to read. Instead, I was left with my wandering thoughts and relentless questions. By eleven, I'd seen no sign of Mom, no indication she was even home, and I'd been left alone with my thoughts for as long as I could stand. And it was probably just as well. Ellmann was supposed to be my phone call if (when) I found Tyler again. That didn't seem like a good idea just now.

I packed it in and went home. Or, to the motel.

Housekeeping had been in the room, as I'd requested, and everything was fresh and clean. I washed my face then carefully tended to my wounds, applying fresh Neosporin and dressings. I read a little in the new book I'd picked up. Half an hour later, my eyelids were heavy. I set the book aside and switched off the lamp. I was asleep almost immediately.

I awoke sometime later because I had to pee. I barely opened my eyes as I fell out of bed and shuffled through the dark to the bathroom. I didn't turn on the bathroom light, either. With only one eye open, I twisted the water on then off again. That was when I heard it.

I wasn't sure what *it* was, but all the little hairs on my body were standing up. My muscles were tense. Suddenly, I was completely awake. I strained to listen through the deafening silence. I could hear nothing over the roaring thump of my pulse in my ears. Too late I realized there was movement outside my door. I heard the lock beep and then retract.

Another, more potent, dose of adrenaline rushed into my bloodstream, and I was in fight-or-flight mode. With nowhere to fly to, I had to fight. Something told me this wasn't Ellmann. And I very much doubted it was housekeeping.

As the door opened, I sprinted for the bedside table and my gun. A figure dressed in black and a ski mask came in and raised a gun. A part of my brain recognized it. The same gun Figure Two had used at Pezzani's.

The intruder fired off several shots as I ran. There was a sting in my left shoulder, followed by a horrible white-hot burning. I heard a cry of pain, but didn't understand it was my own. The rest of my brain was focused on reaching my gun.

I flung myself forward, landed on the bed, and slid, my right hand outstretched. I seemed to watch in slow motion as my hand inched closer to the weapon. Finally, I reached it.

The shooting persisted. Snatching the gun up, I rolled onto my right side. I was already squeezing the trigger.

I continued to fire. I attempted to aim, but more important was pushing the shooter out of the room. I was a sitting duck. It was a miracle I'd only been hit once.

At my return fire, the figure stopped, lowered the gun, and sprinted out the door. He or she may have been trying to kill me, but I'd never been one for shooting a person in the back. I lowered the muzzle and squeezed off a few more shots.

When the figure was out of the room, I scrambled up and hurried to the open door. I heard a car door and the screech of tires, but was unable to see the vehicle from this side of the building. I was disinclined to go after him or her, given how close they had come to accomplishing their task tonight. Too close.

I heard sirens already. I went back into the room and flipped on the light. I ejected the clip from the gun and set both pieces on the table. In the bathroom mirror, I looked at my shoulder. There was an ugly red hole in the front, just below my collarbone. Nothing on the back. The bullet was still in my shoulder.

Soon, the expected blue and red lights were dancing on the walls. I snagged a front-zip sweatshirt and pulled it on carefully, clenching my teeth at the pain. I had just gotten it on when Frye appeared in the open door, his weapon held in front of him by both hands.

I stopped and let him see my hands.

"We have to stop meeting like this, Frye."

He looked around the room.

"That would be nice."

"I'm alone. My gun is there." I pointed to the table.

He lowered his weapon but continued to hold it in front of him.

"Okay," he said. "Why don't you just take a step to the side? I'll have a quick look in the bathroom."

I did as instructed. Only after he'd confirmed the room was empty did he holster his weapon. He retrieved latex gloves from his belt and pulled them on, then took possession of the weapon as he had before. He herded me out of the room as two more patrol cars pulled into the lot. One of them was Pratt. My eyes rolled involuntarily.

Frye took charge, issuing directions. The others obeyed. I walked over to my truck, parked near the office, lowered the tailgate, and sat down.

A few minutes later, I gave my verbal account to Frye. This time, I had no helpful information, like car make or model or even color, no license plates, nothing. The crime scene van pulled into the parking lot and Troy got out. A short time after that, the coroner arrived, parking outside the office. I reached out and tapped Frye on the shoulder.

"Shit, Zoe, you don't look so good. You look . . . white. You okay?"

"Why is the coroner here?"

He glanced over his shoulder in the direction of my gaze, considering the best choice of words. Finally he said, "The night clerk was shot and killed. We think that's how they got the key to your room."

Someone was dead because of me. Someone *else*, more accurately. I felt dizzy, and there were black spots in front of my eyes. I leaned forward and put my head between my knees.

There are people who can go their whole lives, live eighty, ninety, even a hundred years, and not kill another person. Some of them make it without even hurting anyone else. Like Buddhist monks. Who don't even hurt spiders. At twenty-five, I had at least five bodies to my name, and this situation wasn't over yet. How many more would there be by the time it was all said and done? How did those people live so long without hurting anyone?

———————————

The navy blue Charger tore into the lot about fifteen minutes behind everyone else. Ellmann barely got the car turned off before he jumped out. People started talking to him immediately, but he wasn't listening. He was looking around for something, or, more accurately, for some*one*. He spotted me sitting on the tailgate of the truck, and I could see the relief wash over him. He hurried forward, winding his way through people and vehicles. When he reached me, I saw him resist the urge to grab me up.

"Are you okay?" he asked, his voice tight.

"Yes."

"What happened?"

I hit the highlights.

He turned to Frye. "Can I have a couple minutes?"

Frye nodded and walked away.

Ellmann turned back to me. "I was on my way over here," he said. He sounded guilty, like he felt responsible. "I stopped at my house to get a couple things. Then I was coming here. I should have been here."

"That wouldn't have changed anything."

This was a reversal of the conversation we'd had in my mother's basement a few days ago. I'd felt guilty for not being there when Stacy Karnes had needed help the most. Ellmann had pointed out then that something similar or worse might have happened to me had I been in the lobby when Stacy was attacked. Now I was telling him the same thing, and it was true. If Ellmann had been in that room when the shooter had come in, he could have been shot, or worse, much worse. For that reason, I was glad he hadn't been. I really did like Ellmann, a lot. I didn't want anything to happen to him. Still, I knew from personal experience this argument wasn't likely to lessen the guilt he was feeling.

He went to see about things, and I finished my statement. Like anything else a person does over and over again, I was getting pretty good at these things. I figured if this continued, I'd be able to write an entire report in five minutes flat.

The body was removed, and the coroner van departed. Troy and one of the other crime scene guys finished up in the office and went to my room. Ellmann was moving around the parking lot, talking to the other cops, interviewing witnesses, directing the activity. I was beginning to wonder how long I should stay. The fire in my shoulder had caused it to go numb, but that feeling was equally painful. The entire left side of my upper body was stiff, and I could feel the blood running down my arm and shoulder. Had the sweatshirt been a lighter color, it would have been obviously saturated.

Ellmann started over toward me again, and I decided to ask him about leaving. There was nothing else I could do here, anyway. He was a few feet away when Troy emerged from the room and called his name. He stopped and waited while

Troy hurried up to him. The tech held several little plastic baggies in his gloved hands, each containing small bullet fragments. He held them up for Ellmann to see while he talked.

I realized I was swaying slightly. I felt lightheaded, and the little black spots were back. I gripped the edge of the tailgate to steady myself.

I listened as Troy explained the problem. Basically, the bullets they'd pulled out of the wall were too damaged to be useful. Something to do with the way the structure had been changed during the remodel. Something had been added to the walls to help eliminate the noise from other rooms. The point of the story was, it would be impossible to determine if the bullets they'd found in my room were fired from the same gun as the bullets recovered from Pezzani's place or the restaurant.

"Actually," I said, drawing their attention. "There is one more bullet."

They both looked worried when they turned to me, and Ellmann hurried forward.

"What bullet?" he asked. "Zoe, you don't look well."

I pushed the sweatshirt off my shoulder as a particularly strong wave of dizziness swirled around me.

"This bullet," I said.

Then I was falling. I remember the terrified look on Ellmann's face and nothing else. Just blackness.

19

I was in the lobby of Elizabeth Tower. Stacy was standing beside me. We were facing a figure dressed in black, wearing a ski mask. The figure's eyes were as black as the mask. I didn't know the shooter. I was scared. Stacy was screaming.

I reached over and grabbed Stacy's arm. I wanted to push her out of the way. But the gun barked. Her body jerked as bullets struck her: one, two, three. Suddenly her body was falling, her weight pulling me with it to the floor. Blood poured out of her in dark red rivers. It covered her body and the floor around us.

I sobbed, horrified. I clung to Stacy's body, unable to move, to run, to defend myself. I looked up, and the shooter was standing over me. The gun was pointed directly at my forehead. I heard another scream. Then someone was squeezing my hand. I looked down. Stacy was gone. Ellmann was beside me.

Gasping, I came fully awake and tried to throw myself backward, away from the threat that didn't, at that moment, exist outside my dreams. My chest heaved as I sucked in air and sweat ran down my face.

"It was just a dream," Ellmann said, squeezing my hand. He reached his other hand out to touch me then hesitated. I could only imagine the look on my face.

It was daylight. I could feel a horrible pain just out of reach under the numbness brought on by narcotics. Normally, such medications clouded my thinking, causing me to feel the constant, inviting tug of unconsciousness. But the adrenaline that had been dumped into my bloodstream by fear temporarily countered that side effect.

I could feel the worry radiating from Ellmann. I tried to slow my breathing. To satisfy myself I was safe, I had a look around. I saw enough to tell me I was in a hospital. I tried to sit up, but the movement only caused the pain to reach right through the buffer layer of numbness and bite me. I winced and lay flat.

"Don't try to move. Here." Ellmann reached out and pressed a finger to a button I couldn't see. The head of the bed began to rise. "There's no one else here."

He was right; the room was empty. My breathing was returning to normal. The fear was receding. Ellmann sat with me, patiently holding my hand.

After a few minutes, the pharmaceutical barrier was back in place, and the pain had subsided. As the adrenaline burned off, the foggy effect of the narcotics moved in. I rolled my head to the right and saw Ellmann. Even in my drugged state, I could see he didn't look good. His eyes were bloodshot and ringed by the dark circles of fatigue. His hair was a mess, he hadn't shaved, and he was wearing the same clothes as he had the day before. I saw dark red stains on his t-shirt and knew what they were.

I squeezed his hand, then pulled mine away and lifted it to my left shoulder. Under the blanket, I saw a clean white gauze dressing. I picked at the tape, ignoring Ellmann's protests, and peeled up one side of the bandage. I saw the orange stain Betadine leaves behind and lots of black stitches.

"What time is it?" I asked. My throat was hoarse. No doubt from being intubated.

"A little after eleven."

I'd had surgery. Ellmann, no doubt, had been up and by my side every minute since I'd collapsed in the parking lot.

"When was my last dose of narcotics?" I asked.

"I think you got a dose this morning, a couple hours ago. Why? Do you need more?" He reached out toward the call button.

"No," I said quickly. "I can't have anymore. I may have to work today."

"Work?"

"Oh, yeah, I forgot to tell you. I got a job at King Soopers. If I didn't actually get fired last night, I need to work."

He rubbed a hand over his face then back through his hair.

"Zoe, you've been shot. You just got out of surgery. Forget about work."

"I don't want to get fired for real. Getting fired from two jobs in a week is excessive."

"You didn't actually get fired the first time, and I think your boss will understand in this case."

I reached up for the IV and thumbed the line closed. I twisted the line free from the buff cap in the back of my hand. Then I punched the call button for the nurse.

It helped to be awake and moving. The numbness was lessening, and I felt the drug beginning to lose its affect again. I threw the blanket back, against Ellmann's wishes, and struggled to sit on the side of the bed.

"Where are you going?" he asked.

"I have to pee."

"You have a catheter."

"Oh."

A motherly-looking woman with graying brown hair came into the room. She looked surprised and worried to find me sitting up, half out of bed, the IV disconnected. The syringe pump on the IV pole had begun to alarm, no doubt alerting staff to a malfunction caused by the interrupted flow. She hustled around the bed and fussed with the pump until it was quiet.

"What do you think you're doing?" she scolded. I noticed there was still caring and love in her tone. She was probably a wonderful mother. I've never been scolded out of love or affection, and I think people who have are very lucky.

"I was going to go pee."

"You have a catheter," she said.

"I know that now. But it took so much work to sit up, I didn't want to just lie down again."

"Did you unhook this IV?"

"Yes. No more narcotics."

"There's an antibiotic in this. You need that."

"Are there also narcotics?"

"Well, yes, but—"

"I'll take antibiotics, but no more narcotics. Can I see the doctor, please?"

The woman looked at me.

"I'd like to leave," I said. "I'm guessing that sort of thing has to go through a doctor."

"Oh, my word," she said. "You've been shot! Why on earth do you want to leave? You need to rest. You need medication."

"I'll take the medication and rest at home. I have a thing about hospitals."

An hour later, after threatening to sign out against medical advice, the doctor was finally paged. He arrived half an hour later. Tall, stocky, balding on the crown of his head, he wore glasses on his nose, corduroy pants, and a white lab coat. DR. EUGENE ALLEN was embroidered on the jacket, just above the pocket. He strolled into the room and took up a seat on the end of the bed. He shook hands with Ellmann then turned to me.

"I'm Dr. Allen," he said, offering me his hand. "We didn't get a chance to be formally introduced when I saw you earlier."

"It's nice to meet you."

"And you. I'm glad to see you awake. So awake, in fact, I hear you want to leave."

"I'd like to recuperate at home, in my own space." Never mind the fact I didn't actually have a home at the moment. "I have a thing about hospitals."

Allen leaned toward me. "Me, too," he whispered. Then he chuckled.

I couldn't help a smile.

"Is there any real reason I should stay here?"

"We typically like to keep patients like yourself for twenty-four hours or so for observation. But there are no hard or fast rules about this sort of thing. If you're feeling up to it, I don't see any reason why you can't rest at home. Of course, I'll need to see you in my office first thing Monday morning. I'll have an appointment made for you."

"That sounds fine."

"If you have any problems, any at all, in the meantime, don't hesitate to call my service and have me paged. Okay?"

I agreed, and he left. He returned twenty minutes later with the nurse and handed me his card.

"Eight o'clock Monday morning in my office," he said. "The address is on the card there."

Fifteen minutes later, Ellmann pushed me down the hall and to the front lobby, then instructed me to stay put while he went and got the car. I was too drained to argue. I was exactly where he'd left me when he returned. He helped me into the front seat of the Charger then left the wheelchair with an elderly volunteer.

———————————

Ellmann's house is huge and not what I pictured for him at all. Located off Timberline, south of Harmony, the neighborhood is deceptively new looking. The mature trees in the yards are the only real indicator the place has been around a while. That, and the occasionally dated design or feature on some of the houses.

Ellmann pulled the Charger into the driveway and raised the garage door. Inside, I could see an 80s-era Jeep Wrangler parked beside a first-generation Camaro with the hood up. Turned out Ellmann has great taste in cars.

The garage opened to a large tiled mud- and laundry room. I followed Ellmann out of the mudroom and into a large kitchen. It was all tile and marble and dark mahogany wood. And now that I was inside, I could see the place was even bigger than it appeared from the outside. How much were cops making these days?

The kitchen counters were empty, with only a toaster and coffee maker visible. A dish drainer held a single bowl and coffee mug. To the right, the kitchen opened into the rest of the house: a large office, a spacious dining room, and a living room beyond that. A large staircase led to the second floor. To the left, a short hallway led to the back of the house and the master suite. This was where Ellmann took me.

The French doors were standing open, the curtains closed. Ellmann went to the windows and opened the drapes. Warm sunshine filled the space. The king-sized bed was made of oak and seemed to fit Ellmann somehow. A large, worn recliner sat in one corner, a small table beside it. An open doorway led to the bathroom and closet. My duffle bag sat on the end of the bed.

"I grabbed a few of your things," Ellmann said. "I figured you'd want to take a shower."

"I do. Thank you." I paused. "You know, I really appreciate everything, but I can't stay here."

He looked up at me. "I know. I had the motel manager transfer you to a new room, and I moved the rest of your stuff. I just brought you here because I need to do a couple things." He walked over to me and kissed my forehead.

"It can't be a good idea for you to be spending so much time with me. I'm the number one suspect in the cases you're working."

"I'll worry about that."

Showered and dressed, my stuff repacked, I left the bedroom and went to the office.

The office was located in front of the house, the large windows overlooking the yard and street. There were two sets of French doors, both of which were open. A large oak desk sat in one corner with a desktop computer, printer, and other assorted office equipment arranged on it. Ellmann was sitting in a leather chair, talking on the phone, a couple files open in front of him. I went to the brown leather loveseat and sat down. Well, mostly fell down. I lay down with my feet on one armrest, crossed at the ankles.

I was just beginning to relax when my phone rang. I dug it out of my pocket and answered.

"Would you be able to come in?" Karen Lerman asked. "I think it will be easier to discuss things in person."

She didn't sound mad, but she didn't sound totally reassuring either.

"Sure," I said. "I was planning to be there for my shift anyway."

"Great. See you then."

I punched the phone off and dropped it on the coffee table as Ellmann turned to look at me.

"What's the word?"

"Report at four," I said.

I saw the barely perceptible shake of his head as he turned back to whatever he was doing.

Exhaustion pulled at me, and the next thing I knew, Ellmann was shaking me gently and calling my name. I awoke and found him sitting on the coffee table, his elbows on his knees.

"It's close to three thirty," he said. "Did you still want to go to work?"

No. I felt like shit. What I really wanted was to go back to sleep. "Yes."

I groaned as I pushed myself up. The last of the pain medicine had definitely worn off, and my entire upper body was stiff. Ellmann helped me get the sling back in place and then drove me to King Soopers. I was sweating by the time I got to the podium, and all I really wanted to do as I clocked in was sit down. For the first time, I appreciated just how long this shift was going to be.

The podium was unoccupied. I looked around for someone wearing a black vest, then spotted a middle-aged man with brown hair, warm brown eyes, and glasses. He was walking my way with Karen beside him.

"What on Earth . . ." Karen began when she got closer, her eyes wide. "Are you okay? What happened?"

I assured her I was fine then quickly introduced myself to the man beside her, pulling her attention away from my injuries.

His smile was genuinely friendly, his handshake firm and confident. He introduced himself as Mike. I learned he normally worked at the store on Timberline and Drake (my favorite of all Fort Collins King Soopers locations) but was helping out here because of the current staffing problem. I liked him immediately.

"If you're ever in, find me and say hi," he said. "I'm not sure how long I'll be helping out here, but I'll be back where I belong soon enough." He chuckled.

"I might have to do that. It's nice meeting you."

"Karen needs a quick word, then hurry back. I don't know much, but I'll teach you what I do know about this job."

Smiling, almost lightheaded with relief that I wasn't working with Tony again, I fell in step with Karen and followed her up to her appropriated office. I was slightly dizzy when I finally collapsed into a chair beside her desk.

Our meeting was brief. She confirmed Tony did not have the authority to fire me, and that his behavior the night before "might have been" considered out of line. She'd arranged for him to take a couple days off; he was obviously stressed. I asked if he would be reprimanded, and she told me she'd contacted regional management for guidance on what to do next. She was waiting to hear back. I left her office without many definitive answers.

I returned to the front end and met up with Mike, who informed me I was white as a sheet. I assured him I was fine and drank some apple juice I quickly purchased. An hour later, Karen returned and pulled me aside.

"I just heard from corporate," she said. "No reprimand will be given to Tony."

"Really?"

"Further, I'm afraid a formal complaint and a warning for yesterday's incident will go into your file."

"Excuse me?"

She sighed. Actually, she seemed kind of annoyed. "The customer is always right; that's a policy King Soopers takes very seriously." She indicated a document she was holding. "I typed up the warning for you to sign. I'm afraid this also means your trial period will be extended. If you incur another warning, you'll be terminated."

"Let me make sure I understand," I said. I was aware of my tone, but I couldn't be stopped at this point. Blame it on the gunshot wound. "I didn't do anything wrong. Tony was out of line and incredibly inappropriate, blatantly overstepping his authority. Yet, *I'm* the one who will be formally reprimanded while Tony gets a bonus vacation?"

"Look, none of this is up to me." It was clear now her annoyance wasn't directed at me. So that counted for something. But not much, because she was going to carry this out anyway.

I struggled out of the vest.

"I appreciate the opportunity you gave me, but this isn't going to work out." I handed the vest to her.

"I understand," she said, accepting the vest. She offered me her hand. "Personally, I'd do the same. I wish you the best of luck."

I clocked out and said goodbye to Mike, promising to look him up the next time I was in his store. Outside, I went to the employee lot and sank to the ground, my knees drawn up in front of me. Ellmann had been planning to pick me up when my shifted ended at midnight, and I knew he'd be busy until then. I dialed Sadie.

While I waited, I had my eyes closed, periodically opening them to scan the parking lot for ski-masked, gun-wielding murderers. Fifteen minutes later, Sadie's red Lexus IS convertible rolled to a stop in front of me. Powering down the window, she leaned out and peered at me.

"What the hell happened to you?"

"It's a long story," I said.

Straining, I tried and failed to get up. Sadie came over and hauled me to my feet, then watched over me while I got into the passenger seat and buckled up. The soft black leather interior was exceptionally comfortable. I love Sadie's car.

"You look like shit," she said in a faint Southern drawl.

"And you look perfect."

She slammed my door shut.

Mercedes Salois is tall and thin, with long legs and naturally blonde hair and blue eyes. She's incredibly fashion savvy, ultra modern, and downright gorgeous. On top of all this, she's active, adventurous, and fun. If she liked any of the horde of men that followed her around, she could have been married ten times over, and she'd only just turned thirty.

Sadie slid in behind the wheel, then leaned over and pulled the collar of my shirt open, peering at the bandage she'd spotted there. I stole a glance myself. I could see the blood seeping through the white gauze dressing. She sighed and let go of my shirt.

"Don't bleed on the car," she said. But her voice was tight, and I knew she was worried.

I dozed on the short ride to the motel. When we arrived, I struggled out of the car and went into the office. A clerk I didn't recognize was behind the counter, eyeing me suspiciously. No doubt she was a little edgy after last night's events, and I couldn't blame her. Actually, for her sake, I hoped she had a shotgun under the counter.

It was a very long ten minutes for her to triple-check my ID, confirm I was who I said I was, and get me a key to my new room. I was sweating by the end and knew Sadie was watching me, waiting for me to pass out and fall down. She took the key from the clerk then wrapped an arm around my waist and guided me out of the office.

Sadie had been mostly quiet since she'd picked me up. A couple times she'd tried to ask me what had happened, but I'd blown her off. I didn't want to talk about it. And she didn't push.

"Here," she said, pointing. "Forty-two."

She let us in and steered me over to the bed. I mostly fell onto it. She shut the door and flipped on the lamps, knowingly leaving the blinds closed. She dumped her designer bag on the table as I reached into mine (not designer) for Krupp's gun.

Glancing at the gun, she dropped her keys on the table beside her bag.

"New gun?" she asked lightly.

"Yes. Do you like it?"

My gun had been confiscated and taken into evidence last night. The third gun from my house was also in police custody, having been used by someone else to kill Margaret Fischer. All the rest were in a gun safe in the back of my storage unit.

This gun, a Vietnam-era M1911, was Leonard Krupp's, or at least it had been. And I was glad to have procured it when I had. I was going to need it the next time someone with a ski mask and gun came to visit me. And I'd bet anything there would be a next time. How fortunate I already had a box of .45 caliber bullets.

Of course, I'd prefer to avoid having the police look at this gun. I couldn't say for sure where Krupp had gotten it, or what he'd done with it. I'd noticed the serial number was still intact when I'd cleaned it, but that would only make it easier to trace.

"You never carry a gun," she said as she went into the bathroom, flipping on the light.

"I know. But I'm kinda mixed up in something."

"No shit." She poked her head out of the bathroom. She held a bottle of rubbing alcohol and a package of gauze. "Take your shirt off. Let's get that cleaned up."

"You don't have to help me."

"I know. But since I don't know what's going on, it'll make me feel better. Then I'll do whatever you want. If you want me to stay, I'll stay. If you want me to go, I'll go." She ducked back into the bathroom, then stuck her head out again, this time pointing a finger at me. "But I expect you to explain all this to me one day."

Eternally grateful to her for just being a friend, I complied. Shedding my shirt, which now also had blood on it, I went into the bathroom and sat quietly on the toilet while she slipped into nurse mode and made quick work of cleaning and redressing my wound. She asked me no questions and made no comments, although I knew she'd been an ER nurse long enough to recognize a gunshot wound when she saw one.

As much as I would have appreciated the company, I thought it too risky for her to hang out with me right now. And I was just too exhausted to worry about anyone else. I happened to know Sadie had her own gun in her expensive designer bag and wouldn't hesitate to use it, but I didn't want to put her in that position. As promised, she left without protest, simply reminding me I owed her an explanation (which better be good) and ordering me to take care of myself.

I watched around the heavy drapes as she returned to her car and motored away. I hadn't noticed anyone suspicious when we'd returned to the motel, and I didn't think we'd been followed from King Soopers. I was learning quickly how to spot a tail and other suspicious activity. It's amazing how easily that happens when your life depends on it. I swept another glance around the parking lot, confident nothing was out of place.

I put the gun on the bedside table, along with my phone after sending Ellmann a text about no longer needing a ride. Then I crawled into bed and passed out.

20

I woke up to the sound of my phone ringing. It felt late. I reached for the phone and winced, the pain in my shoulder hot and throbbing, my upper body stiff. Finally, I managed to snatch the thing up and answer before the call went to voicemail.

"Yeah, hello."

"Zoe, sorry to wake you," Ellmann said. "I wanted to call you instead of just coming in."

"Okay, sure," I said. "I won't shoot you." There was only a trace of humor in my voice. I remembered all too well how close I'd come to pulling the trigger last time.

"Good. I'll be there in a couple minutes."

I pushed myself out of bed and shuffled into the bathroom, taking the gun with me. (I'd learned a valuable lesson last night.) In the bathroom, I stood before the mirror. My hair was down because I couldn't lift my arm to put it up. Still shirtless, I inspected the dressing Sadie had placed earlier. It was intact and, by some miracle, still dry.

My bag was neatly arranged on the luggage rack where Ellmann had set it. I pulled out a tank top and had it over my stiff, aching left arm when I heard the door. I couldn't help feeling a jolt of panic, even though I was sure I knew who it was. Grabbing up the gun, I stood in the bathroom doorway, weapon at the ready.

"Zoe?" I heard Ellmann call as he pushed the door open.

"Here."

I said hello then returned to the bathroom. I worked my other arm into the shirt and reached for the sling when Ellmann appeared in the doorway. He took the sling and gently helped me into it.

"I'll get some ice," he said. "You could probably use an ice pack."

"That sounds good."

"I filled that prescription for pain meds the doctor sent home with you. Don't suppose you'd want one?"

"I'll try some Tylenol first." I wanted to be stone-cold sober the next time someone tried to kill me.

I dug a bottle out of my bag and shook two capsules onto the table. I found some Ibuprofen as well. Ellmann went to get ice, and I looked in the pharmacy bag. There were more dressing supplies, the narcotic painkillers, and some antibiotics. I shook out a dose of antibiotics and swallowed them down with the rest of the pills.

Delicious food smells were coming out of a second bag. Chinese, by the scent. I confirmed this when I peeked inside and saw the square takeout containers. My stomach growled.

Ellmann returned and filled the ice pack the hospital had sent home with me. I tucked it under my shirt, placing it over the bandage. He began unpacking the food.

"I picked up dinner from Saigon Grill."

"My favorite."

"Good. Your choice of beef and broccoli or sesame chicken."

"Chicken."

"Egg drop soup?"

"Yes, please."

We sat at the table and sipped our soup.

"You shouldn't be here," I said softly.

"Any particular reason why?"

"I'm a suspect in the murder you're working. It won't look good—for either of us—if we're spending all this personal time together."

"First, you're the *only* suspect in that murder. Second, I'm not working it anymore."

"What? Why not?"

"Because of our personal time. I had my captain assign another guy to take lead: Darrel Koepke. I've agreed to stay out of it. Of course, that's only on paper. Koepke will keep me in the loop and let me tag along. For the record, he doesn't think you did it, either."

"That's good, I suppose."

"Except you look like I just gave you bad news."

"Isn't it? I mean, isn't this bad for your career or your reputation or something?"

"Don't worry about that. This sort of thing happens sometimes. Granted, it's usually witnesses, not suspects, but hey."

I sighed. "So what happens now?"

He shrugged. "We keep working the case. I think everything is connected somehow. Koepke doesn't agree, but he's a good investigator; he'll get to the bottom of it. He'll probably want to talk to you tomorrow."

"That's fine. I'm free all day."

He looked at me. "Why'd you leave work early?"

"I quit."

He continued looking at me. "So you weren't fired this time either?"

I explained.

"What's your plan?"

I told him about Hobby Lobby. Apparently I'd passed whatever personality test I'd been given in lieu of an interview. Helen had called to offer me the position. I'd called her back after leaving King Soopers and accepted, arranging to start the following day.

"When one door closes, another door opens, huh?" He was leaning back in his chair, chopsticks in one hand, takeout box in the other.

"How philosophical of you, Detective."

"Guess I'm also superstitious, 'cause I'm starting to believe there is such a thing as luck. And, baby, you've gotta be the luckiest person I've ever known."

_____

Another night passed without any intruders, gunfights, or other interruptions. I felt much better, though the pain and stiffness were still there. Ellmann was awake beside me. I tried to look at the watch on my left wrist, but that hurt. Instead, I shot a glance at the clock beside the bed. It was after nine.

"Do you have the day off?"

He shook his head. "No, but I'm not lead anymore, so I don't have any reason to be there early."

"How long have you been awake?"

He shrugged a shoulder. "A while. How did you sleep?"

"Great. I feel a lot better. Did you sleep?"

"Yes. Do you have any big plans for this morning?"

"No. Why?"

"Would you like to have breakfast?"

I smiled. "Yes."

Ellmann drove us to the Silver Grill. On another day, I might have walked. But I didn't want to expend all of my energy right out of the gate; I had a whole day to get through.

We were seated at a booth for two in the middle of the dining room. Ellmann took the seat with a view of the windows and the door, and I didn't protest. (Another energy-conservation move.)

We ordered then sat quietly for a while, watching the people around us, listening to their conversations. My mind drifted and eventually settled on the first morning I'd had breakfast with Ellmann. I remembered the two cops who had tried to give him a hard time.

"Do you remember our first breakfast?"

He smiled. "How could I not? I've never met a girl who could eat almost as much as me."

Great. That wasn't the part of the morning I had really wanted him to remember. And, for the record, "almost" was a horrible exaggeration. I didn't even come close to eating everything on my tray, as he had.

"Not that part. The part with the cops."

He chuckled. "I've seen them around the station a couple times since. They avoid me like the plague."

"They said dating was a sensitive subject for you. What did they mean?"

He hesitated for a moment. "I had a bad relationship end very publicly."

I was curious to know more, but I could see he wasn't willing to share any more at this point. I understood well how he felt. I didn't enjoy rehashing the details of my failed relationships, either. But, I thought this was a case of show-you-mine/show-me-yours. If I put myself out there first, he might be more inclined to do the same.

"When I was eighteen," I began, setting my coffee cup down, "I started dating a guy named Matt. My close friend Brandi had introduced us. She said we were perfect for each other. Boy, was he charming. He asked me to marry him and I agreed. I ended up dropping out of school, quitting my job, and moving to Denver for him, for the relationship I thought we had. I thought I was happy. I was planning a wedding, preparing for a life together, all of that.

"Everything was fine until I got a call from the doctor's office telling me they had the results back on my pregnancy test. That was interesting, considering I hadn't been to the doctor or taken a pregnancy test. Apparently I was nine weeks along. Then it occurred to me. Brandi and I were always getting each other's phone calls because our phone numbers were the same except for one digit. I asked the lady whom she was calling for and, sure enough, it was Brandi.

"Naturally, I was excited for my friend. Although, I was surprised she hadn't told me she thought she was pregnant, and I wondered whom she was seeing since she'd broken up with her boyfriend a few months earlier. I called her with the news and we celebrated.

"Several weeks later, I was trying to coordinate a time with Matt to look at this great wedding venue. I dropped by his office for lunch, and the lady called me back about an appointment when he stepped out. His planner was open on the desk, so I looked it over, trying to figure out a time that would work for us both.

"I saw 'ultrasound' scheduled for the following Monday. The same time Brandi had her ultrasound. When he came back, I confronted him. He tried to deny it, but I knew. I just knew." My voice had gotten soft, sad. "I can still remember how I felt standing in the office with him that day. I couldn't breathe. I had a horrible pain in my chest. I felt the world spinning around me, out of control. It all hit me at once. All the lies, all the things that didn't quite add up, all of it. I'd never felt so stupid in my entire life."

As I spoke, tears filled my eyes. It was all too easy to recall what I had felt that day, and to feel it all over again now.

"Brandi tried to convince me I was wrong, that it wasn't what I thought, that it had just been a one-time thing. I never spoke to either of them again after that, except once. I ran into Brandi right before her baby was born. She told me she'd found out Matt was seeing someone else."

I wiped my eyes and sniffed.

The waitress delivered our breakfast and then departed.

Ellmann was sitting very quiet, very still. He seemed to have his cop face in place, because I couldn't get a read on him. After a few minutes and a few bites of breakfast, he finally spoke.

"Her name was Kristen," he said softly. "We met in our last year of college, and she was so different from the other girls. I'd played football for all four years of college and most of high school, so I had all sorts of girls chasing me, you know? But she was smart and pretty, focused on her schoolwork and her future career. We started dating, but things didn't get serious very fast. I was way into her, but I just always came second.

"A couple weeks before graduation, she called to tell me she'd taken a pregnancy test two weeks earlier and that it had been positive. She wanted me to know she'd been to a clinic and had it taken care of. That's what she said: 'I had it taken care of.' Without consulting me. It was over and done before I could say anything."

He shook his head as if he was reliving the phone call all over again. Whatever mask he'd had in place was gone now, and I could see the hurt and regret and terrible sadness he felt in his eyes. The tears in my own eyes were spilling over my lashes and running down my cheeks. My heart broke for him as he told his story.

"Not a day goes by I don't think about that baby. I'll lie awake at night and wonder if it would have been a boy or a girl. I would have been happy with either, but I usually end up deciding it was a girl. She would be eight now. I imagine what it would have been like to hold her, to watch her take her first step, to teach her how to tie her shoes or read a book. I would have taught her how to throw a baseball or swing a bat, how to play soccer and football.

"I have tried and tried, but I can't keep myself from hating Kristen for what she did. All she could think about was her stupid career, her goals, and her timeline. There was never any place for anyone else, certainly not a baby."

I sniffed and wiped my cheeks, trying to get a grip on myself.

Several minutes later, I spoke. "You said the break-up was public."

"I managed to pull myself together and get through finals. As graduation got closer, I thought I was fine, getting over it. Two days before the ceremony, I realized I was nowhere near fine. I spent the next two days pouring over every abortion statistic I could find and compiling hundreds of pictures. I put together a very provocative PowerPoint presentation. Kristen was valedictorian, of course. Before her speech, I hijacked the audio/visual equipment from a nerdy sophomore who may or may not have believed I'd beat him up if he tried to stop me. When she started her speech, I played the presentation.

"I managed to lock myself in the equipment room, so the whole five-minute presentation played. Half the audience was in tears. Half of those who were crying left. A lot of people vomited, a couple passed out. Kristen didn't know what was happening on the screen behind her until a minute into her speech. At the end of the presentation, I put her name up, so everyone would know what she'd done. Those two cops, Topham and Olvera, they were in our graduating class. They saw the presentation and know our history.

"She still hasn't forgiven me. I suppose that's fair, because I haven't forgiven her, either. I'm not sure either of us ever will. And, you know, some good did come out of it. Because of what happened, I got involved in a lot of pro-life organizations. They still show my presentation at conferences, rallies, demonstrations, stuff like that."

"I'm so sorry," I said, my voice a hoarse whisper.

"Me too," he said. "Unfortunately, there's nothing I can do about it now."

"What does she do now?"

"She's an attorney. She does a lot of women's rights crap, including abortion cases promoting a woman's right to choose. Not that women's rights is all crap," he added quickly. "It's just—"

"I get it."

When I'd asked him about dating, I'd had no idea his history was anything like this. I now had a whole new dislike for the two cops I'd seen poking fun at Ellmann, and in a moment of hateful vengeance, I wished their big, gay secret would get out for all to know. I also thought my own history was far less hurtful than Ellmann's. The betrayal I felt from my friend and fiancé was minimal compared to what Ellmann's girlfriend had done to him. She was on a whole different level, and I thought maybe I should be grateful my experience was what it was, understanding now how much worse it could have been.

We finished breakfast, though neither of us really had an appetite. When we returned to the motel, I invited Ellmann back inside. He agreed and followed me in. I think it was the deep-seated hurt in our stories, but I felt a need to reach out to him, to connect with him.

I kissed him, wrapping my functioning arm around his neck. He pulled me to him until I winched from the pain in my shoulder. He immediately loosened his embrace.

"Are you okay?"

"Yes, I'm fine. Please, don't stop."

"Maybe we should wait."

I lifted the sling over my head and eased it off my arm, dropping it onto the table. "If you don't mind a few bandages, then I don't want to wait. We just have to go slow."

And that's exactly what we did.

———————————

I reported for work ten minutes early. Probably I shouldn't have been driving. The truck is a manual, and I was severely limited in the use of my left arm. Driving seemed reckless.

My new boss, Helen, was waiting for me at the framing counter.

"Oh, my goodness, dear," she said, a hand fluttering against her chest. "What happened?"

"I had a little accident. I'm fine. It looks worse than it is." This lady was going to wonder what the hell was wrong with me; every time I saw her, I had new and worsening injuries.

"Well, are you sure? You don't look good."

"I'm sure. Kendra's training me today, right?"

"Yes. She's waiting for you."

I was outfitted with a blue vest with an orange logo on the left breast and a plastic name tag with ZOE handwritten in black Sharpie marker. After the grand tour, Helen walked me through how to "clock in" and "clock out," which consisted of writing my name and the time in a logbook kept near the employee lounge. Very complicated. Very high tech.

After this, Helen connected me with Kendra, whose position I was actually taking. It was another *Groundhog* experience. I shadowed Kendra for a while. Then I shadowed people in various other positions.

I spent the last hour of my shift training on the cash register. "Cash register" is probably too generous. It's a large, expensive adding machine. Every item that came through was stickered with a price tag. I simply punched each price into the machine and hit "plus" between them. When the last item was entered, I hit "total," and that was the end of the story.

I learned the population of Hobby Lobby shoppers is largely middle-aged and elderly women, most of them demure-looking housewives working on one craft or another. I listened as almost every one of them proceeded to describe their projects to me, explaining why they were buying each item. I recognized immediately this would get old very fast.

Kendra sent me packing fifteen minutes early, commenting that I looked "tired." This was probably a nice way of saying I looked like I'd recently been shot. I "clocked out" and left.

Likely just out of habit now, I cruised past Tyler Jay's house and then his mom's house. I saw no sign of him, the Honda, or his Escalade. Too tired for a stakeout, I didn't stop, motoring over to the motel. My phone rang as I let myself into the room.

"Zoe? This is Henry Davis. Do you have a minute?"

"Sure, Henry." I dumped my bag onto the bed and sat beside it, digging in it for Krupp's gun. "Is everything okay?"

He sighed. I didn't know the man well, but I sensed he was stressed.

"I can't do this."

"Do what? What's the matter?"

"This job! I can't do this job! I thought I could, thought I *wanted* to, but I can't . . . and I don't. It's only been a week!"

"Exactly," I said reassuringly, closing my hand around the gun. I carried it with me to the armchair, where I sat and crossed my ankles on the ottoman. I set the gun on the side table. "You've only been doing the job a week. And it was dropped in your lap. You have no one to show you the ropes, and you're two people short in your office. Of course things are a mess right now."

Mark White had big plans for Henry Davis, and the more focus White gave to others, the less he gave to me. I couldn't afford for Davis to crap out now. He needed to perform. There was no way in hell I was taking over the Greeley office, and I was getting tired of turning White down. I needed Davis to pull it together immediately.

"We're about to lose a dozen clients," he whined. "And some woman named Patricia Newell has threatened to pull her entire account. She refuses to work with anyone other than you. Do you realize she has nearly forty properties with us, two of them apartment buildings, many of them duplexes?"

Yes, I was aware. I'd been managing Newell's properties privately since I'd met her at a function in Denver years before. I'd brought her with me when I'd gone to White Real Estate. I'd told her I was on vacation, but Newell is the type of woman with an obscene amount of money and far too much time on her hands.

"I'll call Patricia," I said. "She's not going anywhere."

"All your clients love you," he went on. "They're all calling, wondering where you are, when you're coming back, bitching about the people I have covering for you. They hate me. They're all going to leave. White's gonna fire me. Oh, this is terrible!"

"Henry, get a grip. I've been doing this longer than you have, that's all. I've known some of my clients for years. They know me personally. They trust me. You just need to prove yourself, and you'll be fine."

"You're right," he said, sniffling. "You're absolutely right. I'm overreacting."

An understatement, but I'd take it.

"It's gonna be fine," he went on. "I can do this."

"There you go. That's the Henry Davis I know."

We talked for another thirty minutes. He told me the details of the problems he was having, and I walked him through solutions. Unlike at my other two jobs this week, here *I* was the expert; I was the one who knew what she was doing. I didn't have anyone lording over me, trying to tell me what to do or how to do it. For a moment, I sincerely missed the job I had waiting for me at White Real Estate, and my thoughts veered to the job White had been offering me for years. For one inexplicable moment, I considered accepting it. Suddenly horrified, I wrapped up the call with Davis, sending him off with the best pep talk I could pull together on the fly.

21

Saturday morning dawned early and full of pain. As I woke, I realized I was sweating, tense, and breathing too fast. But it wasn't a nightmare. This time it was the screaming pain in my shoulder.

I eased myself out of bed, hoping not to wake Ellmann, and tiptoed to the bathroom, carrying the gun with me. Inside, I closed the door and flipped on the light, wincing at the brightness.

The bandage was peeling off, and the gauze was dark red. I removed the dressing and remembered I'd been dreaming. Not a nightmare, but disturbing all the same. It came back to me in broken, disrupted fragments. I'd been running away. There had been masked gunmen. I didn't remember seeing my father this time.

As I struggled to redress my shoulder, I seriously considered swallowing some of the prescription painkillers with a swig or two of Jack Daniels. But fear got the better of me, and I took more Tylenol, skipping the booze altogether. I went back to bed and tried to sleep.

By six A.M., I'd tossed and turned all I could for one night. I got up and showered. In no hurry, I stood under the hot water for a long time.

When I emerged, Ellmann was sitting at the table, talking on the phone. He was dressed except for his shirt, which was draped over his knee. He smiled when he saw me.

"Yeah, got it. Text me the address, and I'll meet you there. Yeah, later."

He disconnected and stood. Tossing his shirt onto the bed with his phone, he walked over and wrapped me in a gentle hug.

"When someone isn't trying to kill you and you're not in the middle of a huge case I'm not supposed to be working anymore, we're gonna spend the night at my house, and I'm gonna cook you breakfast."

I tipped my head back and looked up at him.

"When my house isn't a crime scene and I can find a new place to live, I'm gonna cook you dinner, and we can spend the night at my place."

"Promise?" he asked.

"Promise."

Smiling, he kissed me, then retrieved his shirt from the bed.

"You didn't sleep much," he said.

I thought he'd been asleep. If he'd been awake, he hadn't let on. He got points for leaving me alone.

"I got enough," I lied.

"Maybe you should take a day off. I'm sure the Hobby Lobby lady will understand."

"I'll be fine. In any case, I don't want to risk getting fired. Losing three jobs in two weeks is ridiculous."

He collected his things and left, wishing me good luck (his personal joke) and telling me to take it easy.

I arrived at Hobby Lobby in the middle of a rush. I was sweating by the time I got to the back of the store to clock in. I ran into Helen as I started out of the lounge, and she confirmed I looked worse for wear.

"Oh, dear," she said, her hand fluttering over her chest. "You look terrible. Are you all right?" What was she doing here on a Saturday, anyway?

"I'm fine, just a little tired."

She couldn't hide her doubt, though she made no effort to try. "Well, I'm glad you're able to work. You haven't earned any time off yet."

"If I called out sick, what would happen?"

"Unfortunately, if you do so before you've earned sick time, you'll be fired."

"Good to know."

So much for understanding.

"You don't look good at all," she said again.

With that warm endearment ringing in my head, I skirted around her and made for the front of the store in search of Kendra.

All three registers were open, two manned by women I hadn't yet met. Kendra was on the last. She gave me the same what-the-hell-happened-to-you look when I walked up, but kindly refrained from comment or question. I was charged with manning a register of my own and did well for the first hour. Then the drain of standing got to me, and I nearly fell over. Kendra brought me a stool, and I was able to continue without further incident.

Just as the rush died down, I heard my name paged overhead. Helen was requesting my presence in her office. I slid off the stool and hiked through the store. I wondered if I'd be stuck on a register all day. So far, I felt comfortable with the check-out procedure, and was unsure of my actual job duties.

I was slightly out of breath when I reached Helen's door. She was sitting behind her desk, reading glasses perched on the tip of her hooked nose.

Before she offered, I went in and took a seat, knowing I'd collapse if I didn't.

"I just got a call from the drug-testing company."

The tone of her voice suggested I should be concerned about the nature of this meeting. If I'd had more energy, I might have been able to muster some up.

"They called because there's a problem," she went on. Or, at least, I expected her to go on. Instead, she sat staring at me, as if waiting.

"What problem's that?" I asked.

"Your pre-employment drug screen came back positive."

"Not possible."

I don't do recreational drugs. And I'd taken the drug test before my narcotic-filled stay in the hospital.

"It is possible. I've spoken with the company myself. They assure me these sorts of tests are accurate. Unfortunately, your employment with us was conditional upon passing that test. So, I'm sorry, but I'm going to have to fire you."

I was feeling a lot of things: confused, angry, and absolutely exhausted. I was sweating, my heart was beating too fast, and I wasn't sure I'd be able to walk back through the store. I've done a lot of dangerous, self-destructive stuff in the past, but drugs weren't one of them. I knew there was some sort of mix-up regarding the urine test. I also knew this wasn't a problem I would be able to fix right now. And I didn't have the energy to spend fighting, anyway. I struggled out of my vest and laid it on the desk.

I stopped and clocked out, then worked my way back to the front of the store. The front door swung open for me at the same time a forty-something-year-old guy started out. He glanced at me sideways as he came up beside me, then turned and looked at me more carefully.

"You don't look so good," he said. "Are you okay?"

I looked up at him as we walked out onto the sidewalk. He seemed fairly clean-cut, like a regular guy. He had a plastic sack in his hand, and I could see it was full of beads and glitter. Either he was purchasing those items for himself, in which case he was the sort of man who liked those types of things, or they were for his wife or daughter. In either scenario, I had a hard time believing he was any kind of threat.

"Where are you headed?" I asked.

"Uh, north: Vine and Shields."

"Great. Mind giving me a lift?"

———————————

After returning to the motel, I fell promptly to sleep. When I awoke, it was still daylight. The room was intact, and I hadn't dreamt. I was still tired, but I felt a lot better. I finished a bottle of water I found on the table then changed into jeans.

My first phone call was to the drug-testing company. I spent a fair amount of time on hold and being passed between people until I finally spoke to a woman named Mary. She sounded busy, but not distracted.

"Now, tell me exactly what the problem is," she said.

I did.

"Okay, tell me your name again."

"Zoe Grey."

"Oh, yes. Hobby Lobby, right?"

"Right."

"Let me see." I heard some shuffling as she looked for something. "Ah, here it is. Okay, yes, I thought so. Ms. Grey, I'm very sorry for the mix up. I called a woman named Helen Auwaerter and explained. There was a small problem with the computer. Your sample was mixed up with another. Your results were negative."

"When did you call Helen?"

"About six o'clock yesterday. I thought for sure I'd miss her, but she was still there."

"Interesting."

"This didn't affect your employment, did it?"

"Yes, I was terminated."

Mary scoffed with disbelief. "Now, why would she do that? I called her myself. I explained to her the mistake was totally on us and that your urine was absolutely negative."

Yes, why *would* she do that? I had no good answer. I thought, all things considered, I had done an outstanding job on the adding machine for my two shifts. And, given a chance, I might even make a fine manager. I'd worn the blue vest with pride (or obligation, whichever), and I'd served the blue-haired hobby community without compliant, in sickness and in health.

Mary offered to call Hobby Lobby again on my behalf, but I declined. She apologized again, I thanked her, and we hung up. Then I dialed Helen.

"It's Zoe Grey."

She didn't say anything, but I could tell she wasn't happy.

"I wanted to talk to you about the drug test."

"Yes?"

"I've just spoken with Mary at the testing company. She told me about the mix-up."

"Mix-up?"

"Yes. My sample was confused for someone else's. My results were negative."

"Really?"

"Yes. Mary told me she called you last night, around six, and explained everything."

"I'm not sure who she spoke to, but I'm unaware of any mix-up. As far as we're concerned, you did not pass the drug test. You are not eligible for employment here."

I sighed. "Really? This is the way you're going to play it?"

"Listen, Zoe, you're an okay girl, but the bottom line is, you're not going to get your job back. I'm sorry. Even if there was a legitimate mix-up at the testing company, it's just not going to work that way."

Probably for the best. I didn't like Helen, and I didn't particularly like Hobby Lobby.

"Can you at least put me down as a resignation instead of a termination?"

"Yes. Like I said, I am sorry."

"Yeah," I sighed, "but that doesn't help me."

Any optimism I had about lining up another job before I needed to give Mark White an answer was dwindling fast. It was time to face reality. I would need to consider accepting one of Mark White's promotions. Maybe I could insist on a contract, put a time limit on the new position. A year, maybe. That sounded reasonable. And it would act as some kind of failsafe for me—protect me from what I feared most.

Still working this over in my head, I called for a cab and got a ride back to my truck, which was still in the Hobby Lobby parking lot. An hour later, I was back on the road in my own vehicle, trying to decide what to do with the rest of my day. I stopped for coffee then figured today was as good a day as any to drop back by Tyler Jay's mom's house. It was Saturday, so she wouldn't be at work, or at least she *might* not be at work. Perhaps she would spend her day visiting her fugitive offspring. I could only hope she hadn't already left her house.

Armed with a book, a snack, and an empty bladder, I parked in a new place with a moderately good view of the house. On my cruise past, it had appeared the same as it had on every other visit. I couldn't tell if Mom was home or not. There were no other cars in the driveway or parked at the curb. I settled into the passenger seat with my book to wait.

While I waited, the book dragged and there was a whole lot of nothing happening at Mom's house. My mind began to wander. I resisted the urge to let it, trying to rein it back in and focus it on the book, but only for a while. Eventually, I just gave up and set the book aside.

I wondered what Tyler Jay did with his weekends. It seemed unlikely he would go to church, but it has been my experience you can find some of society's most dangerous people at church. Maybe Tyler's mom went to church. I pegged her as Catholic. I wasn't sure why, but it seemed to fit.

My thoughts went back to my first visit with Tyler and to the Honda in the driveway. Ellmann said the DMV records showed it belonged to the now-dead guy, Derrick Bilek. Derrick Bilek was six and a half feet tall and three hundred pounds. At least. That subcompact car was intended for girls, or five-foot-tall Japanese people. DMV records or not, I didn't believe that was Bilek's car for a second. So, then, whose car was it? Someone small. No, someone smaller than *Bilek*. Great. That left most the population.

I thought about Tyler and if he'd heard the news of Stacy's death. I wondered how he felt about it. The brief time I'd spent talking with him, I'd gotten the distinct impression his feelings for Stacy were deep and genuine, so very much in contrast to the big, bad murderer everyone had painted him to be. Not to say he wasn't a murderer. It just went to show even murderers have feelings sometimes. Was he heartbroken? Was he feeling depressed? Did he feel responsible? Was he responsible?

How was it he had continued to evade the police? If Ellmann was being truthful, and I suspected he was, then the heat had been turned up on Tyler Jay something serious. It's one thing to keep ahead of the police when no one's actively looking for you; it's something else entirely to stay one step ahead when everyone in the county is looking for you. Tyler Jay was no doubt an experienced fugitive, but he seemed small-time. I couldn't help but think if he could manage to avoid capture on his own, he would have never spoken to me that day at his mom's house. The risk was too high that I could have been a cop. Did this mean Tyler Jay had help? What kind of help did he have?

I went back through my memories of the night in the lobby of Elizabeth Tower, the restaurant, Pezzani's house, and my motel room, and tried to discern some helpful information. The gun in the restaurant had been the same as the gun used by the first intruder in Pezzani's house, the man I'd shot. That didn't necessarily mean the same person had held the gun both times. I considered my memories of the intruder. I hadn't gotten the impression he was tall. I thought Pezzani was tall. I thought Derrick Bilek was huge. I thought Ellmann was beyond tall. I'm average. The intruder definitely wasn't tall. He had been closer to my height.

Hmm. Now that I was thinking about it more clearly, the gun-wielding figure in the restaurant had been tall. And, the figure from Elizabeth Tower had been short. Thinking back now, I thought it was possible I was taller than that person. I hadn't gotten a clear look at the second intruder at Pezzani's because they'd never come up out of the stairwell. I couldn't say how tall that person was.

I felt something tickling the edge of my brain, but I couldn't quite put my finger on it. I thought there was a connection among all this information, but I couldn't see it. I fumbled in my bag for a piece of paper and a pen and began making notes. I went with the same method as before, randomly jotting down names, facts, ideas, and questions then drawing lines between them. I'd found this to occasionally help illustrate an elusive connection, but so far that wasn't happening now.

My phone rang, and I was glad for the distraction.

"Koepke's looking for you," Ellmann said after greetings.

"That doesn't sound good."

"Well, I don't think it's bad. It'll just be a formal interview, an *interrogation*, if you will."

"I'd rather not."

"Zoe, you don't have much of a choice. You can come to him, or he'll come to you. The second way is much worse."

"Okay, I get it. Is he going to call me?"

"Does he need to?"

"Yes."'

There was a beat of silence. "You're stubborn beyond reason," he said. "You know that, right? You know how unhealthy that can be?"

My left shoulder ached and two-dozen lacerations over the right side of my face and arm burned in attestation to the fact that I *did* know how unhealthy it could be. Still, habits and all that.

"Hey, what was the name of the dead guy at Pezzani's?" I asked.

"Steven Pengue. Why?"

"Pengue? That doesn't sound very Hispanic."

"*Ellmann* isn't Italian or Russian, and I'm both. Sometimes names are just names."

"Hmm. How tall was he?"

"What?"

"How tall was he? I'm sure the coroner made note of that. Could you find out?"

"Why? What does that mean?"

"I'm not sure. Maybe nothing. Something's bothering me, that's all. Also, do you know what sort of car he drove? Do you usually look into that when you find a dead person?"

"First, we didn't *find* him dead. Second, we work cases like his a little differently. We're not interested in who killed him or why; we're interested in why he was breaking into Pezzani's place in the middle of the night with the same gun used in an earlier crime."

"You did, didn't you? You looked it up. Tell me, what's he drive?"

"Do you ever get the feeling you're dancing on the edge of trouble?" he asked. "Do you ever realize that? If you do, is it ever in time to back away before you wind up falling into it?"

"I'm not in trouble."

"That's a matter of opinion."

We hung up, and I looked at the name Steven Pengue I'd written on my notes. I wondered if he wasn't the right height for a teeny, tiny, souped-up Honda. Was he connected to Bilek or Tyler?

An hour wore by, and my head was still buzzing. No matter how many ideas or questions I wrote down, I couldn't get them all out. Fortunately, my phone rang—a welcomed distraction. Welcomed, that was, until I answered.

"Ms. Grey, my name is Darrel Koepke. I'm the detective that has taken over the Stacy Karnes, Derrick Bilek, and Margaret Fischer cases from Detective Ellmann. I'm going to need to speak with you about those cases, as well as some other things. I need you to come down to the police station."

As I listened, I saw the souped-up Honda turn the corner and roll down the street toward Mom's house.

"Okay, sure," I said, only a fraction of my attention on the conversation now that I thought I'd gotten lucky. I was more than curious to know who was driving the car. I also wondered why they had come back to Mom's house. "Happy to help."

"I need to speak with you sooner rather than later. How soon can you get here?"

The Honda approached Mom's house but didn't slow. In fact, there was no sign the driver intended to stop. Instead, the car cruised steadily past the house toward the end of the block.

"What?" I said under my breath, unaware I'd spoken aloud until Koepke replied.

"I asked how soon you could get to the police station."

I've already explained I'm not an expert on speaking with the police, but I am pretty good at reading people. Even still, it didn't take any great sensitivity to know Koepke's patience had just about run dry, either with me in particular or the case in general. (I did think I was part of it, though.)

"Right," I said as the Honda rolled toward the corner. I threw myself across the cab as best I could with my left arm in the sling and my right hand holding the phone. It was awkward to say the least. "I can be there today."

I tried to pinch the phone between my chin and right shoulder while I reached for the key, but it fell into my lap. I could hear Koepke talking, but couldn't make out the words. I twisted the key, released the brake, then eased away from the curb while I picked up the phone.

"I'm sorry, can you repeat that?"

His tone was tense, and his words clipped. "What *time* today?"

"Oh, uh . . ." I paused to shift into second, clutching the phone in my right hand as I pulled back on the shifter. "I'm not sure."

I watched as the Honda turned right, disappearing from view.

"Listen, I really need to go," I said. "I'm sorry. I'll get over there as soon as I can."

"Ms. Grey, I don't get the impression this is a priority for you. Now, I understand you have a personal relationship with Detective Ellmann, but I will not extend any courtesies to you because of that. Do you understand? I will treat you the same way I treat all the other suspects in my cases. Is that clear?"

Suspect. Wonderful. It never sounded any better, no matter how many times I heard it.

"Crystal."

I stopped at the stop sign and shifted back to first, easing around the corner. I spotted the Honda a couple blocks ahead.

"One last note, then," Koepke said. "I will speak with you one way or the other. The easy way is for you to come to the station yourself. The hard way will not end as well."

I shifted to second.

"A threat—got it. Absolutely clear, Detective. Shall I call before I come in?"

"I'll give you until five o'clock, Ms. Grey. After that, it's the hard way."

"Okay, great. Thank you so much for calling."

I punched the END button and dropped the phone into the cup holder.

What a day this was shaping up to be. I was likely to find Tyler Jay for the third time. And there was a real chance Ellmann wouldn't be able to make good on his promise to pick up Jay if I did. That would mean the police would miss him for the third time, and I'd still be out the reward money. Not to mention, Jay might be the one trying to kill me, and if the police missed him again, he'd have more time to try to accomplish his goal. It was also a real possibility Koepke wasn't as inclined to believe in my innocence as Ellmann had claimed. In which case, I was likely to walk into the police station and not walk out, because instead I'd be arrested for murder, with maybe a few other charges thrown in.

Yes, overall, this vacation blew big time. There had been no sleeping in, no lounging around, no reading books, or watching TV. So far, all I'd gotten were crack-of-dawn wake-ups, assault with a deadly weapon, embezzlement, a couple police investigations, a family quarrel, a hasty move, the loss of three jobs, mechanical trouble and extortion, an attempted murder, a gunshot wound and surgery, suspicion of murder, and a manhunt.

22

The Honda drove through town to Highway 14 and turned east. It went as far as I-25, where it pulled off into the parking lot of a Motel 6. I followed at a fair distance, and, for fear of being spotted, I waited for an unnecessarily long break in oncoming traffic before I turned left and went into the same parking lot. By the time I drove around the building, the Honda was parked and the driver was already inside. I hadn't seen where he or she had gone. The Honda was parked in the middle of the rather-full parking lot. It was impossible to know which room the driver had entered.

I cruised over to the Waffle House next door. The restaurant had a great view of the backside of the motel. Inside, I snagged a window seat and sat facing the door. I could see the Honda and most of the doors on that side of the building.

I only ordered coffee from the waitress, who was obviously disappointed the ticket (and thus the tip) wouldn't be larger. But I couldn't order a meal. Who knew how long I'd be here.

As I studied the motel parking lot, I thought back to America's Best Inn. It might have been premature to say Tyler Jay was known to stay in motels, but I could say it wasn't unheard of. I couldn't be certain he was in this one, but I had a feeling he was. That was it—just a feeling, intuition, nothing more. Intuition was enough for me, but I didn't think it would fly with anyone else, like Ellmann.

I had a pretty clear view of most the vehicles on this side of the lot. I pulled the notes out of my bag and looked over the makes, models, and license plate numbers I'd recorded for the cars parked outside the Inn the night I'd spotted Tyler Jay. I ran through the list, comparing them. I found none in common except one. There was a white Saturn sitting two spaces down from the Honda, with the same license plate as the white Saturn that had been parked outside the Inn when Tyler's mom had dropped by with dinner. Incidentally, it had also been a little white car that had been the getaway car for the shooter in the restaurant.

No such thing as coincidence, I thought.

The waitress warmed my coffee as my phone rang. I dug it out and checked the ID before answering, wanting to avoid another phone call from Koepke, who was, sadly, probably not one of my biggest fans. It was Ellmann.

"Did you get that information?" I asked.

"Did you really blow Koepke off when he called you about coming in?" Ellmann's voice was tight, angry. It also held a note of fear. I thought that was probably bad news, though very interesting.

"No, I didn't *blow* him *off*. I was trying to drive, and I'm already an arm short; I needed to get off the phone. It's dangerous to talk on the phone and drive, even under the best conditions. I told him I would come in, and I will."

"Zoe, you understand this isn't something you can just blow off, right? This won't just go away."

"First of all, yes, I'm aware of that, if for no other reason than that I'm no stranger to trouble. I know how it works. Second, blowing things off and burying my head in the sand, as appealing as it sounds most the time, isn't my style. I'm a face-the-music type of girl. Now, either tell me why you're worried, or let's talk about something else. I'm not up for lecturing today."

"I'm not worried," he lied.

"New topic it is. What did you find out? How tall was Pengue, and what kind of car did he drive?"

A heavy sigh. "His driver's license says he was six feet, but the coroner notes him as being five-nine."

"What about the car? What'd he drive?"

I thought I knew. Intuition again.

"DMV reports him owning a 2002 four-door Saturn, white."

Bingo!

"How does Pengue connect to Bilek or Tyler Jay or Stacy Karnes?"

"Zoe, I can't be discussing this with you. I'm already way over the line as it is." The tension in his voice ratcheted up a notch.

"One last chance to tell me what you're worried about."

"Will you please just come in and talk to Koepke? The longer you avoid him, the worse it looks. And you can't afford for things to look any worse right now."

"What does that mean? Either I look like a murder suspect or I don't."

"I really can't discuss it."

"I get the feeling the rest of the conversation will just repeat from here. I'm hanging up. I'll talk to you later."

I sat in the Waffle House long enough to have ordered three meals and consumed them without interruption. There were the occasional nasty looks from the waitress as I sipped the coffee and read my book, which I took in stride, smiling and occasionally waving when the look was especially dark. I took frequent breaks from reading to jot down more notes or reread existing notes for the hundredth time. I made a few new connecting lines or circles or boxes or question marks, but no life-changing, earth-shattering, case-breaking insights came along. The elusive tickling at the edge of my mind persisted.

I was holding the pen, staring at the name TYLER JAY, when I saw movement out of the corner of my eye. I turned and saw door number nineteen open. Tyler Jay and another man of similar age, who looked vaguely familiar, walked out and climbed in the Saturn.

"Shit!" I hissed.

I scrambled out of my seat as if it had suddenly caught fire. As I ran for the front door, I worked to stuff the book and the notes into my bag, an awkward and painful task with the limited use of my left arm. Fortunately, I'd already had cash on the table to cover the bill and a generous tip. I sprinted for the truck and threw myself and my bag inside. I pulled out of the parking space as the Saturn turned onto the highway heading west.

I checked for oncoming cars then eased out of the parking lot. When I'd found a comfortable position in traffic and a speed to match the Saturn's, I lifted the sling over my head then gently pulled it off my arm, dropping it on the seat beside me. I retrieved my phone and dialed Ellmann. Then I held it in my left hand and winced against the pain as I struggled to lift my stiff arm. Finally, the phone was near enough my ear I could hear almost everything.

"Please tell me you're calling because you're on your way to the police station."

I glanced at the clock. 4:16. I had little doubt I'd miss my five o'clock deadline. Well, I've never been one to take the easy route.

"No. Sorry. I found Tyler Jay."

I could hear the strain in my voice as I struggled against the pain in my shoulder.

There was silence for a beat. "Again?"

"Yeah."

"How?"

The Saturn changed lanes, and I thought they were preparing to leave the highway.

"I don't have time for details just now. He's headed west on Highway 14, approaching Riverside. Can you come get him?"

"You don't sound so good." There was concern in his voice. It was different than the worry that had been there earlier.

"I'm fine. He's turning left onto Riverside."

"You're following him." It wasn't a question.

"Yes. I feel like I should explain. We'll have to do that later."

Sweat had broken out across my face and chest at the pain.

"Pull over now. Do not pursue him. He's dangerous."

"Maybe. But he's slippery. You need to know where he's going if you're going to catch him."

"Damnit, Zoe." I heard a muttered string of curses.

I wish I could say this was the first time Ellmann had cursed me.

"Okay, now a right on Prospect," I reported. "Where are you, exactly?"

There was another silence, this one longer.

Then I knew.

"You're not coming, are you?"

"Zoe, there are things I can't tell you," he began.

"That's just great, Ellmann. I have to go; I have to call the tip line."

"Zoe, wait, don't hang up. Please, Zoe—"

I hung up.

The Saturn turned south on Lemay. I sat two cars back feeling a rush of emotion and a whirlwind of thoughts blowing through my mind. What the hell was going on?

The Saturn rolled through town and I followed, staying far enough back I was certain I wouldn't be spotted. Ten minutes later, we were in a familiar neighborhood, and I had a pretty good idea where we were going. I dropped back even farther. Two minutes later, I caught up with the Saturn, finding it parked outside Stacy Karnes's house. The driver and Tyler Jay were nowhere to be seen. I parked behind an SUV one block over, where I could see the front of the house, then picked up my phone and dialed. The tip line message began to play. I only heard the first part.

Through the open driver's-side window, a gun barrel reached in and touched my temple. I knew without looking the person holding it would be dressed in black from head to toe, replete with a ski mask. I couldn't figure out where he or she had come from.

"Hands up." The gunman (or gunwoman) was intentionally attempting to mask his or her voice, speaking in a husky, whispered croak. It was impossible for me to determine if the speaker was male or female.

Turning my head ever so slightly to the left, I could better see the position of the figure. I was ninety-eight percent sure he or she couldn't see my right hand or the phone I was holding. Carefully, mindful not to be noticed, I lowered my right hand and pushed the phone into my pants pocket as I slowly worked to raise my left, praying the call hadn't been cut off.

"Both hands," the gunman clarified.

I continued to work on the left and raised the right.

"Where'd you come from?" I asked, sincerely curious.

"No questions. Get out of the truck."

"Mmm, no, I'd rather not."

The gun dug deeper into my temple.

"It isn't an option."

"Actually, it is," I said, working to ignore the bite of the steel against my skin. "If you're going to shoot me, I'd rather you do it here, in this semipublic place outside Stacy's house, where the chances of you being caught are just that much higher."

My mouth was dry. I had absolutely no doubt this person had every intention of shooting me. Shooting me *dead.* It was very unsettling to think of myself dead. I'd been slightly cavalier about that outcome previously, but I wasn't nearly so confident now. My advantages were next to nil. I was in serious trouble. As an expert in trouble, I could recognize that fact. Panic crept in, and it was all I could do to resist succumbing to it.

The gunman scoffed. "I heard you were stubborn. Won't quit, won't shut up, won't go away, won't die."

"Add 'won't cooperate' to that list."

"You're going to want to cooperate. There are worse things I can do to you than just kill you."

"Oh, you mean torture?"

There was no verbal response, but I got the message all the same.

"I hate to correct you again, but I'm afraid you're wrong. Torturing me will only give the police more time to find me and, by extension, you. Again, that works in my favor."

"No one is even going to think to look for you until it's too late."

"Uh, no, I'm afraid that isn't true, either. See, I have an appointment with a detective at the police station in a few minutes. Coincidentally, the detective looking for *you.* Anyway, he's promised to send out everyone short of the National Guard to find me if I don't make that appointment." I lowered my voice as if I was confiding something of top-secret importance. "I'm a suspect in your crimes. If I don't show up, I'm sure an arrest warrant will be waiting."

"You're lying."

The gunman didn't sound sure.

"No, I'm sorry, I wish I was. You don't know how much I wish I was. I'm pretty sure I'll be arrested. The charges might be dropped later, I don't know, but I don't think I'll walk out of the police station tonight. Believe me, I'm not looking forward to that. I don't like jail. Plus, I hate the color orange."

"You are such a pain in the ass. Has anyone ever tried to kill you before?"

"Unfortunately, yes. But it was a long time ago, so I hardly count it."

"Not surprising. Now, get out of the truck."

"What are we going to do if I get out of the truck? Are we going somewhere else? Are we going inside Stacy's house? Are we going to another house around here? What exactly is your plan?"

"Stop asking questions. Stop talking. Just *stop*. Do as you're told. Get out of the truck."

"Oh, you should add 'won't take orders' to your list. I've just never been good at it. I'm sorry."

"You think you're funny? You think this is some kind of joke?" The gun dug into my temple, and I tried to lean away, wincing at the pain in my shoulder. I fell onto my right elbow on the seat. "This isn't a joke, okay? This is for real."

I heard the sound of shoes on the pavement: heels. They were moving fast. I couldn't see anything from my position on the seat. I went to sit up. At the same time, the truck door was wrenched open, and I felt a hand on my left arm, forcing me back down. I cried out at the pain, little white bursts of light erupting behind my eyelids. Then I felt something cold and hard press into my neck, and everything went black.

————————————

When I came back around, my shoulder was screaming in pain. The entire left side of my torso throbbed with it. I could feel a layer of sweat covering my body. I opened my eyes, but all I saw was blackness. I blinked several times as I shook loose the last of the cobwebs. Then I was sure—I was awake, and my eyes were open. It was just pitch black.

I was lying on a hard, cold floor, something like concrete or stone. My hands were secured behind my back with handcuffs. I was on my right side, but the strain on my left shoulder from the twisted angle was horribly painful. The air was musky and dank, ripe with the earthy scents of dirt. As far as I could tell, everything was still—no movement, no sound, no breeze. And this place was cold. I thought that narrowed the possibilities of where I'd been taken.

The complete absence of light was unnerving and incredibly disorienting. I'm not afraid of the dark. I don't believe in ghosts. I'm not particularly upset by bugs or rodents, although I didn't like the idea of either. But the impact of perfect darkness on one's psyche is a well-documented phenomenon. Two minutes after waking up, I realized I'd be no exception. The panic I'd been feeling earlier was back and had increased exponentially. I was having more and more difficulty keeping it at bay.

I may have been down, but I wasn't ready to count myself out just yet. I knew I'd be as good as dead if I lost control and succumbed to the panic.

All I really needed to do was stall for time. Time enough for a rescue or an escape. The exchange in the truck had been recorded on the tip line after I'd dropped the phone into my pocket; I was sure. Or, I had to hope, anyway. Of course, I realized it was stupid to bank on such a hope, considering it was my life hanging in the balance.

I had a feeling I was no longer at Stacy Karnes's house. That being true, if someone did eventually get my message and figure out it wasn't a prank, the police would now have to track me down. In which case, I sincerely hoped they had more information than I did, more information than I thought they did, and that there were a limited number of places I could be right now.

I was also sure my five o'clock deadline had past. I prayed Koepke would make good on his threat and come looking for me. Even if he showed up with an arrest warrant in one hand and handcuffs in the other, I'd be damn glad to see him.

Struggling, biting my lip to keep from screaming in pain, I worked to sit up. Every time I pushed with my right arm, the cuffs pulled my left and made me dizzy, the pain in my shoulder white-hot. It was a real possibility the stitches had been pulled loose. Finally, I got myself sitting up, my arms cuffed behind me, my legs straight out in front of me. I sat bent forward at the waist, panting and sweating, trying to suck in air and fight off the vertigo and nausea.

After a moment of recovery, I turned back to business. I wanted to know if the phone was still in my pocket. I thought the chances were good the phone had been discovered and taken from me while I was unconscious, which I guessed had come from a stun gun. If I still had the phone, perhaps it would be possible to make a call.

Wincing at the pain, I reached down with my right hand, pulling my left along. I felt my pocket, finding it empty. I sighed and sagged forward. I hadn't really expected it to be there, but I couldn't deny the disappointment. The disappointment only served to fuel the panic, however, so I quickly switched gears.

Time to start thinking about how to get out of here. A rescue would be great, but I wasn't willing to put all my eggs in Koepke's basket and sit around waiting for him to show up. For all I knew, he was all bark and no bite, and had no intention whatsoever of tracking me down and hauling me in for questioning.

I needed to get up. Then I could feel around the room and perhaps find a door. There was always the chance they hadn't bothered to lock the door because they thought I was unconscious. Or maybe they assumed I'd be too weak to get off the floor even if I did wake up. Whoever I had talked to in the truck outside Stacy's house had seemed mostly cocky, until I'd cracked that confidence and instilled doubt. Cockiness would lead a person to make a silly mistake and underestimate an opponent. A silly mistake like leaving the door unlocked.

It was thin, oh so thin, but it was all I had. Either that, or wait. And I've never really been much for waiting. I tried standing straight up, but the pain in my shoulder made balance all but impossible, and I kept falling back down. Instead, I tried getting to my knees. It took a couple tries, but I finally got it and was able to stand from there.

I was panting, doubled over at the waist, sucking in breath. The air was stale and rank, and I felt like it was difficult to breathe. I decided this was the panic playing to my fears, so I quickly worked to put it out of my mind. Even if it was getting harder to breathe, if I was running out of oxygen, thinking about it—*worrying* about it—wasn't going to get me anywhere.

When I could stand upright again, my left shoulder sagging uselessly against the restraint, I began to move. My best interpretation of my senses was that this was some kind of cellar or basement. I got the distinct impression it was below ground, and I was definitely inside. Operating on that conclusion, I began moving very slowly.

Being unable to see where I was going was a huge hindrance to the process. I was afraid to move, afraid I'd run into something I'd prefer not to. I was also afraid of knocking something over, or causing some other kind of noise that would alert my captors to the fact that I was awake. I shuffled forward inch by inch, leading with my right shoulder. Whatever I ran up against, I didn't want to lead with my face.

In order to keep the panic from settling in, I tried to keep my brain moving. Questions seemed the easiest way of accomplishing this. The first, most-obvious question was, who took me? The next was, why? I didn't think the person who had appeared at the truck had come after me before. The way they spoke, the way they commented about my reported reputation, made me think they had no personal experience. I like to think of myself as memorable. At least, I thought I would be memorable to a person who had confronted me in the lobby of an apartment building, chased me through a restaurant with a gun, or showed up at the place I was staying in the middle of the night and tried to kill me. I supposed the most obvious answer to the "why" question would be my connection to Stacy Karnes and Tyler Jay. I had seen Stacy Karnes attacked, and I'd been looking for Tyler Jay. (Well, looking *and* finding.)

I came up against something solid. The scent of dirt was stronger. I turned my back to it and touched it with my hands. It was a concrete wall. My cellar theory was looking more and more likely. Keeping my arm and hand on the wall, I shuffled forward slowly, still leading with my shoulder, on the alert for any sign of a door.

Who would have cronies? I'd already seen Tyler Jay's entourage. Maybe those people could be described as cronies. It seemed they were already doing his bidding, staying with him while he hid all over town, running interference for him when people wandered by (or knocked on the door). If Jay was as bad as they said he was, then it was entirely possible he was behind this. If it was Jay, I was having a hard time coming up with a reason. Who was I to Jay that he would want to kidnap me, possibly murder me?

Where had that person at the truck come from? I'd only just parked and had enough time to put the phone to my ear before the gun was pressed against my head. I hadn't heard anything through the open windows or seen anything in the mirrors. If that person had hid in another vehicle or behind a vehicle or bush, how did he or she know where I was going to park? I hadn't heard any car doors after I parked; it seemed unlikely the gunman had come out of a car. So what, then? He or she didn't just drop out of the sky or ooze up through the ground.

I came to another corner. The cold concrete of one side met another at a ninety-degree angle. I changed my direction and continued with my chore, using the same approach. So far, I had come across nothing that could be a door or an outlet, no furniture or fixtures, no objects of any sort. I had also counted fifteen paces from where I had started to the corner. When I came to the next corner, I had counted twenty-three paces, give or take. Because I had nothing else, I adopted the working theory the room was square.

I was ten paces along the next wall when I heard the unmistakable sound of a key in a lock. So much for the unlocked-door theory. I froze and listened as a doorknob turned, creaking from age or disuse or both.

23

The door, heavy by the sound of it, swung in, squeaking on its hinges. A long bar of dim light appeared on the floor and grew wider as the door opened. I now saw I was standing against the wall with the door. In the light, which was blinding after the total darkness, I could see a large shelf beside me, laden with jars and cans, pots and pans, and several glass vases. I hoped it would temporarily shield me from whoever had come to check on me, and that whatever delay it provided me would be the extra few seconds I would need.

The light pouring in through the open door was natural but dim; I'd been unconscious from the stun gun longer than I'd estimated. My five o'clock deadline with Detective Koepke was certainly long past. It also told me whatever room I was in opened to the outside, which supported my cellar theory. There were a lot of older homes in Fort Collins, and I thought it seemed likely any number of them had cellars. But something deep down caused me to doubt I was still in Fort Collins. Actually, it was the fact that the cellar was so cold—too cold, I thought, to be in town, where temperatures had been in the nineties for three days straight. Either way, it did limit the number of places I could be.

The room was indeed square, made of cold concrete, and very dirty. There was nothing in it aside from several large shelving units near the door. And no source of artificial lighting.

Around the edge of the shelf, I saw the muzzle of a gun first, then a black gloved hand. As the figure continued forward, obviously confused about not finding me on the floor, he or she began looking around, a large flashlight in a second hand. Now that I could see the figure fully, I saw the expected bad-guy uniform complete with ski mask. This was not someone I thought I'd met previously, however, because I didn't recognize the gun, and it was held in the left hand. None of my other visitors had been left-handed. The figure looked to the left, shining the light into the deepest corner behind the shelf and seeing nothing. Then the figure turned to the right. I took a breath then closed my mind to the pain I knew was coming.

I held my weight on my right leg and lifted my left, striking upward at the gun. There was a cry of surprise and the report of a gunshot. The arm flew up, the person pulling the trigger reflexively, the shot landing in the concrete ceiling. The figure stumbled backward but managed to keep hold of the gun. I was afraid he or she would kill me out of retaliation or self-preservation, even though he or she didn't seem to have come down here for that reason. Before the shooter could aim, I kicked forward for all I was worth, the sole of my shoe connecting with the figure's chest. There was the sound of air rushing from the figure's lungs, and I was sure I also heard the snap of bone. I kicked again, this time sinking my foot into soft belly.

The figure doubled over and stumbled backward. I moved with him (I now felt sure this one was male), keeping the distance between us minimal and my eye on the gun. The figure crashed to the floor, landing heavily, and I rushed for his left arm, stomping on it with a foot and pinning it to the ground. Now the gun was pointed harmlessly toward the wall. The figure had dropped the flashlight, and it rolled across the floor, coming to a stop against the wall with a flicker. His right arm was banded across his chest as he writhed in pain, trying to suck in a breath.

I considered my next move as the light from the open door was interrupted. Looking at the door more closely now, I saw there was a very small slab of pavement between it and concrete steps leading up away from the cellar. I couldn't see the top of the stairs, but I imagined they opened to a backyard.

I saw black boots on the stairs. Then a second uniformed figure appeared, this one with a familiar gun held in both hands—the gun the shooter at the motel had used. It was pointed steadily at my forehead.

"Back away," the newcomer croaked. It was impossible to tell from the voice if the person was male or female, but based on the height, which I guessed to be about six feet, and the narrow hips, I was positive this person was also a man.

"That doesn't seem like my best move," I said. I was panting, exhausted from the pain and exertion.

"I'll shoot you if you don't."

He was serious. Nothing about his posture, his dark brown eyes, or his demeanor gave any indication there would be a moment of hesitation.

"All right," I said. "You've persuaded me."

Slowly, I lifted my foot off the first guy's arm and took a step back. Step after step, I backed away. I was briefly worried the first guy would shoot me as payback. The second man seemed to sense the same thing.

"Don't," he cautioned the first. "Get up."

"The bitch broke my ribs!" the first guy croaked. He was not trying to disguise his voice, however; he was simply in pain and out of breath. My guess as to gender was still only that: a guess. But it felt right.

"Just get up."

We waited, watching while the first guy struggled to stand and leave the cellar. The entire time, the second man held the gun on me without ever wavering, displaying no doubt or hesitation. This man was certainly thin enough to be Tyler Jay, but I thought he was too tall. Of course, the last time I had seen Tyler Jay, we had not been on equal footing, so my estimations might have been off. Still, I didn't think it was him. Based on the cool confidence, the level of control, I was considering this person to be the leader. The only reason I doubted it was because I thought for sure the leader would be someone I'd already met. With the mask, it was difficult to be certain, but I didn't think I knew this guy.

————————————

The men left and secured the door behind them. Neither had bothered to collect the dropped flashlight. There were still parts of the cellar that were dark, but the light helped immensely in warding off the confusion and despair I had experienced before, in total blackness. Even if it was getting dimmer.

I decided it was pointless to try to get through the door, because I'd clearly heard the lock engage. What would be more helpful would be to get the damn handcuffs off. I thought I could use the flashlight to search the shelves for something with which to pick the lock. Lock picking is something of a pastime for me. It had also been a required skill during my brief walk on the other side of the legal line.

Picking the lock on the cellar door would likely be impossible from this side, but picking the cuffs was another matter entirely.

Handcuffs have the type of locks that can be picked with any number of items. I wasn't sure what I'd find on the shelves, but I thought I might be able to find something useful. A small knife, maybe, or a screwdriver, even a paperclip or—

Oh!

A hairpin. Like the bobby pins in my pocket.

Already I felt the pain surge through my shoulder at trying to retrieve those pins. I walked over and stood in the beam of the flashlight. It blinked off then on again. I cursed the damn thing and the idiot who'd dropped it. Just like a kidnapper to drop a flashlight with shitty batteries.

Leaning my left shoulder against the wall, I twisted my right hip backward as I pulled my right hand forward. My left arm screamed with pain, and sweat ran over my skin. I knew I was holding my breath, but I couldn't seem to make myself exhale.

My fingers found my pocket. Twisting a bit further, tears filling my eyes and squeezing past my pinched eyelids, I finally got my fingertips into the pocket. I began pulling up, working the fabric up and out of my pants. After what felt like forever, I had reached the bottom of the pocket. A bit of careful searching found the pins, and I pulled them out, relaxing. I resumed breathing, my chest heaving, as I leaned back against the wall.

Soon, I sank to the ground, knowing full well I'd have to get the cuffs off if I had any chance of getting back up. The exertion so soon after being shot was draining me quickly. Soon I would be drawing on reserve strength and after that . . . well, I didn't want to think about after that.

I slid one pin into my back pocket for safekeeping then worked with the other. I held the pin in my left hand while I used my right to feel around the cuff, trying to locate the lock. If the kidnappers put them on with the lock facing away from my hands, then this chore would be much more difficult. After a moment of carefully searching the cuff, I felt defeat pressing in on me. Then, finally, my cold, nearly numb, trembling finger found the small opening.

The second problem would be the double lock. I have made mention of my familiarity with trouble. So familiar at one point, it was appropriate to use the word "intimate." This means I know a few things about a few things. One of those things is handcuffs. What I know is, back in the day, after being handcuffed, people would try to get the cops to take the cuffs off so they had an opportunity to escape or fight back. One such trick was squeezing the cuffs tighter around the wrists. To stop this, handcuffs were later equipped with a double-lock feature. This type of handcuff prevents the cuffs from closing tighter after the double lock had been engaged. To release this type, the double lock must be opened first. Double-locked cuffs, for this reason, would be much more difficult to break out of with a hairpin.

Fortunately, mine were not double locked.

I retrieved the pin with my right hand and set to work. I pulled the two ends apart and stripped the plastic coating off the straight end. The most time-consuming step was actually getting the pin into the lock. Once in, I bent the pin and gently twisted it until I felt the tension on the piece I was trying to manipulate.

The flashlight blinked again. I didn't want to be stuck in the dark again, but I didn't need the light for my current task. If I could stay focused.

I had no idea how much time had passed since my captors had been to visit me. It seemed like an eternity. I didn't know how long I'd been working on the cuffs, either. One minute? Five? Thirty? It was impossible to tell, and it felt like forever. I used to be much more proficient at this task. Obviously, some of my skills had slipped in the years I'd spent obeying the law.

Beyond the door, I heard sounds, like muffled voices. My captors had returned. And I had a feeling this visit wouldn't be as peaceful as the last. I twisted the pin firmly. Finally, the cuff popped off my wrist.

Quickly, I pushed myself up and stood leaning against the wall, huffing. I heard the lock slide back and clasped my hands behind me. The doorknob creaked and the hinges squeaked. The door swung inward, and this time three uniformed figures appeared in the doorway. Each of them held a flashlight and a gun. I used my foot to spin the flashlight around and pointed it at my visitors.

One of the figures, the one on my right, I recognized as the man who had come to see about the first person earlier. He had the same gun, the same posture. On the left was the shortest of the three. This one was several inches shorter than me, and though it was difficult to tell from the black clothes against the dark, I thought I caught the impression of hips and a narrow waist. My guess was a female. The figure in the middle was the tallest. A few inches taller than the other man, he was also much wider, fuller, stronger. The lighting was horrible, and I couldn't get a clear look at any of them, but there was something familiar about the man in the middle.

Something familiar and commanding. I guessed this man to be the leader.

"Not very nice what you did to my friend earlier," the leader whispered hoarsely, lowering his weapon and holding it at his side, pointed at the floor.

The other two held their aim steady.

I shrugged my right shoulder casually. "So far I think *you're* ahead in not-nice points. Either the stun gun or the cellar would have put you over the top. Together, it's game over."

He snickered. "Always so mouthy. I have to confess, I've always really liked that quality in a woman. It's too bad we came down on different sides. Maybe we could have had something."

I noticed the way the woman flashed a look at the leader at his comment. I filed the reaction away.

"Different sides of what, exactly?"

"I'm on a pretty tight schedule; I don't have time to explain. And, what does it matter? You're going to be dead in a few minutes anyway."

"If I'm going to be dead anyway, what's the harm? And if you're planning to kill me, why the masks? It won't make any difference if I see your faces."

A wry chuckle from the leader now.

"You always have something to say, don't you? And such a strong personality. I could have used someone like you, I think. It has been very difficult to find a partner."

There was that look from the woman again. This time I was sure it was jealousy. It seemed a shame not to exploit it.

"Is it too late to join you?" I asked, adding a small amount of sultry to my voice.

Another chuckle, this one amused.

"Unfortunately, there are events in motion that cannot be undone. I wish things had turned out differently."

"Events even you can't undo?" I inquired, deciding to play to his ego. "Seems hard to believe."

"How very unlike you, Zoe," he said with a *tsk, tsk* sound. "Stroking the ego of a man. That's a whole new low for you, I'd imagine."

There was a sense of intimacy between us, and while I couldn't really explain it yet, the woman had more than picked up on it. Still, I was playing on instinct, gambling everything. I had no real idea who this man was or how we knew each other.

"You know I'm resourceful," I said. "I'll do what needs to be done, even if it's a bit out of character."

"And what are you trying to do? Create an emotional bond between us, or appeal to my attraction to you in order to keep me from killing you?"

Another flash from the woman, this time I saw more than a little anger.

"We already have an emotional bond, and your attraction to me already has you regretting your decision to kill me."

A small smile, though I couldn't really see it. "So true."

"Then why the rush to kill me?" I infused my tone with more than a little suggestion. "There's always tomorrow. Or the next day. Or even months from now . . . *if* you grow tired of me."

He laughed, and I knew it was familiar; I'd heard it before. Where? Who was he? I felt the same tickling sensation on the edge of my mind as I tried to think. Something obvious was eluding me.

"That's more like the Zoe I know. Mmm, what I wouldn't do for a night with you."

The woman was barely containing her annoyance, jealousy, and anger now. I wondered if she could be pushed far enough she would turn the gun on him and pull the trigger.

"What's stopping you?"

There was a long pause, in which I knew he was calculating his plans, testing them for any leeway he might be able to use to satisfy his desire. The woman seemed to tremble. Good. Progress.

"I'm afraid the heart of the problem is location. We're wearing out our welcome here and need to get moving. Dragging you along simply isn't an option."

I shrugged a shoulder. "Let your people take care of that. Take me somewhere else. Just you and me."

Just you and me, so you can rape and murder me in private? Maybe not the best plan.

Again, I could see he was thinking about it. So could the woman. She'd finally reached her breaking point.

"What the hell?" she snapped. She did little to disguise her voice, and I thought it was also familiar, though I couldn't place it.

Her voice agitated the tickling sensation I felt at trying to remember where I'd heard it before.

"Not now," he said to her over his shoulder, maintaining his croaky voice.

She scoffed. "You want us to just leave then? Give you two some time alone?" She was being sarcastic.

I smiled at the leader.

After a moment, he said, "Yes, actually. Leave us."

Another scoff from her, irritated, hurt.

Now the second man spoke. He used the same voice he had earlier. "That's not a good idea. We don't have much time."

"I'm aware of that. You and the others continue on with the plan as scheduled, and I'll take care of her. I'll catch up when I'm through."

I could see the other man thought the decision was an unnecessary risk, but he didn't further argue the point. Instead, he backed out of the cellar, pushing the woman with him.

"I'll post someone outside, just in case," he said.

The leader nodded.

When the man reached the stairs, he finally lowered the gun and turned around. He was careful never to expose himself to the threat, even though this threat (me) was unarmed.

Once his partners were gone, the leader turned and pushed the door shut. It latched, but it was unlocked. He tucked the gun into the waistband of his pants and reached for the mask, pulling it off. Then he turned around.

I'd told myself to expect the face I would see, to show no surprise. I hoped the dark had hidden what I'd been unable to keep private. Seeing that face felt like a sucker punch to the gut. The tickling sensation I'd been feeling morphed into a sharp sting that reached out and smacked me as I recognized the man standing before me.

"Joe."

24

Pezzani smiled as he moved toward me, tucking the ski mask into the back pocket of the black jeans he wore. "I thought you'd be more surprised."

I shook my head. "You might have been nominated for the Oscar, but you wouldn't have won."

That was the most bogus thing I'd ever said. His performance all along had been award-worthy, but his finale in the parking lot outside his condo had been a work of art. I'd had absolutely no idea any of it had been the least bit false.

I struggled to keep my breathing even.

"I don't know," he said thoughtfully. "If it wasn't an Oscar, maybe an Emmy. It was good, you have to admit."

"It was good, but not great. I do have to compliment you on one thing, though. You took an awful lot of risk."

He laughed. "I thrive on risk. A born gambler, I get off on the high. Even losing is a thrill."

"Did you seek me out from the beginning, or did I come along later?"

"Actually, you have dear old mom to thank for all this."

It was easier to keep a straight face with this revelation. I still didn't know how it all fit together, but I am never surprised to hear about my mother stabbing me in the back.

"That sounds about right."

Pezzani shook his head. "Bridget, you know, she's a real piece of work. But she's fucking brilliant with money. And when she's high, she's quite the talker. Few months back, she told me a story that was just too good to pass up."

"She's got a vivid imagination." I didn't doubt for one second whatever story she'd told Pezzani had been absolute truth.

He chuckled. "Well, she certainly likes to ride high. But no, turns out this story was very true. I had it verified myself. After that, it didn't take me long to see the benefit of getting close to you."

"What benefit would that be?"

He shrugged. "There's been quite a bit of heat lately. I was trying to figure out the best way to clean up the messes and get out. Then you came along. At first, I thought I could use you to help with one mess, maybe two." He laughed. "But you just kept pushing, kept digging, kept turning up where I didn't plan for you to be, right in the middle of everything." He spread his hands, smiling. "You became the perfect fall guy for the whole thing."

"Fall guy?" I repeated. "That was your big plan? That doesn't even make sense. What, exactly, did you want me blamed for?"

"I had a list of people I needed to get rid of. I'd originally been toying with ideas of how to kill them myself, but everything seemed too messy or obvious or connected to me. What I needed was someone else to kill them. Even better if the police didn't look into those deaths very closely. What kinds of deaths don't the police look into? Natural causes and . . . *self-defense*.

"That little story your mom told me? It was the one about how you shot your father dead. With that history, and being so familiar with guns, I guessed you wouldn't be afraid to pull the trigger again. So, all I had to do was set it up so these 'messes' I needed cleaned up would come after you. Then you'd knock them off." He grinned. "It worked perfectly. You're a deadly shot. Well, almost perfect, anyway. Like I said, you just kept pushing. Things got a little out of hand before I could have you finish the job. I had to kill the last of them with the gun we took from you." He shrugged. "It will look like you managed to kill and fatally wound your captors before they killed you."

It was a bit frightening to think his plan had worked as well as it had. Maybe all the pieces didn't fit perfectly, but I was the one and only suspect in at least two murders. And I had killed at least one of his "messes" in self-defense. Who knows how much worse things could have been if I'd sat back quietly and played along. I'd probably be in prison by now. Of course, even I could appreciate that irony; if I'd been in prison, I wouldn't have been standing in a cellar somewhere with the man who'd kidnapped and planned to murder me.

I grinned at him. "You don't work security, do you?"

He waved a dismissive hand. "That's a consult-based gig. I am in security, and I consult with several businesses around town. Including Home Depot. That's how I happened to run into you that day. Also King Soopers. I was there when you came for your interview. The managers were quite impressed with you, by the way. It's a shame you got the boot."

"Actually, I quit."

"Whatever. It took a little bit of planning, but I knew Wolf Security had done business with White Real Estate in the past. If I could create a threat on one of their properties, I figured it would be enough for them to call us in. Even better if it was one of your properties and I could have the chance to meet you." He grinned. "That part worked out better than I'd hoped."

I really, really hate when people explain to me just how easily I've fallen face-first into whatever little trap they've laid for me. And it's always that much more insulting when they do so with such self-satisfied glee.

"Anyway," Pezzani went on, "the mess I needed cleaned up was my full-time business, which had recently fallen under increased police scrutiny."

"That business being?" I had a guess. If my mother was connected to Pezzani, that significantly narrowed the possibilities.

"Ecstasy." He said this as if it should have been obvious. And it turned out I'd been on the right track. My mother is a partier, but it was annoying to learn she was more involved than that.

"I dabbled in manufacturing," Pezzani continued, "but the truth is, it wasn't worth the headaches. Every time we got set up somewhere, we barely got a batch made and we had to move again. Distribution is much less hassle. We find a place we can use for several days, maybe as long as a week, then put the word out. The kids call them raves. I call them paydays. It hasn't been difficult to find a place, and with two major universities and all the community colleges, not to mention the high schools, there is no shortage of paying customers.

"For several years, I had a permanent location. A partner and I opened the club, originally thinking it would be a sound business investment, Fort Collins being the party town it is. Then we were approached with another business opportunity and branched out, started selling X. Everything was great until my idiot partner got ripped on the shit and plowed into a minivan full of middle-schoolers last year. Cops started sniffing around, got wise to the business expansion, though they couldn't prove anything. They settled for a bunch of charges that would get his liquor license yanked. Which meant mine, too. No more club." He shook his head. "Fortunately, my partner isn't a problem anymore. Still, I have plenty of messes to clean up. It's time to move on. Too much heat around here."

"My mother doesn't constitute a problem?" I honestly wasn't sure what I felt at the thought that she might be on Pezzani's hit list. Now that I was thinking about it, I hadn't seen her since I'd picked her up at the courthouse a week ago. For all I knew, she could already be dead.

Pezzani shrugged. "As big a pain in the ass as she is, she's too valuable. No one can do with money what she can. And that's the whole point: money."

I realized it was relief I felt at hearing Pezzani had no intention of killing my mother, even if only a small degree. No matter what else she'd done, she's still my mother, and apparently that counts for something with me.

Her arrest Sunday night made a little more sense now. No one had said as much, but I now suspected she'd been at one of Pezzani's raves when the police had busted her. And if Pezzani's business was under increased scrutiny, as he claimed, it wasn't surprising the police had crashed the party. Her party habits likely also explained how she and Pezzani had gotten together in the first place. I didn't think she would have volunteered to work with him, or sought him out, but if he'd threatened to expose her, she would have complied. Hiding the extent of her darker habits from her legitimate business partners has always been a driving force in her life.

Pezzani was standing only a couple feet in front of me now, the flashlight held in his left hand and pointed straight up. The light from the beam was enough to illuminate both our faces. I studied his and saw nothing of what I expected. I had hoped to find he was crazy; it would have explained some, if not all, of his behavior. Instead, I saw he was perfectly sane, totally in control and aware of his behavior, his decisions conscious and deliberate. I thought that was worse.

He stepped even closer, and I saw the dark gleam of desire in his eyes. He hadn't been kidding about his attraction to me. I was sweaty, dirty, and blood had begun seeping through the shoulder of my shirt. But none of that seemed to slow him down.

"I should have pushed you a little harder that night before Pengue showed up at the house," he said. "That would have been so much more . . . comfortable . . . than this."

He leaned toward me, his gloved right hand on my cheek, and kissed me. Then he stepped forward, and I felt the gun press against my abdomen. I knew it was now or never. I had to make a move. More than that, I *wanted* to make a move; I didn't want him touching me an instant longer.

As if I was getting into the kiss, I shifted my weight to my left foot. Then I did several things at the same time. I lifted my right knee, bringing it up forcefully into his gonads. I also brought my right hand around in front of me and snatched the gun out of his waistband. Finally, I brought my head down hard against his, stunning him.

"What?" he gasped in a tortured whisper.

"You didn't double lock your cuffs."

I swung the gun, bringing the butt of it down against his temple with a sharp *crack.* He crumpled to the floor in a pile, inert.

Stepping back, I put some distance between us as I brought the gun up in my right hand. My left was hanging mostly useless at my side. After a pause to catch my breath, I squatted beside him and felt for a pulse in his neck. He had one.

Satisfied I'd only incapacitated him and not killed him, I held the gun in my left hand while I searched his pockets with my right. I found the handcuff key I was hoping he had and freed my other wrist. I finished my search, pocketing the cell phone and keys I found, then rolled Pezzani onto his belly and, after stripping off the black sweatshirt, handcuffed his hands behind his back.

I examine the weapon, ensuring it was fully loaded with the safety off, then chambered a round and stood. Pezzani hadn't had any additional ammunition, nor did he have an extra round in the chamber, so I was limited to the fifteen shots in the magazine. Keeping my ears open for sounds beyond the heavy door, I again held the gun in my left hand, standing well away from Pezzani, and examined the phone with the other. I saw what I'd expected: no bars. Cell reception is usually poor in cellars.

"Hey, boss!"

I jumped as the guard outside pounded on the door and yelled. My heart hammering against my ribs from the scare, I quickly pocketed the phone and transferred the gun to my right hand.

"Everything all right?"

"Yes!" I snapped in an imitation croak. "Don't bother me!"

"Sorry, boss."

I wondered what my chances were of getting out of the cellar alive. And if they were any better than my chances of getting off the property alive.

I worked my left arm into Pezzani's sweatshirt and pulled it over my head. Then I raised the gun and reached for the doorknob. Any hope I'd had of opening the door without notice was wiped away practically the instant my hand touched it. It creaked loudly, and the hinges squeaked.

Quickly, I pulled the door open.

"Hey, boss," the guard started, not attempting to hide his voice. He was on the third step when he stopped and made to turn around.

I rushed forward and pressed the barrel of the gun into his back. He froze, instinctively bringing his hands up.

"Back down the stairs slowly," I directed.

I couldn't see it, but I swear the guy rolled his eyes.

"I should have known," he said as he obeyed.

"Walk backward into the cellar."

I moved with him, keeping the gun steady at his back.

"What's the plan?" he asked.

"Ask you a few questions and hit the road."

He scoffed. "You won't get anywhere."

"We'll see. Now, where am I?"

"Take a peek."

"Neighborhood or a compound of some sort?"

He shrugged. "Neighborhood, but very rural. That's the appeal."

"How many people are here?"

"Just you and me. Well, Joe, too, unless you killed him. Did you kill him?"

"No. Contrary to popular belief, I don't like killing people. How many people are outside?"

"I told you, it's just us."

Yeah, right.

In one quick move, I swung the gun toward his head. It cracked against his skull solidly, and he went down with a small groan.

Keeping my eye on the door, I ripped the ski mask off his face. It was the guy I'd seen leave the motel with Tyler Jay, the one who had driven the white Saturn, the one who looked familiar. Actually, he kind of looked like Pezzani.

I made quick work of emptying his pockets, stuffing his cell phone and the two sets of keys he had into my pockets. I found little else of interest, aside from a gun and pocketknife, which I also took.

I hadn't found another pair of handcuffs. I guessed he was out for the count, but I thought it was a wise move to ensure there was one less bad guy to contend with on my daring escape. I untied his boots then pulled the laces free. I used my foot and rolled him toward Pezzani unceremoniously. Then I used the laces to tie his hands and anchor him to Pezzani.

Bad guys neutralized, I moved toward the door, took a breath, and left the cellar.

———————————

One set of keys I'd taken from the second guy fit the cellar door. I locked it then pocketed them. I paused long enough to pull on the black ski mask I'd taken. I was already wearing the black sweatshirt. It wasn't a complete costume—my jeans were blue—but I thought it might be enough to cause even a small amount of confusion. Which I would then exploit to the fullest.

I listened for any sounds around the stairs but heard none. Of course, my pulse was pounding so hard in my ears I probably couldn't have heard anything else anyway. Trying for casual, I simply climbed the steps, holding the gun at my side. I moved slowly, taking in everything as I emerged out of the ground.

I had been right about the cellar stairs leading to a backyard. From what I could see in the dark, it was expansive, with no visible fence. The temperature was significantly lower and it was chilly. I thought this was weird, but I couldn't settle on why. Big, dark, heavy-looking clouds had settled over the area, and I could hear the low, deep rumblings of thunder. It was going to rain, and it was going to rain soon.

The cellar was directly under the house, which rose behind me. To the left of the cellar stairs were two steps leading up to a backdoor. The light beside the door was on, but the dim bulb did little to penetrate the darkness.

I shivered against the cold (maybe the exhaustion and blood loss, too) then hurried up the last few steps and out into the yard. The house stretched in both directions from the cellar, with most of it sitting to the right. I hurried that way, cautiously rounding the corner away from the backdoor.

Now that I was really thinking about it, there were a lot of evergreen trees here. With the pinecones covering the ground, the absence of nearby neighbors, the drastic drop in temperature, I now suspected I was no longer in town. I was in the mountains somewhere. Great.

I stopped and leaned against the house, pulling out the second confiscated phone. No bars. I waved it up and down through the air in front of me several times, then checked it again. Bingo. Now it was roaming. Of course, I didn't care; it wasn't my bill. I started to dial Ellmann's number until I realized I wasn't sure what it was. I'd programmed it into my cell phone and just selected his name from my contact list when I called him.

Shit.

I closed my eyes against the tears and took a ragged breath, trying to steady myself. I was on the verge of falling apart. I was tired, I was in pain, I was cold, I was scared, and I was feeling very alone. The monotonous life I'd had a few short weeks ago suddenly seemed very appealing. Obviously, the fatigue and panic were affecting my perception.

A door banged shut, then there were voices. Color me surprised; there were still others here.

"Where's Paul?"

I slipped the phone back into my pocket and took up the gun again. I eased back over to the corner I'd just come around and peered through the dark at two black-clad figures approaching the cellar stairs from the backdoor.

"I don't know."

They drew their weapons and descended the stairs, pounding on the door and calling Pezzani's name.

I saw a huge flaw in my bad-guy neutralizing plan. These guys could simply unlock the door and free Pezzani and his friend.

"Hey, man, you got a key?"

"No. Don't you?"

"No. Why don't you have a key?"

"What? There are only three keys."

Perfect.

So far my luck was holding.

I didn't hang around. These guys didn't seem like great problem-solvers, so I thought I would maximize my head-start. Mindful of my step, I worked my way along the side of the house, which seemed more like a cabin, toward the front. I squatted down then rolled my head around the corner.

It had started to rain big, fat drops that fell slowly at first. I'd found the front of the house. The yard here was equally as expansive. At the edge of the yard, a gravel driveway sloped to the left and away from the house. It was too dark and there were too many trees to see beyond the edge of the yard.

To the right, vehicles were parked randomly in front of a large three-car, unattached garage and into the grass. A sidewalk led from the front porch to the garage and driveway. There were lights mounted beside the front door and on the garage, but like the one on the back of the house, they provided very dim light.

From what I could see, there was no one standing guard, no lookouts, no one around at all. Wincing, I struggled to get my left hand into my pocket and dig out the keys I'd taken. Pezzani's key ring held several dozen keys, one of which I imagined was for the cellar. There was also a remote-entry keypad for a car. I pointed it at the cars and hit the unlock button, as I didn't recognize any of them as belonging to him. A Volvo station wagon parked on the far side of the driveway chirped and its lights blinked.

Next I tried the keys I'd taken from the other guy. This time a Chevy Tahoe parked in front of the garage beeped in response. As I took in all the vehicles, I guessed them to have one thing in common: four-wheel drive. And I had a feeling four-wheel drive would be an important feature before all was said and done. I pocketed Pezzani's keys, choosing the Chevy, not because I thought it was superior in four-wheel drive or off-road capability, but because I'd driven a lot of Chevys in my time (which I suddenly realized was too short) and couldn't recall ever having been in a Volvo. I would be familiar with the Chevy. It was a safe bet I was going to be pretty distracted; I thought one less thing to figure out was a good idea.

The Tahoe was a few years newer than the truck I'd once owned, but the dash arrangement would be identical. Holding the keys and trying to think several steps ahead, I stood. The car alarms beeping off and lights flashing hadn't seemed to call any attention. I hoped that was true and that they weren't just lying in wait. Although, I did still hear banging on the cellar door, so I wasn't convinced they even knew I was missing yet.

I took a fortifying breath and moved around the corner. Keeping my eyes peeled and my ears open, I marched across the lawn toward the Tahoe. I shot a glance back at the house; the front door was closed and the curtains drawn. Now I heard more voices from the back, including a woman's. Their focus was on the cellar and the absence of someone they called Paul. (Probably the guy I'd boot-laced to Pezzani.)

I reached the Tahoe and pulled the door open with my left hand, but just barely. As expected, the dome light came on. A quick look at the dash confirmed it was a familiar arrangement. I hit a button and the light blinked off. Using the running board, I climbed inside and closed the door. I tossed the flashlight onto the passenger seat and placed the gun in my lap while I started the car.

The radio came on, blaring. I jumped and immediately punched it off. I made quick work of the heating controls, then put the Tahoe in gear and hit the gas pedal, angling the nose around the cars that had blocked it in the driveway and cutting across the front yard. I struggled with the controls, trying to move the seat forward, then with my seatbelt. I was just about back on the driveway when several figures—some in masks, some not—came flying around the corner of the house, guns drawn. I saw one face clearly, and I felt the tickling sensation vanish after recognition bit me.

I ducked down, trying to keep an eye on the road, as the bullets started spraying. The sound of glass shattering was all I could hear for a moment. The passenger-side mirror ruptured and then banged against the door, dangling by the control cabling. The rear window shattered, and several bullet holes appeared in the front windshield. Several more shots bounced off the Tahoe and hit the trees around me. Then I was far enough down the slope I was out of range. For the moment.

Must have found Pezzani and Paul.

25

As the Tahoe barreled forward, down the unfamiliar road, with the windshield wipers working against the rain, I harbored no illusions the reprieve was temporary. Pezzani's cronies were no doubt piling into their cars and giving chase. And, they had every advantage. They knew where they were. They knew the terrain. They were greater in number. I suppose this was a note-to-self moment. The next time I find myself in a life-and-death situation where bad guys are going to give chase, I should spend a little time incapacitating their vehicles.

I took a corner a bit fast, and the SUV drifted on the gravel. I flipped the switch to 4H and regained control. Keeping my eyes open for pursuers, I pulled out the cell phone and checked for service. Mercifully, it was still roaming. I dialed a number, my best guess as to Ellmann's number, then put the phone to my ear. The line rang three times before it was answered.

"Hello?"

It was a sleepy-sounding older woman. The connection wasn't that great, I noticed.

"Is there a Detective Ellmann at this number?" I asked, knowing the answer.

"Who? No, I'm so—"

I wanted to apologize, but every second counted. I punched the END button and tried again, dialing my next best guess of Ellmann's number. This time there was no answer. When the machine picked up, I heard a man's voice I knew was not Ellmann's tell me through the periodic crackle of static I had reached the Wright family.

Giving up, I dialed the police station. That is one number I know by heart.

"Dispatch. Do you have an emergency?" The dispatcher, a woman, was calm, with an efficient way of speaking.

It was tempting to say yes.

"No. But it is urgent. I need to speak with Detective Ellmann."

"Who's calling?"

"Zoe Grey."

"Is he expecting your call?"

"Yes." More or less.

Behind me, in the mirror and through the shattered window, I saw the first flash of headlights.

In the light of the high beams, I judged the road in front of me. Deciding on distance, I switched back to 2H and toed the gas. The SUV picked up speed, and I worked to avoid and then compensate for any loss of traction.

I heard nothing to indicate I was on hold and frequently checked the display to ensure the call was still connected. After what felt like a lifetime, the dispatcher came back on.

"Ma'am? I'm sorry, I can't reach Detective Ellmann. Would you like to leave a message?"

Not good.

"Listen, I'm not trying to be a pain in the ass, but I'm in more than a little trouble here. Did you try all his numbers?"

"What did you say your name was again?" she asked. I heard some shuffling.

"Zoe Grey."

"Ah. I thought that sounded familiar. Okay, Ellmann let us know you might call. He said if you did, we were supposed to do whatever it took to get ahold of him. I've tried all his numbers—no answer. I don't have any word of him being out in the field, but let me see if I can reach his sergeant. There is a *chance* he might know where Ellmann is. Slim, but possible."

I was back on hold. The headlights flashed behind me, and this time they stuck. The first of my pursuers had caught up.

I approached the first crossroad I'd seen since leaving the cabin. The road I was on looked relatively untraveled. By contrast, this crossroad, I could see even from a distance, looked well traveled. I shot a glance left then right. I had absolutely no bearings. It would have been more accurate to toss a coin. Holding the wheel with my knee, I reached out and flicked the switch to 4H, then pulled right. The rain was coming down fast and hard, turning the gravel roads to soup. But the wheels bit and gripped, pulling the SUV around the corner.

I could see the other headlights behind my nearest pursuer now. They were coming in force. The nearest, a Subaru, slid across the road as the driver jerked the wheel to the right.

There was a momentary pause while the driver regrouped, and then the chase was on again. The sound of several gunshots rang out, only one of them hitting the Tahoe.

"Ms. Grey?" the dispatcher said.

"Yes, I'm here."

"The sergeant doesn't know where Ellmann is. Not surprising. But I talked to another guy he works with. Apparently Ellmann is working with Koepke. They had a lead on a kidnapping case and went to check it out. I'm trying to reach them by radio. Unfortunately, it's not too difficult for the radios to get out of range, especially in areas like the mountains."

I had very little doubt I was that kidnapping case.

The Subaru was gaining, as were the others. I studied the road ahead and made another decision. Gambling, I switched back to two-wheel drive and hit the gas. I wanted to put as much distance between us as possible on the straight shots. I saw several more crossroads coming up, and I was calculating, trying to formulate a plan.

Several more shots rang out, this time most of them hitting the Tahoe.

"Were those gunshots?" the dispatcher asked. She managed to maintain her calm.

"Uh, yeah. Say, listen, is it possible for you to trace this call?"

"Yes." I heard some rapid-fire typing. "Who's shooting at you?"

"I'm not sure."

Not complete truth. I had recognized one face. But by far the shortest answer.

"Is it a cell phone?"

"Yes. And it's roaming."

"Okay, that just takes more time. Do you know where you are?"

"No. The mountains somewhere, but I don't know anything more specific. I haven't seen a road sign or a mile marker. Did you leave messages for Ellmann?"

"Yes. Stay on the line. It takes a couple minutes for the trace. I should ask if you're okay. Except for the gunshots, you sound pretty good."

"I'm okay for the moment, but I have no doubt my luck is about to run out."

"We can work with that. Let me try Ellmann again."

The line was silent again.

I had watched as the other cars had hurried around the corner, nearly all of them sliding as the Subaru had. This could mean they were so excited about the chase they had forgotten how to drive. It could also mean they had deliberately chosen speed over traction. But, I hoped it meant at least some of them didn't really know how to drive.

I chose the road I wanted and shifted down one gear as I held the wheel with my knee and switched straight to 4H. Without touching the brakes until I was already into the turn, I pulled the wheel to the left, the tires holding to the road. I shifted back up and switched out of four-wheel drive, allowing the downward slope of the road to pull me forward and increase my speed. I realized I was at incredible risk for losing control, a risk that increased proportionately with my increase in speed, but it was a risk I was willing to take. I had few options available to me, so I decided it was time to go for broke.

In the rearview mirror, I watched as the lights turned after me. I saw some sliding, but overall everyone seemed to have learned their lesson. Except one. Someone near the end whipped around the corner and slid off the road. The car started down the hill, back-end first, and slipped out of sight.

One down.

"Ms. Grey?"

"Please, call me Zoe."

"Okay. I left another message. No word yet. The trace is—"

There was a crackling sound and then nothing. The phone winked off. Cursing a blue streak under my breath, I redialed. The damn thing kept blinking NO SERVICE, NO SERVICE.

Shit.

———————————

The change in direction and elevation had caused me to shake one pursuer but cost me my lifeline. I wasn't sure it was worth it.

Headlights drew nearer in the remaining mirrors, and the rainfall was heavier, officially a downpour now. Even on high, the wipers were basically useless. And this only contributed to the fact that visibility was basically nil.

Holding the wheel with my left hand, I waved the phone around, trying to pick up any cell signals. Finally, after a minute, the thing was back in roaming. I quickly redialed.

"Dispatch. Do you have an emergency?" This was a different woman.

"My name is Zoe Grey. I was just speaking with a dispatcher. I didn't catch her name."

"Let me check. One moment."

My anxiety ratcheted up several notches as the silence stretched on. I worried the call would be dropped again. Finally, someone came back on the line.

"Zoe? Is that you?"

"Yes. Was I talking to you before?"

"I can barely make you out. My name is Rita, in case that happens again. I've restarted the trace, but it still needs time."

"How much time?"

"Two minutes, give or take."

"You hear back from Ellmann?"

"Not yet. I'm still trying. Hang in there."

The Subaru had the same idea I did and was closing the distance between us at a frightening rate. I thought I knew his plan. I rolled my eyes.

"I have to put the phone down," I said quickly. "If I get disconnected, I'll call back. Keep trying Ellmann; it's urgent."

I didn't hear her response. I dropped the phone into a cup holder in the center console and switched back to 4H, the motor crying out in response to the sudden change, but immediately slowing the SUV. It was a split second before the Subaru smashed into the rear bumper. The impact threw the Tahoe forward, and I jerked hard against the seat belt, wincing at the strain on my shoulder. But the car clung to the road. I saw the Subaru pulling back for another run, and I waited. Choosing the right time, I let off the gas and stomped on the brake. The Subaru plowed into the Tahoe, the back end beginning to fishtail. I steered a little in the other direction, the battered bumper pushing the front of the Subaru in the wrong direction, exacerbating the fishtail. Then I hit the gas, putting some distance between us.

I watched in the mirror as the driver tried in vain to regain control. Ultimately, the car spun off the road and down a small embankment where it stopped against a line of trees.

Two down.

I snatched up the phone.

"Rita, still there?"

No answer.

I started to redial, until I saw something new bouncing on the passenger-side floorboard. I shot a look at the mirrors then chanced a longer look. It was a handheld microphone on a curly black cord—a radio mic. I wanted a better look but couldn't look away from the road just then.

I got back on the line with dispatch and, a moment later, with Rita.

"Are you okay? I heard crunching."

"A quick game of bumper cars," I said. "I won. Any luck with that trace?"

"Some. We've got a general idea. We still need time. How are you doing?"

I glanced down at my shoulder. Even in the dark, I thought I could see the bloodstain had spread to my neck and halfway down my arm; the area was shiny and wet-looking on the black cloth of the sweatshirt. I was feeling the damage more profoundly now.

"I've been better."

The road straightened out, and I took a better look at the passenger-side floorboard. A small CB radio was mounted under the dash, the microphone having bounced off the hook during the impact with the Subaru.

"Hey, I've got a CB radio here," I said.

"I still need the cell phone for the trace, but maybe that radio would help eliminate the interference in the line."

She gave me a channel to try.

I hit the speakerphone button then dropped the phone into the cup holder again. The static on the line had been horrible, and I could only hope the call wasn't dropped. Holding the wheel with my left hand, gritting my teeth against the pain, I leaned down and fiddled with the buttons on the radio. Without any light, and only a second here and there to look at it, it was difficult to find the right knobs. Finally, I got the damn thing on. The display on the right held two little red numbers indicating my channel. I found the knob I needed and rolled over to the one Rita suggested. Then I picked up the mic and tried calling out.

"Oh, no," Rita came back over the speakerphone. "That's no good."

She gave me another channel, and I tried again.

"Better," she came back over the radio. "How is it for you?"

"Loud and clear."

"Good. Oh, Zoe, hang on. I'll be right back."

With the Subaru gone, the next car in line raced up and closed the gap. The road ahead began to slope upward. I'd passed several crossroads, but none had seemed right. I didn't pretend to know where I was going, but I was operating on intuition, which almost never steered me wrong. I'd had no strong feelings about changing direction. That is, until I got to the top of the next hill.

The crossroad stretched out on a fairly flat plane for as far as I could see. The car behind me raced ahead. I did some mental math, and when the timing was right, I switched back to 4H and pulled the wheel to the right. Again, without much hesitation, the wheels gripped and held the road as they pulled the SUV around the corner, propelling it forward. I flipped back to two-wheel drive for a bit of distance. The car behind me had been racing ahead, intending to follow me on a straight path. My sudden detour came as a surprise, and the driver was unable to compensate. As he reached the top of the hill, he pulled right, trying to make the corner, but the car spun off the other side of the hill and out of sight.

Had none of these idiots driven before?

"Zoe? Come in, Zoe."

Rita's voice crackled over the CB radio.

I picked up the mic from my lap and pressed the button.

"Yeah, I'm here."

"The trace is complete. I've got you. I'm tracking you through GPS now, in real time."

"Excellent. How about some directions?"

"No problem."

A round of gunfire rang out. I dropped the mic and ducked down as several bullets whizzed over my head, putting a few new holes in the windshield. Immediately, water poured in, running down the glass into the recesses of the dash. Fortunately, it wasn't my car. Otherwise, I'd have been pissed.

"Zoe! Are you there? That sounded like more gunfire."

I couldn't answer her and keep the Tahoe on the road.

I flipped back to 4H and felt the tires grip the road with more surety. When the gunfire had stopped, I chanced raising my head, ready to duck again. No more shots rang out. I could see the cars were close, on my tail, but the drivers had stopped shooting. For the moment.

"Zoe! Come in, Zoe!"

"I'm still here," I said.

"Good grief, you scared me half to death. There will be a crossroad coming up in about four hundred yards. You'll want to make a left."

"Copy that. Where am I?"

"Up near Walden. Three hundred yards now, Zoe."

I strained to see through the wall of water. It was useless; I couldn't see enough to differentiate a crossroad ahead.

"A hundred and fifty yards, Zoe. And good news."

"I could use some."

"I've got Ellmann on the line."

26

"How close am I? I don't see a road."

The dark landscape stretched out in front of me in waves of hills, the entire area covered in evergreens, but I could distinguish no road. The rain was too heavy now to make out anything but large, looming shapes.

"Fifty yards," Rita answered, her voice steady and even.

"Count it down, please."

"Forty, thirty-five, thirty . . ."

I knew I should be slowing down, but the best I could do was let off the gas. I could see no differentiation between the road Rita was directing me to and the rest of the dark, wet surroundings.

"Fifteen, ten, nine," she recited.

My heart hammered. I decided to turn even if I couldn't see the road. Seemed like I had less to lose that way. And the Tahoe was an SUV, with an off-road package; that's what it was for.

"Five, four, three . . ."

I reached for the four-wheel drive controls, and the wipers swiped past. I caught the briefest glance before the water was a wall against the glass again. And I saw it. There! The dark outline of a road.

"Two, one, now."

I flipped the control to 4H and pulled the wheel to the left. As it had each time before, the SUV gripped the road and shot forward, though I could tell the rain was taking its toll on the dirt road. Behind me, others slid, but none lost control. I grabbed up the mic.

"Okay, now where?"

"It'll be a couple miles on this road."

"What's Ellmann have to say?"

I thought there was the slightest hesitation.

"He was upset to hear about the gunshots and bumper cars."

"That's a nice way of saying he's pissed."

"Yes. Turns out they were headed your way all along."

"Where are they now?"

"On the other side of Walden. I'm hoping you meet in the middle."

Another round of gunshots rang out, just to remind me how dire my situation was. I was extremely fortunate none of the bullets so far had put a tire out or hit the gas tank and barbequed me. I wasn't sure how long that would last. I kept my head down until the shots let up.

"I'm not sure I have that long," I said.

"I've notified all units in the surrounding area. No one is very close, and the rain isn't helping, but I've got everyone and their brother headed your way. Hang in there."

I roared ahead, almost blind from the downpour, along an unfamiliar, indistinguishable road in the middle of nowhere, and I tried to keep my spirits up. I was sure things could be worse, but I didn't know how. Of course, I'd learned my lessons about wishing, so I didn't spend any time wondering just how much worse they could get. I didn't want to find out.

More shots rang out, and I ducked. I couldn't help the tears in my eyes. It was probably the fatigue. Or the exhaustion. I mean, I can handle stress. And I had survived worse than this. But I was just so tired. I was sure that was it.

When the shots stopped, I grabbed the mic.

"Is there any way to put me in touch with Ellmann directly?" I asked Rita.

"Zoe, is everything okay? You don't sound so good."

"I'll be fine. What about my question?"

There was a beat of silence. "Give me a minute."

It was a long minute. There were two more episodes of shooting, two skids, one near loss of control, and one more bumper-kiss from the guy right behind me. The driver's side mirror erupted, the glass shattering and falling away, although the unit itself remained affixed to the car. The rear quarter-panel window on the driver's side was also shattered. Several more holes adorned the windshield. Rain poured in from all sides. And the heater, even at full blast, could no longer adequately combat the cold wind blowing through the drafty car. Too much more of this shooting crap and the windshield would be toast. When that happened, I'd have a hard time continuing on; it would be damn near impossible to see through a river pouring into the front seat.

"Rita!" I cried into the mic. "Rita! How far to the next turn?"

A few more bullets whizzed by, and I groaned in frustration, smacking my hand on the steering wheel.

"Aaahhh! Stop *shooting*!" I snatched at the mic. "Rita! Damnit, come in!"

"Zoe! I'm here. I'm sorry, I'm here."

I blinked away the tears, and they streaked down my cheeks like little ice cubes.

"Where am I going?"

"It's a little over a mile before you reach the next road. I've been talking to Ellmann. He's going to switch to the civilian frequency we're using. I'm trying to work it out on this end, because he and Koepke will be out of touch with dispatch once they do that."

"They'll still have you, right?"

"Yes, but that eliminates a lot of the fail-safes we use. It requires a bit of adjusting."

I sighed. "I just need to talk to him. I'm sorry."

"Please, as if I could stop him."

I couldn't help but chuckle.

I hit the button for the mic as another round of bullets peppered the car. I dropped the mic in my lap and ducked down, trying to keep the car steady.

"Zoe, let me hear from you."

It was Ellmann. His voice was tight with worry. I knew he'd heard the gunshots.

I had to wait until the gunfire ceased. With each second that ticked by in radio silence, I knew Ellmann's anxiety was ratcheting up a notch. Mine wasn't anxiety anymore. It was despair. I was feeling the effects of the blood loss and fighting off constant nausea and dizziness now. I wasn't sure how much longer it would be until I passed out.

When the shooting stopped, I picked up the mic.

"I'm here," I said. I didn't have to add, "for now."

"Are you okay?"

"Yes. I'm sure I need to explain some things."

"Right now, I'm not interested in that. You don't sound okay."

"And you sound scared."

"That's because I am."

"Me too," I confessed.

It had been a very long time since I'd been truly scared, had felt the type of fear that grows out of the deepest part of your being and spreads its icy-cold substance through your body like a cancer. Before I got mixed up in this case, it had been thirteen years, six months, two weeks, and two days. I remembered it well. And that was what I felt now, oozing through me. It had reached the base of my spine, wrapped itself around, and slithered upward. It made my hair stand on end.

———————————

"Zoe?" Rita still sounded calm and collected. I was very grateful it had been her who had taken my call. "You're turn is coming up. Make a right in about five hundred yards. Want me to count it down?"

"I'll let you know. If you don't hear from me, assume the answer is yes."

I didn't have to see Ellmann's face to know the look it held at my words. I was glad he didn't say anything. I was already having enough trouble.

When a person is faced with the very real chance of death, they suddenly see all the things they should have done, should have said, should have appreciated, should have celebrated. I saw all those now, and then some. I could think of every situation in which I should have been nicer, more patient, more understanding, more loving. I could hear all the words I should have said to my family, my friends, my coworkers, complete strangers. All the things I'd taken for granted, all the times I'd pushed too far, come too close, given up too soon. All of it. I saw all of it.

Blinking away tears, I keyed up the mic.

"Rita, I just want to say, I'm really glad you answered my call."

There was a beat of silence.

"Oh, honey," she said. "I'm glad, too. Unless you're giving up. That would seriously piss me off."

I chuckled, then sniffed back tears.

"Ellmann," I said. I could no longer keep the tears from my voice.

"Zoe, don't," he said sharply, before I could continue. "Don't even think about it."

"But if there isn't another chance—"

I stopped and released the mic key, unable to even form the words.

"No," he insisted. There was something in his voice I'd never heard before, something I didn't like, didn't want to name. He was trying to hide it, but wasn't quite pulling it off. "No way. You have something to say to me, you say it in person."

It sounded good, and the idea appealed to me, but I felt the fight seeping out of me. Probably in direct proportion to the blood running out of my shoulder.

Keeping one eye on the last remaining mirror, I searched for the road I was supposed to take up ahead. Mostly all I saw was rain and darkness. I hadn't seen any homes, any cars that weren't chasing me, or any street signs. I was about to ask Rita to count it down when there was more gunfire.

As if reading my mind, her voice came over the radio.

"Three hundred yards."

It was impossible now for me to steer with my left arm, the damage to my shoulder finally taking its toll. I scrunched down in the seat, keeping my head out of the line of fire as best I could while still being able to reach the wheel with my right hand. I drove with little more guidance than a glance here and a glance there.

"Two hundred yards."

I swerved to avoid at least some of the bullets. I could hear them hitting the exterior.

"One hundred yards."

They had to be running low on ammo by now. How long until they exhausted their supply?

"Fifty yards."

I bobbed my head up after a long pause in the gunfire and looked over the road. In the rain, visibility was twenty feet at best. If I'd had more energy or more sense, I would have been more worried about my situation and the potential outcome. Instead, I was focused on nothing more than the next task: get to the turn.

"Forty yards, thirty-five . . ."

I put my effort into keeping the car on the road and not much else. Straining to see through the wet onslaught did nothing but suck energy I didn't have to spare. And I felt my brain struggling to keep up now. Planning ahead was becoming difficult. It was much easier to simply follow the directions at hand.

"Fifteen, ten, nine, eight . . ."

More gunshots rang out, and I slipped down in the seat. Two bullet holes appeared in the windshield directly in my line of sight, having zinged over my head, so close I'd felt them pass.

"Five, four, three . . ."

I'd reached the turn.

I touched the brake while switching to 4L, then, on Rita's count, I pulled the wheel to the right. Cutting the corner a little short, I felt the tires on the passenger side roll off the pavement briefly then bounce back onto it. I switched to 4H and hit the gas.

The spray of bullets had hit the passenger side of the Tahoe directly during the turn, shattering two more windows.

"Zoe?"

Ellmann's voice was calling me. But I was still hunkered down in the seat, trying to keep away from the bullets. I didn't have a hand to answer him. I felt the mic on my lap, but I couldn't let go of the wheel. I tried to reach for it with my left hand.

"Zoe, answer me."

I couldn't make my arm move, but my fingers were still working. I pulled the baggy sweatshirt to the left, until my fingers found the mic.

"Rita, is the car still moving?" Ellmann asked. His voice was so strained I hardly recognized it.

I hit the button on the mic, but realized Rita had hit hers at the same time. I released mine and heard the last part of her transmission.

"—moving toward your position."

"I only got half of that," he said, more hopeful. "Someone keyed you out. Zoe? Tell me you did that."

"Yes," I called as a bullet tore through the headrest of the passenger seat and pierced the windshield. "Bad timing. Sorry."

"I hear gunshots."

"Yes. The little bastards won't stop shooting!" I cried, more out of frustration than anything else. I was really, *really* tired of gunshots.

"Rita, where is she? How far away?"

"There was a lot of interference with the cell connection, and we lost it. Last known position was approximately ten miles from you."

"Where am I supposed to turn?" I asked.

"You don't worry about that," Rita said. "I'll reroute everyone else to meet you on this road."

"Hurry," I said over a soundtrack of gunfire.

When there was a break in the shooting, I sat up, though the effort was enough to cause unconsciousness to dance at the periphery of my mind. I could see a structure through the trees on the left: a house. As I flew forward, I saw another house on the right.

The more populated area led me to believe I was closer to town, and hopefully closer to Ellmann, Koepke, and their backup. I heard Rita and Ellmann on the radio chattering in official cop tones, using cop phrases, and I realized it was coming to me through a fog.

With the more-frequent dwellings was more light. As I passed beneath a streetlight at the end of a long driveway, I caught a glimpse of my arm. The blood had soaked through the sweatshirt to my elbow, the material hanging heavily on that side.

I didn't know how long I'd been on this road, but it felt like forever. The battle to keep myself from passing out was a losing one, I knew. I flew by another house on the left, visible through the trees, as the others were. A ways down the road, I made out a clearing in the trees on the right. Through the rain, I could see a cabin sitting in the clearing with lights on in the windows. I also saw, too late, the road curve around to the left.

I was going too fast. I reached for the switch at the same time the bullets started flying again. I managed to get it to 4L, but I lost control. I touched the brakes and tried to direct the Tahoe to the left, but one of those bullets finally hit the tire, which had, statistically speaking, only been a matter of time. The tire blew as the SUV was rounding to the left. The combination caused the tire to lift off the ground and push the Tahoe over, off the road.

For a moment, the SUV seemed suspended in the air, two tires still touching the ground, everything else frozen in time and space. Then, as if someone hit the PLAY button, everything was moving again. The SUV pitched up and over, landing on the passenger side and sliding down the embankment, away from the road. I felt the momentum continue to pull the Tahoe over, but the initial jolt flung me around and I hit my head. The unconsciousness I'd been forestalling closed in around me, and, in a blink, everything went black.

27

When I came back around for the second time that day, freezing wind and water were blowing onto my face. I was suspended in the seat by my seatbelt, lying on my left side against the door. I blinked, trying to clear away the last of the cobwebs. Raising a hand to block my eyes from the rain, I glanced through what was left of the splintered windshield. The SUV was lying on the driver's side.

I heard the crackle of the CB radio and vaguely recognized Rita's voice as it issued a message to Ellmann. From beyond the SUV somewhere, I heard other voices. Then the squish of boots in the mud.

They were coming for me. And there was no question about their intention. I had to move.

I released the seatbelt and crumpled against the door, gasping at the pain that burst throughout my shoulder. I struggled to get up, distantly aware of the glass cutting into the skin of my hands and through my jeans. What wasn't soaked with blood was quickly soaked with rain, my clothes becoming heavy, cumbersome. As I worked myself out from under the steering wheel, I looked around for the gun. I could tell my brain still wasn't firing on all cylinders, but I was slightly rejuvenated, the adrenaline of the crash fueling me.

I still (by some miracle) had one gun tucked into the waistband of my jeans, at the small of my back, but it held only fifteen shots. My odds would be better if I had twice that many. I spotted the second gun lying against the back window behind the driver's seat. Once upright, I reached back and picked it up.

Bracing myself on the seat, I kicked at the damaged windshield. It broke free in a crumpled sheet with minimal effort. I kicked it away, then eased myself through the opening, gun at the ready.

Now that I was out of the SUV, I could see it had spun slightly in its trip off the road. The nose was pointing away from the road, just enough to shield me from view of those I knew were stomping down the hill after me. I hurried behind the vehicle and contemplated my ability to run the distance between it and the trees. It was probably only thirty feet, but I'm not a runner on my best day. Today was not my best day. It was a silly risk.

I also knew standing behind the Tahoe waiting for five pursuers to close in on me was stupid. I really didn't want to kill anyone else, but I wasn't about to roll over and die; I just don't have it in me. I stumbled to the back of the SUV and leaned around it, gun raised. I saw the five of them, still dressed in black, all without masks now, marching toward me in a wide line. Horrified, I realized I recognized a second and third face among the crowd. I fired at the guy on the end. He stumbled and fell back, and the others scrambled to decide what to do.

Two of them raised their guns and squeezed off several shots, which struck the roof of the Tahoe. Another began running, sprinting toward the opposite end of the vehicle. I hurried to the other end and came around the front bumper in time to surprise him at ten feet. I squeezed off two shots, both of which struck him center mass.

Stepping around the SUV a bit further, I fired on the pursuers from the new position, hitting one. The two remaining redirected their fire, and I fell back. Over the ringing in my ears, the pounding of my pulse, and the rain, I swore I heard something very much like an engine.

"That's the rest of our team," Tina Shuemaker called.

Not good.

I was already outnumbered. Any more joiners to the party would put a serious cramp in my style, and this whole thing would end very badly for me. Of course, there was a chance it would end badly regardless.

Now I was certain I heard the sound of an engine. The engine was running high, and I thought it was approaching quickly. I tried to determine where it was coming from but wasn't certain. My best guess was the direction I'd been heading before the crash. I leaned around the bumper, enough to see the road but not to draw fire from Shuemaker or her companion. Soon I saw the bounce of headlights. Then I saw the flickering glow of blue and red lights.

This wasn't her backup; this was *mine.*

My hope was quickly overshadowed by panic as I saw the Dodge Durango race over the side of the road and down the embankment, heading into the clearing and straight toward me. Shuemaker and her friend had realized the same; this wasn't the rest of their people. The two began firing on the Durango. I heard the bullets hit the body and the glass. The passenger side window was open, and someone was returning fire.

I leaned around the bumper and took aim, firing the last of my first fifteen shots. My opponents were in the worst possible position, and they were now painfully aware of it. They were totally exposed with nowhere to run. The SUV flew forward, toward me, and the gun in my hand clicked empty. As I moved around the bumper, I noticed the first guy I'd hit was no longer on the ground.

I tossed the empty gun aside and grabbed the second from underneath my sweatshirt as I turned toward the other end of the Tahoe. I raised the gun in time to see the missing guy stumble around the SUV, gun in his hand, slumping forward and slightly to one side, bleeding from the abdomen. I saw him flinch and knew he was about to fire. In the same instant, the Durango slid into the overturned Tahoe. The Tahoe jumped with the impact, slamming into the guy just as he pulled the trigger. The shot went wide, and he flew backward. Hurrying away from the Durango as it continued to slide, I aimed at the guy as he landed in the mud several feet away. He struggled to raise his arm to take another shot, but the only sound was the report of my gun. He slumped back, his body limp.

The hurried movements had zapped my strength. I collapsed to my knees in the mud behind the Durango as the driver's-side door flew open and a large man I'd never seen before spilled out. He was on his feet, hurrying around the back of the SUV then kneeling in the mud, firing at the others.

I leaned forward, bracing myself with my gun-hand on the ground. I knew I needed to get up, to at least aim the gun at the back of the Tahoe should one of them come around it, but I could barely hold myself upright. A second man shot out of the Durango. This one I recognized. I must have looked as bad as I felt, because I'd never seen Ellmann look so white, not once in the whole week and a half we'd known one another.

"Got another SUV approaching," reported the cop, whom I assumed was Koepke.

"Copy that," Ellmann acknowledged.

Ellmann hustled over to me and easily lifted me up, helping (mostly carrying) me over to the Durango. He lifted his gun and kept it trained on the exposed end of the Tahoe. I saw his jaw flex several times as he looked me over.

Keeping his eye on the exposed side, he went back to the open door of the Durango. Reaching a long arm inside and peering through the open window, he grabbed up the mic. After identifying himself to Rita, he relayed critical details of our situation and requested immediate medical response.

"Copy that," she replied. "Contacting Flight For Life now. Zoe, hang in there."

I would have thought it impossible for a helicopter to fly in such a downpour, but I guess they aren't as affected by the rain as I'd thought. Lucky for me. Who knows how long it would have taken an ambulance to arrive all the way out here.

On the other side of the SUV, I heard another vehicle slosh down the muddy embankment and stop, followed by the sounds of car doors and voices.

"Looks like five or six more guys," Koepke reported.

"Backup en route," Ellmann answered. "ETA: three minutes."

"That's a long time."

Koepke said aloud exactly what I'd been thinking. Three minutes was a lifetime.

"Zoe, how many shots do you have left?"

I looked at Ellmann and tried to focus. It was difficult. Next, I tried to think. That was even harder.

"Fourteen."

"You sure?"

"No."

"It's shoot-to-kill here, Zoe," he said.

"Way ahead of you," I said, thinking of the three I'd already taken out.

"Hey, you better not die on me. Understand?"

"You and me," I said, my mouth dry, "we're on the same page there, too."

He reached into the SUV again and withdrew a water bottle, which he handed to me. I accepted it and worked the lid off while he moved away toward the end of the Tahoe. Tossing the lid aside, I lifted the bottle to my lips and took a long drink. I felt the water rush down my esophagus and into my empty stomach. When half of it was gone, I pulled the bottle away and exhaled with a big sigh.

"Hey, Zoe?"

It was Koepke calling me.

"Yeah?"

I didn't have the energy to get up and move just then.

"There're eight of these guys now. Are any of them a good shot?"

I'd recognized one guy who definitely knew his way around a gun: Officer Pratt.

I reported this to Koepke. I shrugged as I lifted the water bottle, one thought swirling toward the forefront of my mind. "But I'm a better shot."

"We're gonna need all the help we can get here," Koepke said. "Any way you can get a sight?"

I was tired. I just wanted to lie down and sleep for a week. I didn't want to fight anymore. And I didn't want to kill any more people.

I sighed. "What are they doing right now?"

I took another long swig of water while he answered.

"I can't see them. I'd guess they're making a plan for attack. It's what I'd be doing."

I finished the water and tossed the bottle aside. I actually felt a little better. With the water in it, my stomach was much less upset, and the nausea faded to manageable. I hoped I didn't hork up everything I just drank.

"And *our* plan of attack?" I asked.

"It has to be defensive," Koepke answered. "Offense is too risky."

"So we just wait for them to come to us?"

"Basically."

"I need your spot."

I struggled to my knees. Leaning against the SUV with my left arm, I shuffled toward the back of it, the mud pulling at my jeans. I couldn't help but notice the dark red smear I left against the white paint, not completely washed away by the heavy rain.

"Here they come," Koepke said as I started around the back of the car.

Koepke and Ellmann both fired. The bad guys returned fire. I realized Koepke couldn't move now.

Moving away from the SUV, I struggled forward, very unbalanced on my own. Coming up beside Koepke, I was panting, sweating. I paused to catch my breath.

The bullets peppered both SUVs and pounded into the ground near our knees. I wasn't going to get any stronger. If I was going to make a play, it needed to be now.

I raised the gun and leaned around Koepke. I saw the eight of them had come around a Ford Explorer and formed a line, moving forward, side by side. They all had their ski masks back on, and the differences in mass and height were the only things distinguishable now. They were difficult to see through the heavy rain. The headlights did little to illuminate the scene. What gave them away was the muzzle flare of their guns.

I aimed for the one on the far right and fired. The bullet struck, and he went down. My arm was shaking from fatigue as I lined up the next shot. I noticed Koepke hesitate for half a second.

It was equal measures luck and skill. Maybe what Ellmann said about me having an overabundance of both had merit. Plus, I'd had *a lot* of practice, starting at a young age. I didn't stop to explain any of this to Koepke, however.

I pulled the trigger again, and one on Ellmann's end staggered back and fell. I saw him practically bounce off the ground, back onto his feet. I swung my gun left and fired. This time when he fell, he didn't get up.

Koepke fired off the last of his magazine, hitting one in the shoulder, then dropped back to reload. I aimed at another and fired, the bullet flying harmlessly past the person and landing in the mud beyond. My arm was dropping; I was too weak to hold it up. What I needed was another shot of adrenaline.

As if in answer, the remaining shooters focused on me. A spray of bullets whizzed past my head, one so close it grazed my temple. I dropped back, and the shots struck the ground just behind me, mud spraying up with each. Now my heart was hammering, and I felt another dose of adrenaline dump into my bloodstream. The open wound on my temple burned from exposure and the heat of the bullet. That bullet had been too close.

From the other side of the SUV, I heard a grunt of pain. Ellmann had been hit. I heard one of the bad guys say, "There! Go!"

I shot up onto my knees again and leaned around the SUV, aiming the gun. I went left, picking off the one running forward to finish off Ellmann. I squeezed the trigger, and the figure fell forward, splashing into the mud. The bullets were already flying my way again. Once Koepke had reloaded his gun, he leaned out and resumed the fight, his fire helping to ward off some of what was being directed at us—at *me*.

"Ellmann!" I called.

I didn't know how injured Ellmann was, or if he could defend himself any longer. I lined up my next shot, trying my best to ignore the ones fired at me, and pulled the trigger. The figure went down. Another shot made it permanent.

Out of the corner of my eye, I saw one of the remaining three fall. The figure dropped to his or her knees, gun still raised. Koepke fired again. The figure fell back, the gun splashing into the mud.

"Ellmann!"

Panic closed in around me until I finally heard a reply from the other end of the car.

"I'm fine!"

Relief washed through me just as a white-hot pain exploded in my right thigh, the fire rushing over my leg and pelvis. My shot went wide, hitting an arm. I fired again, this time my aim true.

"Son of a bitch!" I cried at the last guy standing. "I'm tired of getting shot!"

He was moving forward quickly, his gun held in front of him by both hands, his aim better than any of the others'. And he had not stopped firing for my outburst. I was certain this was Pratt.

His fire had driven both Koepke and me back behind the SUV. I could hear the slosh of his boots in the mud over the report of the gun and knew he was close. Koepke and I were both kneeling. He'd been aiming low.

My last idea hit. I threw myself at the bumper of the SUV and struggled to get to my feet, groaning at the effort. I could feel each second tick by as I strained, my strength beyond drained. Then it was as if everything was in slow motion. Each footstep squished in a prolonged sound. Each gunshot was drawn out.

Leaning on the heel of my right hand, still clutching the gun, I got my left foot under me. Another footstep. Giving it every last thing I had, I pushed up, managing to get the other foot under me. Another footstep. Panting, I leaned on the SUV as I pulled myself upright. Another footstep.

Taking a breath and leaning heavily against the vehicle, I raised my arm and pushed myself to the left, leaning over Koepke and around the edge of the SUV. I was surprised to find Pratt a mere three feet from the barrel of my gun. As expected, he'd been aiming low, at the place I'd just been. At the sight of me, his eyes widened, and he swung the gun up. But not before a shot rang out.

He was thrown backward from the impact of the shot. His arms flew open and the gun fell from his hands. For a moment, everything was suspended, as it had been in the split second the SUV had gone over the side of the road. The gun hovered in the air just below his gloved hands. His arms seemed to hang in the air. His feet were mostly off the ground. The gunshot rang out and seemed to pause. Then it was over. The sound of the shot rolled away and everything moved again. The gun splashed as it hit the ground. Pratt flew backward and landed on his back, mud spraying up around him, his arms out to the sides, a large hole oozing in the middle of his chest.

It was over. I heard sirens in the distance and the unmistakable sound of helicopter blades cutting the air. Suddenly I was falling, sliding down the back of the SUV into the mud. My left arm hung uselessly at my side, and my right, still clutching the gun, draped over my leg. I noticed my jeans were covered in mud, and my traumatized brain wanted to focus on this.

Suddenly Ellmann was squatting in front of me, stuffing his gun back into the holster on his hip. His clothes were soaked, and his dark hair was plastered against his head. Through the fog, I realized there was blood on his left arm. The blood on my right pant leg didn't fully register, though.

"What, you needed a matching hole?" I asked. It came out as little more than a sorry, pained whisper.

He took the gun from my hand. At first I clung to it, refusing to relinquish it. He gently pried my fingers away, and I let go.

"What were you going for? The trophy?" He waved his hand at my thigh.

My gaze dropped back to my leg, and I saw the dark red stain spreading around the burned, frayed hole. The pain began to register, slowly at first, then more powerfully as the significance of it penetrated my understanding. I'd been shot. *Again.*

"I need to close my eyes for a minute," I whispered.

The sirens were closer now, as was the helicopter. I heard car doors and Koepke shouting directions to the new arrivals.

"No, Zoe, stay awake," Ellmann said, reaching for me. He touched my face, tipping it up to look at him. "Stay with me."

I smiled. Or, at least, I attempted to smile. It may have come across as a grimace. "I'd never leave you."

"Zoe. Zoe!"

His voice seemed to be coming to me through a tunnel now, echoing and growing more distant. I felt his touch, felt him shake me, then I was moving upward. Had Ellmann picked me up? I could no longer fight the blackness. Everything faded away, replaced by unconsciousness.

28

When next I became aware, it was daylight, warm, mostly quiet, and I wasn't feeling much of anything, pain included. Information came to me in layers. I became aware of lying in a bed. Then of someone holding my hand. Then of a *SportsCenter* reporter speaking. When I recognized the steady beeping of something nearby, I had a suspicion as to where I was.

I cracked an eye open and gazed around. Sure enough, it was a hospital room. In fact, it looked very similar to my last. Opening my other eye and blinking away some of the blur, I looked to my right. Ellmann was sitting in a chair beside the bed, his feet propped beside mine, crossed at the ankles, my hand lying in his. There were bandages visible under the sleeve of his t-shirt, and there was a sling in his lap. He was watching TV. I squeezed his hand.

Immediately, he looked at my hand then up to my face. Seeing I was awake, he dropped his feet to the floor as he switched off the TV. He turned in the chair to face me, leaning closer. He was smiling.

"How was your nap?"

"Maybe one of my best."

He chuckled softly and reached his long fingers out to brush a strand of hair back from my face.

"Did I have another surgery?"

"Yes."

I rolled my eyes. "I've never been in the hospital before. Now I feel like I spend all my time here."

He lifted my hand to his mouth, pressing a kiss to it. "How's your pain?"

"Whatever I'm on this time is *way* better than last time," I said. "I feel pretty good."

He grinned. "Good, I'm glad to hear it."

"Hey, how's your arm?"

"Nothing to it. Just a nick."

The nurse bustled in, a tall blonde woman I didn't know from my last stay, which I thought was good. She carried a syringe in her pocket as she rounded the bed for the IV. She greeted me and inquired how I was feeling. I began to answer as she twisted the syringe onto the IV line. She depressed the plunger, and an instant later I felt whatever she'd injected hit me. Suddenly very tired, I trailed off midsentence and fell asleep.

———————————

I awoke again Monday morning. Ellmann was still beside the bed, with his feet propped up beside mine, the paper open in front of him. I saw no sign of the sling. I could see the date on the front page, but couldn't believe I'd basically skipped Sunday.

I bumped my foot against his. He put the paper aside and turned to me, smiling.

"Hello, again."

"No more nursing trickery," I warned.

He grinned, attempting to play coy. "No idea what you're talking about."

"I'm serious."

He kissed my hand. "It's been almost thirty-six hours. That's longer than your last stay. I'm willing to be a bit more open-minded now."

"I don't want to see that nurse again."

"Don't stress yourself out, okay? How are you feeling?"

The pain was there, just beyond the insulation of narcotics, as it had been the first go-round. Whatever I'd been on yesterday had been much better. Yesterday, someone could have probably cut my arm off and I wouldn't have felt a thing. Not so today.

"Well rested, thanks to you and your Nazi nurse."

"You're welcome."

"Oh, please." I tried to look around. "Could you sit me up, please? No funny business."

Making a point of showing his hands, he reached out with a single finger and hit the button to raise the head of the bed.

I noticed he was wearing different clothes. He'd been home to at least shower and change. And I noticed the bandage I'd seen yesterday was gone, or, at least, was smaller. That was good. I wondered if he'd also been home to sleep, though I did notice the dark circles under his bloodshot eyes. I asked him.

"I've mostly slept here," he said. "I had to do a bunch of paperwork yesterday, then I moved your things out of your motel room. Seemed pointless for you to pay for a motel room you weren't using. I took your stuff to my house and showered. Otherwise, I've been here."

"Thank you."

"You're welcome. Oh, you'll be glad to know your house is no longer a crime scene."

I sighed. "Great. I can move again."

There was a knock at the door, and a young woman with short brown hair and pretty blue eyes came in. I glanced at Ellmann questioningly. He raised his hands.

"Wasn't me," he insisted.

"I'm Melinda, your nurse today. I just stopped in to check on you. Glad to see you're awake. How do you feel?"

I started to answer when Ellmann whispered in my ear.

"I was a little vague on details when you got to the ER."

Good to know.

"I feel great." I smiled at her. "All things considered."

"Wonderful." She grinned. "You have a visitor. Are you up for it?"

Obviously I hadn't called anyone. I figured it was Sadie. She always seemed to be working. Probably she'd been in the ER when I'd been brought in. It wouldn't have been difficult for her to find my room number.

I also figured this meant my promise of an explanation had come due. It didn't seem right to put her off when she was already here. So I nodded to the nurse.

Smiling her approval at my compliance (I easily imagined the horror stories she'd heard from my past nurses), she went to the door and opened it, waving in the visitor I still couldn't see.

I heard a male voice, not Sadie's. I glanced at Ellmann, who squeezed my hand reassuringly and stood.

The door closed behind the nurse, and a moment later footsteps carried a very uncomfortable Zach into the room. He was as uneasy as I was confused. Stopping barely inside the room, he stuffed his hands into the pockets of his jeans, and his eyes darted around. They glanced to me a couple times, and each time I was sure I saw him wince.

Ellmann walked over to him, his hand extended. Zach, clearly uncertain about the much bigger guy, carefully placed his hand in the one offered to him, as if resigning himself to the idea he might not get it back.

"Glad you could make it," Ellmann said. "I thought you should know what happened. And that you two could use a minute together." He turned and shot a very pointed look at me.

I glared back. Up to this point, Ellmann had done an outstanding job of staying out of my private thoughts, my personal problems, and my family drama—at least as much as our recent situation had allowed. I couldn't deny that was one of the things I truly appreciated about him. He wasn't Mr. Fix-It, running around butting his nose into stuff he really didn't understand.

Zach continued standing near the door, trying his best not to fidget but failing miserably. I was going to have to discuss this with Ellmann immediately. He couldn't make this a habit. I've been dealing with my family my whole life; I understand the dynamics better than he ever could. He was going to have to respect that, or this wasn't going to work.

"I need to make a couple phone calls," Ellmann said, taking a step toward the door, his movement forcing Zach another two steps into the room.

Zach watched Ellmann leave then turned back to me. He didn't move any closer.

"So, uh, when did you get a boyfriend?"

There was a trace of indignant accusation in his voice, reminding me he was not only my younger brother, but also a boy who had always depended on me like a mother. I felt a pang of guilt. And, privately, I was willing to admit Ellmann may have had a point calling Zach here today.

"Honestly, I'm not sure. He just sorta showed up one day."

Zach looked at me for a beat, the longest he'd looked at any one thing since arriving, and I knew he was trying to decide if I was being serious. He must have seen that I was.

"Oh. Well, I, uh, I kinda like him. I mean for you, obviously. He, uh, he's very serious."

I nodded. "He's a cop. I think they have to be that way to get the job or something."

"Huh? Right. No, I meant about you. He's very serious about you. I like that part."

"Oh."

This was an interesting perspective on the relationship between Ellmann and me, one I hadn't considered before. It also made me acutely aware of the fact that Zach had never seen a healthy romantic relationship in his entire life. Our parents certainly didn't count. And I had a string of failures behind me. That wasn't to say what Ellmann and I had fit that description, but the revelation was valid all the same. And, I could certainly hope Ellmann and I would have it one day.

"Thanks for coming," I said, steering the conversation back around to what I thought might be safer ground, for both of us.

"No problem. I mean, when the guy, uh—" Zach turned and pointed a finger at the closed door.

"Ellmann."

"Yeah, when Ellmann called, I wasn't sure what to think. I mean, I probably wouldn't have known you were here."

That blow landed directly on target. Then it was my turn to wince.

"I hope he didn't make it sound worse than it is," I said lightly. "I'm fine. I'll be released in a couple days, tops."

I could see it was best to play this down for Zach. He was actually scared.

"Well, I mean, what happened?" He was back to shuffling from foot to foot, eyes darting everywhere but to me. He wasn't on the verge of tears, but they weren't totally out of the picture, either.

"Hey," I said, reaching out to him with my uninjured right arm. "Come here."

Requiring no further prompting, he darted forward and practically flung himself onto the edge of the bed, wrapping his arms around my shoulders and squeezing, like he'd done all those times as a child when he'd sneaked over to my room in the middle of the night and asked if he could sleep in my bed. My body tensed, and I froze as the pain jolted through me, both from my right thigh and my left shoulder.

He immediately released me and jumped to his feet, as if the bed had caught fire. "What's wrong?"

I blinked the tears out of my eyes and forced a breath. "It's okay," I said, my voice tight. "Really, I'm okay. Just sore. Here, sit." I scooted to the left of the bed and patted the empty space.

He was eyeing the bed and me, obviously unsure.

"I promise, it's okay."

I held my hand to him again.

Finally, he took it, and I pulled him closer. He sat slowly, carefully, watching me with slightly wide eyes for even the tiniest hint of pain. I smiled and squeezed his hand.

Someday I would need to explain to him what happened to me. But that day was not today. It would have been too much.

"Are you sure you're okay?" His voice was a whisper.

I smiled. "Yes. I promise; I'm not going anywhere."

I finally understood. That was his real fear. If he didn't have me, he wouldn't have anyone. He needs me. And he knows it. The little shit.

We both had tears in our eyes now. I pulled him toward me and hugged him. He was stiff at first, resistant, worried about hurting me again. But soon he was squeezing my waist, his head on my shoulder.

For a moment, I was back in the stolen Tahoe, driving through the dark and the rain, bad guys chasing me. I remembered what it had felt like to experience a moment of doubt, a moment in which I wasn't sure my future would be very long. All those wasted moments, those missed opportunities, the mean words, the withheld gestures—they all came back to me. Most of my regrets had to do with Zach. I'd been a child trying to raise a child in unthinkable circumstances, but those excuses didn't change the mistakes I'd made.

"Zach, I love you. More than anything else. No matter what happens, no matter how angry or disappointed I am, that's always true. You know that, right?"

He nodded against my shoulder.

He was quiet for another minute then said, "Do you love me enough to give me my ID back?"

Our tender, touching moment was over.

"Absolutely not."

He sat up. "Zoe, it cost me a hundred bucks!"

"Mom's probably given you five times that this week alone."

"That's not the point. It's a waste of money. I'll just buy another one."

"No, you won't. You're going to pay Donald for the damages to the Lincoln. And you're going to think long and hard about what I'll do to you if I catch you a second time."

He did his best to maintain his carefree expression, but I saw his Adam's apple bob as that thought hit home.

"There is no damage to the Lincoln! I already told you."

Not surprising.

"Well, then, you can fill the gas tank for him."

"I already did."

"Good."

"I even told him he could park it in the garage now, too, but he said no." He shrugged as he stood. "I think he likes parking on the street, to show it off."

I was looking at him closely now. "Why could Donald park the Lincoln in the garage?"

Zach turned back to me. "Because Mom won't need it anymore."

Immediately I thought Ellmann had talked to her, even though I'd asked him not to. Was this the kind of guy he really was? Meddling in other people's personal affairs? If so, I didn't like it.

Then my thoughts drifted to another conversation I'd had not so long ago, and I thought there might be another explanation.

"Why won't she need it? Did she move out?"

"Sorta. She's in jail."

"Jail?"

"Well, prison, technically. The cops say not even *her* lawyer can get her off this time."

29

Zach had gone, and Ellmann was back in the chair beside my bed. He seemed to have made all his "phone calls." I guessed he'd really been standing in the hallway outside my room, waiting until Zach left, because he reappeared almost the instant the door opened.

"How are you?" I asked, extending my hand to him. "How's your arm?"

He took my hand, leaning his elbows on his knees. He kissed my palm then held my hand in both of his.

"I'm tired, and I've never been so scared in my life, but I'm fine." He indicated his shoulder. "Through and through. Very little damage. Light duty for a couple weeks. How'd it go with your brother?"

I nodded. "Fine. Thanks for calling him."

Ellmann grinned. "Maybe I did the right thing after all?"

"That's all you're going to get from me," I said.

He chuckled.

"Ellmann, did you know about my mother?"

The smile fell from his face. He nodded slowly. "Yes. I was going to tell you, but I didn't get the chance before your brother showed up."

If Ellmann had been willing to use whatever he'd found in her room as leverage simply to get her to move out, I didn't think he'd suddenly be compelled to arrest her. So I didn't ask him if he had. But I thought I knew who had.

"Did Koepke arrest her?"

Another nod. "Yeah."

"So . . . he connected her to Pezzani?"

Only a small part of me questioned what Ellmann had done with the information he had about my mother. Small as it was, I still needed to know.

He leaned forward and clutched my hand, imploring me. "Zoe, I never said a word to anyone about what I found in her room when I searched it. I told you, Koepke is a good investigator. He made the connections on his own. Once he did, he got a search warrant, found everything she had stashed anyway."

"There was still something to find?"

"Of course. I found it, but I didn't take it. I couldn't have all that shit on me. The best way for me to use it was to leave it there, let her think everything was fine, then confront her, threaten her. That's all it would have been good for, because the day I'd found it, we were looking for connections between *you* and Stacy."

Ellmann was slightly more devious than I'd previously given him credit for. I liked it.

I nodded. "Sorry. I . . . it's the drugs. I'm not thinking straight."

He shrugged his uninjured shoulder lightly. "I know you don't totally trust me yet," he said, kissing my hand again. "Just give me time to prove you can."

I squeezed his hand. "I'm trying, believe me." My voice was a soft whisper.

After a moment, Ellmann shifted slightly in his chair and redirected our conversation.

"So, have you put it all together yet?"

I nodded. "When I saw Tina Shuemaker, a lot of pieces fell into place. The rest came when I saw Officer Pratt in the clearing after the Tahoe had rolled over. I am curious, did you ever find Tyler Jay?"

"He wasn't involved in this, surprisingly."

"No, I know. But still, did you find him?" I studied his face. Then I smiled. "Ah, you did, didn't you? Where was he? Was he at his mom's?" Another subtle change. "He was, wasn't he? I *knew* it." I shook my head and laughed. "It's nice to hear *that's* over."

"Aren't you going to ask about the reward money?"

"No. I'm past that. By the end, it was just about catching him. I suppose that's ultimately what got me in trouble."

"I told you going after him was dangerous."

"Yeah, yeah, yeah. But who else do you know has tracked down Tyler Jay *three* times?"

"I'll give you that," he conceded.

"Saturday, after I'd been 'fired' again, I decided to take another crack at finding Tyler. I was sitting at his mom's house when Bilek's Honda drove by. I followed it to the Motel 6. But it had been a ruse to lure me to the motel. While I was sitting in the Waffle House, Tyler's friend Paul called his friend Tina. Tina ordered someone to come to the Waffle House. I guess we were there a while because it took that long for someone to go home and get his bad-guy uniform then report for duty. While I was watching the motel, someone climbed into the back of the truck. The lock's been busted for a year, and I've never fixed it.

"Anyway, I saw Tyler and Paul leave the motel room, and I'd been so focused on following them, I hadn't noticed I wasn't alone. Plus, the stowaway was on the floor, behind the seats. When I parked at Stacy's house, the stowaway slipped out and proceeded with the initial kidnap attempt. Of course, when I didn't cooperate, Tina had to come in with her stun gun."

I rubbed my hand over my neck and felt the two small burns left by the stun gun.

"I knew you were going to call the tip line," Ellmann said. "So I had someone listen to the messages. We got yours right away, but by the time I got to Stacy's house, you were gone."

"Where were you headed when Rita got in touch with you?"

"To the cabin where you were initially held. When I went back through Tyler Jay's file, I found a connection to the club Pezzani had once co-owned. There was also a list of known associates. When I ran through the list, I found Paul Dortch also had a connection to that club, and to Pezzani specifically. The only reason I started looking into Pezzani with any real intent was because I didn't like him. From the first night I met him, I thought he was a prick. Then I turned up the cabin that belonged to Pezzani, left to him by his uncle, Paul Dortch Senior."

"You know, I thought they looked similar. Not quite brothers, but a family resemblance."

"Cousins. Anyway, the cabin was fairly remote, and it seemed like as good a place as any to take a kidnapped victim. While dozens of other units checked out dozens of other places, Koepke and I headed to the mountains."

"Pezzani and Tina Shuemaker were an item."

Ellmann nodded. "I went back over the security-camera footage from the Elizabeth building around the time of Stacy's attack, focusing primarily on the exterior shots. I found a few seconds in which Tina was unmasked, walking toward the building. After the attack, there was a very clear shot of her getting into a red Mustang. I ran the plate, and it came back registered to Pezzani. That started to connect a lot of dots for me."

"I never liked that car."

He gave a small chuckle.

"Tina had begun dispensing ecstasy with the food to her customers at the Olive Garden," I said, "which helps explain how her place was so well furnished and she was always so well-dressed. My guess is she'd gotten Stacy involved in the same thing. The fight they'd had in the kitchen not long before Stacy was attacked was probably about Tyler finding out. He'd made a comment to me about Stacy being a goody two-shoes. I think his feelings for her were genuine, and while he's a bad guy, he didn't want her to become a bad girl because of him. He probably would have been angry if he'd known she was selling drugs."

I realized now, Tina had recognized me from Elizabeth Tower the day I'd shown up at her door. That's why she'd been so weird. She'd been trying to figure out how I'd gotten on to her, what I knew, what I was trying to figure out, and above all, she'd wanted to put me on to someone else, like the criminal boyfriend Tyler Jay. I'd been right when I'd speculated the attacker in the lobby would surely recognize me if I waltzed up to their door, but I hadn't anticipated that person being so good a liar and thinking so quickly on his or her feet.

"Rather than risk Tyler finding out, Stacy would have quit," I went on. "I think Tina threatened to tell Tyler what had been going on if Stacy backed out. That's what they were fighting about. I think that's also why Stacy was in such a hurry to move out. She was done with Tina and the drug business. And she likely planned to tell Tyler herself after she was out rather than risk him finding out from someone else.

"But Tina couldn't have that. Pezzani's business was already in jeopardy. With Tyler Jay being at the top of the Most Wanted list, the last thing they needed was someone a step away from being caught possessing information worth trading for. So Tina followed Stacy to her meeting with me. And their attack was well planned; they'd even sent someone into my office to delay me. I'd recognized the guy among the cronies at the cabin.

"On the security video, when Stacy turned around, it was as if she knew the person behind her. It was only after seeing that person in a ski mask that she was afraid. But those stab wounds didn't kill Stacy, so Tina had to finish the job. The day Stacy went into cardiac arrest, you told me you'd run into Tina at the hospital. An air bubble injected into the IV line would have been enough to cause a heart attack. But Stacy survived that, too. So Tina had to try again. The second time I went to the hospital, I ran into Tina as she was leaving. A couple minutes later, Stacy was dead. I suspect that time she used some sort of poison."

Ellmann nodded. "Sort of. Tina's a biology major. Somehow she managed to get her hands on a big dose of potassium. It was enough to cause another cardiac disturbance, which was more than sufficient to kill Stacy in her fragile state."

"It was also Tina who killed Derrick Bilek," I said. "Derrick had probably gotten mixed up in Pezzani's business somehow and was a part of the 'mess' he'd talked about needing to clean up. I was supposed to be the fall guy. Pezzani had helped me move the day before, so he knew where I lived. All he had to do was tell Tina. Then, while I was out to dinner with Pezzani, Tina and Bilek went to the house. Tina shot him, and we found him later."

"Bilek had been a bouncer at Pezzani's club. After the club closed, he worked 'security' for the raves they threw around the area."

"As the fall guy, I was supposed to shoot the people Pezzani needed dead. The most efficient way he thought to do that would be to have them try to kill me. Then I would kill them in self-defense, a situation the police don't really look into. Pezzani needed a public attempt on my life, something like at a restaurant. I think the best shooter Pezzani had was Pratt, a cop who had some training and lots of practice. He couldn't have just anyone come into that restaurant and shoot at me, because, one, he would be right beside me, and, two, I couldn't actually get shot. Any marksman will tell you it takes skill to hit a target and even more skill to miss. After the restaurant, Tina took Pengue to Pezzani's house, where Pengue was under the impression they were there to kill me. Of course, I shot and killed Pengue. I also hit Tina."

"You did. The coroner noted a flesh wound on her left arm. Initial blood testing indicates it was her blood we found on the stairs."

"Margaret Fischer must have been killed because she interrupted something, saw something she shouldn't have. She'd gone to the house after work to assess the damage, but I'm guessing Pezzani was there. He was trying to set me up as the fall guy, so I'm thinking he went there to find a weapon, which he did. It was a stroke of seriously bad luck he had to kill Fischer and leave the gun there to incriminate me. It would have taken him more than a few minutes to get that lockbox open."

"He told us Pratt had looked up your registrations. He knew you had a handful of guns registered to you. He was more than a little pissed off he only found one of them and then had to leave it behind."

"Having a cop in the inner circle would go a long way in helping Pezzani stay ahead of the police. Plus, it also meant he got access to all sorts of information, like my history. And, I'm guessing it was how Tyler managed to stay one step ahead of you guys every time I tipped you to his location. Pezzani didn't care if Tyler got pinched, but timing was everything. If Tyler got picked up too early, it would have affected his plan."

"Pratt tipped off Paul, who spent most his time with Tyler. The coroner said Pratt had levels of X in his system when he died, and rather significant damage to his brain, thought to be the result of prolonged usage of the drug. Pezzani was likely blackmailing Pratt into cooperation after learning of his drug problem. X wasn't the only thing Pratt liked, apparently."

"Really? He was a decent shot. Think how great he could have been sober."

"Probably a good thing he wasn't, then."

"Yeah, probably."

Although, it was a little unsettling to think he'd been high when he shot up the restaurant that day. Especially since I'd been in the restaurant.

"Speaking of, I'd still like to know what happened to my mother."

"When she was arrested last week, she'd been at one of Pezzani's raves. And the X I found in her room had the same stamps as the stuff Pezzani is known to distribute. Now that we have Pezzani, he's doing some talking, trying to buy himself a better deal. He gave her up."

Like any other bad guy making lots of money doing something illegal, Pezzani couldn't just deposit his ecstasy profits into the bank. It had to look like it was coming from somewhere legit. This was where my mother came in. It would have been nothing for her to take Pezzani's money, run it through a couple legit businesses, and make it all look like he'd earned it on the up-and-up. And in her compromised mental state, she'd somehow aligned herself as Pezzani's partner. But, sound decision-making has never been her strong suit.

And, for once, the cops had been telling the truth: not even Bridget Grey's sliver-tongued lawyer could slither her out of trouble this time.

"Zoe? You have that look again, the happiest-kid-in-the-world look."

I realized I was still in the hospital, still sitting with Ellmann. I'd forgotten myself for a moment. I'd been daydreaming about my mother in a bright orange jumpsuit, living behind bars for the next fifteen years. I realize for most children, such a thought would be sad or scary. For me, it was a *huge* relief.

"Sorry," I said. "Hey, how's Koepke? He still mad at me?"

"He's fine. He's still drowning in paperwork, but he'll survive. He's only a little bit mad at you."

I scoffed. "He should be thanking me. I blew his case wide open."

"You became the number one suspect in two homicides, blew off a homicide detective, got yourself kidnapped, and proceeded to take your show on the road, leading a band of murderous drug dealers through the mountains during a record-setting rainstorm for more than thirty miles while trying to bleed to death. Eighteen people are dead. When I think about it like that, I realize *I* should be mad at you. I've never been so scared."

"Okay," I conceded. The guilt I felt was almost entirely the result of Ellmann; I didn't want him to worry about me. "Maybe I was a tiny bit reckless. I see that now."

Annoyance flashed in his eyes.

"It's the best you'll get," I said softly.

"Is there any point asking you to promise you won't do anything like that ever again?"

I wanted to say yes. But I didn't have the heart to lie to him. I had no plans to ever repeat any part of what had just happened to me, but I knew my ability to wind up in big trouble better than anyone. It was too risky to rule anything out.

"Probably not."

"Yeah, I didn't think so."

He kissed my hand again, then sat holding it tight between his, as if he might never let it go.

30

The following day, I was discharged from the hospital and Ellmann drove me home. Or, he drove me to his place, as I was temporarily homeless. I spent the afternoon napping and watching TV. In the middle of the night, I woke up sprawled across the sofa, covered with a blanket. I swallowed a couple more pain pills then shuffled off to the bedroom, where I crawled in bed beside Ellmann.

Ellmann had taken a week off. He assured me he had plenty of personal time, but I figured part of his reason for the vacation was needing time to recover from the stress of worrying about me, which had likely driven him dangerously close to a stroke. I knew Ellmann had been seriously wounded once before in the line of duty, but it had been little ol' me that had almost done him in. Go figure.

Wednesday, I switched to Tylenol. My left shoulder was horribly bruised, the deep black and purple coloring spreading from the middle of my arm to the base of my neck, and down my chest and back. I'd been right when I'd guessed the sutures had pulled loose. In fact, every last one of them had been. Dr. Allen had had to repair the wound again when he'd gone in to tend to the bullet hole in my thigh.

My leg wasn't nearly so bruised, and, as a result, it was far less tender, though I still walked with a limp. I was fortunate that bullet, like the other, had missed everything vital.

Actually, Allen had said it was the blood loss that had been the most dangerous for me. If I had been any longer getting to a hospital, my ending would have been much different.

Thursday afternoon, Ellmann took me to run a few errands. We stopped by King Soopers, and I picked up my one and only paycheck. Hobby Lobby had already mailed me theirs. Then we went to Fort Collins Property Management. The snooty little receptionist appeared much more reserved today. When I got a bit closer, I could see her eyes were bloodshot. She had taken the loss of Margaret Fischer hard.

"Cindy Grogan took over your account," she said, reaching for the phone. "She's in her office; let me see if she has a few minutes."

A moment later, the girl hung up the phone, and a nearby office door opened. A petite woman with short, curly blonde hair and brown eyes walked up to me. She was wearing heels and a gray skirt suit. I guessed her to be in her forties. After shaking my hand and Ellmann's, she led us back to her office.

"I'm really sorry about Margaret," I said sincerely. I hadn't liked her, but I didn't wish her dead.

"Thank you. Margaret was a very passionate woman. She will be missed. Now, I've read the notes on your account, but I think I'd like to hear from you what's going on."

I explained the situation to her. She asked a few questions, took lots of notes, and then when I was finished, she set her glasses on the desk and leaned back in her chair, looking between me and Ellmann.

"I'd like to suggest we charge you a weekly rental fee, pro-rated, of course, to cover the partial second week. As these circumstances were beyond your control, I see no justifiable cause to hold any of your deposit." She reached for a prepared document and laid it on the desk in front me. "If you're agreeable to the weekly rental charge, this would be your balance. The difference," she said, reaching into her drawer and withdrawing a check, "would be refunded."

I stared down at the check. It was most of the money I had paid to the management company. Making out better than I had dared to dream, I quickly agreed, signing the paperwork and tucking the check into my pocket before she could change her mind. We shook hands, and I left.

Next, we stopped by the bank. Ellmann parked, and I reached for the door handle.

"I'll be right back," I said.

He leaned over and opened the glove box, withdrawing a small note. He handed it to me.

"What's this?"

I unfolded it and saw it wasn't a note. It was a check. The check was made out to me in the amount of fifteen thousand dollars. I knew my eyes were wide when I turned to Ellmann.

"What's this?" I asked again.

"It may have just been about catching Tyler Jay to you, but it wasn't to the police department or the sheriff's office. And, like you said, no one has ever found the guy three times. You deserve it."

"That is awesome!"

Smiling all the way into the bank, I deposited the money into my account. Suddenly I felt much better about my job situation, and I was reconsidering my previous decision to accept White's promotion, even if temporarily.

Ellmann and I spent the afternoon looking at houses for rent. Around four o'clock, we ended up in a nice neighborhood near Front Range Community College. Most of the homes sat on spacious lots full of mature landscaping. They were starter homes for people buying their first house or raising their families. But one of them, obviously a bit smaller than the others, sitting on one of the biggest lots at the end of a quiet cul-de-sac, appealed to me even from the street.

We met the landlord and took a tour. It was slightly smaller than the place I was moving out of, with two bedrooms and an office, a smaller living room and kitchen, and almost nothing of a formal dining room. But it had the attraction of never having been a crime scene. The two-car attached garage and enormous yard were what finally did it for me.

The guy had a contract ready for me to sign right there. I paid the security deposit and first month's rent then took the keys.

The place needed some work, but I could move in immediately. That was ideal, because I'd signed an agreement with Fort Collins Property Management saying I'd be out of their place by seven o'clock the following evening. The landlord left shortly after our business was completed. Ellmann and I sat on the front porch, the evening quiet and warm around us.

"Have you thought any more about what you'll do for work?"

I shook my head. "Not really. I'll go back to work at White Real Estate for now. Nothing else has really worked out for me. Maybe that's a sign."

"I think I may have a job for you."

"Really?" I asked, surprised. "Doing what?"

"Well, you tend to wind up knowing things other people would prefer you didn't. You're pretty good at finding people who don't want to be found, or at least having people who don't want to be found find you. I think you could put that talent to work."

"Sounds interesting. I'm listening."

"Bond enforcement agents get *paid* to track people down. That's sort of your thing."

"What's a bond enforcement agent?"

"A bounty hunter."

At the height of my recent ordeal, I'd just wanted my life to go back to the way it was. But, really, my life could never be the same. And not all the changes were negative.

I no longer lived with my mother (or roommates who used all my shower products). I was growing fonder of my truck now that it drove without any issues, and it had been more than a week since I'd entertained ideas of pushing it into the reservoir or in front of a train. And the last few days of my vacation were really looking up. I'd slept in three mornings in a row, no one had tried to kill me, and no one had accused me of a crime. Yesterday afternoon, I hadn't move from the sofa. I'd watched hours of TV, and I'd already finished a whole book.

My relationship with Ellmann was, without question, the best thing to come out of it all. We were still working on getting to know one another, but I felt hope and confidence growing every day. Only time would tell regarding our longevity, but Ellmann is different; that much I already know.

My mother going to prison for a very long time was a close second. Our relationship now had the buffer of time and distance, and that was already helping. As predicted, she'd fallen into depression. The prison had put her back on her meds, which she was, so far, taking compliantly. In a few more weeks, she'd be leveled out again. A few months after that, she'd want to stop taking the pills, starting the whole cycle over again. This time, however, the prison psychiatrists would be monitoring her. It would be more difficult for her to be noncompliant—not impossible, just more difficult (this is *my* mother after all, and I'd gotten it from somewhere).

Work would also be different. With Paige and Sandra serving prison sentences of their own, the office would be a friendlier place. I ran almost zero risk of being fired by White, and I had never appreciated White or my job more than I did after the recent fiasco of trying to find a new one. I still felt the best thing for everyone, including me, was to find something else for the long-term, but I was content in the short-term.

So, I signed up for the certification course to begin my bond enforcement career. I didn't know if it would work out, but Ellmann had made some valid points: I am pretty good at finding people, and I do have great instincts (or luck, as he calls it). I thought the least I could do was give it a try. I also figured it would be more like self-employment, which might make it more difficult for me to get fired.

On top of it all, I was making regular trips to see my therapist again. And she was having a field day with all the new material. Killing people, being kidnapped and shot, having people try to kill me—it had all provided the means for several more weeks of therapy.

Oh, and I'd lost eight pounds. Turns out, getting shot and spending two days in the hospital aids weight loss.

All in all, I was adjusting to my new normal. And I thought I could get used to it.

But then, I should have known, I have never been *that* lucky.

About the Author

Catherine Nelson has worked in healthcare for the last ten years. She is a Colorado native and currently lives in and writes from Fort Collins, Colorado. Be sure to follow her at catherinenelsonbooks.com and visit her Facebook page at facebook.com/CatherineNelsonBooks.

Preview of *The Trouble with Theft*

Turn the page for a preview of the next book in the Zoe Grey series.

The trailer park off Harmony Road is almost completely obscured by the shopping center that had been constructed a few years before. Now, only those who already know it's there ever spot it. I found I was spending quite a bit of time here recently.

It was five a.m. on Thursday morning, and this was my second trip to this particular trailer park this week—the third to trailer parks total. I made my way through the roundabouts then made the first right, cruising around the periphery of the park until I came to the lot I was looking for. It was a double-wide, and plain white, though someone had tried to spruce it up with pink shutters (horrendous even in the dark) and a window planter. It was late June, but the planter was empty.

Albert Dennison was out on bail and had failed to appear for his court date earlier this week. Not only did the court not appreciate that, but the bond company, which I work for, didn't either. Now here I was, cuffs in my pocket and capture paperwork in my bag, assigned to haul his dumb ass back to jail.

Of course, I don't do this kind of thing for free. Each skip I drag back to the pokey is worth ten percent of his or her bond. In Dennison's case, eight hundred bucks. Bonds vary, but some capture fees are six figures. I haven't tracked down any of those guys yet, but I've only been doing this four weeks.

I drove past Dennison's mother's trailer and made a left down the next street. I turned around in an empty driveway and parked near the corner, eyes on Dennison's place. I'd been assigned Dennison on Tuesday. This was his third bond this year alone. He almost always skipped, but he wasn't hard to find. He was something of a "starter" case for newbies like me. All the other guys had taken their turns, and now it was mine.

When I'd first shown up at Sideline Investigations and Bail Bonds with my toy-like badge and course certificate asking about work, Dean Amerson, the office manager, had taken one look at me and paired me up with an old school PI and skip tracker named Roger Blucher. Blue, as he was called, spent three weeks showing me the ropes. Dennison was one of my first cases working solo, assigned to me because I was lowest on the totem pole and needed the experience.

The majority of Dennison's arrests were alcohol related. There were notes in his file about his favorite watering holes. Turned out, he wasn't hard to find. But he was slightly more difficult to *catch*. He may have been a middle-aged drunk, but he was fast. Both times I'd found him, he'd bolted before I'd had a chance to put a hand on him.

I will admit a small degree of culpability in this, as I am not a runner. I don't want to run, I don't like to run, and I'm not any good at running. In the last six weeks, this reality had become painfully clear; I'd discovered this new job of mine involved a great deal of running.

But this job isn't one I'm willing to walk away from. Six weeks ago, I'd been more or less fired from a string of jobs for circumstances largely outside my control. One of the most appealing aspects of my new job is that I'm something of an independent contractor; it's much more difficult for me to be fired. Also, I'm good at this. Call it luck like my boyfriend Ellmann does, or dumb luck like Amerson does, or instinct like I do; I have an uncanny knack for finding people who don't want to be found. Even if that sometimes means *they* find *me*.

So if I can't run my skips down, it just means I have to outsmart them. This isn't usually difficult. Which brings me back to sitting outside Albert Dennison's mother's trailer at five in the morning. If I couldn't catch him when he ran, I had to make sure he couldn't run.

I'd followed Dennison last night. He was on his third bar by the time I'd finally called it quits. I was betting he'd closed down whichever one he'd ended up in last and would be sleeping it off right about now. His mother was home, but from my search of the place, I knew she took sleeping pills. Plus, she was seventy. I didn't see her posing much of a threat.

I got out of the truck, stuffing the capture paperwork into my pocket and holding a flashlight in one hand. I hustled over to Dennison's place and bypassed the front door. The trailer had lots of windows but only two doors. I'd expected a sliding glass door off the kitchen but instead found a regular one. I went to the back and found a square shovel propped against the siding with some other yard tools. I arranged it under the door handle and reinforced the other end with a couple cinder blocks that were serving as steps. Then I returned to the front door.

When I'd searched the house, I'd also discovered a spare house key in a drawer in the kitchen. I'd pocketed it, because

I'd quickly learned those things come in handy. And it did now.

I let myself in and closed the door, taking time to lock it. If Dennison slipped past me, that would buy a few seconds. Immediately, I heard snoring. I grinned inwardly; my plan was working.

I moved down the hall to the bedroom on the left I knew to be Dennison's. As my hand twisted the knob, I felt all the little hairs on my body stand up. Something was wrong. The snoring had stopped.

Shit.

Before I could make my next move, the door at the end of the hall swung open, and I saw the business end of a double-barreled shotgun. An instant later, there was an enormous *boom* and a burst of orange light. I threw myself to the floor. I felt the round spray over me and heard it pepper the furniture in the living room.

As I scrambled forward, toward the shooter, I heard the pump rack the next shot. My shoulder burned in pain as I desperately charged the shooter. An instant before I closed the distance between us, I caught a glimpse of fuzzy slippers and a pink bathrobe.

Great, I thought, *I'm going to get shot again by a seventy-year-old woman. I'll never live that down.*

I shot to my feet, my left hand closing around the gun and forcing it upward, my right hand gripping the front of the pink bathrobe and pushing the woman back. The gun boomed again, this time spraying the ceiling. Then Dennison's door crashed open.

"Let go!" the woman squawked at me, batting at me with her free hand. "Give it back! Let go!"

I tried to yank the gun from her hand, but she refused to let go, displaying unnatural strength born of deep conviction.

"Lord, forgive me," I groaned as I let go of her robe and reached for her neck.

I closed my hand around the front of her neck, squeezing her carotid arteries closed, interrupting the blood flow to her brain. Within seconds, her obdurate grip on the gun slackened. I ripped it away and turned back in time to see Dennison fumbling at the lock on the front door.

"Stop, Albert!"

"Fuck you!" he slurred, practically clawing at the door.

I charged forward, but I heard the lock retract. That drunken bastard was a second away from slipping past me again.

In a moment of blind desperation, I hurled the shotgun at Dennison. I hadn't been necessarily aiming, and it never crossed my mind I was giving a gun to a bad guy.

The gun flew through the air and banged into Dennison's shoulder, knocking him off balance. He cried out in surprise and pain and went down on one knee as the door swung open. Then I was on top of him. There was a loud crash as I collided with him, and we landed in a pile on the smelly carpet.

A brief struggle ensued, in which I nearly vomited from the old beer stench clinging to him, then, after a lot of swearing and name calling, I finally got him face-down under me. I held his right hand behind his back as I reached into my pocket for handcuffs. Before I could get them on, there was a screech behind me.

I flung myself forward, lying flat over Dennison, as I glanced back. The old woman had grabbed up a lamp, still plugged into the wall, and chucked it at me. Clearly, she'd recovered from my assault.

The lamp jerked against the cord and crashed to the floor a foot from me, shattering. With another screech, she flung herself forward. In the faint street light pouring through the open door, I saw her face, wrinkled with age, contorted with anger and a dose of madness, her eyes black and her mouth open. She had two snaggleteeth remaining, and they just made her look that much more demented.

"Shit," I hissed, straining to keep hold of Dennison struggling beneath me. "Lady, stop. Stop!"

To be fair, I think she was too far gone to hear me. She barreled into me. Had she weighed more than a hundred pounds, she would have knocked me over. As it was, she mostly bounced off, landing on the floor on her ass. Her spindly legs stuck out in front of her from underneath the bathrobe, which was frighteningly askew.

"Stop, now," I said again, cinching the cuff on Dennison's right wrist. "Just stay down."

Her black eyes were fixed on me, and she worked to get to her feet. She seemed oblivious to the broken lamp as it cut into her legs and hands. Dennison continued to struggle, and as I finally got hold of his left wrist, he shot a glance at his mother. Even in the poor light, the blood was obvious. Dennison screamed.

"Mama!" he cried, wrenching his wrist away from me.

I groaned my annoyance and increasing desperation and flung myself forward again, pinning his face to the floor.

"Stop!" I ordered him.

I caught his wrist again and managed to get it behind him, ignoring the pain in my own shoulder. The old woman got to her knees. On all fours, she came at me again. She crashed into me and clawed at my face and neck.

I didn't want to hurt her. Bottom line, she was old. Her body was fragile. If I threw her around like I knew I could, like I so badly wanted to, I could very easily cause serious damage, even kill her. I had enough bodies on my conscience; I didn't want another. But that was hard to remember as I felt her talon-like nails tear into my skin.

"Mama! Mama!"

The old woman was screeching in my ear, her rancid breath hot on my cheek.

I couldn't take any more. I threw my shoulder into her, knocking her backward.

She squealed as she fell, and Dennison howled. I roughly clamped the cuff on his wrist and squeezed, hearing the satisfying click over the racket. Then I was up.

The old woman was righting herself, ready to make another run. I wished I hadn't left my damn cell phone in the truck. Not only did the woman need medical attention, but I thought a few cops would be useful right about now. I couldn't remember seeing a phone when I'd been in the house the first time.

She threw herself at me again, stumbling slightly over her son as he thrashed on the floor between us. By some miracle,

I managed to get a hold of her around the middle, pinning her arms to her sides. She twisted and fought against me, but she was no match. I lowered her to the floor, holding her in front of me as she fought for all she was worth, screeching all the while. I began to worry she would give herself a heart attack or a stroke. And I was seriously wondering what to do now.

When blue and red lights began to dance over the walls of the trailer, I was almost giddy with relief. A moment later, two uniformed officers came to the front door, guns drawn and flashlights on.

"Zoe? I should have known."

The taller of the two, Derek Frye, is a patrol officer for the Fort Collins Police Department. Frye, tall and lean with dark hair and brown eyes, is a nice guy and a good cop. The shorter of the two was obviously young, with blonde hair cut in a high and tight. I'd seen him before, but I didn't know his name.

"Hey, Frye. I'm really glad to see you."

He pointed his flashlight at the old woman and Dennison floundering on the floor. Then he tipped his head to his partner.

"Have a look around," he said.

The second officer moved down the hall toward the bedrooms, searching for anyone else inside.

"Neighbor called 911," Frye said to me. "Reported gunshots."

Frye and I went back a couple months, to shortly before my bounty-hunting days. I'd been mixed up in a big drug/murder case in which people kept trying to kill me.

Incidentally, that's also how my shoulder was injured: gunshot wound. Also, Frye's a friend of Detective Ellmann's. I was coming to think of him as my friend, too.

"Thank God. I wasn't sure I could handle her on my own. Speaking of, will you call an ambulance?"

"Sure," he said, holstering his gun. "Wanna explain things to me?"

I tipped my head at Dennison. "He's FTA. When I came to escort him back to jail, his mother took exception. She shot at me and then attacked me. She's not well."

Frye looked from the old woman, still struggling in my arms, to the rest of the living room and then the ceiling. I saw him shaking his head.

"Things got a little out of hand," I admitted.

"No shit."

"Hey, it's clear," the second cop said, holstering his weapon. He glanced over to me and the old woman and chuckled. "I've heard about you," he said. "Zoe Grey, right? Ellmann's girl?" Then he laughed. "This is great."

"Ellmann's girl?" I repeated, looking between them. "Is that what you guys call me?" I gave Frye a pointed look.

Frye had the wisdom to look cautious and slightly embarrassed. The other guy just chuckled again and nodded.

"Yeah," he said. "But it's true, isn't it?"

I sighed. I wasn't sure how I felt about my identity as "Ellmann's girl." True or not.

"Whatever. Mind giving me a hand here?"

They looked at each other then back to me. After a very long minute, they stepped over Dennison and each took the old woman by an arm, easily hauling her up.

"Don't let her go," I said, getting to my feet, a wary eye on the woman. "Not until I'm long gone."

Frye looked me over. "She do that to you?"

I was almost afraid to know what the damage had been. From what I could see, there was blood on my jeans and shirt, and my shirt was torn. My left cheek and the side of my neck burned where her nails had clawed me, and they felt sticky with blood. The chunks of hair that had come loose from my ponytail were stuck in it.

"Yeah."

"You need an ambulance?"

"No. I'm fine."

"Better take your skip and go then. We'll stay with her until EMS gets here."

I didn't wait around to be told twice.

"Thanks. Appreciate it."

I went to Dennison, grabbed an arm and his belt, and pulled him to his feet. The pain bloomed in my shoulder again, and I winced.

"Should you be working?" Frye asked, having seen my face.

"It's been six weeks. The doctor released me." Technically a true statement. Technically.

"He know this is what you're doing?"

No. That was the rub. But I had sat around for as long as I was able.

"I'm fine," I said. "Good to see you, Frye." I looked at the other guy. "What's your name?"

"Brooks. Jason Brooks. I just started a few weeks ago. I'll probably see you around." He grinned again, amused.

"Right. Well, Brooks, tread lightly."

Confusion pinched his eyebrows together. He glanced at Frye, who gave a small nod.

I steered Dennison out the door and off the porch.

Mr Frank Harris
7373 E 29th St N Apt E131
Wichita KS 67226-3438

71989374R00265

Made in the USA
Middletown, DE
01 May 2018